I0555790

Surviving

the Bicentennial Tour

A Novel

R.G. Shannon

Pamelia Publications LLC

Surviving the Bicentennial Tour
Copyright © 2017 by R.G. Shannon

This is a work of fiction. Any references or similarities to actual events, real people, living or dead, or to real locales are intended to give the novel a sense of reality and are used fictitiously. Any similarity in other names, characters, places and incidents is entirely coincidental.

ISBN-10: 1-946857-00-9
ISBN-13: 978-1-946857-00-2

Cover Design by Illumination Graphics
www.illuminationgraphics.com

Published by Pamelia Publications LLC
Troutdale, OR 97060
www.pameliapublications.com

To the adventurers of the world—those who refuse to conform and set out on the path less traveled; those whose minds shun the boardrooms and wonder what lies beyond the next hill.

1. A Bold Idea

Saturday, November 19, 1974

*T*all and thick with fish-scale bark, stood a lone Sitka spruce. It was a holdover, a remnant of times past. Twenty-one feet thick at its base and 150 feet tall, it was here before the time of Christ. Hell, it was already a hundred years old by the time the Great Savior was making a nuisance of himself in what is now the Holy Land.

It had survived the hot summer fires the Mother started over the years. More surprising, it had survived the greed of the timber barons whose men had laid waste to this land during the last century.

A strong, cold wind whistled through the massive tree's branches, causing a shudder that ran its length. The wind roared southward over the thin strip of flood plain that lay between the Coast Range and the Pacific Ocean. It sliced through the ancients at Ecola State Park, occasionally snapping a limb off of one of the giant trees and sending it hurdling to the ground like a missile. At a time like this, the coastal forest could be a very dangerous place.

The wind blew the heavy rain sideways and continued from the heights of Tillamook Head down onto the beach below. It rattled through Cannon Beach, a small village that sat on the very edge of the coast. Many of the locals, having survived another tourist season, were now enjoying the first of many powerful winter storms.

While most of this story takes place a long way from this remote location, every story has a beginning. This one starts here with a suggestion made on this stormy, Oregon evening.

The travelers of this tale, Larry and Connor, took refuge from the storm in a small cabin on a narrow, gravel road just off of the famous Pacific Coast Highway. While it had no electricity or city water, the occupants enjoyed the warm glow of gas lights and water piped in from a nearby artesian spring. A glorious Irish-made cookstove stood against one wall. The heat from the roaring stove was quickly drying their rain-soaked clothing hung on a line for that purpose and was warming the travelers to the bone.

Larry and Connor were on the second of a three-day hitchhiking trip. They left Portland after work on Friday and thumbed a ride to Lincoln City on the central Oregon coast.

While they both owned cars, they preferred the adventure of hitchhiking over driving. A mutual friend had invited them to a birthday bash at his parents' beach cabin. It was the perfect excuse to hitch.

Connor met up with his girlfriend, Diane, at the party. She drove his Firebird down from Portland with three of her friends. The partiers gave him and Larry guff about hitchhiking instead of driving.

"We tried to talk them into taking two cars," Diane explained, "but they just wouldn't do it. You know how stubborn they can be." She wanted everyone to know she didn't approve of hitchhiking, either.

What mystified the partiers even more was their intent to hitchhike 120 miles north to Astoria the next day. When asked, Larry replied, "For a bowl of chili at John's Cafe."

Most of them knew about John's famous chili, and while great, they didn't think it justified the trip. They looked on in disapproval. "It's not just the chili, man!" Larry said with a grin, "It's the adventure of getting there!"

Early the next morning after a hearty breakfast, hungover, but fully caffeinated, they took off. As they left, several of their friends reminded them of their disapproval and referred to the endeavor as a stupid and dangerous folly. The travelers just smiled.

Diane gave them their first ride just north of town. She dropped them at a nice, wide spot where Connor had hitchhiked several times before.

He explained why he liked the spot. "It's the first good place to stand just north of the Portland turnoff. Everyone on this road is now going in our direction and not toward Portland."

They climbed out of the Firebird and pulled their packs from the trunk. Dressed in heavy flannel shirts, light jackets, and jeans, they were ready to conquer the road. They both sported bandanas on their heads. Larry's was red, and Connor's, blue. Diane loved it when they wore their bandanas in this way. She thought it made them look like gypsies.

After a hug and a kiss goodbye, Diane pulled a U-turn and headed south. Before she was out of sight, Connor and Larry had already gotten their first ride of the day. It put them nine miles north. After a half-mile walk, they waited at another good spot.

The next ride was with the Tepee People, who took the two home with them for a noon meal. They manufactured tepees for customers all over the world. They lived in communal fashion and often invited hitchhikers in for a meal if the vibes were right. Connor produced some Colombian green bud, which had been the right vibes.

Larry shared some of his father's homemade, huckleberry wine that he had brought along. Lunch was a wonderful vegetarian cuisine, using good, organically grown food. Everyone enjoyed the meal, the good company, and the conversations about life and tepees.

After the meal, they played some Frisbee football and enjoyed more weed. Before they realized, they had stayed longer than they should have. The goal of making Astoria that afternoon had become unlikely. The two gathered their belongings, thanked their host and continued their way northward.

The travelers walked two miles through a narrow, winding section of the highway and stopped at a pullout. They stood on a 150-foot bluff overlooking the ocean.

On the Pacific Coast, the weather forecast always sat on the western horizon. The view from the bluff was exquisite except for the ominous bank of storm clouds, blue to almost black, that was building and slowly moving toward the shore.

The wind picked up as they stood on the exposed highway. They smelled the moisture in the air and felt the increasing power of the storm as it bore down upon them. Finding refuge was more important now than that bowl of chili in Astoria!

They made it as far north as Cannon Beach, another eighty miles up the coast. That is how they came to be in the cabin as the storm raged outside. Larry had known the location of the cabin but still had trouble finding it in the fading light and stormy weather.

Now safely inside, the travelers were stripped down to their skivvies and lay stretched out on their bed rolls. Both nursed a bottle of locally made, Himalayan blackberry wine they had scored at a nearby market along with some breakfast goods for the next morning.

Connor was the bigger of the two, average in height at just under six feet tall. His build suggested he did many sit-ups and push-ups each morning, but he also worked very hard in the steel industry.

He didn't have much of a beard, so he kept his face clean-shaven. His straight, dishwater blonde hair came to his shoulders.

Larry was shorter and wiry compared to Connor. That's not saying he wasn't built—he was. But when he stood next to Connor, he looked slight.

He was also clean-shaven with curly, blonde hair that was a little shorter than Connor's. They both were blessed with big, beautiful smiles. Connor said this was their best asset for getting rides.

Connor was in the beginnings of the fabrication of the perfect joint. He always said the pursuit of the perfect joint should be every dope smoker's goal. After painstakingly sifting out every seed, husk, and stem, he worked the weed between his thumb and forefinger into a sticky, meal-like consistency. Next, he deposited the perfect amount onto a rolling paper with an indention in the middle of the mound. With a bit of rolling back and forth until it was just right and a quick lick on the edge, he sealed the prize.

It was a one-revolution roll with just enough overlap to seal in the gift from the Mother. It looked just like a tailor-made, filterless cigarette on its completion.

Connor held the completed roll out in triumph, and then lit it and inhaled, mixing one-third smoke with two-thirds air for the maximum assimilation of tetrahydrocannabinol, or THC. He passed the joint to Larry.

"There for a while, I didn't think you were gonna find this place," said Connor. "Too bad we couldn't make it to Astoria, but we'll get there tomorrow."

Larry spoke around the smoke in his lungs. "It's been a year and a half since I was here last, and this place is hard to find even in the daylight. We're lucky as fuck to be here!"

He had led them through the semidarkness down three different dead-ends before he finally found the right trail. It zigzagged three times over a short distance and went over a small hill before it led to the cabin.

"The guy who built it didn't want it easily found. Wait till daylight, and you'll see what I mean. This place is really hidden! He planted all those bushes at the beginning of the trail just for camouflage."

Bob, an old friend of Larry's from north Portland, had built the cabin. Larry knew him since he was fourteen before his family made the break to the suburbs. He had helped Bob with the construction.

Bob built the cabin on a small, dry swell in a swampy corner of his grandfather's dairy farm. It was nestled in a dense, mossy woodland of red alder and bigleaf maple. Young cedar, hemlock, and Sitka spruce trees grew in their shade, waiting to get tall enough to dominate the forest. A thick undergrowth of salmonberry, salal, and Oregon grape filled the spaces between the trees and surrounded the pasture.

The cabin was small, just twelve-by-twenty feet. The roof was built with salvaged, rough-cut studs and galvanized sheets of tin. The plywood walls and floor came from a used-building-materials store.

The cedar shake siding for the exterior walls was the final touch. Bob's grandfather had been on hand for this step. He showed them an old growth cedar log that had lain in the rainforest for over thirty years with barely any sign of rot.

He gave them a quick lesson on making hand-split cedar shakes. First, he cut a twenty-four-inch round from the log with a chain saw. Next, using a four-pound, single bit axe, he split out all the good, straight-grained wood to make the shake bolts. Finally, with a fro and wooden mallet, he split off a shake from one of the bolts, using the short handle of the fro and pulling it slightly toward him to give it a taper. He turned the bolt over and split another shake in the opposite direction.

He left the rest to Bob and Larry. By the end of the day, they split enough shakes to complete the siding. A week later, the cabin was finished. The work had been hard, but it earned Larry a place to crash whenever he was in the area.

After the joint, Connor and Larry sat in the warmth of the cookstove and in the glow of the weed and wine. "This Bob dude definitely knew what he was doing," said Connor. "I mean, there's no door or window on the south wall where the worst of the winter storms come from. The three windows are all on the north end around the cookstove so, if it's hot in the summer, you can cool the place down. This is really nice."

During the biggest storms, the wind-driven rain would blow through the cracks around any exposed doors and windows, soaking the floors and walls. It wasn't wise to put them on the south or west sides of a building.

"Wait till morning. That cookstove is plumbed for hot water," Larry explained. "There's a thirty-gallon, insulated water tank up on the roof. An hour after you build a fire, you have enough hot water for two showers with enough left over to wash all the dishes.

"Bob and I buried a five-hundred-gallon fiberglass reservoir on the hillside across the pasture. It's fed by a spring that flows year-round. Then we buried a plastic supply pipe to the shower and the cabin.

"The shower is just outside. You can't see it coming in. Man! The water pressure will take the top layer of your skin off!"

Larry got up and walked over to a box that looked like it was used for food storage. He opened it, pulled out a couple of pieces of wood and fed the fire.

"Well, fuck me runnin'! It's a woodbox!" Connor's admiration of the place was steadily growing.

"You don't know the half of it. You load the wood in from the outside, so there's no tracking mud inside every time you need to fill it." Larry sat back down, grinning like a proud parent.

They fell into silence, quietly enjoying the high and sipping their wine. Grateful to be dry and warm inside, they listened to the wind whistle through the trees outside and the rain drum a steady refrain on the tin roof. It was a wonderful symphony to the ears of a northwesterner.

A mosaic of art created by previous visitors adorned the interior walls. It had evolved into a collage of landscapes and cosmic interpretations of spiritual deities and mythical creatures. When stoned, it was like reading a fantasy book.

Connor broke the silence. "You know, I was up in Centralia a couple of weeks ago. I got a friend who's a mechanic in the open-pit coal mine they got up there. He gave me the twenty-five-cent tour of the place. It's really amazing.

"The most interesting thing I saw was this big chunk of dirt. It had to weigh like ten tons. He said they got it from right above the coal seam, about 250 feet under the surface. It had thousands of fossils in it and they were all sea life, you know, little shells and weird-looking fish. It got me to wondering how the sea life got that far under the ground."

"That's bullshit!" Larry said. "How did they get under the ground, a hundred miles from the ocean?"

"Sixty miles from the ocean," Connor corrected him. "But that's what I wondered. So I said, 'Self, you need to look into this shit!' So for the last couple of weeks, I've been studying the Continental Drift theory at the library."

"Jesus, Connor! That is what's so strange about you! Why, the fuck, do you do things like that? A lot of people think you're really weird, you know!"

Connor took a couple of deep breaths, suppressing the urge to slap Larry upside the head for being so ignorant, and he went on. "Fuck you, Larry! Sometimes I run across a puzzle and need to know the answer. If I cared what everyone else thought, I guess I wouldn't be weird.

"Anyway, getting back to what I was sayin'—It's cool as hell! Turns out, Oregon and Washington have been under the Pacific Ocean a couple of times before."

"That's more bullshit, Connor!"

7

"It's *not* bullshit. Listen, you got these two tectonic plates, the North American plate and the Pacific plate, and they're heading in opposite directions. The Pacific plate is diving down under the North American plate, creating what they call an *uplift*." Connor held his hands up, palms down, placing one hand over the other. "Now and then, the Pacific plate collapses under the pressure. When it does, *bam!*" He quickly dropped his hands a few inches. "Just like that, Oregon and Washington are under water."

"And you believe that bullshit?" asked Larry. "Because that's all it is, a bunch of bullshit!"

"Listen, you ever heard of fossil fuels, man? Well, how the hell did that coal seam suddenly appear 300 feet underground? That's plants and animals that were, one day, growing and eating and shitting, going along minding their own goddamned business. When all of a sudden, their whole goddamned world's under water! There they sat under the weight of all that water and compressed into coal. How the fuck else did all those sea fossils get there?"

"You ever thought that maybe God put them there?"

Connor was starting to raise his voice a bit. It was normally loud and carried easily so it didn't take much to make him sound pissed off. "God? Damn you, Larry! Every time you get confused, you pull that God shit on me! Well, I'm here to tell you this old planet's been here several billion years longer than that poor excuse of a Jewish deity of yours showed up!"

"Fuck you, Connor!"

"Well, shit, Larry! Did you know that Oregon is made up of a bunch of small islands that used to drift around in the ocean? They're called *terranes* and every time one hit the mainland, it would create a mountain range. The Blues, Strawberrys, Siskiyous, Cascades, even the Coast Range are all there because of terranes hitting the West Coast.

"Kind of like the front fender on your Rambler when your bro wrecked it. For every action, there's a reaction." Connor was laughing now.

"Connor, you're so full of shit! Where do you get all this stuff? But it's all just theory. That means there ain't no proof! And fuck you about my fender!" Now it was Larry's turn to get pissed.

"There is, too, proof! About a million years ago, maybe more, I'm not sure, there was this terrane that was floating across what is now the Pacific. Well, it split in half. Half landed in central Idaho and half in Alaska. They drilled core samples in each half, and they were identical. Now, shit-for-brains, explain that! That's proof. It's like a fingerprint, man!"

"There ain't no arguing with that, Connor, but I still don't have to believe it!"

"You know, Larry, the earth used to be a lot hotter and shit was a lot more liquid. Look at the Hawaiian Islands. They were all formed by the same hotspot out in the middle of the Pacific. The movement of the Pacific plate's starting to slow down, so each island gets progressively bigger."

"I tell you what, Connor, you just keep on thinkin'. Why don't you roll us up a Thai joint?" Larry pulled a bag out of his pack. "It might make you a little less belligerent." Larry laughed. He really liked Connor when he went off on his little tangents so he would get him charged up on purpose.

"Gotta love those Thai folk! I got five or six seeds out of the last ounce I bought. Think I'm gonna cross-pollinate them next fall with my best plants. I hear Thai weed buds real early."

"That's a good idea" said Larry. "What do you say we do a crop together next spring?"

"If you're okay with it," said Connor, "I'll do a ten-plant plot with you. That way, you won't be stuck with that shit you and your brother grew last season. But don't tell anyone, including any of your fucking bigmouthed brothers!"

"That's not fair. It was our first try. How long have *you* been growing?"

"My first crop was in '67. Sativa. I had eighteen-foot-tall plants. They were from Mexican seeds, so they didn't bud worth a shit this far north.

"I cross-pollinated my earliest males and females every year. By 1970, I was already starting to bud in late August. If it wasn't for the draft, I'd have much better plants by now.

"This Thai infusion should just do the trick. Shit! In a couple of years, I'll be budding in July," Connor said with a smile.

9

"By the way, I learned all about growing at the fucking library! I guess that's what makes me so fucking weird, huh!"

Connor twisted a pinner this time. That's all the Thai they required. That didn't stop him from twisting the perfect pinner, though. Perfectly round, it was about one-third the diameter of a cigarette and was much more difficult to roll than a normal-sized joint. He gave it to Larry who lit it, took a hit and passed it back to Connor.

"Life is good, Larry." Connor took a hit off of the joint and a pull from the wine. He kicked back on his pillow and exhaled. He licked his fingertip and moistened one side of the joint to stop a run up the side and passed it back to Larry. "Yeah, life is real good," he said, staring at the art on the walls.

They finished the joint and sat in silence for a while, basking in the THC and alcohol haze. They took in the wood grain pattern on the plywood, the rust spots growing on the ceiling, and the flickering shadows cast by the flames of the gas lights. It was like sitting inside a Picasso painting.

"You know," Connor said after another long silence, "I been thinkin' the last couple of weeks—"

"What else is fucking new!" Larry laughed.

"Fuck you! Now listen. I've been thinkin' about a bicentennial hitchhiking tour of America. You know, to celebrate our nation's two-hundredth birthday? Just you and me. We'll leave the spring of '76.

"I got friends all over the country from my military days. They'll let us crash for a few days and show us the sights while we're there."

"You just keep on thinkin', Connor." Larry loved saying that. It pissed Connor off every time.

Connor would say something like "Fuck you, asshole! I can't help it you ain't got no ideas of your own!" The snit would never last very long, though, and their conversation would always mellow out after a minute or two.

"I'm serious, Larry. We both got good-paying jobs. We'll just save a bankroll and have someone we can trust hold on to most of it. Then they can mail it to us when we need it."

Larry was silent for a while and then said, "I'll think on it, okay?"

After another silence, he asked, "What do you think God would say about that continental drift shit?"

"*Your* god, Larry. He'd be pissed off that one of his ignorant sheep was thinkin'."

"What do you think your Buddha would say?" He laughed at the thought of Connor's Buddha.

"Buddha was a man of science. He would've said, 'It's about time you figured that out!'"

Connor got up, turned down the lights, closed the window a bit and returned to his bed. He stared up at the ceiling and realized it didn't get better than this. Life was good. He drifted off.

2. No Chili Today

Sunday, November 20, 1974

The next morning, Connor woke up and glanced out of the window. It was still dark, but he sensed it was nearly dawn because he felt rested. Without a watch, he couldn't be sure of the time—a common theme for him in the morning. His head was a little foggy from the wine and weed of the evening before.

He lay there and waited. In a couple of minutes, it came. A nearby robin began his soulful, undulating morning serenade. Then, one by one, other robins joined in to create a robin sonata. It was nature's wake-up call. Minutes later, the eastern sky began to glow.

Connor had been using the robin's morning song as an alarm clock most of his life. Usually the first bird to wake and sing, it started the symphony of morning birdsong. It was soon joined by the chickadee, towhee, junco, thrush, and the many other local and migrating songbirds.

Before it was fully light outside, Connor had a small fire built and was showered. He had the bacon frying, and the aroma went to work on Larry who finally pulled his tired ass out of bed. This was typical.

Connor was an early-to-bed, early-to-rise kind of guy. At the big weekend camping parties, he was normally the breakfast cook for those who got up before he had finished.

He loved to cook over an open fire; so did Larry. Together, they created some real masterpieces and always enjoyed the accolades they received from their fellow campers.

This morning, their timing was perfect. Larry had plenty of hot water for a shower when he got up. Afterward, they enjoyed the bacon, spuds, and eggs they scored the night before. After a quick clean-up, a restock of the wood box, and a thank-you note in the visitors log, they were off.

The main push of the storm had passed over during the night, leaving partly cloudy skies and occasional, light showers. Everything was bright and colorful, having been scrubbed clean by the heavy rain and strong winds. Even the air itself was fresh and clean.

They arrived at the intersection of the gravel road and the Pacific Coast Highway and set up their packs. Looking around at the marvel of the Oregon coast, they could see the ocean but not the breakers though they heard their constant roar. The soft, slightly briny sea breeze combined with the ever-present birdsong to make a little bit of nirvana for the travelers.

The thing about hitching along the coastal highway was there were a lot of people giving rides, just not very long ones. They didn't stand and wait very long, but they did a lot of getting in and out of vehicles. Three rides and thirty miles later, they were in Astoria, the northern-most city on the Oregon coast.

After a short hike, they stood outside of John's Cafe laughing so hard the building was all that held them up. It was Sunday, and it seemed John's was closed on Sundays during the winter season.

"Twelve rides, 120 miles, all for the fun of it, I guess," Connor said with tears in his eyes. "I finally spent the night at Bob's place, though, so I guess it was worth it."

Larry wiped his eyes and looked to the west at some incoming weather. "You know it's gonna rain in a little bit. We ought to find us a place to hitchhike where we can stand under cover if it gets going hard, okay?"

Connor nodded and followed Larry out to Highway 30, the main road through Astoria and the way back to Portland. They decided to grab some lunch elsewhere and walk about a mile to the east end of town before putting out their thumbs.

Most of the coastal residents lived by a code. It took a strong person to live in such a wet climate. Not a physical strength, it was a strength of the soul. They reached out to others, gave them a smile and helped them if they needed it.

The travelers hadn't gone a half block before a guy in a 1956 Chevy pickup pulled over and offered them a ride. The driver said he lived on the east edge of town, and they were welcome to come in and watch football until the squall blew over.

That earned the man a joint that, as it turned out, his old lady smoked with them because he didn't smoke the herb. He *did* drink beer, though, and had a kegged refrigerator on his back porch. Soon, some of his friends showed up, and the football game started. That was followed by more weed and more beer.

Connor and Larry made it out to the highway four times that day. Each time, they were driven back in by the rain. Actually, it was the beer and the football that drew them back.

It was their fifth trip out, and it was getting late. For the first time all day, they were serious about getting a ride.

They set up their packs in plain view, and Connor leaned a sign saying "Portland" against them. Larry pulled out his harp and started playing. Connor found his juggling bags and began juggling and singing to Larry's bluesy harp. As usual, the lyrics were pretty bad. He sang about another rain shower as it approached. Sometimes, the words would even rhyme.

The travelers were having the time of their lives right on the side of the highway. They were there just ten minutes when a guy in a Ford van pulled over and gave them a ride.

"Where you guys headin' in Portland?" he asked.

"We're on our way to the West End Tavern," said Larry.

"Shit! I ain't been up there in a while. I guess it's a good excuse to go back."

"Well," Connor said, "If that's the case, you won't have to buy beer while you're there."

"That seals it!" the driver said with a smile. "To the West End Tavern then.

"You know, I don't normally pick up hitchhikers, but you guys looked like you were having too much fun!"

Larry and Connor looked at each other and smiled a knowing smile. Connor started in on his mantra.

"Presentation, presentation, presentation! You see, we're offering you a product—us. We try to appear as appealing as possible so you'll pick us up. We find a spot on the road with an easy pullout and a good, long viewing distance, so you can really look us over. We're neat and clean. We make eye contact with you, and we smile. Larry here plays the harp, and I juggle and sing.

"Man, it's not an act. We really *are* having the time of our lives. You see, we know we're going to get a ride. Shit! You were probably eating lunch, thinking of that long-assed drive to Portland, not knowing you were gonna pick us up at all.

"Or it could've been someone else, but the absolute here is that someone was going to pick us up. It may be tomorrow instead of today, but the ride is out there. Since we're confident in that knowledge, it's easy to be happy.

"Our job is to present ourselves so that whoever comes along *wants* to pick us up We're *definitely* not rookies here!"

Larry said to the driver, "We need to change the subject. He can go on forever. You smoke marijuana, man?"

"Yeah, you got any?"

"Light 'er up, Connor!"

"Comin' right up, bro," said Connor.

"That's one of the reasons I picked you guys up. You looked like you were stoned!" They laughed as Connor lit the joint.

An hour and a half later, they arrived at their destination. The West End Tavern was a local dewdrop inn. It lay just inside the Portland city limits at the summit of the West Hills. Forest Park, one of the world's largest city parks, was its neighbor to the east, giving it a rural feel.

Connor grew up just down the hill, west of the Tavern. He spent a good deal of his childhood bicycling and horseback riding around Forest Park. His parents owned a small piece of land and raised a cow, two hogs, and a bunch of chickens for food each year. It was paradise to a young, adventurous boy.

There were several boarding stables in the area, and Connor earned money exercising horses that were otherwise ignored. He knew the hills like the back of his hand. He and his friends built tree forts all over. They traveled the woods without a hitch even in the pitch black of night and in the driving rain. It didn't matter to them because they had memorized every square inch. This was the one place on earth where Connor felt at home.

It was Sunday, and the owner of the West End Tavern was enjoying her day off. Because neither Connor nor Larry liked her, Sunday was their favorite day to drop by. Having hitchhiked there, they were confident they could get a ride down the hill from one of their many friends.

The place was crowded when they arrived. They ordered two large pitchers of beer and headed out the back door to the horseshoe pits, fondly known as the Beer Garden. The driver, Dave, followed them out, carrying three pint glasses.

"Well, who left the door open?" asked a friend named Jeff. He had last seen the two travelers as they departed for Astoria the morning before. "I figured you two would eventually show up here."

"Just the way we planned it!" Larry bragged. He went on to fill him in on what had gone down over the last two days.

He introduced Dave to everyone in general, lit a joint and passed it around. One of the sweet benefits of the West End was nobody said anything about smoking marijuana while they were in the Beer Garden.

"Man! I'm really glad I gave you two a ride," said Dave. "I forgot how nice it is here. Plus I didn't know you could smoke the hooch."

Connor smiled at Dave, turned his gaze to Jeff and planted a sloppy kiss on his cheek. "Speaking of a ride, Jeff, you gonna give me and Larry a ride down the hill?"

Wiping his cheek and smiling, Jeff gave out a hoot and said, "After a kiss like that, I guess you'll sit up front!"

Someone yelled for more beer. Another joint was lit and started its way around the group. Laughter rose up from several people gathered around the firepit.

"That's why I came up here," Jeff explained. "I figured you two vagabonds would show up looking for a lift."

"That's right! And don't you forget it, either. I'm nothin' but a fucking vagabond." Connor was smiling.

They sat outside and played horseshoes until the wee hours of Monday morning. Despite being stoned and half-drunk, Jeff managed to get them home safely.

Connor was just crawling into bed beside Diane when the phone rang. He paused to hang his head in disgust and let out a big sigh. Then he crept out to the kitchen to avoid waking her and answered the phone. It was Larry.

"What the fuck, Larry?"

Slurring his words, Larry asked, "You know that idea about the bicenten—, bicentenel—, you know, that tour you were talkin' about?"

"Yeah."

"Well, I'm in."

"Good, it's gonna be a kick in the pants. One thing, though. It's just you an' me. Anybody else wants to come along, that's tough shit. One's no fun and three's a crowd. Okay?"

"It's our tour, buddy," Larry agreed. "Now go to fucking bed, you drunk!"

Connor chuckled. "I'll ring you tomorrow after I get off work to see if you remember this call."

Larry laughed and hung up.

Connor had been saving for a year when he told Larry about his idea for a hitchhiking tour. Larry had been saving, too, and he had more money put away. Connor would be hard pressed to catch up. He figured three thousand dollars apiece would be enough, and he was confident they'd reach that goal if they worked hard.

So, in the beginning, there was Connor and Larry. Connor thought up the idea and together, they formed it into a plan—one that would evolve into a six-month, cross-country, hitchhiking adventure they dubbed the Bicentennial Tour.

3. The Perfect Plan

*O*nce they decided to go on the Bicentennial Tour, Larry and Connor focused their energy on the preparations. They studied maps of the states and talked about where they wanted to go. They researched the latest equipment and clothing options available to them.

Connor got in touch with his Army buddies and let them know of their plans. Larry set up a visit with his aunt and uncle in Florida.

They turned their attention to raising money for the trip. During the summer of 1975, they grew a ten-plant weed crop as Connor had promised. Larry kept his word and never told anyone about it. Connor landed a logging job in southeast Alaska, so Larry did most of the work. Connor managed to get back to Portland in time to help with the harvest.

While Connor made big money from logging, Larry kept busy with his roofing and painting business. When he returned, Connor went back to work in the same stainless steel shop where he worked before he left for Alaska.

With the profit from the crop and their earnings from their jobs, Connor was able to save forty-five hundred dollars and Larry saved over five thousand dollars. But the *real* work of planning the details was yet to come, and they still had to decide on their departure date.

Just after the New Year in 1976, Diane moved into a three-bedroom condo with two of her friends, Melissa and Lynn. It was decided that Connor would move in with Diane to save money.

Saturday, January 10, 1976

Larry stopped by to watch football and brought beer and fried chicken. He had been trying to get Connor to commit to a departure date for the tour and wasn't leaving without one.

After dinner and during halftime, Larry said, "Listen, Connor. The one thing I want to nail down tonight is our departure date. I don't want to bid a big job and then not be able to finish it because you want to leave."

"Yeah, yeah, I know," said Connor. "The game is about to start again. Let's talk about it later."

Larry patiently waited for the end of the game. Afterward, he pressed Connor again. "A date, my friend, a date," he insisted.

Connor stared at Larry for a moment. "You talk to Dudley lately?" Dudley was one of Larry's brothers.

"Haven't seen him in a week or so."

"Well, I want to leave in March, and the other day, I was talking to your bro, the Dudmeister. He said he was gonna leave for Death Valley on February 27 and was gonna stay there for two weeks.

"I figured Death Valley should be our first destination. So, what do you say about the third of March?"

"I like it. Fuck yes!" said Larry. "Okay then, everything is focused on the third of March. Jesus, that was easy!"

Friday, January 23, 1976

In the evening, Larry arrived with a shorty of beer and a nice bag of Colombian Gold for a sit-down meeting with Connor to talk about the trip.

"Let's go get our backpacks tomorrow," said Larry. "We both need bigger packs to carry all the shit we're gonna be needing."

"Okay, but listen," Connor said. "I talked to Steve, my lead man at the stainless shop, about fabricating us some new frames out of aluminum tubing. He's done it for several other people and says there's no commercial frame on the market that's as strong. Plus the tubes are bigger inside so we can stash our weed there."

"Won't it just fall back out?"

"That's the trick part to this tubing," Connor explained. "There's a plug we use for the air systems on the trailers we build. This plug has a left-handed thread that fits it perfectly. All we have to do is tap the tubing. And we have the thread tap we need at work. Just leave that part to me."

"How long is that gonna to take?"

"It'll be done this weekend. I told John I'd help him with it. Now, I can get the tubing for free since we use it for centrifuge repair for the local dairies, but it's gonna cost us a shorty of beer and a joint for John to do the work. It'll be worth it, trust me!"

The next day, they went to a local outfitter and scored the biggest packs they had in stock. Then they began the pain-in-the-ass task of making a list of the equipment and supplies they would need. They relied on their experience as a guide through this process.

Connor was never a stranger to the outdoors. His fondest childhood memories were of hiking and fishing in the wilderness. He had spent two weeks at a time in the backwoods every summer since he was four. That first summer, he had caught his first fish during a visit to Pamelia Lake, three miles into the Mount Jefferson Wilderness, just east of Salem.

The majesty of the Cascade wilderness held a special place in Connor's heart. Sometimes, when troubled, he would fight the problem for hours, or even days. These were struggles that troubled his inner peace. Finally, he would retreat to a quiet corner and envision the forest, with its tall firs, dank sphagnum moss, singing birds, and cascading streams. It wouldn't be long before the trouble would take a back seat to the peacefulness of the envisioned wilderness.

As an adolescent and young adult, Connor spent many nights in the forests surrounding Portland. These were lessons he still used as an adult. He was well-versed at living out of a backpack.

Larry had grown up doing many of the same things as Connor and was just as comfortable in the outdoors. When he first got to see the new pack frames, he couldn't believe their strength despite being so light. While he had backpacked many times before, he had never used anything as big as the packs they'd chosen. Packs this large were new to Connor, as well. Even with the light frames, they would need to acclimate to the heavy loads necessary for such an ambitious undertaking.

Getting ready for an extended trip required a great deal of planning and creativity. They poured over their list again and again—first adding, and subtracting, and then adding again. Throughout this process, they struggled to keep the weight and bulk to a minimum. Soon, the dickering began. Just like two stubborn mules, they argued and bitched at each other well into the month of February.

Connor conceded that an eight-inch cast iron pan was a necessity, although only on the insistence that Larry would carry the heavy fucker! They both bought summer sleeping bags that were light but still warm down to twenty-eight degrees. Connor insisted on a wool blanket from the local army surplus store, and Larry insisted he carry the heavy fucker! Larry bought a cotton blanket that he would carry. In a pinch, the blankets were big enough to go over both of their bags as extra layers.

They argued for days about their shelter. Larry had ideas about several different styles of tents, but Connor held firm on an eight-by-twelve-foot tarp.

To test it out, Connor set the tarp up outside the girls' condo, and they spent the night under it. A half inch of rain fell through the night, and Connor woke Larry up six or seven times to see if he was staying dry.

Finally, at five in the morning, Larry conceded to the tarp. He lit a wake-and-baker. They smoked it and fell back asleep until the girls woke them for pancakes. Connor agreed to carry the tarp, but they split the tent poles, tent stakes, and lengths of parachute cord used as guy lines for the poles.

They both had one pair of swimming trunks, a pair of jean shorts, two pair of long pants, three T-shirts, two long-sleeved flannel shirts, and a hooded pullover sweatshirt.

They argued over Larry's coat. He really wanted to take it. Connor finally convinced him they were going to be in the south until it warmed up enough north of the Mason-Dixon Line that he wouldn't need his sacred coat.

They did, however, score two OD-green army ponchos from the surplus store. Connor knew how handy they'd be as covers over their backpacks while they served as endcaps at each end of the lean-to tarp.

They each had a mess kit and shared all the kitchen utensils. They both packed a towel, a washcloth, some all-natural liquid peppermint soap, a toothbrush, and toothpaste. They included two eight-inch Bowie knives that would always be in sight either on the outside of the packs or on their belts. Connor would carry a small hatchet, and Larry would carry a small wood saw.

That left room for a week's worth of food. This included spices and the staple of all staples: Instant pancake mix. They split a five-pound bag between them in plastic containers. They planned to score small amounts of additional food and drink wherever they went.

Despite the fact that neither had heavy beards, or maybe *because* of that fact, they both packed shaving kits. Connor's philosophy was that clean-cut people get picked up, and that rule would be firmly enforced, most of the time anyway.

So, after three weeks of effort and many compromises, the preparation for the trip was finally completed. They were packed and ready to go, each carrying about forty-five pounds.

It was the second week of February. Larry had been neglecting work he had promised his clients. He worked twelve hours a day until he got the house he was repainting done, both inside and out. Connor came along to help on the weekends.

4. The Secret Weapon

Monday, February 9, 1976

Connor was in Diane's room doing push-ups. He had begun an exercise routine to get in better shape for the trip. There was a knock at the door. "Yeah, come on in."

It was Melissa. "Hi, Connor. Could you come downstairs? We want to talk with you."

Connor noticed the concern on her face and thought he'd done something wrong. When he got downstairs, the three girls were sitting on the couch with worried expressions.

Diane started. "Listen, we've been talking about you and your stupid hitchhiking tour with Larry. Do you understand how dangerous it is to hitchhike? Not so much here, but what's gonna happen when you're down south with all those rednecks?" They had seen *Easy Rider*, apparently.

When Connor tried to talk, all three girls started in at once. He raised his hand, and they stopped. "Listen, you may not know this, but I can take care of myself."

He looked from one set of eyes to another and smiled, "Anyway, I have my secret weapon that none of you know about."

"What's that, Connor, your good looks?" Diane asked. The three girls giggled. Connor smiled and shook his head.

"Are we still going camping this weekend?" he asked. They all nodded. "Good. This weekend, I'm gonna show you something that even Larry doesn't know about. Only a few people I grew up with know about this, and even they don't know how good I've gotten since I left for the military.

"And for the record, if I had to rely on my looks, I would be in serious trouble!" Connor wrinkled his nose and mouth into a grimace, and then he smiled again.

"Connor, we think you're being a little naive about the dangers involved with this trip of yours," Lynn said in a motherly tone.

"Just listen. You can talk to me this weekend after I show you my secret weapon. I've been planning on showing Larry, anyway. Since you're concerned, I'll show you, too."

Saturday, February 14, 1976

Early Saturday morning, Larry stopped by, raring to get started. Connor was packed and ready, too. The girls were dragging their feet, though. They had partied late and weren't happy with the early start. Eventually, they got it going and were eager once Larry reminded them about Connor's "goddamned secret weapon".

The party was on the John Day River in central Oregon, about 180 miles from the condo, so an early start was important. Once in the semi-arid climate just east of the Cascade Range, Connor pulled off of the interstate at Biggs Junction, a small truck stop on the Columbia River.

He drove right through the one-intersection town and up onto the bluffs overlooking the river. A short time later, he turned onto a narrow, gravel road and drove for another mile. He pulled into an abandoned gravel pit and stopped.

Without a word, Connor got out and opened the trunk of the car. He pulled out a couple of two-by-six boards about a foot long with a small bull's-eye painted on them. He walked to the back of the pit and leaned the boards against the wall about ten feet apart.

Meanwhile, everyone had gotten out of the car and stood watching with puzzled expressions. As Connor counted out paces away from the wall, Larry started laughing and said, "What! So you're gonna throw boards at them? Are you seri—"

His mouth fell open when a knife suddenly appeared in Connor's hand. It flashed through the air and hit the bull's-eye of the board on the left. Before Larry could say another word, a second knife appeared and landed dead center in the other board.

Larry and the girls stood there stunned as Connor pulled off his shirt to reveal a harness that held a sheath for two throwing knives snugly between his shoulder blades. It was custom-made for comfort and stealth with thin nylon straps over his shoulders and under his arms. The straps were adjusted to his size with a simple clip that released with a twist of his fingers. It was easy to conceal, and the knives could be pulled with no resistance at all. He could pull them with his eyes closed and hit his target as far away as twenty feet.

"So, what do you think of my secret weapon?" He returned to the boards, pulled each knife free and sheathed them with a precision and speed that let them know he'd been doing it for years.

"I had the harness made in Germany when I was in the Army," he explained as he walked toward his friends. "That's where I got the knives, too.

"I've been throwing since I was ten or eleven. Started with a hatchet, then I found a throwing knife downtown at a hock shop when I was fifteen. Whenever I got pissed at my old man or just for something to do, I'd go out behind the barn and practice."

Connor turned his back so they could get a better look at the harness. Still speechless, his friends just stared at it.

Connor continued. "About a month after I got to Germany, I saw one of the German nationals that worked in my accounting office with a throwing knife. I asked him where he got it. He said I'd just hurt myself if I had one and shined me on. I didn't get mad because I never let inexperienced people play with my knives, either.

"At lunch, I made a target and brought it back to his cubicle. I set it up against the wall and was gonna ask to use his knife. Before I could say a word, he threw the knife and bull's-eyed the target.

"I got the knife and set the target back up. I took my turn and nailed the target about a half-inch away from his mark. You should've seen the look on his face! He fell all over himself to give me his address and invite me to his house that weekend."

"So he's the one who got you the harness?" Larry asked at last. He reached up and tugged at one of the knives. He pulled it out of the sheath, admired its sharp edge and carefully sheathed it.

"Not him, a friend of his. Over in Europe, they have knife-throwing clubs with events and tourneys. I never got involved with that shit, but I was welcome to practice and was invited to a couple of their get-togethers. They were really good people. The quality and balance of their blades was like nothing I'd ever seen before.

"So, over the next six months, I paid for this stuff," Connor stood proudly with his thumbs tucked under the front straps of the harness.

"I was allowed to go down in the basement of this ancient building and practice anytime I wanted for the next year. Shit! There were knife-throwers in that club that were so good they could hit bull's-eyes from thirty-five feet.

"Not that I'm a hack, but they were surprised that an American could throw as well as I could. They couldn't believe I was self-taught. I just liked doing it and wanted to be as good as I could."

Connor took several strides toward the wall and suddenly dove to his right. Before he hit the ground, a knife streaked through the air and hit one of the boards. As he rolled back up to a standing position, the other knife flashed and hit its mark in the other board at almost the same instant. "I'm just about as good left-handed as right."

Diane ran up and hugged him saying, "I've known you for over a year and you're just now telling me this?"

"Jesus fucking Christ! I've known you for over three years and I've never even seen you *hold* a throwing knife before!" said Larry, impressed with Connor's acrobatic performance.

"Well, there's only a few people who do know. None of my family knows about this harness. I tend to keep it to myself. You guys don't know how many times I've had it on at parties where I didn't know the people, or when I scored weed from a stranger, or when I've hitchhiked."

"Wait a second! Is that why you had so much trouble taking your sweatshirt off when we were down at the cabin? I wondered what the problem was." Larry smiled as he thought of how Connor had struggled to get his sweatshirt over his head, and how he turned his back just as it came off.

"Yeah, it's not easy getting the harness over my head, but I manage, don't I? It's also why so many of my tee-shirts have hoods. It helps to hide the sheath."

He turned, half dragging Diane over to the boards to extract his knives. "The point is, I'm not Superman, but I'm a handful for any redneck, hippie-hating asshole I run into."

"Besides," said Larry, attempting to placate the girls, "we're both gonna cut our hair and shave this scruff before we leave. Shit! They'll think we're just down-on-our-luck rednecks. They'll probably stop to offer us a lift."

"So here comes the disclaimer," said Connor. "I'll deny any knowledge of this if you guys tell anyone, not only this weekend, but anytime. That's why none of my old friends I grew up with talk about it. They know better than to piss me off, and they're also good friends. I hope I can trust all of *you* to be good friends, too."

All four fell all over themselves and agreed at the same time. Connor looked at each of them in turn, cementing their promise of secrecy with an intense gaze.

He returned the boards to a hidden corner in the trunk of the car and said, "Come on. Let's get a move on before they start this party without us!"

5. Farewell

Tuesday, March 2, 1976

The night before their departure, the girls held a going-away bash at the condo. Five neighbors participated and most of the other tenants were invited, so there was no problem with noise complaints. A gallon jar sat on the living room coffee table for donations. It was Diane's idea, and it was a good one.

The travelers were upstairs packing the last items in their packs. First was a quarter-pound of Thai sticks, the best quality marijuana in the world.

They had driven to Seattle to score it from a friend who had made connections in Bangkok during his tour in Vietnam. He flew over every six months and shipped weed back in the Buddha statues he sold in his emporium, which he used to launder his weed import money.

They wrapped the Thai sticks in plastic, three at a time, and slid them up inside the pack frames. After the weed, Connor inserted three more containers that were also wrapped in plastic.

Two of the containers were the components of Connor's Special Smoke. The first was a leather pouch containing a special blend Connor had perfected over the last couple of years. It was a mixture of dried liberty cap mushrooms, dried peyote buttons that he had cleaned and pulverized himself, a wee bit of Thai weed, a touch of tobacco to help it burn right, and a little spearmint to improve the raunchy taste. The second was a leather-encased glass tube with a rubber stopper that contained the bulk of Connor's blend. It just barely fit inside the pack frame.

The third container was another leather pouch holding a handmade, clay pipe. Connor had hiked into the Coast Range to a vein of clay he read about that was used by the local Indians to make pottery. It had taken a while to find the clay, but it was worth the effort. It made a fine pipe that drew the attention of several friends.

They had asked him repeatedly where he found the clay, but he kept that to himself.

Larry had two test tubes with stoppers and a small vial for his generation weed. The second gen was a collection of roaches from their joints. The third gen was the roaches from their second gen joints. The fourth gen was the roaches from their third gen joints and was held in the vial with a screw-on cap. Larry would normally smoke the fourth gen weed as soon as he got enough roaches. He'd make a double-paper joint and add a little tobacco to make it burn because it contained so much resin and would go out after every hit. This all fit neatly inside his pack frame.

The last thing to go inside each side of the frames was cayenne pepper wrapped in cheese cloth as a precaution against dogs. Connor didn't know if it would work, but it was worth a try. They had just enough room for the special, left-hand-threaded plugs. It was just as Connor had envisioned when they bought the packs.

They went downstairs and partied until the wee hours of the morning when the cops came to break up the fun. The Man never could stand a group of young adults having a good time. So, at three in the morning, they went to bed, but not necessarily to sleep.

Wednesday, March 3, 1976

Connor got up at 8 a.m. and began making Italian omelets for everyone. The place looked like a flophouse with people scattered all over the floor.

Two hours later, the travelers' adventure began with a surprise first ride to Eugene, the home of the Fighting Ducks of the University of Oregon. It was kind of a joke since their football team sucked big time and had for years. Larry's brother, Ray, gave them the ride.

Before getting in the car, Connor swapped spit with each of the roommates and told Diane he'd stay in touch. Once on the road, Larry said, "Jesus, Connor! It looked like you were sleeping with all three of 'em!"

"I was, so what," Connor answered. "Besides, I told Diane I didn't expect her to be faithful while I was gone. She'd been fucking around on me all along, anyway. That gave Melissa and Lynn the excuse they needed to fuck me.

"But this last month has really taken it out of me. I don't know how much longer I could've handled it!" He laughed.

Larry listened and shook his head with a smile on his face. He opened up one of the two brown paper bags he brought along. He reached in and pulled out a joint, lit it, and passed it forward to Connor. He hit it and passed it on to Ray.

"That tastes good, man." Connor remarked. "Where'd you get it?"

"Didn't you notice the donation jar last night?" asked Larry.

"You got that from the jar on the coffee table? Fuck, man! How many joints *are* there?"

"One hundred sixty-three joints and two Thai sticks!" Larry announced triumphantly. "Like we ain't got enough of that shit already! The cool thing is we also came away with 658 dollars. There were three hundred-dollar bills from your roommates and two more from our parents. So we're cool for a while when it comes to cash, and weed. We're gonna fill Ray's tank up when we get to Eugene."

"You know, when I thought up this trip so long ago, I remember everyone said what idiots we were," said Connor. "Last night, I couldn't believe all the people who wanted to come along!"

"Yeah, they hit me up, too," said Larry. "You know, I watched two ounces get rolled with a cigarette machine, but I didn't know they were gonna go into the donation jar. I guess that's kinda cool. Shit, man! We won't be going into our stash for a couple of months! It was a banner going-away party for our Bicentennial Tour."

"I find it amazing that we go to all the trouble of hiding our stash, and then we get all this weed that we have to carry outside the frame," said Connor. "We really should keep it hidden as much as possible.

"And you take care of the money. It goes to the trip *only*, though. When we get to Nevada, you're gambling with your *own* money." Connor knew how much Larry liked to gamble.

Larry pulled his wallet out and showed Connor the three hundred-dollar bills in a secret compartment. "That's my mad money. I put it there six months ago. That's what I'm gambling with."

"Yeah, I've got a fifty stashed for the same purpose. I don't plan on dropping any more than that," said Connor.

Once in Eugene they stopped for gas and had some lunch at a ma-and-pa diner with great sandwiches. The travelers were dragging their feet. They were suddenly nervous about starting their adventure. The conversation slowed to a halt and an uncomfortable silence ensued. It was Ray who finally announced that he had to get back home and got the show on the road, literally.

Once on the side of the highway, the travelers quickly set up their packs and displayed a sign saying "SF". It wasn't long at all before they were playing music and dancing around. Their genuine happiness was showing to all the people heading south. Connor began singing:

> *We're standing in Eugene*
> *By a flowing stream,*
> *Our Bicentennial Tour goes*
> *Just like the water flows,*
> *Because we're standing in Eugene*
> *It's the beginning of our dream,*
> *Just standing in Eugene by the river side*
> *Waitin' for our first Bicentennial ride.*

"Jesus, Connor! That really sucks!" complained Larry.

"Yeah, I hope the next ride is better than that," Connor replied, laughing.

Eugene was a liberal college town, a great place to start a hitchhiking tour of America. Connor's rule about appearance was in effect.

Their sign let everyone know they weren't local and not to be offended when they turned down a short ride across town.

They were moving to the rhythm and smiling with happy faces when the first car pulled over. Connor turned down the twenty-five mile ride and Larry got a little miffed.

"I don't know, bro. That might have been bad luck."

"That set the precedent. *We're* in charge of this tour. *We're* the ones who decide who's gonna benefit from giving us a ride. We're definitely not going to break Rule Two right off the get-go." Connor was on his hitchhiker's pulpit once again.

"You just keep on thinkin', Connor." Larry laughed.

"Fuck you, Larry!" Connor laughed, too.

It was the fourth offer, a ride to Roseburg that finally got the tour underway. A nice, Christian couple was coming back home after spending a week at a Jehovah's Witness retreat. The husband constantly preached at the travelers. All the while, his wife rocked back and forth with a crazy-looking smile on her face and added a *praise-the-lord* now and then.

It made Connor feel a little queasy. He didn't say anything, not wanting to jeopardize the ride. Larry, however, joined right in.

A couple of hours later, they were back on the side of the road once again, laughing about the holy rollers and "counting their blessings" for the beginning of their next big adventure.

The next ride took them from Roseburg to Ashland, the home of the Shakespearean Festival. It was the last exit in Oregon where they could stand on the freeway and present their wares to every passerby. Their ride had been going to Weed, California. Connor made the call and asked to be let out in Ashland.

Larry was confused. "Sometimes, this Hitchhiker's Rulebook of yours don't make any sense. The guy was heading fifty more miles up the road."

"Yeah, you're right. But you ever been to Weed? It's nothing but a farming and logging town. Don't get me wrong, it's beautiful, but we don't want to hitch a ride from there.

"It's gonna be dark soon, and I've spent several nights over in those woods before." He pointed to a thicket of firs not far from the exit.

"Just the same, I liked the sound of Weed." Larry chuckled.

"Speaking of that, let's head on over there and scope out a spot to sleep. Then we'll eat before it gets dark and smoke a going-away joint."

"Now you're talkin'. You know what I like best about the going-away joints?" Larry laughed.

"No, what?"

"You never know what you're gonna get!" Larry continued to laugh as they headed toward the small copse of thick, Oregon forest.

Well-fed and happily stoned, the travelers returned to the highway. They set their packs up and began their roadside act once again. For two hours, they waited. Connor was getting tired of juggling, and Larry had long since quit playing the harp. They were about to call it a night when a VW bus pulled over. The driver said he was going as far as Red Bluff. They jumped in.

It was close to midnight when the VW dropped them off. They quickly found refuge under a bridge that spanned the American River. They spread the tarp out, using the soft, sandy bank as a mattress, and went to sleep to the muted sounds of the river slipping by.

Thursday, March 4, 1976

They spent four, long hours in Red Bluff, and Connor was beginning to second-guess his decision when a gay lawyer in a brand-new Olds gave them a lift.

Connor parried the lawyer's come-ons while Larry sat in the back seat, grooving on the music. It was worth it for the lift out of Red Bluff and down to I-80, just north of Sacramento.

> *Well, I never had a man*
> *I guess that ain't good*
> *Cause that fuckin' lawyer*
> *Wanted to suck my wood.*
> *I'm going over to Nevada*
> *With these California blues*
> *Going on up into Reno*
> *Got some money to lose.*

"You can be one sick puppy sometimes!" laughed Larry.

"You were in the back seat listening to the music the whole time he was trying to put the make on me!"

The next ride took them into Reno. It was with a couple on their tenth anniversary, and they were looking to score a stash of weed. Larry gave them ten joints, one for each year of marriage. Everybody was happy.

The third ride proved very interesting, mostly because Larry was willing to leave Reno after hardly gambling at all. He met a couple of girls from Boise that were on their way to Las Vegas and offered to give them a ride all the way to Death Valley.

33

Connor was surprised because Larry was normally too shy to talk to strange girls. He usually spoke very little until he got to know them. But Larry seemed to really like these girls, especially the one named Tanya. Connor was just happy to get out of town after winning twelve dollars.

He sat up front with the driver, named Lisa, and made small talk while Larry was in the back seat, cementing his relationship with Tanya. The smell of sex was in the air. Connor was in shock.

He filled their tank and scored some beer at a gas station. Lisa drove to a small motel in Bishop where they had reservations. Connor slept in the back seat of the car, Larry in the front.

Friday, March 5, 1976

The next morning, Connor showered in the girls' room, and he took Lisa to breakfast while Larry and Tanya showered the sex off of themselves.

Lisa told Connor she had never seen Tanya act that way. Connor was still suffering from the shock of it all with some envy thrown in, as well.

After breakfast, they all piled in the car and took off. On this leg of the drive Connor learned that Lisa was pregnant and on her way to get married in Las Vegas. Tanya was her best friend and maid of honor. Where Larry fit in, he figured he'd find out later.

6. Dropped at Death Valley

They arrived in Death Valley around noon and searched for Dudley's camp. Back in Portland, he had showed Connor and Larry where he and his friends planned to camp. After a few unsuccessful tries, the travelers finally found his campsite.

They unloaded their packs from the top of the rig and traded some small talk. There were hugs and one real wet kiss, and then the girls were gone.

"Well, lover boy, did she leave you an address?" Connor asked.

"Shit, Connor! She left me an address, a phone number, and the directions to her parents' house! I think I'm gonna see her again when our tour is over." Larry smiled. "It's better than anything I could've imagined."

Dudley and his friends, the Dud-ettes, as Connor called them, were standing in camp with their mouths hanging open in disbelief. "Jesus! You guys close you mouths!" said Larry. "You ain't seen a woman before?"

"There's a story that needs to be told," said Dudley. "Larry, you tell it. I can't believe you, Connor." He and Connor weren't the best of friends and spent a lot of their time fucking with each other.

"Well, I'll tell you what," Larry proposed. "Let us put our warm beers in your ice chest and drink some of your cold ones to wash this dryness out of our throats, and I'll tell you one of the most amazing stories I'll ever tell." Four beers and a couple of shots of whiskey later, Larry finished the story.

Connor lit one of the going-away joints. "Damn! Larry, that was good. The whole damned, three-day adventure. A little more than I needed to hear. But now that we're all on the same page, let's think about dinner, and while we're at it, maybe breakfast in the morning.

"What say you, Dudmeister? I'll buy, you fly? Or better yet, let Larry use your van and we'll go."

"Fuck you, Connor!" Dudley retorted. "I can't trust Larry as long as you're around. *I'll* drive and I'll go in half on the food. But *you* guys are buying the beer because I brought a whole case of bourbon."

"What do ya say, Larry? Let's do stew. Okay?" asked Connor.

"As long as you're cooking, let's do stew."

It was eight in the evening, and the sun had long since disappeared below the horizon. Everyone sat around eating oxtail stew.

Connor referred to the oxtail as the asshole of the back strap. He said the famous cuts like the fillet mignon, the rib eye, the New York strip, and the porterhouse always got all of the attention, but the oxtail had all of the flavor and was tender as soft butter when it was cooked long enough. He would sear them to seal in the juices and add them to the stew. He knew what he was doing, and no one turned down seconds.

While he was eating, Connor noticed the new tent the Dud had scored before he left Portland. It hung loosely from several dead juniper limbs that were tied together with nylon twine.

"Fuck, Dud! Is that the brand-new, nine-by-twelve-foot tent you bought right before you left? It looks like a typhoon ripped it apart!"

Dudley laughed and said, "The first night we were here, we camped down there in the open." He tipped his head to the left, pointing to an open area devoid of trees or brush.

"We had sixty mile per hour wind gusts! Shit! We're in Death Valley, supposed to be one of the hottest places on earth, and we woke up to six inches of snow!

"It all melted by ten o'clock and, by noon, you couldn't even tell it had stormed. Everything was dry except for the Devil's Golf Course and *it* was flooded."

One of the Dud-ettes said, "Some of the tent poles were all bent and fucked up so we moved up here. We only had two good tent poles left. Dudley had to go buy some rope, and we found those branches. It looks better than I thought it would, though."

"Yeah, right. It looks like a hobo camp! But that's to be expected, isn't it?" Connor chided. "So, Dud, what did you do? Pay these guys to come down here and be your camp bitches?"

"Fuck you, Connor! At least I'm not hitchhiking, like you."

"What do you mean? That's a matter of choice, asshole! My Firebird's a much better rig than this battery-eating, piece-of-shit van of yours!" Connor pointed at Dudley's dilapidated, old van. "And, your brother's paying his own way. I'm not paying for everything, like you do."

"Yeah? Well, everyone back in Portland thinks you're crazy."

Larry interrupted, "Not everyone, Dud. Before we left, seven different people asked if they could come with us, and we turned them all down."

"Well, not me."

"You're just jealous, and too lazy!" said Connor, "But ya know what, Dud? We never woulda had those adventures if we drove." He walked over to the make-shift tent.

"I mean, Jesus Fucking Christ, Dud! It sounds like you and the Dud-ettes have been having the time of your lives the last couple of days!" Connor threw another verbal jab, "I mean, a fucking snowstorm in the middle of the frickin' desert?"

"You know, I don't believe half of that fucking story, anyway." Dudley was getting pissed.

One of the Dud-ettes said, "What do you think, Dudley? They paid those girls to drive them here and swap spit with 'em just to convince us. And did you notice the Idaho plates?"

"Shut the fuck up, asshole!" Dudley was getting *more* pissed.

"That's why you pay their way, huh, Dud." said Connor. "So you can have someone to order around and yell at. Someone to do all the shit work. Right?"

"Fuck you, Connor! And my name is Dudley, you asshole! One of these days you're really gonna piss me off, and I'm gonna kick your ass!" The words were no more than out of his mouth when he knew he might've stepped over the line. The Dud-ettes froze.

Just in time, Larry stepped in and went into action. He looked over at Connor, smiled and put a hand on his shoulder. "So, what do ya say, Connor? You want to go smoke a special after-dinner J?"

"Sounds good, but first, I want to point out one thing to the Dud." He stood up and walked over to Dudley and leaned in. "Bring it on, old man!" Silence followed as he stared at Dudley until the Dud looked away.

The tension was broken when one of the Dud-ettes asked if they could come with them. The Dud-ettes were two guys who partied with the gang back in Portland. Most of the time they were tolerable, but they were always broke, and both still lived at home with their parents despite being in their mid-twenties. It was odd to see them standing side by side. One was over six feet tall, and the other was only five foot two.

Connor pointed up at the tallest of the bluffs behind the camp and said, "We're gonna be up there in an hour. Come on up as soon as you two get done with the dishes and whatever other shit work the Dudmeister wants.

"Be sure to bring flashlights. It should be easy enough to see, as long as the moon is up. But I'd bring a flashlight, anyway, just in case."

The travelers had walked some distance away with Larry carrying a military, OD-green laundry bag he borrowed from the Dud. It was lined with a garbage bag and had a shorty of beer and some ice inside.

"We're not going up there, are we?" Larry asked.

"No! We're going over there." Connor pointed up at a bluff a short distance away. "Who wants to hang out with a couple of human sponges?"

Once they made it to the top of the bluff, they looked at the steep trail that led up the tall one Connor had pointed out to the Dud-ettes. They were on the last of the beers and were nicely baked when they saw two flashlights nearing the top.

"They're gonna be pissed, you know." Larry smiled.

Suddenly, they heard yelling in the distance. "Fuck you two!" The Dud-ettes had seen Larry's flashlight.

Connor and Larry were laughing it up pretty hard when they noticed four people coming up the trail toward them. The four were talking among themselves, unaware that they were about to run into the two travelers.

They were only ten feet away when Connor asked, "How you all doing tonight?"

The kid leading the group just about fell over backwards and let out a high-pitched squeal. "Man! You guys scared the shit out of me!"

"Sorry, but I thought you were gonna walk right over us," Connor replied.

Earlier in the day, he had noticed a school bus from some town in Illinois drive into the campground. He had seen about twenty school kids hanging around in their camp. Connor looked at the two girls and two boys standing before him. He figured they were out to do a little necking.

"Are you guys part of that group from Illinois?"

The taller of the two girls pointed at the two boys and said, "They are. It's a high school field trip. We're just tagging along." Then she held out her hand and said, "I'm Carol, and this is Becky. That's Jim and Dave. We were out for a walk when we saw your tracks. We thought you were friends of ours."

Connor pointed to a group of people on the next ridge over. "You mean them?" The four kids looked over and they all nodded, realizing it was their friends.

Connor lit a cigarette he'd just rolled and finished his beer. He waited for the question he knew was coming.

"Was that weed I smelled when we got here?" asked Dave.

Larry lit what appeared to be another cigarette and took a hit. The smell of the smoke quickly gave it away as some good, green Colombian weed. It was one of the going-away joints.

The kids settled in close to the travelers. Larry passed it to Dave. Dave hit it, choked and passed it on to Jim, who also choked. So, too, did Carol and Becky, who passed it to Connor. He took a hit and sent the joint on another round. The kids did a lot better with their second effort and even better with their third. Larry put the roach away in his second gen container.

"So, if you're just tagging along on the field trip, what did you do? Stow away in the luggage compartment or something?" asked Connor.

"Well, we're all members of the Geology Club at school," Carol explained, "and we had all sorts of fundraisers, like car washes and bake sales, over the last two years to pay for this trip.

"But Becky and I graduated in January and weren't allowed to ride on the bus because of some insurance liability. So we followed them out here in my VW Bus. My dad made it into a camper for me."

39

"The fucked thing is Carol used to be the president of the club," said Jim, "and she did most of the work to get us here. Then because she graduated early, she's being punished."

"We had a bake sale last month just to pay for their gas. It turned out to be the biggest fundraiser of them all," Dave added.

"So you guys study geology?" asked Connor. "Is Death Valley what you expected?"

"Absolutely!" said Carol. "Out that way about twenty miles"— she pointed out into the darkness—"is some of the oldest exposed rock on earth. Not too long ago, it was pushed upward by the California Plate.

"We've been looking forward to coming out here for two years. We've all been studying about it, and we have experiments we're doing. Completing the experiments and the getting results will earn college credits for me and Becky."

"What do you think of the weed?" Larry asked.

"That's a question that Becky should answer. She looks the most stoned!" said Carol. They all laughed.

"I don't think I've ever been this stoned. That was some serious shit!" Becky confessed. "Hey, I think we should be heading back. I don't want Mr. Simpson to catch us."

"He ain't gonna get out of bed." John laughed. "Didn't you hear him snoring? We did, and he's not gettin' up. Besides, I think he's scared of the dark!"

"I don't care. I'm outta here. Thanks for the high, and I hope to see you guys again, but I got to get back to camp." Becky stood to leave.

Jim stood up, too. "Don't leave without me. I'd probably get lost on the way back, then we'd all be in trouble."

"All you have to do is follow our tracks," said Carol. She turned to Connor and asked, "You gonna be here tomorrow night?"

Connor pointed up to the tallest bluff where he'd sent the Dudettes. "We'll be up there. Come on up, and we'll smoke some of the good shit with you. Say ten o'clock tomorrow night?"

"Can I bring my friends?"

"Fuck, yeah!" answered Connor.

"We'll see you tomorrow night then."

All four kids were standing now, and they started back down the hill. After they were out of earshot, Larry said, "Jesus, Connor! She's a little young, isn't she?"

"I think she's eighteen, asshole! And besides, I'm not thinkin' of pussy. I'm thinkin' of a ride to Illinois."

"Hey! Now that's a thought!"

"Yes, it is. I think the VW Bus she mentioned is the one parked across the street from the high schoolers' camp. If it is, she's got plenty of room."

"You're just trying to get laid."

"Hey, listen. The most important thing is a good, long ride if we want to make it to Florida fast," said Connor. "Speaking of getting laid, how are you feeling?"

"Like I was rode hard and put away wet! My friend, it was the best time of my life. I think Tanya and I are gonna hook up in the fall." Larry smiled.

"Yeah, you already said that. I think it's just one of many stories you'll be able to tell the buds back home. It might be the best one, but I'm sure there's gonna be more. If everything goes good, a ride to Illinois with two young girls will definitely be one of 'em!" After smoking one more joint, they meandered back to the Dud's camp.

"What the hell? What were you two doing on that other bluff?" one of the Dud-ettes asked.

"What do you mean? We were right where we said we'd be," Connor lied.

"Bullshit! You said you'd be up there on the tallest bluff," the other Dud-ette complained, "and it was a *bitch* getting up there!"

"I'm sorry, but I pointed to the one to the left of the tallest one," he lied again. He pulled a doobie from his shirt pocket and threw it at him. "Now don't be smokin' that shit around here."

Larry pointed back toward the draw they came down and said, "See that draw? There's a party that way. A bunch of those high schoolers from that school bus down there. Who knows, you might get lucky."

The Dud-ettes gathered up a bottle of bourbon and the doob and headed for the draw. "How far up the draw, Larry?" one asked.

"It's up there a ways. You'll hear 'em before you see 'em."

41

Away they went on another wild goose chase. Connor and Larry had heard some people up there as they returned to camp. They were singing gospel songs. If the Dud-ettes found them, they'd be in for a big surprise. Who knows, maybe they would join in! They looked at each other and almost fell over laughing at the thought.

The travelers sat in front of the campfire for a while. It was down to a warm glow. They could hear the Dudmeister snoring from inside his van. Larry was exhausted and ready to call it a night. He found his way to the tarp and crawled inside.

Connor headed into the hills until the lights from the campground disappeared. He lay back on the ground and stared up at the stars. He'd seen more stars in darker skies before, and he'd even seen the northern lights. But lying there feeling the warmth of the sand, smelling the fragrance of the desert and watching the bats and nighthawks darting here and there, he was at peace. He was thinking that Death Valley certainly was more than he expected, and he drifted off to sleep.

And that's where he woke, freezing his ass off. He got back to camp, into his sleeping bag and threw the woolly on top.

"Where'd you go?" asked Larry.

"Fuckin' out to look at the stars. I fell asleep out there, and it's colder than shit! Death Valley, one of the hottest places on earth, my ass!" They both laughed and went to sleep.

7. Trolling for a Big Ride

Saturday, March 6, 1976

Connor was up early, like normal. He had gone out and salvaged kindling left in empty campsites. Together with the wood already in camp, he was able to get a good cook fire going without having to use an axe. This was a favorite time for him. The crisp, cool morning offset by a small, but hot, cook fire. The juniper wood was like incense.

He was using the Dudmeister's gallon coffee pot. He filled it about halfway with water and waited for it to boil. Once he had a rolling boil, he added a half cup of coffee grounds. After five minutes, he carefully drizzled cool water over the surface to send the grounds to the bottom.

He had the hobo coffee done for no more than a minute when Larry and the Dud showed up with coffee cups in hand. It was good coffee, and they quietly enjoyed the moment.

Realizing the Dud-ettes were nowhere in sight, Dudley asked, "Where are the other two?"

"We gave them a joint about ten-thirty last night. They took off that way with a bottle of bourbon, looking for a party that wasn't there." Larry pointed to the draw. "What do ya think, Connor? They lost, or sleeping it off?"

"Hell, they might've found a party and got laid by some Christian girl, but I doubt it. I tell you what, though, I'm doing omelets. When we finish breakfast, if they're still not back, let's go look for 'em."

"I ain't lookin' for those jerks!" Dudley announced.

"They'll be back as soon as they smell food," said Larry.

Connor hadn't gotten the veggies cooked yet when a park ranger's truck pulled up to the camp. Out crawled the Dud-ettes. They both looked like they had rolled in the dirt and were limping.

"There you two are," said Dudley.

"So they're camping here, then?" asked the ranger.

"We been lost out there all night. We went back that draw a long way and never did find anyone," said the tall Dud-ette as he gave Larry a dirty look. "Then we decided to walk up to the top of those bluffs out there." He pointed to nowhere in particular. "We were just walking along, and next thing you know, we're falling and rolling down a cliff. We both fucked up our knees. We wandered around for a long time before we finally found the road."

"Yeah, and he insisted on walking the wrong way," said the short Dud-ette.

"I found them hitchhiking to the other side of the park about four miles down the road. Lucky thing I found them before they got a ride. They may have never gotten back." The ranger shook his head and turned to get back in his truck.

"You feel like an omelet? We've got plenty," Connor asked the park ranger.

"No, thanks. I appreciate the offer, though." The ranger opened the door of the truck and paused. "Do me a favor. Don't let these two go walking at night anymore, okay?"

"You got it, officer. Have a good day. You don't know what you're missing."

After the ranger left, Larry asked the Dud-ettes, "Where's the fucking bottle of bourbon?"

"We lost it when we fell down that cliff, man! I swear, we looked all over for it."

"So, did you guys find the party?" Connor asked.

"We heard someone talking and singing, but we never could find anyone," the tall Dud-ette answered.

"Hey, Connor. You think you could do us up an omelet?" the short Dud-ette asked.

"Sure, that's why I hitchhiked down here, for the breakfast chef position." Connor rolled his eyes.

After breakfast, Larry and Connor found the Dud-ettes' trail, and not much later, found the bottle where they had left it, empty. They never did find a cliff, but they found the hill they rolled down and where they left the trail and took off in the wrong direction.

"Your brother sure can pick 'em, dude."

"Yeah. They're the only guys that'll take all the bullshit that the Dud dishes out.

"By the way, did I tell you that my dad has started calling him *The Dud* because of you? He saw how much Dudley hates it when you call him that. Some of the people at his job are doing it now, too.

"I usually don't, but every now and then, when he's being a particularly *large* asshole, I do. I know it pisses him off, so I do it, and then I run!" Larry had that famous shit-eating grin on his face.

"You know, I do like him most of the time," Connor said. "It's just the way he always hangs with high schoolers, and he's in his thirties. It's kinda creepy, you know? I mean, he's the guy my mom told me to watch out for."

Connor paused for a moment and continued, "When it's just him, though, I kinda like him. That's the reason I wanted to come on down here. That, and the warm weather."

"Speaking of high schoolers, do you think the girls will give us a ride?" asked Larry.

"Won't know till I ask. But you can bet I'll be up on that bluff tonight hoping they show.

"The thing I'm gonna do today is walk through the campground and talk to everyone that's friendly. I can size 'em up for a ride outta here. I mean, the less time we're waiting at exits on the highway, the better I'll feel."

"Illinois is a little far north. It's still freezing every night up there, ain't it?"

"I don't know. You're probably right. One of my Army buddies lives in western Kentucky, so, if push comes to shove, we'll show up a month or two early. He won't care. Besides, our next goal is to get to your aunt and uncle's place in Florida. A big ride outta here to Illinois would be a big chunk of that."

"Okay, Connor. You just keep on thinkin'."

"Fuck off, you little piece of shit!"

"You love it, and you know it." Larry laughed and Connor joined in.

They headed back to camp to flip the Dud-ettes shit about the bottle, but they had already gone to bed to catch up on their sleep.

Connor walked away from the camp up a rise far enough that he could take in the whole campground. It was a typical national park campground with over 100 campsites. It had two rows of sites designated for tents with parking spaces cut at an angle off of the road to allow easy parking.

Each site had a fire pit about fifteen feet beyond the parking space. The width of each tent site depended on the location of cleared areas among the brush. Each site was a mirror image of the site across the road to afford more privacy.

There were two more rows, closer to the highway, which were designated for RV's.

Connor sat down and listened to the din coming from the campground. Dozens of conversations blended together into an unintelligible noise. He studied each group of campers trying to determine which ones might provide a ride out of this desolate lowland.

Then he got down to business. He figured that working the crowd couldn't hurt. He went from camp to camp, talking to anyone willing, feeling out their situation, and moving on.

The worst scenario would be the Dudmeister dropping them off in Las Vegas. They would hitch across the lower tier of the states, which, as far as weather was concerned, was the best way to go. Connor was determined to get a ride farther east than Vegas.

Meanwhile, Larry drove his brother's rig to the camp store and scored on some fixin's for some more camp stew. It was Larry's turn to cook, and he did it as only he could. He started with the fixin's to make a good base. On this day, his secret was adding beer to make it truly excellent.

When Connor got back to camp, Larry was just moving the pot away from the hottest part of the fire for an afternoon of slow cooking to meld all of the flavors into a wondrous stew.

"What do ya say we do a dayhike out to those tall hills way back over there, so we can get a better view of this bleak fucking place?" asked Connor. "Then let's go down to the visitor center to get all that tourist shit they give out. I need to learn a little about the geology of this place."

"Yeah, a hike sounds pretty good about now," said Larry.

He had devilish smile on his face and added, "You're goin' after that high school girl. Jesus! She's just eighteen, Connor."

"Fuck you! I'm not lookin' to get laid! I'm looking for a ride outta here other than hitchhiking across the fucking Hoover Dam. Besides, she's not in high school anymore, and Diane's just eighteen, too, asshole!"

"I ain't concerned one way or the other." Larry was in a huff.

"Yeah right, it sure the fuck sounds like it. So fuckin' drop it."

Later, they went for a hike to look around. It was the driest place they'd ever seen with a green golf course right in the middle. It had a certain stark beauty and was about as opposite a climate from a rainforest as was possible. Having come from a wet climate, it was definitely not a place they could ever get used to. The lowest place in North America was a shallow lake created by a snow storm that had ruined the Dud's tent.

They hit the visitor center where a cute little lady sold Connor a book on the geology of Death Valley. "Here's the thing," Connor explained why he bought the book, flipping it in the air. "I know you don't want to know about this stuff because it smacks in the face of your Christian Creationism theory. You know I can't do that shit!"

"So when Carol said she was looking to be a geologist, it kinda fed that interest of mine. I was thinking that if I showed a little knowledge on the subject, maybe we could get a ride from her."

"And maybe you'll get laid."

"And maybe I'll get laid, but believe me, she's the one who's going to play the sex card. You watch me. This is all about us getting a decent ride first. Second, it's to expand my knowledge, and third, if I'm real lucky, I might get to sleep with that beautiful thing."

Okay, I'll play along. But if you get laid out of this, you'll never make me believe that this geology angle was anything but a ruse."

"Whatever, asshole."

They got back to camp, and Connor crawled under the tarp to begin his cram session. He wanted to be ready for the geology class in store for him that evening.

About nine o'clock, the Dud-ettes began to get antsy. The Dudmeister was feeling ill, and the alcohol reserves were running low. The Dud wasn't coughing up another bottle, so they kept a close eye on Connor and Larry. They weren't going to let them sneak off and ditch them like the evening before.

Larry walked over to the ice chest and started loading a shorty of beer into his brother's laundry bag.

The Dud-ettes got more nervous. "Say, you ain't gonna take all the beer, are you?" one of them asked.

"Just the shorty we plan on taking up there tonight," Larry said, pointing up to the tallest of the bluffs and smiling.

Connor grabbed the short Dud-ette by the arm and said, "Come here. I want to tell you something." He led him back to where the tarp was set up and handed him a pint of the cheapest rotgut whiskey he could find at the market.

"I know Dud's not feeling well, so I picked you two up a pint of this stuff. And here,"—he shot a glance toward Larry and handed off some weed—"don't tell Larry, but I rolled you two a couple of joints."

"Where you two going tonight, really?" He whispered so Larry couldn't hear.

"Same place as last night." Connor pointed up to the tallest of the bluffs.

"Fuck you, man! I'm not falling for that shit again!"

"Listen, we *were* going up there, but we found some footprints and followed them instead. We saw a group of foxy little things and just followed our noses. Tonight, we'll be up there." He pointed to the tallest bluff again.

"We almost fell last night trying to get up there," said the short Dud-ette, "and you two weren't even there. Then you sent us up that draw, and we *did* fall. Tonight, we're not going on another wild goose chase!"

"Have it your way. But you just remember this—I provided you two with a bottle and a couple of doobies. So you can just thank me and go have a good time."

Connor walked over to Larry, acting a little pissed. He winked at Larry and said, "Let's get the fuck outta here."

When they left, they took a route that headed away from their destination. But as soon as they were out of sight of the camp, they went straight up the steepest bank they could find. Then they cut back to the bluff where the geology cuties were going to meet them.

Once they reached the top, they stayed back from the edge so they couldn't be seen. They found a nice flat spot with a good view, settled in, chugged four beers apiece and smoked a joint.

Just then, the Illinoisans showed up. It was just the two girls, which was unexpected.

Larry asked, "Where are your friends?"

"They didn't believe you'd be up here," Becky answered.

Connor started laughing, "There's a lot of that going around." He turned and walked out to the edge of the bluff. Larry and the girls followed. Looking down where they'd been the night before, they could see the Dud-ettes and about six or seven of the high schoolers. Connor started laughing again.

"What's so funny about that, Connor? It'll keep them out of our hair for the whole evening," Larry said as they returned to their flat spot and sat down.

Connor didn't bother answering Larry, but offered the girls some refreshments instead. "You two want a beer? There's enough for one each. It'll help with the cotton mouth you're gonna get when you smoke the good stuff." Connor had with a grin on his face.

"What's the good stuff?" asked Becky.

"You ever heard of Thai weed?" replied Larry. Both girls shook their heads.

"Well, it's the only thing I've found, so far, that came out of the Vietnam War that's worth a shit. It's the finest-tasting, smoothest-smoking weed to ever hit the Americas," said Larry, smiling in anticipation.

He reached into his pocket and pulled out a wooden match holder, opened it, and revealed four of the baddest joints in the world. He carefully pulled one out and lit it, turning it ever so slowly to insure a good burn and handed it to Carol.

"Don't take a big hit," he cautioned. "It'll expand in your lungs and kick your butt!"

Connor sat back and watched the show as Larry tutored the newbies. He turned down the first go-round just to see the looks on their faces as the marijuana took effect.

Carol remarked, "This is amazing! It has kind of a weird taste, but I like it."

Connor shared the next time around, taking two hits, and passing the joint to Larry. He got up and walked back over to the edge of the bluff overlooking the lowest place in North America. He could see the lights of the golf course and the little village where the employees lived. They were mostly old retirees who work the winter in the sun, and then leave before the scorching heat of summer.

Suddenly from the bluff where they had partied the night before, Connor could hear the Dud-ettes yelling up at him. "Fuck you, Connor! This is bullshit, man! Fuck you!"

He chuckled, and laughed a little harder as one of the high school kids with a powerful flash light shined it up his way. When it landed on him, he smiled and waved at them. Connor's voice was a low baritone and powerful, so with little effort, it carried to the other bluff.

"Get that flashlight out of my eyes and quit yelling or I'm gonna *spank* you when I get back to camp!"

The flashlight went out immediately. He could hear someone shush the group, and then silence. Larry and the girls were curious and had followed him out to the edge again.

"What did you do to piss them off tonight?" Larry asked.

"Well," Connor paused to let out a few more laughs, "First, I told them we were coming up here, and they didn't believe me, so they went down there. Then," he paused again to let out more laughter, "then I gave the short one two joints that I rolled that were mostly tobacco! I think that's what really has them going!

"But they're hangin' with a bunch of high schoolers, so they're probably lovin' it. Problem is, those kids are way smarter than they are. I mean, we're talking about Tweedle Dumb and Tweedle Dumber." Connor continued to laugh and the others joined in.

"Who are those two?" Becky asked. "They walked by us the other afternoon. Kinda gave us the creeps."

"They're friends of my brother's," Larry explained. "They're worthless drunks. My brother paid their way down here because he didn't want to camp by himself. They're both unemployed idiots. Just the kind of people my brother hangs with."

"We chose Death Valley as our first destination because Larry's brother was camping here," said Connor. He went on to tell them about the Bicentennial Tour, where they'd been so far, and where they planned to go.

"This really is an amazing place. And here's my first question for my new geologist friends—What happened to create this basin?"

What followed was a flood of information from the girls. It was as though he'd turned on a geological seminar. Connor had read enough about the local geology to ask them some good questions. He was really enjoying the discussion and was learning quite a bit.

A half hour passed, and Larry had been patiently listening and waiting for Connor to bring up the kicker. He finally shot his friend a look of boredom, and Connor reluctantly changed the subject.

"So, how long are you two gonna be out here?" he asked.

"We've got four more days here, but we're gonna make a few stops on the way home. Right, Carol?" said Becky.

"Yeah, we're gonna hit a few geological hotspots." She smiled for a second, glanced at Becky and asked, "Why? You guys want a ride?"

"We were thinking of accepting, if you offered." Connor was smiling.

"Well, before this goes any further," Carol gave Becky another quick look, "I've got to call my mom and talk to her first."

"Yeah, right. She's gonna call home to ask *her mom* if she can give a couple of strange guys a ride across the country!" Becky retorted.

Carol gave Becky an unhappy look and continued, "That, and one other condition—no sex. I'm a virgin, and I plan on staying that way. So if we're riding together, there won't be any sexual overtures from either of you." She looked right at Connor and pointed her finger. "Especially you."

Connor sat there with a sheepish look on his face. Larry leaned over to him and said sarcastically, "Jesus, Connor! She's got *your* number!"

Connor thought for a moment and said, "Okay, but let's talk sleeping arrangements. Larry and I don't want to spend money on motels all the way to Illinois, but we will help pay for gas."

"That's cool. We camped all the way out here and took our sweet time. We smelled pretty bad by then. That first shower once we were here was one of the best I've ever had!" Becky said, laughing.

"Amen!" agreed Carol.

"Okay, then if Mom says we're good, when are we leaving?" Larry asked.

"In four days," said Carol.

"That would mean three nights before we leave, right?" Connor asked. "We've got to have a Special Smoke party just to make sure the spirits are with us, and we're gonna need a day to recover the lost sleep."

"Now you're talking! I've been wondering when you were gonna pull out your Special Smoke again." Larry said excitedly.

"What is your Special Smoke?" asked Becky.

"It's a combination of psychedelic mushrooms, peyote, and weed with a little spice to hide the bad taste," Connor explained. "It only takes a little bit, and you won't believe what your wonderful Death Valley turns into! It'll be love at first sight."

"I don't know if I'm ready for that." Carol paused before going on. "We both did acid a few times, and it was a little scary. I liked it when I was with my friends, but not when I went home and was alone in my room. After the third time we tried it, Becky and I talked and decided it wasn't for us.

"So is it okay if we meet you up here the day after tomorrow? I'm not promising that we'll do your Special Smoke, but we'll definitely give you an answer on whether you'll have a ride to Illinois. Deal?" asked Carol.

"We'll see you then. And don't worry, you won't freak out. This shit ain't a purple mini-tab or anything like that," Connor reassured them.

"You'll have the time of your life!" Larry added.

After the girls left, Larry and Connor kicked back. Connor lit a going-away joint, took a long draw, held it in and slowly exhaled. He laughed and asked Larry, "So, what's your take on her I'm-a-virgin shit?"

"Well," Larry replied, "I'd say she's got a big crush on you and needs your help to keep her out of your bed."

"Yeah, that pretty much spells it out, alright. I'll tell you what. If she gives us a lift, I promise you this, I'm not going for that sweet thing at all."

Carol was a slender beauty, almost as tall as Connor. He was startled at how alluring he found her whenever she walked away from him. She didn't even seem to realize how beautiful she was and that just added to her appeal.

"Besides, if she's a virgin . . ." Connor didn't finish his thought. "Let's just say that the two virgins I've had really weren't worth the trouble. Shit, I thought one of them was going to shoot me the next day!"

"I remember, she sure thought a lot of that hymen, didn't she!"

"What was so fucking bizarre was *she* came crawling into *my* tent saying it was time for her to become a woman. Shit! She was *nineteen*! The last thing I expected was that fucking scene she made the next morning!

"Anyway, she must've gone cryin' to her big brother, because he called several times and threatened me. I finally told him that if he called me one more fucking time, I'd come over there and give him a *chance* to kick my ass! That finally ended it."

"Yeah, now she's a slut. Any guy can fuck her."

"And not a goddamned one of them, including you, ever called me to say, 'Thanks.' Yeah, that's right! I heard about you!"

They both chuckled and finished the joint. Not long after, they slowly made their way back to camp for a good night's sleep.

That night, Connor dreamed he was lost in the desert. He was following a talking burro that told him to "get the fuck out of my desert!" He woke up thinking just that. It was time to go.

Sunday, March 7, 1976

The travelers spent the the next day touring the park. Afterward, they found a bar and played some pool. Once back at camp, both of the Dudettes went down for naps. Larry and Connor took off and walked with Carol and Becky until dinner.

8. The Long Ride

Monday, March 8, 1976

Dud and the Dud-ettes left on a beer and whiskey run. They were passed out by the time Larry and Connor were ready to go have their Special Smoke adventure with the girls. They walked down to the girls' camp to see if they were up for it.

Carol asked, "Hey you two, are we still on for tonight?"

"Sure," said Connor. "Are we on for an Illinois adventure?"

"Yeah. My mom's actually *glad* you're coming along. She believes it's safer for us to travel with two guys. We aren't going to be following the bus back, so she's all for it. And, she's looking forward to meeting you two."

"Wow, I didn't realize you were gonna take us all the way to your house. But, if she's looking forward to meeting us, you must've really told her some lies!" Connor grinned.

Becky laughed. "She told her you belonged to a church group!"

"Well, hell, I do! It's just not a *Christian* church. I'm a Buddhist," Connor said, grinning. "Not a good one, but I'm trying! Larry, here, is a fine upstanding Christian man!"

"Hey, you guys up for the Special Smoke tonight?" asked Larry.

Connor noticed they were packing some of their belongings. "You guys leaving early or something?"

"Yeah, tomorrow morning, early," said Carol. "Are you okay with that? We were gonna come by and let you know. We thought you'd be flexible, though."

"Shit, yeah! We can be ready in fifteen minutes easy. Less if we're in a hurry," Larry answered.

"I tell you what," Connor proposed, "you guys come on up and get us when you're ready to go. We'll do some packing tonight so we won't be rushed in the morning."

Carol agreed. "We were thinking about six o'clock."

"Well now. That *is* an early start. What's the agenda?" Connor asked.

"We'd like to get to the Grand Canyon by tomorrow evening."

"Don't worry, we'll be ready."

The guys returned to Dud's camp and hung out until it was time for their Special Smoke adventure.

About an hour later, the girls showed up at their camp. They hadn't gone far when Becky told the guys they weren't ready to do the Special Smoke. "We just want to get a good night's sleep. We're in for a long day tomorrow."

"That's okay. Shit! We're not gonna force anything on you, I promise," said Connor.

Larry added, grinning, "That includes anything in the way of sex. Right, Connor?"

"That's what we agreed to. I'll hold up my end of the bargain." He smiled and said, "I just hope these two can hold up *theirs*."

That got laughs all around and two slugs in Connor's arm from the girls. *Foreplay!* Connor smiled.

"So, what do ya say we just do a short walk tonight, then get a good night's sleep for an early start tomorrow," Connor suggested. "We can wait to do my Special Smoke till after we get to the Grand Canyon."

He paused. "So why the early out? What happened to change your schedule?" Connor could feel the tension rise in the girls.

"Our geology teacher is being a jerk. I think he's pissed because Becky told him he isn't in charge of us. The last couple of days he's been suggesting that we shouldn't even follow the bus. That didn't happen of course. The class kind of rebelled a bit so he backed down. So we want to get out of here before he gets up."

Tuesday, March 9, 1976

At five-thirty in the morning, Larry and Connor were packed and eating a breakfast of omelets and hobo coffee. The girls showed up at a quarter to six as they sat and enjoyed their second cup of joe. With a little arm twisting, they accepted the offer for breakfast.

Just as the guys finished the dishes, the Dudmeister got up and sweet-talked Connor into one more omelet before they took off.

Connor cooked and made another batch of hobo coffee while Larry and the Dudmeister talked to the girls.

Like clockwork, the Dud-ettes got up and put in a breakfast order that Connor declined. They were in the midst of whining about having to burn their own breakfast when Becky walked over to the tall Dud-ette and slapped him across the face. He reeled back on his heels at the force of the slap.

"*That's* for your foul mouth the other night!" Becky growled. "You don't talk to my friends that way!"

"I didn't say it!" the tall Dud-ette muttered as he rubbed his cheek and pointed to the short Dud-ette. "*He* did."

The short Dud-ette was still laughing about the slap when a second one caught him squarely on the jaw and he went down. "You're a perverted asshole!" Becky eyes flashed with anger.

The short Dud-ette jumped up and yelled, "You fucking cunt! No woman hits me like that!" He lunged toward Becky with his fist raised just as Connor arrived. He blocked the intended blow and landed a left to the side of the short Dud-ette's chin.

"Well now, Becky," said Connor, "You didn't tell me he offended your friends, and you didn't say you were gonna kick his ass."

He looked at the tall Dud-ette and said, "Jesus, dude! She would've kicked both your asses if I hadn't stepped in when I did. Now get your buddy up before he pukes all over himself."

Connor turned to the Dudmeister. "I hope I didn't fuck up your help too bad. At least he'll have trouble talking for a few days."

"You did me a favor," said Dudley. "Now get the fuck out of here and take care of my little brother."

"I don't need a babysitter, but I'd rather have him in my corner than anyone else, if you know what I mean." Larry gave the Dudmeister a hug. "Later, bro."

The girls waited in the bus as the guys put their packs in and waved goodbye to the Dud camp and to Death Valley.

As it turned out, a week after the short Dud-ette returned to Portland, he had his jaw wired shut and spent the next eight weeks sucking his food through a straw. Connor had broken his jaw in two places but never owned up to it. He always maintained it had been Becky.

"Jesus, Becky!" exclaimed Larry. "At least give a guy some warning before you go and slap someone like that!" Larry was laughing now.

"That guy was an SOB! My friends were crying after he called them a bunch of sluts. But I didn't intend on hitting him until it happened. I've never done anything like that before."

"It was a nice one!" said Connor. "You're lucky he didn't hit you back before I stepped in. That guy may a dumb-shit, but he *does* know how to fight."

They managed to leave the park without any further incidents and, before they knew it, our travelers crossed back into Nevada.

Connor had them stop at the border while he and Larry climbed to the top of the state line signs for both Nevada and California, and Becky took their picture.

"I'd like to do that at as many borders as possible," said Connor.

"How about a Nevada joint, girls?" asked Larry as he pulled one of the going-away doobs out of his shirt pocket.

"How many of those going-away joints do you have? Where'd you get them?" asked Becky.

Larry told them about the going-away party held for them back in Oregon and the donation jar. "We were surprised it worked out as well as it did."

"Yeah, it was kinda like one of those bake sales you had, except we provided free beer. Once we got them drunk, they were very charitable," Connor laughed.

While they smoked, Connor looked out of the window at the landscape. It was so foreign compared to his home. The broad, sweeping valley was parched with little more than sparsely-growing cactus and a few low, prickly bushes.

Giant rock outcrops rose from of the desert floor. Made mostly of sandstone and ancient volcanic ash deposits, the color of the rocks was a muted rainbow of yellows, reds, browns, and grays. On their flanks, about eight to ten thousand feet in elevation, grew sagebrush and other similar groundcover. Only on the very top of the highest summits did he see any green. This green color, though, was yellowish and faded, nothing like the deep, dark green of his native western rainforest.

He said to no one in particular, "You know, this place reminds me of the first time I went skinny-dipping and got my ass all sunburned. The next day, my pants kinda grated on it all day long. Irritated the fuck out of me! This place looks like a dried lake bottom. Reminds me of a sunburned ass!"

They stopped and had lunch at a casino near the Hoover Dam. The travelers showed the girls an old trick of pilfering food from the buffet. They took fried chicken, baked potatoes, bread and butter, and anything else that would travel. They wrapped the food in paper napkins and hid it in their daypacks.

"This is a trick we use when camping to save money for more beer," explained Connor.

9. The Best of Friends

Lucas, Alex and JJ

Lucas Brown, Alex Groan, and Jerry Johnson were "one for all and all for one" like the characters in *The Three Musketeers*. It was their mantra, their secret since their days in the FBI Academy in Quantico, Virginia.

They managed to get through the school even though they were unpopular with the instructors and the other students. It was, in retrospect, the reason for their friendship. No one else really liked them.

After graduating from the Academy, their assignments scattered them to three different regions of the country. This, after all three had put in for the Miami Field Office, the hotspot in the country for the import of illegal drugs from Colombia. The thought of the friends being assigned to the same office had brought nightmares to the administrators of the school.

Each had been a police officer in a major metropolitan area and dreamed of becoming an FBI agent. As a police officer, each worked his tail off in hopes of qualifying for the Academy.

While off-duty, each dedicated himself to earning his Bachelor's in Criminal Justice by attending night school and correspondence school.

All three were in their late twenties and were above average in height with very muscular and imposing figures. They had never met before attending the Academy, but formed a tight bond while there. They were generally considered egotistical jerks and shunned by everyone else.

While at school, they shared stories from their childhoods. It was then they realized they all came from abusive families, and it infected them in similar ways. They managed to hide their deep-seated hate and frustration from the world.

When they were alone with each other, however, they could vent the anger that had been beaten into them as children. It was a relief to finally speak of the hurt that followed them through their lives, and it was the cement that bound them together.

On graduation day, they made a pact to keep in touch and to meet in Chicago for a week each year. Then they parted ways, each to his first assignment as an FBI Agent.

Lucas

Lucas became a member of the Mafia Division of the New York Field Office in New York City. In just a few years, he was on the take and warning the mob of impending investigations. It wasn't the money that drove him, though. It satisfied the resentment he felt toward his superiors who routinely passed him over on promotions.

He stood about six feet four inches in height and had a stocky build. His face was scarred from his father's abuse and from fighting as a teenager. They added character to otherwise homely features. This didn't stop him from being popular with women. Those he pursued were charmed and happy to have his company, at first.

He married and divorced twice in the next three years, each wife citing physical and mental abuse. He had a child from each marriage and the alimony and child support payments took a good chunk of his paycheck.

After his second failed marriage, he could barely afford his efficiency apartment. He began drinking heavily, and it started to show on the job.

One day, he sat alone in his favorite bar. He only wanted a drink to mellow him after another boring day of watching some pawn shop suspected of bringing heroin into the city. One drink led to two, and two led to ten.

A stranger sat down on the stool next to him and bought him a drink. Then he just laid it out. "You keep my bosses informed of what's going on in the FBI investigations. We pay you for it. Move you into a nice apartment. Get you a little cash bonus when you save the organization money."

Lucas was a classic target for the mob and was easily recruited. Once turned, he actually became a better agent. At their urging, he reduced his drinking. He began showing up for work cleaned, pressed and ready to go. He even showed a little more respect and friendliness toward his fellow agents. Everyone figured he had hooked up with future wife number three.

Once a week, when he was off-duty, Lucas would drive to a quiet little house in eastern Pennsylvania for a meeting with his handler. Over a wonderful dinner served by two beautiful women, he would casually give the man all the information he had gathered during the week. After dinner, the handler would leave, and the two women would stay and serve Lucas.

He was in heaven. He just needed more money. That came with the promotion he felt was long overdue. He answered to the Regional Director and had an office to himself. The first time he sat at his new desk, he smiled inwardly at the irony. He had to become a snitch for the mob to finally get his long-sought promotion.

Just as ironic, with the promotion came more mob money. He put a down payment on a townhouse and bought a new car. His handler began introducing him to the big bosses.

Things were finally looking bright for him. Still, with all his success, he could not sit alone at night in his dark apartment without reliving the beatings from his parents. He could almost hear their cruel comments and constant reminders of his shortcomings.

One night, while at the bar, he met a woman who came home with him. She introduced him to marijuana. He tried it and discovered the mellowing effect the herb had on him. While using it, he could relax and let go of the hatred he always felt.

Alex

Alex went to the Bank Robbery Division of the Los Angeles Field Office. In the beginning, he excelled. He quickly rose to the position of Section Lead and performed well in his new job.

His one mistake had been marrying the boss's daughter. It was commonly thought that his promotion came, in part, because of the marriage. He quickly fathered two beautiful baby girls. They were the apples of their grandfather's eye.

As time went on, he began to withdraw within himself. He didn't understand why at first. Most nights, he fell asleep on the basement couch in front of the television. Night after night, his wife's pleas landed on deaf ears. Alex finally realized the trap he had stepped in. He didn't love his wife anymore and her father controlled his future in the FBI.

At work, Alex was all business. His strongest asset was his amazing deductive capability. This skill had earned him his promotion. Despite this, his fellow agents resented him for that and worked to make him look bad at every chance.

One day, he came home to find a babysitter instead of his wife. She had left him a note, explaining that she would be home late. She was with a friend who had suffered a death in the family.

From that day forward, he could feel a change in the marriage. There were no more complaints about his withdrawn and aloof behavior. Alex continued to spend most nights sitting on his basement couch and staring into space.

He silently retreated to his memories of abuse from his father that had intensified after his mother left for another man. She had told him she loved him, but couldn't live with his father anymore. She promised to come back for him as soon as she could, but that never happened. He never forgave her for that.

He felt the same thing happening in his marriage. The deep-seated resentment of women caused by his mother's abandonment was gradually beginning to surface. He could no longer contain the anger he felt from all of the beatings and sexual abuse he had endured as a child at the hands of his father and his father's friends.

At work, he noticed that people were smiling and snickering behind his back. He knew something was up, and it began to weigh heavily on his mind.

It all came to a head the evening his wife told him she was pregnant. Alex hadn't slept with her in months, so he knew it wasn't his. She told him that she wasn't sure who the father was, but it was most likely one of his fellow agents. She had slept with several.

Alex broke. He blacked out after the first punch, and was not aware of the next four. He could only recall seeing her lying on the kitchen floor, unconscious and bleeding. When she came to and struggled to stand, he sat on a chair, staring at his wife—his broken life and destroyed career—slowly get off the floor.

She stood on unsteady legs and ordered Alex to leave. Her parents came and took the kids while she went to the hospital. Despite her broken nose and bruises, no charges were pressed.

She quickly filed for divorce. He was to pay alimony and child support for his two kids and the yet unborn baby. Knowing the third child, a boy, was the son of an agent from his office made him want to kill.

His wife had ruined him. His fellow agents openly laughed at him and mocked him. He was demoted and transferred to the Drug Smuggling section of the San Diego Field Office. Some rumors followed him, but nothing was ever said. He wasn't ridiculed and was generally treated better than he ever was in Los Angeles.

He was broke and alone, and spent most of his days working in the field. He enjoyed being outside rather than behind a desk all day. But while his partners went home to a life, Alex worked late in the office until exhaustion sent him home to his empty apartment.

Before long, his efforts caught the eye of the Station Chief, and he was promoted to Team Leader. This time, there was no resentment from his peers, but he knew he was not well-liked.

Even with the increase in pay, he was still living in a small, studio apartment and riding the bus to work to save on gas. His ex-wife moved to St. Louis to follow an agent she had been living with since their divorce. When Alex protested, she took him to back court and won full custody of the kids with no visitation for him. To make matters worse, she also got an increase in child support. He was again living below the poverty level.

That year, he called Lucas and told him he couldn't afford to come to Chicago. Lucas sent him a plane ticket and a thousand dollars for spending money. He included a note, promising to talk to him about side work that could improve his financial situation.

During the Chicago visit, Lucas pulled Alex to the side and told him about his mob connection. At first, Alex resisted, but he reconsidered once Lucas told him how much money he could make. Lucas explained that he would just help with the logistics of getting drugs across the border.

Lucas had told his handler that he planned to recruit Alex during their visit and he came prepared. He told Alex that if he accepted, he would be given a handler and would meet with him once a week. Lucas described his weekly dinner dates. Alex was intrigued.

Seeing his interest, Lucas opened a briefcase and revealed thirty thousand dollars. He explained that it was a signing bonus. Dumbfounded, Alex agreed and was given a phone number.

Jerry

Jerry Johnson, JJ to most, was the least popular of the three at the Academy. He had been unpopular his whole life. It was his ego. He always talked about how good he was, and he never gave credit to anyone around him for anything. He just wasn't a team player. These qualities endeared him to no one.

He was a cruel, sadistic bully and was very tough. When he was young, his father beat him and his mother during drunken rages. His mother took him and left his father when he was six.

Life did not improve for Jerry, though. His mother brought home a series of boyfriends who inflicted him with beatings and the torture of watching his mother getting beaten. The abuse had been etched into his mind. He couldn't understand how she could be drawn to such violent men.

JJ stood around six foot six inches and was built like a wedge with broad shoulders and a narrow waist. His nose had been broken several times, and he carried scars over each eye.

He received the scars as a teenager when he dreamed of being a heavyweight boxing champion. That dream faded as he was beaten by boxers with better skills and speed. He was good, but not good enough.

Later, he and his mother moved to Detroit with a black man. There, he was a football coach at JJ's high school. He was the best man his mother had ever been with and the first that JJ respected.

He taught JJ how to focus his anger on the linemen of the opposing teams. Soon, scholarships poured in, and he chose to attend the University of Michigan. A career-ending knee injury forced him to turn to law enforcement.

Soon after switching his major, JJ took his first job at the Robbery Division of the Detroit Police Department. He played the bad cop in the good-cop, bad-cop routine. He was brutal.

After graduating college, he applied to and was accepted by the FBI Academy where he barely graduated. His test scores were good, but his bad attitude threatened his success.

He was unable to get along with anyone, except Lucas and Alex. It was their advice that helped him fool his instructors into thinking he was a team player. He hated kissing ass, but it got him through the Academy and helped him control his violent rage that was always just below the surface.

His instructors smiled when they sent him to the smallest field office they could find: Fairbanks, Alaska. It was staffed by three agents and a field chief, and he quickly became the fifth wheel. Like everywhere else he'd lived, no one liked him. He had nothing to do but keep his nose clean and wait until he acquired enough seniority to transfer out of purgatory.

He had a series of relationships, but all were short-lived. Two, however, resulted in children, and he dutifully paid his support. JJ never played a role in raising the two boys because both of their mothers had filed restraining orders against him.

At the third annual Chicago gathering, Lucas told JJ about large shipments of heroin that had been coming in through Fairbanks. If he wanted to supplement his income, the mob needed someone in the Fairbanks Field Office to keep them informed of any investigations concerning their dope. JJ accepted the offer. Lucas had now recruited both of his friends.

JJ's job was easy since the shipments were coming in under the radar. He received monthly payments that he deposited in a Swiss bank account.

Like the others, JJ met his handler once a week. The meeting place was a hotel near the airport in Anchorage. He enjoyed room service while giving the weekly report to his handler. Then he would receive his money and spend some time with an East Coast hooker. These weekly meetings were the only exception to an otherwise solitary life.

During their fourth annual Chicago gathering, they talked about President Nixon's plan to reorganize the Justice Department. They had read reports that he intended to merge the Bureau of Narcotics and Dangerous Drugs with the Office of Drug Abuse Law

Enforcement, thereby creating the Drug Enforcement Administration, the DEA.

Lucas' handler encouraged him to apply for the new agency. He would get an extra hundred grand if he was accepted. Lucas brought applications for both of his friends to their Chicago gathering. The offer was extended to all three. On JJ's urging, Lucas and Alex each set up their own Swiss accounts. They were very excited by the possibilities.

Six months later, the FBI approved their transfers. All three were suddenly top agents, according to their superiors, who just wanted them out of their hair. The DEA had just acquired all three "musketeers".

On July 28, 1973, the three friends stood on the podium behind President Nixon as he signed the proposal for the DEA and introduced the new agency to the American public on national television.

They were part of an army of agents, all in identical black suits, white shirts, and black ties, that were, once and for all, going to end the mob's dominance over the drug trafficking around the country. In reality, they were just another agency full of informers and snitches that would keep the mob in the business of supplying drugs to America and the world.

The mob had silently set up in Colombia. No one knew of their influence in the cocaine and marijuana trade that was just beginning to dominate the drug scene in America. In their newly-formed symbiotic relationship, the Colombian Cartel provided the drugs and the mob used its extensive distribution network to sell them.

As part of Nixon's famous "War on Drugs", the DEA targeted the Colombian Cartel, making them the new bad guys. All the while, the mob sat back and collected their share.

In accordance with the DEA's mandate, the American Embassy in Bogotá got three new undercover agents for their security detail. The three friends finally got their wish, and beyond their wildest dreams, they now collected drug money from both the mob *and* the Cartel.

They were all dirty, all together, and all left on their own. It was a recipe that was destined to come to a bad end.

On October 23, 1973, they flew down to Colombia. On their first night at the Embassy, the three dined with the Ambassador. Fully aware of their undercover status, the Ambassador's role was nothing more than advisory. The agents reported directly to their superiors at DEA Headquarters in Washington, D.C.

After dinner, the Ambassador laid out the strategy that the DEA had sent him. The agents were to discover where the cocaine was being manufactured. They would turn their findings over to the Colombian Army who would then destroy the operations.

On the agents' third night in Colombia, they dined at a secret location where the food was much better. Their hosts were bosses of some of the most powerful drug cartels. The three were directed to turn over all information the American government had on their Colombian informants. In return, the agents would be given information on manufacturing plants that had been shut down to make them look good to their bosses. After dinner, they enjoyed American scotch, Cuban cigars, and Russian whores.

Over the coming months, they became a formidable team and worked diligently to uncover their government's informants. Lucas, the mouthpiece for the team, would deliver this information as promised. The Cartel would then eliminate the informant, keeping the agents' hands clean.

Their ability to extract information from their captives was becoming an art form. They were brutal. Each was discovering his own niche in the finer techniques of physical and mental torture. To further their advantage, they became fluent in Spanish. It was a valuable tool that enabled them to do their dirty work without the need of a translator.

The Cartel set them up in a house in a small town just outside of Bogotá. With a soundproof basement, it was a secure location where they could bring their captives, and the inevitable screams would go unheard.

It was in this house that a change came over Alex. One night, in a drunken haze, he brought home a cross-dressing man. Not knowing his sex until the next morning, Lucas and JJ walked in as Alex stood over the bed, staring at the guy. None of the three had realized it was a guy when Alex had brought him home.

They took him into the jungle and put three bullets in his head. Alex realized it had been the best sex he'd had in some time. Since they held no secrets, he told Lucas and JJ.

Alex began to incorporate sex, and rape, into their interrogation routine. It was very effective in getting information, and he enjoyed it immensely. Lucas and JJ got off watching.

They had been in Colombia for almost two and a half years when their whole world came crashing down around them. The Cartel ordered them to arrest a man and to use their talents to get some sensitive information.

When they went to the address, they detained the wrong man. He was the son of a high-ranking government official. They were unaware that witnesses saw them force him into their car.

They took him to their basement to extract the needed information. During the interrogation, JJ snapped and killed him with his fist. They dumped the body in the jungle and were seen doing that as well.

The next day, all three were flown to Washington and put on desk duty while under investigation. They explained to the investigators that the man had been involved with the Cartel and they assumed he died of a heart attack while being questioned.

Six weeks later, March 9, 1976, they were cleared of all charges and reassigned. Their new post was the one they had first sought as FBI agents: Miami, Florida. They would all be working together as part of Operation Stopgap out of the DEA's Miami Headquarters.

10. Smoke and the Big Ditch

"So, we gonna make the Grand Canyon before we stop tonight?" Connor asked.

"We'll get close, but I think we should stop and camp in the forest just south of the park," Carol answered.

"Trees. Sounds good to me. If I remember right, we'll be in Ponderosa pine. We've got plenty of that in the high desert in central Oregon. I love the look of a good Ponderosa forest. It's wide open, hardly any underbrush. Great for camping."

Connor paused and looked over at Carol. "I just want to thank you again for the ride. This is better than anything we could've hoped for."

"Becky and I have planned this trip for almost two years. That's the reason for all the extra credits and summer school last year. We knew my dad was gonna give me this VW Bus as a graduation gift. We figured there was a chance, if we both graduated early, we'd be *forced*"—she made air quotes to emphasize her double meaning—"to drive if we still wanted to come on the Death Valley field trip." Carol looked over at Connor and smiled.

"Anyway, we've been pouring over the maps forever," she continued. "We wanted to chart a course back home so we'd hit as many national parks and geological hotspots as we could.

"The one thing that's been giving us headaches is the price of gas. We paid fifty-four cents a gallon in Vegas. But with you two footing half of the bill, we'll be able to take the scenic route we had planned. That's gonna take about three weeks. You don't mind, do you?"

"No problem. Like I said, this is better than anything we could've hoped for. Larry and I've been planning for over a year, too. The thing about hitchhiking is you kinda set yourself adrift. You go with the flow of whatever comes your way. You know what I mean?

It's exciting, standing on the side of the road not knowing where your next ride's gonna get you."

"Well, I think you're crazy!"

"And that may very well be. I mean, I'm not naive about the possibility of running into bad people. I shudder at the idea of you, or any other female, doing what we're doing." Connor paused at the thought.

"Carol, one of my best attributes is that I don't panic. My mind stays clear in situations where other people freeze up. Believe me, I don't know why I'm that way, but I am. It's saved me more than once in a fight. I hope it will take care of me and Larry on this trip if we're ever confronted. By the way, I think Becky is the same way."

"*She's* the one who scares me!" Carol remarked. "Her temper is going to get us into trouble one day, you watch. I don't think she's *anything* like you."

"Ah, hell! She's not that bad. Shit! I remember all the dumb-assed mistakes I've made just because my temper got to me. It makes me wonder how I've lived to be twenty-two."

"Oh yeah. You're almost old enough to be our dad!" Carol joked.

"I turn twenty-three next month. You come back and tell me if you ain't fucking a little more in control of yourself when you're twenty-three! I mean, hell, by then, you ought to be working on your masters in rocks!" Connor laughed.

"You're so much more than I was four and a half years ago. Shit! You'll probably be running the University of Illi-fucking-nois by the time *you're* twenty-three!"

"Or I could be a housewife with three kids, wondering what life could have been."

"Bullshit!" Connor pulled a going-away joint out, lit it, and offered Carol a hit. She declined, so he one-manned it. He put on the Marshall Tucker Band and enjoyed the ride. The thing about a loaded 1972 VW Bus was that a two-hour drive usually took three hours. There was no hurrying it.

And it was about three hours later when Connor noticed something way out on the horizon that he'd not seen since the Tahoe forest. He smiled and pointed. "You see that over there?"

"Yeah, so what?"

"You see, that's the difference between you and me. You see everything through the eyes of a geologist, but I see a forest on those hills."

"You're right. I didn't notice the trees."

Just then, Larry sat up straight, looked out at the hills and smiled. "Shit, Carol. We were *born* in a forest. Of course we're gonna notice the trees."

"He's right. See how the mere mention of a forest brings Sleeping Beauty back to life?"

"Shit! I just woke up," said Larry as he pointed to the roach sitting in the ashtray. "What do ya say we get some beer for the camp tonight?"

Connor laughed and handed Larry the roach. "You just keep on thinkin', Larry, just keep on thinkin'."

Larry smiled and said, "Fuck you, Connor. That's my line!"

The forest turned out to be Williams, Arizona. They took a left and headed north toward the Grand Canyon, leaving the little oasis of green behind. They stopped for refreshments and gas. That's when Becky woke up from the dead to announce that she was famished.

A few miles further, they found a narrow, side road and slowly drove until they were out of sight of the highway. They came on an old campsite and stopped. They broke out the daypacks and were soon drinking cold beer and eating the deep-fried chicken and spuds they had scored at the casino.

Larry and Connor poured over a map of Arizona for a place to spend the night. Carol and Becky were amused as they watched the two study the map, point and discuss, and then study again. This went on for several minutes.

Finally, Connor poked the map and said, "I say here. What do you three say?"

They all nodded. Carol walked to the bus and crawled in back. "Becky, you get in back with me and let the great white campers find us a spot to camp."

Larry said, "Sounds good. Let's stop first and get fixin's for breakfast. Connor's cooking in the morning because he's always up first and making the best damned hobo coffee for us caffeine junkies. Come on, Connor. You drive and I'll look for the camp."

They continued to drive north toward the Grand Canyon. Soon, the rise in elevation put them back in the forest.

So, on the eighth day of their Bicentennial Tour, the guys had travelled eleven hours in a VW hippie bus, found a camp, set up their tarp, built a fire, and were roasting the wienies they scored with the last of the casino tailings being used to round out their meal.

"All in all, today was a very productive day," Connor said. "We started within the confines of Death Valley, California, and traversed the narrow end of Nevada. We've now travelled into our third state and are enjoying hot dogs, the great American food source!

"What do ya say we do my Special Smoke for dessert?"

No one said anything for a few seconds, and then Larry spoke up. "God, yes! We're in a forest, now's the time."

They finished eating and cleaned up the camp. Connor and Larry went out and foraged for some breakfast kindling while the girls changed. The western sky was finishing up its evening light show as they settled in around the fire.

Connor carefully removed the handmade, clay pipe and his Special Smoke from his pack frame. He began to load the first headrush for Larry.

"Now, ladies, I know I've already told you this. But as a reminder, I want you to know this is a very mild high. You won't get the hallucinations you got from LSD. I promise you an evening of laughter and wondrous feelings and thoughts. You may find yourselves laughing till your face hurts!" Connor smiled.

Larry took the pipe, lit it, and took a long draw and held it as long as he could. He took another draw and held it again. He finished the offering and carefully cleaned the pipe before handing it back to Connor.

Next, Connor readied the pipe for Becky. She choked on the first hit and did real well on the next two. As she handed the pipe back to Connor, she said, "Wow! That's an unusual flavor. It kinda took me by surprise."

Carol was next and didn't choke once. She handed the bowl back to Connor and said, "Holy shit! I can already feel it."

By the time Connor filled his pipe, the three trippers were up and wandering around in the evening light, giggling about the weird shadows cast by the fire. He finished his pipe, carefully cleaned it and put his Special Smoke away.

He settled back and waited for the drug to split the two worlds of consciousness and sub-consciousness. He loved the body high, but mostly he loved the way his mind worked while the peyote coursed through his brain.

He acquired a smile and just sat there, listening to the others express their thoughts and insights as his Special Smoke took them places they'd never been before.

It was a night of laughing, music, the swilling of beer and wine, and rolling-on-the-ground blissfulness. They lounged around the fire, listened to the Arizona night and watched the mysteries created by the shadows in the trees that seemed to move in lifelike form.

Wednesday, March 10, 1976

The cackle of dawn was upon them, when the birds sing their sweet nothings to one another and the sky begins to boil into a tie-dyed Monet. A soft, cool breeze scented with pine and sage caressed their faces.

All four enjoyed the heightened sensitivity of a clear, peaceful, drug-induced mind. Each found a power spot and sat contentedly with that shit-eating grin one gets after a wondrous experience.

After the Father Sun breached the horizon and the sky settled on a passion blue, Connor took a deep breath and said, "How about you guys go get more breakfast wood while I start the hobo coffee."

All three jerked when he spoke, startled out of their own private worlds. Becky got up first, walked over to Connor, and planted a kiss on the top of his head. "Thank you for your Special Smoke. Can we do it again sometime?"

Carol laughed, got up, repeated Becky's kiss and thanked him, too. "When can we do it again? That was the best high I've ever had!" She was all smiles.

"We'll do it again soon, I promise," said Connor.

Larry was the last to rise. "That was nice, bro, but don't expect a kiss from *me*! That sunrise was far out, wasn't it?"

"It *was* far out," Connor replied. They were in the final stages of the euphoria that came with the exit of the drugs.

"Now what do ya say you three go get some more breakfast wood," he pressed them. "It's Italian omelets."

"That's my favorite!" Larry announced as he walked away with the girls following him.

"What is breakfast wood?" Carol asked.

"Yeah." Becky asked, "Are we eating wood for breakfast?" The girls giggled.

Larry ignored the pun and said, "Stay with me, grasshoppers! We aren't eating wood. We're looking for wood that makes a good bed of coals in a hurry and other wood to keep the fire at an even temp. Believe me, my geology girls, while you're way smarter than me or Connor, the science of cooking fires is one we've mastered. Matter of fact, I think Connor's gonna write a paper and get 'PhD'd'." They all laughed.

Half an hour later, they sat around the slow-burning fire, drinking coffee and watching Connor create the Italian omelets. Larry fed the fire small pieces of Aspen limbs just enough to keep the bed of coals from cooling down and providing a nice even heat for Connor to work his magic with the eggs. The girls toasted bread with the same sticks they used for the weenies the previous evening. All were quiet until after the meal.

Connor broke the silence and started to talk to no one in particular. "In the fall of '74, I did the mushroom high for the first time. It was just a few, but I could feel the special nature of the high they gave. I knew they had done something to my mind that only peyote had done before. There was no edge you're walking on, like acid can have. I mean, really all acid, mushrooms, or peyote do is magnify what's already there and enables you to see it.

"But mushrooms and peyote are different. They're medicines that the great Mother gave us to help us understand what's in our subconscious so we can free our minds of our fears.

"I remember reading this story about these guys who got kicked out of Harvard for doing illegal experiments on people with acid."

"Richard Alpert and Tim Leary," Carol put in.

"That's right, Ram Dass and *Be Here Now*. Which is all well and good in the world of those who *can* be here now. He describes acid as 'a little bit of heaven' and I agree. For me, it *is* a little bit of heaven.

"There are some people, though, who would describe it as a little piece of hell. Like I said, acid is a magnifying glass on your subconscious. There are people out there who, when straight, are good, level-headed people but with underlying terrors they keep bottled up. Acid releases those terrors. I've seen it a hundred times. The guy you least expect crawls into the corner and starts shuddering. You're there trying to talk him out of a bad trip, man."

"That's kinda how I felt when I did acid by myself," said Carol. Becky nodded in agreement.

"Well, in most cases, my Special Smoke is like acid but without the edge. I mean, there are still fruitcakes out there who should *never* do anything that would open up their minds to themselves."

Connor paused and was deep in thought. Silence returned to the group, and it was several minutes before he continued. He spoke in a low voice.

"I was in the military for two years. After I'd been in for about nine months, through what some would call fate, I picked up a hitchhiker coming out of Munich. It turned out he was going to Augsburg, where I was stationed, to see a friend. He had a bunch of window-pane acid and I bought a sheet for a grand. Never seen the cat again, and if I could thank him, I would."

The others looked at him with puzzled expressions.

"When you get to know me, you'll understand that the *one thing* I can't stand is some ignorant asshole telling me what to do. But here I was, surrounded by ignorant, asshole bosses, and if I punched them out, I'd go to Leavenworth for twenty years!

"You'd get twenty years just for hitting your boss?" asked Becky. "That's hard to believe."

"It's true. It happened to a friend of mine. He'd had all he could take from this moron captain. He went to his house on Thanksgiving Day and knocked on the door. The captain's wife answered and he asked to speak to him, all polite like. When the captain came to the door, my buddy broke his jaw with one punch and put him on the floor, twitching. My buddy turned and walked back to his room and just sat there, waiting for the MP's to come and arrest him. I mean, he was already packed and ready to receive his punishment. I saw him. He was crazy, with a big grin, as the pigs hauled him away!

75

"I felt the same way. I had this pent-up anger toward my superiors, a couple in particular, and was beginning to think I was gonna break, too."

"Well, you're here now," said Becky. "How did you keep from hitting someone?"

"I did the acid. I rode my bike into the Black Forest, set up a lean-to, somewhat like the one over there,"—he pointed at the tarp—"and did acid by myself. I wanted to test the quality before I sold it to my friends.

"You see, in the Black Forest, the Germans built ladders up some of the largest fir trees with seats at the top that go all the way around. I crawled up one of them and spent the whole night up there. I realized how homesick I was and how much I hated my situation. I cried hysterically for more than two hours! I haven't had such a heartfelt cry since. In truth, I don't think I'll ever need one again.

"Then suddenly, I was happy. Well, not really *happy*, but content. I sat up there the rest of the night and watched the Father awaken from his slumber, kinda like this morning.

"I climbed down from the tree later that morning and ate some bread and cheese and just sat there, contented. When I got back, I realized that my anger had left me. I went to work and all the stupid fucking jerks who had been getting to me before, weren't anymore. There was a joy in me that I couldn't believe.

"I told my friends about my experience and twice a month I would have an acid party, with a five-dollar-a-hit admission. I made a two-hit limit. Most of the time at sunrise, you could find me and a bunch of the guys up this huge ash tree at the edge of the military station. We'd sit up there and listen and watch the city of Augsburg wake up.

"Every time I did it, the next day I had no anger toward these stupid, fucking assholes anymore. I really think I'd be in Leavenworth if it wasn't for LSD.

"My brother told me it was my mind, self-medicating. I think it was fate, just like you two are fate, karma, something outside my mind. It could be luck, you never know."

"Well, I've heard acid described a lot of ways, but never as a medicine," Larry remarked.

"That's nothin'. You wait till I relay the message that the little space aliens gave me." Connor started laughing. "Yeah, they got their eye on you, man. They'll be probing you up in their spaceship anytime now."

"There ain't no aliens, God made us in his image. There ain't no one else."

"I wouldn't talk that way around Becky," cautioned Carol. "She's been studying about the possibility of extraterrestrial life for a while."

"I'm not gonna go there today," said Becky. "Just not in the mood to create conflict."

"Another benefit of the peyote. After the introduction of the conscious to the subconscious, there's usually a lingering peacefulness," said Connor.

"Yeah, but you'll be slappin' strange men upside the head again in no time at all," Larry said, grinning at Becky. That sent the whole group into laughter for a while.

They lounged around camp until each one found their way back to bed to catch up on lost sleep. It was early in the afternoon before they broke camp and drove into the park.

The first order of business was to secure a camping permit, and then they stopped for an early dinner at one of several restaurants in the Grand Canyon Village area.

They spent a couple of hours driving along the canyon rim and stopping several times to admire the view. As evening approached, they headed back to the camp to spend one more night.

11. Backpacking Adventure

Thursday, March 11, 1976

The next day, permit in hand and packs on their backs, they began their trek into the Grand Canyon. Frost covered the trail at the very top, but they felt the warmth build as they descended. Soon, they were peeling layers off as the sweat began to flow.

Before they knew it, they were on Horseshoe Mesa, looking for their campsite. After a few moments of searching, Becky found the small sign marking the camp and the fire ring.

Connor and Larry began setting up their tarp. The clouds on the western horizon were part of a cold front, so they went all out. They placed their backpacks at each end of the tarp and covered them with their ponchos. This would keep rain from entering from the open ends. Trenches were already in place, in case it rained. For Connor, though, it was *when* it was going to rain, so he deepened the trenches a little.

Carol and Becky were busy setting up their tent a few feet away. Once finished, they studied the guys' shelter. "I've never seen anybody use a tarp like that. Who taught you that?" asked Carol.

"I got it out of a survival article written back before World War I," answered Connor. "Of course, they were using canvas tarps and ponchos. These are much lighter than the ones in the article."

Connor stared at the ominous clouds and studied the tarp, "You know, I think tonight's gonna be another big test."

After they got the camp set up, they continued down the trail to the Colorado River. Larry found a secluded ledge overlooking the roaring river that provided protection from prying eyes. Connor passed a joint to each of the girls and lit a third. Larry lit one he had in his shirt pocket. Carol and Becky looked confused.

Larry said, "Just smoke as much as you like, then save the rest for later."

They sat on the warm rocks, watched the river flow and talked about their lives until the sun dropped behind the canyon's rim. They stayed as long as they dared and hurried back to camp as the menacing wall of clouds approached.

They quickly cooked a sparse dinner of canned beef stew, using Carol's gas stove. Darkness came quickly as they cleaned up, and the canyon seemed to close in on them.

Connor pulled out a pint of bourbon he'd scored on the sly at a store right outside the park. "What do ya say to a little nightcap? This stuff is like antifreeze. It feels like it's gonna get cold tonight."

He took the first small pull of the bottle, swirled it around in his mouth and swallowed. He winced and said, "Man! That tastes like shit! I think a joint ought to complete the bedtime prescription the doctor ordered." Connor was smiling happily.

The bottle went around several times with everyone taking progressively longer pulls as their bodies gradually accepted the straight bourbon. After the joint, everyone except Connor went to bed.

He walked away from camp out to the edge of the mesa and watched the canyon change as the moon moved in and out of the drifting clouds. In the distance, he could hear the roar of the river.

He thought about Carol's version of the natural history of the place and the irony that she supported his side of the long-running debate with Larry. He went back to the time in the little cabin at Cannon Beach when he first threw out the Continental Drift theory. He lay back and let his mind wander as he enjoyed the beauty of the red canyon.

He wasn't sure how long he'd been there or if he'd gone to sleep. A cold gust of wind caused him to shudder as the first drops of rain fell around him. The clouds had moved in, erasing any light from the moon and slowing his trek back to the camp.

By the time he returned, it was a steady rain. He quickly crawled under the tarp. In just a few minutes, Connor was naked and under everything he could find to cover himself. The rain intensified. The wind gusted and drove the rain sideways.

Larry spoke from within his warm cocoon, "Well, you're right, tonight's gonna be the biggest test yet of your tarp idea."

"I think we'll be alright. But if not, we've got enough cash to buy a good two-man tent. If we wake up wetter than fuck, then the first chance we get, let's go in halves on one."

"Okay, we'll flip to see who keeps it when we get back home."

"Sounds good to me," Connor agreed.

They both slept soundly, warm and dry. Meanwhile, the wind and rain tried in vain to penetrate their little sanctuary.

Friday, March 12, 1976

The next morning, as usual, Connor was up first. He took a moment to enjoy the freshly-scrubbed landscape. The previous night's storm had battered the surrounding sage plants, and the air was filled with the pungent aroma of the plants' bruised and broken leaves.

Before anyone stirred, he had a small cook fire going and some hobo coffee brewed. The smell of coffee woke Larry and he joined Connor. They sat by the fire, quietly talking over their first cup of joe, when they began to hear stirring inside the tent.

"So how'd you two sleep?" asked Larry as the two girls finally emerged.

"Lousy," Becky muttered. "The foot of the tent got wet. We both had to sleep all balled up at the other end. My feet never *did* warm back up."

Connor looked out over the mesa. The sky was crystal clear and steam rose from the ground as it warmed. He looked up to the South Rim and noticed for the first time that snow had fallen up there. He pointed up at the rim.

"Shit! Will you look up there? It looks like a lotta snow!"

"Wow, there's much more snow on the North Rim," said Larry. "I don't think we're gonna hike *there* today as we planned." He looked at the girls "You two should pull your bags out to dry and leave your tent open, too."

They spent the day exploring along the river, listening to Carol and Becky take turns talking about this rock, that vein, sedimentary this, igneous that, and how everything was red due to iron oxide in the rocks. Connor was fascinated, but Larry just sighed and listened as the girls excitedly told them about the origin of the canyon.

The sun was deep in the west when they got back to the camp. They were winded and ready for peanut butter and jelly sandwiches. Connor got the fire going long enough to boil some water for hot chocolate. Then he pulled another pint of bourbon from his pack.

"Jesus Fucking Christ, man! How much of that shit did you buy?" Larry was happy to see the bottle.

"Two bottles for two nights," explained Connor. "Tonight I doubt there will be rain, but it's gonna be cold again. A little more antifreeze should do the trick." He smiled as he held up the bottle in a symbolic toast.

"Well, I slept warm last night, but another nice glow to go to bed with tonight sounds good." Larry was smiling, too.

Carol asked, "So, what time do you plan on getting up in the morning?"

"As early as possible is what I was thinking," Connor replied.

"You didn't need to ask him that, Carol. There's only one answer with him, and you just got it. Although, as early as possible seems good to me, too." Larry was ready to get out of the canyon.

"I'd like to be out of the park before light and drinking coffee in a restaurant, first thing," said Becky.

"Bingo! The earlier, the better." Connor, once again, was surprised by Becky's thinking.

They passed the bottle around until it was gone and shared a joint. Like the night before, everyone hit the rack, except Connor. He hiked to the mesa's edge once again and relaxed. He listened for the last time to the roar of the mighty Colorado.

He wondered, if the river could talk, what would it say about being reduced to a mere trickle before it emptied into the Gulf of California. Instead of being allowed to flow freely, its water was siphoned off as it made its way from Colorado through Utah, Arizona, Nevada, and, of course, California.

He thought about the river's dams and their negative effect on the canyon's fragile ecosystem. The river that used to run red with sand and silt was clear and cold. Most of its banks no longer held sandbars where plants could get a foothold.

Did it strain against the dams in a futile attempt to be free once more? Or, if it could, did the Colorado laugh at the temporary obstacle that Man had thrown up? It had been flowing for millions of years, so what was a dam or two?

Connor chuckled softly. He knew the latter to be true. The river would get its revenge sooner or later. He smoked another joint, which trashed him into a stupor, and walked back to camp in the moonlight and slept.

Saturday, March 13, 1976

Just as Becky had wanted, they were putting the gear in the bus while it was still dark. Because of the icy conditions, Connor drove them out of the park to a restaurant.

While they ate breakfast, Carol laid out their itinerary for the next week. She wanted to visit all five of the national parks in Utah, and then go north to Yellowstone.

Connor nudged Larry and smiled. They both were amazed at how lucky they were to get this ride.

12. Things Get Complicated

Sunday, March 21, 1976

On the ninth day out of the Grand Canyon, they camped just west of Arches National Park at the base of a huge cliff of pomegranate-red sandstone. The late afternoon shadows created quite a show of relief, bringing out the many faults in the cliff face. The sky was a mix of pink swirls and red cotton balls randomly scattered over a deep blue background.

A group of ravens played on the updrafts rising off of the cliffs. Their aerial games of tag and chase were entertainment for the group of young campers. They had hiked most of the day in Arches and were spent.

Larry and Connor decided to make a spit over the cooking coals to rotisserie a small pork loin roast. They had talked about doing it for a while, and finally, the girls told them to put-up or shut-up.

They had bought some firewood and charcoal briquettes from a local store to insure a steady heat. They went down by the Colorado River and cut the green willow limbs needed for the spit.

Three and a half hours later, the roast was ready for carving and everyone salivated over the bounty. Connor made fried asparagus mixed with hot peppers, onions, mushrooms, and garlic to go with the roast. Larry made his prized spiced wine to top everything off.

Like every other time the two friends went all out with a camp meal, all eyes rolled in pleasure and statements of this being "the best meal cooked over a fire that they ever had" fed the travelers' egos. Once again, the guys just credited their good luck.

Under the influence of the wonderful meal, Becky commented, "We both thought that your talk of cooking over a fire was bull. If I hadn't seen you make that rotisserie, I wouldn't have believed it."

She paused for a moment and continued. "I just want to say that I wasn't too happy about you guys coming along with us at first, but you've taught me more about living on the road and camping than I ever thought possible."

Another pause as she raised her spiced wine, and added, "This is to new friends. You have made this trip back home an unexpected pleasure!" With smiles all around, the others lifted their glasses and took a ceremonial sip.

Larry stared at Becky for a few seconds and said, "When Connor first mentioned to me that he thought we should try to get a ride with you two, I had reservations. I mean, I really didn't think that going to Illinois in April fit into our plans. But I've learned from you two as well. Not that the geology of the southwest is my cup of tea, but it's fun to listen to you two talk about it. Your excitement is contagious."

Connor smiled and stared at the fire. Shaking his head slowly, he said, "Sometimes, I feel like there is someone watching out for me." He paused and added as he looked over at Larry, who was about to go off, "And, no, it's not anyone you believe in, asshole!"

Larry let the comment drop and Connor smiled. The weed, wine, and food, together with a twelve-mile hike in the arch-filled national park had mellowed everyone out.

Connor stood and stretched with a moan. He pointed up at the ravens and said, "That's something you don't see much in western Oregon. I've seen ravens in eastern Oregon, but never so many in one spot."

"A flock of ravens is called an *unkindness*," Becky announced. "I remember because we had to read Poe's poem, *The Raven*, and it was a question on a test. Everyone got it wrong." She stared up at the birds, and then finished her wine. "I don't know why I remember things like that."

Connor stretched again. He meandered out of camp, hoping to find a spot up the road to sit and quiet his mind. Before he got fifty feet away from camp, however, Carol came up beside him and snuggled up next to him.

"What's up, girly girl?"

"I don't know. Just thought I'd tag along, if that's alright?" Carol leaned in and snuggled even more than she already was.

"Sure. You're always welcome to snuggle me up like this." He casually put his arm around her. It was a nice fit.

They walked down the road a ways to a rock he'd spotted on the way in. It was a nice, flat rock that sat about fifteen feet above the road. It took an effort to climb up onto it, but once there, they could see some of the arches in the park. They sat in silence for a while and enjoyed the darkening landscape.

"So, who is this Diane girl back in Oregon?"

And there's the second shoe. Connor had been waiting for this subject to come up. "How'd you hear about Diane?"

"I heard you and Larry talking about what was going on back in Oregon. Larry mentioned Diane like she was your girlfriend. I was just wondering who she was."

Stalling for more time, he brushed bits of debris off of his pant leg. "Just a friend I had a relationship with."

He paused as Carol waited expectantly for him to continue. "I was really attracted to her for a long time. She showed up at a camping weekend and let me know the feeling was mutual. We've been kind of a couple for the last eighteen months."

Connor paused once again and sensed that Carol didn't like what she was hearing. He thought about it for another minute and finally continued, "You see, I wanted to be exclusive, but she wasn't built for that. She was always secretly fucking around on me. I would hear about it from my friends. I just kind of accepted it. I knew it wouldn't be long before someone else would come along and she'd be gone. So, we talked and decided on an open relationship."

"An open relationship?" Carol asked. "I could never do that."

"I like her a lot, but she definitely is *not* what I'm looking to settle down with. Matter of fact, I'm pretty sure she's fucking a good friend of mine right now.

"So, I guess you could say Diane is just an old girlfriend of mine, who I really like, but can't get on board with her lifestyle."

"You know what I like the most about you, Connor?" She paused and he looked over at her. "You don't pull any punches. I ask a hard question, and you just lay it on the line."

"The truth isn't always easy, but it's better than a sugar coating. Then you're left guessing. Besides, you only have to tell the truth once, usually. If you're lying, then you're all the time having to defend it."

Darkness was beginning to win the battle, and the red sandstone was gradually turning black. They sat in silence for a while longer. Connor felt the tension and knew why she had asked about his personal life. He felt the urge to run away as fast as possible, yet he couldn't resist the desire to stay. *Why do things always have to be so fucking complicated?*

In the darkness, the way off of the rock was harder than he thought it would be. He helped Carol off the last step and she ended up in his arms. Before he knew what was happening, they kissed. When they separated, Carol said, "I think I have a crush on you."

"Yeah, I gathered that. And I think I may *love* you," Connor confessed. "But we have an agreement and I plan on bringing you back to your mom, cherry intact."

"Never said I wanted to sleep with you!" Carol paused, surprised at his confession. "Well," she waffled, "I do think about it, but I just couldn't do that."

"I know. The thought's crossed my mind, too. But a deal is a deal. Maybe after I get you home . . ." He grunted at the thought and then chuckled. He pulled her in close and kissed her with an intensity she didn't expect. "Let's get back to camp before this gets out of hand," he said, a little out of breath.

They walked back to camp in a tense silence. Just before getting into earshot of their two companions, Carol asked, "How can you possibly think you may *love* me? You hardly *know* me."

"It's just a feeling I get when I see you. It's like something I haven't felt in a long time. I *think* it's love." He fell silent for a moment. "Let's just say, when you're near, I'm happy."

"I've never had anyone talk to me that way," Carol said, surprised. "Back home, I'm the freak geologist who guys don't ask out. I don't know why.

"At the time, it didn't seem that important to me. But when I was never asked to any of the proms at school, it kinda hurt. I mean, I would go, but alone, and I'd just chat with the other wallflowers. I tried not to let it, but it really did hurt."

They arrived back in camp to find Larry and Becky leaning against the rocks, asleep. They startled awake at the sound of their footsteps, just in time to see a colony of bats emerge from a large crack high up in the cliff face. They formed a black ribbon that meandered like a slow, lazy river. The bats flew into the moon's light and the campers were able to see their silhouettes. Suddenly, they were flying right above them and catching bugs that were attracted to the light of the campfire.

"That's cool," Larry said.

"It is," Connor agreed. "I hope they feed well tonight. Get rid of these fucking, blood-sucking bugs."

They watched the bats for a while longer and drifted off to their beds, one by one. Lying under the stars, Larry said, "Becky told me that there's a crush going on. Did Carol say anything to you?"

"Yeah," Connor sighed. "I don't know what I'm gonna do about that. I promised I wouldn't touch, and now she's teasing me."

"That's a bitch," Larry said with false sympathy. "One of the most beautiful girls I've ever seen has a crush on you. Poor thing!" He chuckled.

"I don't think she has a clue how pretty she really is," Connor remarked. "But there's something going on there that she isn't sharing. She's trying to tell me she's never even been on a date. Maybe the guys in whatever bum-fuck, backwoods town she's from prefer animals. I don't know."

Larry was quiet for a while. "Well, I'm glad it's you. I got enough to think about with my own feelings right now."

"Tanya?"

"Yeah. It's serious. If it wasn't for you, I'd pack it in and head to Idaho. Well, it's not just you. This trip has been a real kick so far. What do you think?"

"Well fuck. What do I think? I think that when we were sitting at Red Bluff, I wondered if this whole thing was gonna work out. Since then it's been so much better than I could've dreamed when I first thought it up."

"It's true, it has," said Larry. They both stared at the moon's last quarter and the starry sky, and they drifted into slumber.

Monday, March 22, 1976

The next morning, Connor woke Larry up just as the eastern sky was starting to glow. "Let's do a wake-and-bake up on that rock I was on last night." He had his camera ready. "I think it's gonna be a sunrise to remember and I don't want you to miss it."

After a little grumbling, Larry was up and dressed. "I don't know why the fuck you get up so early," he complained, "but when you drag me up with you, that's bullshit!"

They walked down the gravel road, stirring up little dust clouds as they went, and climbed up to the flat rock. Larry grumbled some more. "The next time you wake me this early, at least have a cup of coffee in your hand."

Connor just smiled at him. He was used to the early morning complaints of the night owls of the world. He knew it was best just to let the bitching go on with no comebacks. It would just piss Larry off even more.

They sat and watched as the sky slowly became brighter and the colors intensified. Connor snapped a picture every now and then. Suddenly, and just for a moment, two of the arches he'd seen the previous evening lit up like a pair of eyes. The sunlight shined through the arches like flashlight beams onto the lowlands to the west. And just as suddenly, it was done.

"Wow, did you know that was gonna happen?"

"Just a guess. Thought of it last night when I first saw the arches. It sure was cool! I hope my pictures come out." Connor paused. "Well, I guess that deserves a wake-and-baker, huh?"

"I can't believe what I just saw! Thanks, bro." Larry pulled a joint out of his shirt pocket and lit it. Around the smoke of his first hit, he continued, "So this is why you're up so early all the time. Still, I think I'd rather be sleeping."

Connor stared off into the morning light and the reddening sky, and said, "Normally, I don't put up with this whiny bullshit. Just be happy I woke you this morning. And don't tell the girls about the sunrise, either, or I'll be hearing it from them."

They sat and watched the Father's show in silence and finished the wake-and-baker. Before long, they crawled down off of the rock and were making dust clouds with their boots as they walked back to camp.

"Thanks again, bro. Let's get that hobo coffee going, okay?" Larry was finally glad to be up.

They were on their second cup and Connor was well into his slumgullion breakfast hash before the girls began to stir. The spuds were cooked tender with onions, garlic, and spiced with habanero peppers for that southwestern flavor. He cut up the remaining meat from last night's feast and was just about to add it to the hash when Carol got up. Their laughing and joking around finally woke Becky. Connor added the eggs once she stirred.

In no time at all, everyone was fed, the dishes were done, camp was broken down, and the bus was packed. The foursome sat around the fire, basking in the glow of the morning sun with coffee in hand.

Larry asked, "So, what's on the agenda for today?"

"One more day in Arches, then I think we're going north to Yellowstone," Becky replied.

"Then south to the Tetons," Carol added.

Suddenly, Connor got up and started dancing around in circles and singing, "We're going to Yellowstone! We're going to Yellowstone! Hey, Boo-boo! We're going to Jellystone!"

Larry got up and they started circling each other, both singing, "We're going to Jellystone!" The girls got up and joined in. They danced around for a couple of minutes and had a big group hug.

It was time to head off to Arches to see Delicate Arch. Contrary to Larry's and Connor's expectations, it was worth the hike out to stand under the arch for a group photo.

That evening, they camped in the same spot as the previous night. Connor warned everyone that he would be up at daybreak the next morning with coffee to insure an early departure to Yellowstone.

"So what the fuck else is new?" complained Larry.

13. Cold Snap and Disappointment

Tuesday, March 23, 1976

The next day, they drove to West Yellowstone, Montana. It was an all-day drive. They approached the west gate of Yellowstone National Park and found it closed. To make matters worse, they had to rent a motel room because the low that night was going to be fifteen degrees below zero. They weren't prepared for that.

The room had two beds that were so narrow that Larry flipped a coin and won. That meant Connor was on the floor.

The guys went out for beer and the girls sprung for a pizza. The television had only two channels with fuzzy reception. One channel was Mormon and the other was so fuzzy they weren't sure what it was. So they passed the time playing the Monopoly game they'd gotten from the front desk.

Earlier that day, the girls had talked about meeting up with a dude, named Jonny, who was a year ahead of them in high school. He grew up in the same podunk town as the girls and had moved to Yellowstone the year before to work. They warned the guys that he was gay and begged them not to tease him. They explained that he was real sensitive and that the boys at their high school had been relentless in their hazing.

Becky won the game, and the pizza and beer were gone, so they all went to bed. The girls wore their pajamas, and the guys were in their skivvies. Cat calls came from both sides of the room.

Lying out of sight on the floor beside Larry's bed, Connor said, "Yellowstone lost some if its grandeur as soon as I found out it was closed."

"Yeah, but we have another first. It's the first time I've frozen my ass off in minus fifteen-degree weather! The guy at the store said it's a little late in the year for this cold snap, but it wasn't that uncommon either. Just a little bad luck, I guess."

"Don't worry, we'll get to see the park," Carol promised. "Jonny says he'll get us through the north gate and that we'll get a guided tour. He said this is the best time to see the park because there aren't any tourists."

"Well, that sounds good, I guess. I've never seen Old Faithful. If we get to see that free of charge and with no tourists about, it'll be worth it," said Connor.

Becky added excitedly, "It's a super volcano. Just think of it. We'll be driving around inside the caldera of a super volcano! I've dreamed of this for a long time. Do you guys realize how much this volcano has influenced the world? There are some who think the last ice age was caused by an eruption of this very volcano!"

Connor sat up and looked over Larry to Becky and asked, "This super volcano excites you, but having two nearly naked men in a motel room doesn't?"

Becky lay there for a minute and then asked, "Why, you lookin' for some company?"

"God, no! Sorry I brought it up!" Connor exclaimed, thinking the whole time that, yes, he wanted someone to crawl in bed with him, but it wasn't Becky.

They all lay there in silence for a long while. Connor finally started snoring. It was all Larry needed to send him into slumber, and he joined in with Connor.

"You still awake, Becky?"

"Yes."

"I really do want to crawl into bed with him."

"I know. To tell the truth, I wouldn't mind it a bit, either." They both giggled and finally went to sleep, too.

Wednesday, March 24, 1976

At first light, they drove north out of West Yellowstone to Bozeman, where there was little snow and it was considerably warmer. The city was surrounded at varying distances by white-capped mountains, and they took a moment to admire the view.

They turned east on I-90 toward Livingston, a city that lies in the path of the wind that comes down out of the park following the Yellowstone River. At Livingston, they turned south through the wind tunnel that was called Paradise Valley. Fortunately, they picked a relatively calm day for the drive.

"No denying why they call this Paradise Valley," Connor said. He surveyed the mountain ranges, the Gallatins to the west and the Absarokas to the east, snow-covered with the sun reflecting off of them. "Kinda reminds me of the Swiss Alps."

Carol provided the required geologic update. "This is a glacial valley and that is a lateral moraine." She pointed to a smooth ridge that ran along the east bank of the river. "It was left there by the glacier that receded from here back up to Yellowstone Lake. I can't wait until you get to see the lake! It's friggin' huge!"

The geologic narration went on until they arrived in the little town of Gardiner, Montana. Straddling the Yellowstone River as it leaves the park, Gardiner sits at the north entrance to Yellowstone, the only year-round access to the park. It's the warmest gateway city, despite being the most northerly, because its elevation is only fifty-five hundred feet, over eleven hundred feet lower than any other gateway.

The bulk of Gardiner's winter population is made up of park employees as well as the owners of the many bars, restaurants, and motels and their employees. They all lay in wait for the hordes of tourists that visit Yellowstone each summer.

It begins in April with a trickle of hardy folk and steadily increases into a mass of idiots from June through mid-September. Once the weather turns cold and unstable, and all the kids are back in school, the flow of tourists returns to a trickle as most of the park closes in the fall.

In no time, they found the little house where Jonny lived. They got out of the bus and were stretching their muscles when the front door flew open and out burst an excited Jonny. He screamed like a girl and ran out to hug Becky and Carol with tears running down his face. He went on about how much he missed them and what a time he had in store for them. Then he turned to the two stunned travelers and quickly dried his face.

"So these must be your companions." Jonny checked the guys out, his eyes scanning them up and down. "You didn't tell me how gorgeous they were!"

He approached Larry, who held out a hand to shake. Jonny slapped his hand aside and moved in to plant a kiss on Larry's lips. Jonny had to settle for the cheek as Larry quickly turned his head, his eyes wide with surprise.

At least Connor had a clue by the time Jonny got to him. He moved real quick and got a surprised and thrilled Jonny in a bear hug. Connor twirled him around once, let him go, gave him a pat on the back and quickly said, "Howdy, partner. I'm Connor. The girls have been saying real good things about you. Been lookin' forward to meetin' you. Say, you got a bathroom inside? I gotta piss like a racehorse!"

"Damn, you're cute! There's a bathroom inside on the left." Jonny pointed back over his shoulder with a flick of his wrist and a tilt of his hip. He demurely tucked in his chin, tilted his head and rolled his eyes up at Connor.

"Knock first! My boy toy may be in there. His name is David. He won't bite!" Jonny's words fell on Connor's back, as he had already turned and retreated toward the house.

Jonny watched Connor walk away and said loudly, "Damn, Connor! You sure have a nice ass!"

Larry, grinning that famous grin of his, had to turn away to hide his laughter as he withdrew to the other side of the bus.

Connor, who was still recovering from his initial shock, turned back to the girls, shot them a pissed-off look and continued toward the house.

Jonny continued to admire Connor until he disappeared through the doorway, and then turned his attention back to the girls. Their expressions betrayed their surprise as well. This wasn't the shy, sensitive boy they knew from back home!

"I was hoping you were gonna get here today," Jonny continued, oblivious to their surprise. "We're gonna have some friends over tonight to celebrate your visit. We would've partied anyway, but it's always nice to have a good excuse." He smiled real big and gave the girls another hug.

Jonny invited Larry and the girls inside and he introduced David to everyone. He seemed nice enough, about thirty and was at least a little masculine. Connor and Larry liked the couple instantly.

David led them up a narrow set of stairs to a small room with one bed. This is for you girls. We don't know where your friends are gonna sleep. They should get several offers to sleep elsewhere before the night is done, though." David winked at the guys.

"Actually, if you don't feel too uncomfortable about it, you guys can sleep up here with us. Okay with you, Becky?" Carol asked.

Becky shrugged and said, "We'll manage it. Let's get our bags up here."

After David left, Connor gave the girls another stern look. "You know, I'm cool with gay people and all, but don't you think a little heads up about Jonny would've been nice? I mean, Jesus Fucking Christ! That guy's more feminine than you two combined!"

"I'm sorry," said Carol, "but we were just as surprised as you. Back home, Jonny was always quiet and reserved. Who would've expected it?"

Larry was laughing and said, "Connor, I thought you were gonna blow a gasket when he said you were cute! Holy shit! If you could've seen the look on your face!"

He was still laughing as he turned to the girls and explained. "The thing you don't know is every gay guy Connor's ever met has tried to put the make on him. Well, maybe it's not *that* bad. But back home, everyone knows what a badass he is. They usually stop as soon as he says something. But here, you made him promise not to offend Jonny or he would've already put his foot down."

"Larry's right, Connor. It *was* kinda funny to watch," said Carol as the stern expression returned to his face. She placed a hand on his arm to placate him. "I told Jonny you both were straight, but Connor, you've got to know what a cute ass you have. I mean, Becky and I have never mentioned it, but we both like to watch you walk away from us."

"Yes we do." Becky chimed in with a smile on her face.

"Okay, I hear ya. It's definitely not the first time I've heard it," Connor admitted, the stern expression still on his face. "Here's the thing, though. If I don't put a stop to it right off the get-go with guys, they take it as an invitation to make more advances.

"Believe me, I was just fifteen the first time I had to knock a queer down. It was in downtown Portland and the guy pinched me on the ass even after I warned him. It's like, 'Hey, motherfucker! Back the fuck off! I'm not gay!' is foreplay to some of those motherfuckers!

"I mean, I'm cool with gay guys who respect my sexuality. Have I tried to force my way on either of you two? No, I haven't! Because you told me no touch, so I don't touch. But how would it make you feel if I ignored that?"

He was still pumped up. Having to keep his voice down so the two guys downstairs couldn't hear was about to give him an embolism. "Fuck this shit! I'm gonna go have a beer after I get my backpack up here. Let's go shoot some pool and get a buzz on, bro!"

The girls followed them downstairs. Jonny gave them directions to his favorite bar and the guys were gone as soon as they deposited their packs upstairs.

On the way, they went under the bridge that crossed over the Yellowstone River and smoked a going-away joint. They sat in the glow of the weed and let the sound of the river take them to places only a river can.

Larry kept an eye on Connor and waited for him to relax before saying anything. "You gonna be alright? I thought you were gonna melt down back there."

"Yeah, I'm cool." He gave a snort and said, "In truth, Carol can tell me I have a nice ass anytime she likes. She's got a fine little ass, too."

He paused for a moment and continued, "I just need to unwind and I'll be fine. But I don't need no shit off a bunch of queers tonight!" Then he laughed. "I think it's your turn in the gay ringer. I'll just say I'm with *you*." He glanced over at Larry with that twinkle in his eye.

"Fuck you, Connor!" Larry said with a smile. They got up and continued on to the bar.

Like in most tourist traps, most of the winter inhabitants were drawing unemployment and hanging in the bars, waiting for the resurgence of tourism to breathe life back into the local economy.

Connor and Larry stood and looked out a window at the nearby snow-covered peak that towered over the town. The bartender explained that it was called Electric Peak because of the frequent

95

lightning strikes at its summit. He said there were so many strikes that the rock at the top had a strange, crumbly texture.

As they watched, dark clouds descended from the flanks of the mountain and began to drop snow. "You don't see that much in Oregon. I'm telling you, this is gonna be the trip you'll tell your grandkids about," said Connor.

"I got to admit, it *is* beautiful here."

After a couple of hours of pool and several beers, their moods were much improved as they returned to Jonny's house. The party was well underway with music playing and beer flowing. They went upstairs and pulled out a few going-away joints. It was looking like a good evening.

Connor walked up to Carol, kissed her and said, "I'm with you, in case any of these guys don't understand what *no* means."

"I thought you'd abandoned us."

"Kiss me again, right now while everyone is looking," he said. Carol looked confused. "Just to let everyone know I'm straight."

She leaned in and gave him a short peck on the lips. Smiling, she took his hand and led him through the family room and out to the backyard. About twenty park employees and locals stood with beers in hand and talked around a fire. She led Connor around with Jonny for the introductions.

When Larry got to Becky, he whispered in her ear for a minute and then she planted a wet one on his lips. Connor put his arm around Carol, lean in and whispered, "Jesus! Maybe I should've said I was with Becky!" She smiled and planted an elbow in his ribs.

Things were going smoothly until Carol went inside to go to the bathroom. She wasn't gone ten seconds when a big guy walked up to Connor and said, "I heard about Jonny's good-looking, new friend, but I didn't realize just *how* good-looking you were. I want some of *you*."

Connor corrected him. "That's Jonny's good-looking, *straight* friend. And I just met Jonny. I'm friends with Carol. *She's* Jonny's friend."

This dude was big, six-foot-six, with a cut to him that said he was ripped under his baggy sweatshirt and coat. He put his arm around Connor's waist and said, "My name is Charles. I'm the park-wide Food and Beverage Manager, and I'm doing some hiring right now. If you want a job, I can get you one. Just give me a call."

Connor was thinking that his worst nightmare was coming true. He grabbed the guy's hand, ducked and spun under his arm. Then he quickly let go and backed up a step.

"Listen closely," Connor said. "Number one, you'll never be my boss because I would never work for you. Number two, I don't like you. So don't touch me again, or I'll fuck you up! If you want a good ass-kicking, just disrespect my personal space again."

Connor made his way inside. Jonny followed him with a worried expression. "I'm sorry about Charles. He has a bad habit of forcing himself on younger men. I'll talk to him."

Jonny hesitated for a second. "I want to ask you something. Are you and Carol really an item? I mean, it's the first time I've ever seen her with a guy."

"Let's just say there's a mutual attraction. And don't worry about Charles, I can handle him." Connor looked hard at Jonny, and then it hit him. "Jesus, Jonny! Did he force himself on you?"

"Well, I'm gay, but it *was* a little more forceful than it needed to be. I enjoyed it, though," Jonny explained. "Charles usually grows bored quickly, then moves on. We were a couple for about a month."

Carol came out of the bathroom and smiled at the sight of Jonny and Connor talking so nicely. Not knowing how beautiful she looked as she walked up to them, she put her arm around Connor and said, "Two of my favorite people talking. Isn't that sweet."

"She must be drunk," said Connor as he smiled at Jonny.

Jonny came close and hugged them both and said, "It's so nice having you here, Carol. And you having a boyfriend makes it even better. I've never seen you with anyone before."

Carol turned and stared at Connor. "Yes. It's nice to finally meet someone who I like."

"Jonny, I need to talk to Carol for a minute." Connor turned to Carol and said, "Let's go out front, okay?"

"I'm not in trouble, am I?"

"Hell, no! But let's talk."

They walked out of the front door and were hit with a cold wind that felt like an eighteen-wheeler. The back of the house was protected by a big fence and the fire warmed the area. The front, however, lay open to the cold wind coming down from the park. Neither of them was prepared for it.

"You ever been in a bar?" Connor asked as he turned his back to the wind.

"No, why are you asking? Remember, I'm just eighteen."

"Yeah, but you can pass for twenty-three. So let's go play a game of pool and have a beer. If they card you, we'll come back here. It's just that there's a dude in there that makes me uncomfortable." Connor looked worried.

"Okay, let's go, but first let me check in with Becky so she won't worry." She stepped inside and was back outside a minute later, smiling. "Becky's gonna tell Larry. Let's go."

They got in the bar with no problem and were playing their first game of pool when Larry and Becky showed up, beers in hand.

"He carded me even though we were in here just an hour ago. I told him that he had been serving me for three hours and my ID was back at Jonny's. He served me." Larry laughed.

"He didn't card *me*." Becky smiled and held up her beer.

They nursed down four or five beers and played pool for a couple of hours when Larry noticed the girls were beginning to slur their words. The guys gathered them up and they left.

It had been a fun time, and they were all ready for bed. They were also drunk enough that, when they got back, they joined the party instead of going upstairs.

Other than Charles having to be told to back off every time Carol left Connor's side, all of the people were really nice. After Larry broke out two Thai joints, everyone got even friendlier.

All four got numerous job offers. It seemed that just about everyone at the party was a manager in some capacity in the park and were looking for workers for the summer season.

Eventually, the partiers trickled away until it was just the two travelers, the girls, Jonny, and David.

Becky asked Jonny if he was ever going back home. He explained how, for the first time in his life, he was accepted for being gay. He said that before he came to Yellowstone, he had lived a lie. Jonny's father was a preacher at the largest church in Podunk.

"When I was twelve and just beginning to become confused about my sexuality, my father sat me down and asked me if I was gay. I lied, denying my feelings.

"Then he announced for the first time that, if I was gay, I would be banished from the family. I spent many nights in my bed crying in fear of losing my family."

"Oh my god! That's terrible!" said Carol. "I never imagined things were so bad for you." She hugged him and Becky joined in.

"Well, things got better when I turned sixteen. One day, I was walking alone down on the river and met a man who said all the right things. That was the day a lot of my confusion left. The lies began to be easier, but my father's inquisition never let up.

"My lover was in his mid-twenties. I was young and I loved him, but we were very different. One day, a little over a year later, he let me know he was married and had two kids. He said he loved me, but he couldn't leave his wife."

"What did you do?" asked Becky.

"He was the one who told me about Yellowstone. He said I should go out west and figure myself out. When I got out here, I realized that leaving all that bullshit back in Illinois was gonna to be a lot easier than I thought. Then I met David and I'm happier than I've ever been in my whole life.

"My family is right here, in the park. Most of those people here tonight look at me as a man, not a gay man. For a long time, I was going to mail my father a copy of my gay manifesto that I wrote when I got first here. David convinced me to let him live in his bullshit world. The truth is, his opinion doesn't even matter to me anymore."

"Was that guy who picked you up at school every now and then your lover?" asked Becky.

"Yeah, I used to tell people he was my piano teacher. He did play the piano and so did I, so that lie worked out well. He was a mechanical engineer and worked at the auto plant just out of town. His office overlooked the park where we met."

Everyone had fallen silent when Connor suddenly announced, "It's been a long day and I'm wasted, so I'm going to bed. It was a good party, other than having that Charles dude hitting on me every fifteen minutes."

Connor was down to his skivvies and in his bag when Carol came in, pulled her bag off the bed and laid it out next to Connor's. She stripped down to her panties and bra and climbed into her bag.

She leaned over, planted a sloppy kiss on Connor and whispered in his ear, "This is our little secret. I think I may love you, too. Don't tell anyone." She was slurring badly, and her head thumped as she lay back on her pillow. Then she was out.

Connor was a little confused, but smiled and surrendered to the drunken haze. His last thought being that this was going to get messy.

14. Lunch with a Bear

Thursday, March 25, 1976

*L*ike most mornings, Connor was up first. He had forgotten the change up in the sleeping arrangements and was confused for a while. Why was Larry in the bed? It came back to him as he was downing his first cup of joe. Carol had thrown the change-up.

He was midway through cooking a pound of bacon in a cast iron Dutch oven when Larry came rolling out of the attic. Trying to be quiet, he slipped off of the second step of the staircase and bounced down the rest to the kitchen floor.

"Good morning, bro. Nice entrance," Connor chuckled.

"Jesus! I don't remember what happened. Did I make Carol sleep on the floor by passing out on the bed?"

"No, I think her head was spinning on the bed, so she decided the floor was better. I was fucked up, too. I'm just starting to remember everything." The last thing he needed was Larry going off about sleeping with Carol, so he put an innocent spin on it.

Connor had the onion, garlic, carrots, broccoli, cabbage, and mushrooms diced into little piles on a cutting board. He put the bacon on a plate and poured off most of the bacon grease into a coffee can that sat on the counter. Then he slid the salad into the pan and let the marriage begin. Five minutes later, everyone was up.

Larry diced spuds in a ten-inch cast iron pan and Connor stirred the veggies. Everyone had a cup of java.

"I hope you're hungry. I got a hearty Yellowstone Montana breakfast on the menu. Lots of grease to soak up the poisons left over from last night's debauchery."

"Fuck you," someone muttered. Connor wasn't sure who. He smiled and began dishing up.

An hour later, breakfast was done. With a short clean-up of the backyard and a joint, they were ready for a day in Yellowstone.

While they hadn't been able to get through the west gate, it turned out employees could go through the north gate just by showing their ID's. David drove his car with Larry and Connor, while Jonny rode with the girls in the bus. The guards waved them all through.

The morning was clear and very cold, but the sun was slowly warming the air that was still freezing at twenty-five degrees. The bitter wind from the evening before had subsided.

"It gets better every day," said Larry. "Inside Yellowstone while it's closed! Hooking up with Becky and Carol has been amazing! I'm just glad you're with me, because no one back home would ever believe half the shit we've done."

They wandered for hours through the Mammoth Hot Springs area. David happened to be a tour guide in the summer. He led them from one geological point of interest to another. The girls were in heaven, Connor was interested, and Larry just listened. They had conversations about this formation, that spring, and blah, blah, blah.

The first thing Connor noticed when they were driving to the hot springs was a sign saying "Liberty Cap". It pointed to a large rock that looked surprisingly like the liberty cap mushroom. Connor pointed it out to Larry who immediately recognized the resemblance. They both were amused.

The girls looked at them as they stood and pointed at the formation. "What do you think? It's a phallic symbol or something?" Carol asked indignantly.

Connor smiled at her and said, "Now that you mention it, I can see your point. No, actually, we were noticing that it looks just like the mushroom we pick out on the West Coast. You know, my Special Smoke?" Carol remembered and smiled.

David, not knowing what Connor was talking about, said, "Hayden named it back in the 1870s. He thought it looked like the hats they wore during the French Revolution."

"I like your version better, Connor," said Larry. He and Connor chuckled.

The terraces of Mammoth Hot Springs were incredibly beautiful, composed of layer upon layer of intricately woven lace. While the springs ran, they were white hot and filled with crystal-clear water. But when the spring flowed to another part of the terrace, those formations no longer fed with water turned gray and began to erode.

Bison hung out near the springs and enjoyed the warmth they provided. They stared at the approaching group with mild curiosity that mellowed into disinterest. Still covered with their shaggy, winter coats, they moved in slow motion when they moved at all.

"Don't be fooled by their docile appearance," warned David. "The bison is the most dangerous animal in the park. People ignore our warnings because they look domesticated and injuries occur all the time." Everyone kept their distance and their eyes on the bison as they continued their tour.

Connor and Larry told the girls they would meet them back at the VW Bus and headed off into a group of trees to answer the call of nature. Once out of earshot, Larry remarked, "I didn't think it could be more boring, but David really takes the cake! I *did* like seeing the bison, but they sure did stink!"

"Well, at least the girls are enjoying it," Connor agreed. "Hey, I saw a spot over that way when we turned around and came back to park." He pointed to a distant tree-covered knob across a meadow. "Let's head over there and get stoned."

Half an hour later, they sat under the low branches of a spruce tree, concealed from prying eyes. They noticed someone up on the road looking toward them with binoculars, so they made sure they were well hidden and their smoke didn't blow in that direction.

As they smoked, they kept hearing grunts of some kind and raven calls coming from down the hill a ways. So, properly stoned, they decided to investigate.

First, they moved downwind from the sounds. Then, on all fours, they crawled toward it. As they grew closer, they realized there were a lot of ravens in the area. They reached a small ridge and slowly peered over the edge to see what was going on.

No more than fifteen feet away, were more than a hundred ravens and a couple of bald eagles clustered around a dead bull elk. Some of the ravens spotted the two voyeurs, squawked in surprise, flew off and circled overhead. When they saw there was no danger, they swooped down and reclaimed their spots.

Suddenly, the blood-covered head of an enormous bear emerged from the far side of the elk's body. He licked his chops as he surveyed his surroundings. Not seeing any competition for the food or the travelers, he went back to gorging himself on the downed elk.

Eyes wide with surprise, Larry and Connor quickly retreated the way they had come. When they got back to the spruce tree, they saw four rangers coming toward them.

"Great. Just what we fucking need!" Connor muttered.

The rangers hadn't noticed them and were intent on the bear. Connor and Larry blended themselves into the puckerbrush as they passed. Once the rangers were out of sight, they made their way back to the road.

Larry laughed and said, "I don't think they were interested in us. They were looking at that bear."

They walked over to the same spot where the rangers had stood. They could barely see it, but since they'd been up close, they knew it was the bear. They could also see the rangers standing considerably farther away than they'd been. They appeared to be taking pictures.

"That was a grizzly!" said Connor with excitement. "They're very unpredictable, especially when they first wake up in the spring. Lucky for us, he had food there. I read yesterday that they look for winter kills after they wake up from hibernation. Builds those fat reserves back up."

"I've never seen a bear that close before! Scared the livin' shit out of me!" Larry exclaimed.

"I saw a lot of grizzlies when I was up logging in Alaska last summer, but never that close. Now that I'm up here on the road, I can say that was pretty fucking cool!"

"Yeah, I hear ya. I was scared shitless!"

They walked back to the VW Bus to meet the girls. When they got there, the girls were a little miffed. They'd been waiting for quite a while. After hearing their explanation, the girls grabbed their cameras and were raring to go see the bear.

Connor got his camera, too, and they retraced their steps. They passed the four rangers and took the girls down to the spot where they had seen the rangers taking pictures.

"You see that little ridge right up the hill from the bear?"

"Yeah," the girls chimed.

"Well, that's where me and Larry were when we first saw him. We could smell the meat and blood, and I think, the bear, too."

The girls looked at the ridge and at Connor with wide eyes. "You've got to be kidding! You were that close?" asked Carol.

"Yeah, you see those two brown streaks heading away from that ridge? That's Larry and me shitting ourselves, getting away from there!" Connor laughed.

"Holy shit!" Becky exclaimed.

They took pictures, making sure to get shots of the ridge and the bear together. That would make a great story back home. When they had all the pictures they wanted, they headed back to the bus.

Famished, they made for a bar in town that served burgers. They had a few beers and played a couple of games of pool, playing partners with Connor taking Carol to even things out. Carol claimed to have a pool table in her basement back home. She couldn't prove it by her play.

Larry and Becky headed back to Jonny's to shower and take a nap. Connor and Carol said they were going for a walk and would be back after there was more hot water so they could shower as well.

Connor led her down under the bridge where they sat and watched the Yellowstone roll by as Connor and Larry had done the day before. They told each other about their families and their hometowns. The tension mounted as they avoided what they both knew needed to be said. Finally, Connor asked her, "So, do you remember going to bed last night?"

Carol answered shyly, "Yes, and I'm sorry for tempting you like that. You're a real gentleman, because I think you could've had sex with me."

Connor was quiet and Carol stared at him, waiting for his reaction. "I've been teased much worse than that, believe me. It's easier for me with you because of my promise to behave."

He paused and looked over at her. "What I was wondering is, do you remember what you told me?"

Carol scooted over closer to him and kissed him softly on the lips. "I'm not drunk now. I've got a buzz on, but I'm not drunk. And yes, I do remember what I said. It's been on my mind all day.

"In my whole life, I've never felt the way I feel toward you. So, while I'm not experienced in such things, I do think I love you."

"Always the scientist," Connor declared. "You make it seem like the logical conclusion of an experiment. That said, I can say that I love you. It's something I thought I'd felt before, but never as strongly as I feel toward you."

He followed that with a kiss that took him to second base and left her trembling. For the first time in her life, she didn't care about her promise to her mom. She wanted sex. Her body screamed for it. She'd never felt this way before.

"I want to sleep with you," she declared.

"Well, that's not gonna happen. I made a promise and I'm sticking to it."

"Jesus! I can't believe this feeling! Now I understand how my sister got knocked up."

"I'll try not to do that again. I just couldn't resist."

"As long as you can resist, you can do that anytime." She smiled.

They returned to Jonny's house hand-in-hand, not saying much, both wondering what they'd gotten themselves into.

Friday, March 26, 1976

The next day they got a great tour of the other highlights of Yellowstone, including Old Faithful.

"Jonny, you're so lucky to live here," said Carol. "This has been such a wonderful visit. Thank you both so much."

"For me too, Jonny," said Becky. "And David, you're the best tour guide ever. Our visit has been a dream, come true."

Connor and Larry added their thanks as well. Then they announced they would be cooking dinner when they got back, and asked for any requests. Everyone just shrugged, so it was on the travelers to get creative.

When they got back to Gardiner, Carol dropped them at the store so they could decide on the menu. Connor left the ingredients to Larry and he zeroed in on the alcohol.

Once back, Larry took over the kitchen. Connor showered and went out back to get the fire started. Carol came out back and they stood holding hands and talking.

"My parents are starting to worry about how long we're taking to get home. So I think we should leave tomorrow morning early."

"I'm just along for the ride. So lead on, girly girl."

"Okay, I'll let everyone else know."

Connor came back inside a while later. The inviting aroma of the pot roast found its way into every corner of the house. Larry went into the kitchen and inspected his creation, and then he announced that dinner was ready.

To go with the pot roast, Larry prepared fresh broccoli and leeks he'd peeled and steamed with boiled onions. The six friends were sitting around the table, enjoying the meal and chasing it with a real nice merlot.

Jonny rose for a toast. He announced that he'd made two new friends and thanked his two best friends from home who had brought them. He thanked his guests for a wonderful visit and sat back down.

And so it went, everyone took a turn, rising to toast everyone else. Larry's turn came last and he took a moment or two. He finally spoke in a quiet voice.

"I know I've said this before, but when Connor first suggested this Bicentennial Tour, I never dreamed of such a wondrous adventure as the one I've had since leaving Portland. Every day, I'm delighted at what unfolds in front of me. So, thanks to all of you, and most of all, to you, Connor. If it wasn't for you, I wouldn't be here right now." Everyone clapped when he sat.

"Thanks, bro," Connor whispered in his direction.

The going-away party was about twice as big as the arrival party. That's what happens when the word of good weed gets around.

Connor and Larry went upstairs and rolled four Thai joints. They also pulled six more of the going-away joints out, leaving them with a measly seventy-four.

The one guy Connor didn't want to see showed up as they were out back getting stoned. Charles came right over to Connor, put his arm around his shoulder real hard, and told him that he was going to fuck him.

Connor easily spun out of Charles' grip. "You know you're a real dumb fuck! Even if I *was* gay, I wouldn't fuck you, asshole! So this is your last warning. Listen real good."

Connor turned to the whole group and said, "I want everyone here to listen. I'm sick of this motherfucker telling me he's going to fuck me!"

He turned his attention back to Charles. "If you touch me one more time, I'll kick your ass! If you think I'm joking, just touch me again, bitch!"

Connor stepped in fast and gave the asshole a two-handed push. Charles flew back about five feet with a smirk on his face. Connor spun and quickly walked inside.

Everyone was silent as Larry walked up to Charles and quietly whispered, "I'm asking you to leave him alone. It's been a very long time since I've seen him this mad. He's never lost a fight as far as I know. So I'm asking you to back off, for your own good."

Charles was an imposing figure, standing ten inches above Larry. He watched Connor intently as he entered the house. After Connor disappeared through the door, he looked at Larry and said, "I like it rough. I hope he does, too, because I think he likes me."

"Don't say I didn't warn you."

A few of the others told Charles to lay off, too. He just shrugged. After a few moments, the tension eased, and everyone returned to their own conversations. Soon the party was going strong again.

Larry walked over to talk to Jonny and David. He could see immediately that they were getting trashed. "I'm warning you guys. If Charles doesn't back off, Connor will fuck him up."

"Fuck Charles," said David. "Maybe a good ass-kickin' will bring him around, and he won't be such a jerk."

"I really think both of you like Charles, and I wouldn't wish an ass-kickin' from Connor on anyone. I was really hoping you'd eighty-six him for the evening."

Jonny answered, "I hope he doesn't get beat up, but I also hope Connor puts him in his place. As for asking him to leave, we just don't do that much in this town."

"Well, if anything *does* go down, it won't be pretty. Don't say you weren't warned." Larry turned and walked inside to see Connor.

He was upstairs with Carol. Larry joined them, and Becky showed up last. They decided to go back to the bar for beer and more pool.

On the way to the bar, they walked through town and out to a trail they'd heard about at the party. It led them down a steep embankment to the river. They found a spot to sit and passed a Thai joint around. They each stared at the Yellowstone, lost in their own thoughts, and listened to the river slip by on its way to the Gulf of Mexico.

Connor told them about a book he'd read where the author described the sound a river makes as the word, *Om.* "For me, growing up with rivers all around me, I have always tried to make time to just sit on their banks and listen. They're all different in tiny ways, yet the same. I really think of all things the Mother has given me, the sound of a river is one of my favorites."

They headed back to town, this time, Connor and Carol walked with their arms around each other, whispering. Becky and Larry slowly pulled away until they were out of sight. Connor pulled Carol under the bridge once again for some serious making out. She was new to this and lay bare to whatever Connor wanted to do. When he couldn't take it anymore, they continued to the bar.

The foursome played a few games of pool. Then they decided that, since it was a going-away party for them, they really should make a showing.

Once back at the house, Connor went upstairs to read a book on the fauna of Yellowstone. He listened as the partiers gradually left. Thinking the coast was finally clear, he headed downstairs and out back to the fire.

Jonny, David, Larry, and the girls stood around the fire and four or five others hung out by the keg. Connor headed toward the fire not seeing Charles until just before he reached in to kiss him on the lips.

What happened next was over so fast that, when asked, no one gave the same account of how Charles got knocked down. Most of the partiers had seen Charles go in for the kiss, but they weren't sure how he ended up choking on his own blood and having to be turned over on his belly so he could breathe before going out cold.

Larry's account was the most accurate. "He went in for the kiss. Connor gave him a right elbow to the solar plexus, a left hook to the jaw and, as he went down, a kick to the face. All in about one or two seconds."

109

Larry gave Connor a high five and said, "It ain't like you didn't warn him. I mean did anyone *not* hear Connor tell the dickhead to back off or he'd fuck him up?"

One of the guys administering first aid to Charles, who was beginning to come around, said, "Listen, we all heard what you said, and the whole time you were gone, he said he was going after you if you came back. We all tried to tell him not to, but Charles don't take *no* for an answer."

"I didn't say, 'No,' I said, 'Fuck, no!' That punk-assed piece of shit thinks because he's big, he can lord that shit over whoever he wants. Well, I just hammered home a conflicting opinion, is all."

He walked over to Charles, who was beginning to become coherent again and said, "You ain't such a pretty boy now, are you, Charles? Now that I bent that big-assed nose all over your face!"

Another guy said, "One thing you need to know—one of Charles' boyfriends for the last six months is a ranger. They keep it on the down-low, but everyone knows about it.

"So when he gets up in the morning, he's gonna go find his ranger boyfriend and tell a story that'll be a lot different from the truth."

"You were talking about an early start? That would probably help a lot," David said. "We all saw it. When they get here in the morning, we'll tell his boyfriend what really happened. Charles initiated the fight even after being warned to back off. Everybody here heard it.

"You know, a lot of people don't really like Charles, so you don't have anything to worry about. If he pushes it, he's the one who could get in trouble. But he has good survival skills. If it looks bad for him, he'll shut up and back off."

Charles was sitting up, but still unable to talk so he could be understood. He mumbled something about his nose that, upon close inspection, had been broken. It was bent over in a bad way with blood still flowing freely all over his sweatshirt and coat.

Carol walked up to him and slapped him across the face. Charles winced and let out a painful moan. "He told you to keep your hands off. Now *I'm* telling you. You better keep your filthy hands off my boyfriend!"

Come on, Connor, let's go inside," Larry suggested. The four went upstairs. Connor immediately stripped down to his skivvies and crawled into his sleeping bag. The adrenaline rush was gone and all he wanted to do was sleep.

The girls sat on the bed with Larry while he repeated his version of what happened. They talked for a while and Larry told them about how Connor was no one to mess with, that he never picked fights, but he'd never lost a fight, either.

"That's the second time I've seen him fight. Both times, it only lasted a couple of seconds," Larry explained. "There are all sorts of stories about him from when he was in school. Back in Portland, it's a given, you don't mess with Connor."

They grew quiet as they pondered the events of the evening. Presently, they heard Connor softly chuckling. Carol lay down alongside him and cradled him.

After a minute or two, he said to no one in particular, "I never like hitting anyone, but I won't let them, especially a fucking piece of shit like that, get away with that kind of bullshit! I hope he'll think twice the next time someone tells him to back off."

No one said a thing. Nothing else needed to be said. Carol gently brushed his hair out of his face and softly kissed his forehead. He looked up at her and smiled. He slowly closed his eyes and drifted off to sleep.

15. Into the Sacred Valley

Saturday, March 27, 1976

*E*arly the next morning, the VW Bus headed north, back through Paradise Valley. The cold spring wind pushed them along as they followed the west bank of the Yellowstone River. Along the way, they passed several bald eagles perched in trees beside the river, waiting patiently to begin their hunt for breakfast.

The passengers watched the sun come over the white-capped mountains. The colors of the sunrise became unbelievably beautiful, so they turned onto a side road that took them down to the river.

They waited as the sun rose just to the south of a mountain named Emigrant Peak. A large, calm pool in the river reflected the orange sky as they smoked a wake-and-baker to savor the moment. The updrafts off the mountains caused havoc as the warmer air from below mixed with the frigid air above to create a series of lenticular clouds that broke the sunlight into a mixture of pinks, oranges, and blues. The morning sky looked like a masterpiece from the Renaissance.

It was cold as they sat on the river's edge. No one complained as the pot grew around their brains. They watched in silence as the Mother and Father's live act took place in front of them.

***

Meanwhile, back in Gardiner, there was a knock on Jonny's door. It seemed everyone was getting an early start. A lot of people had come over for an impromptu breakfast, so they could hear all about Charles' ass-kicking. Jonny was greeted by several officials when he opened the door. Both the county sheriff and state police were represented as well as the park rangers.

"Well, hi!" Jonny said, smiling and turning on a bit of the flare he'd shown when Connor and Larry arrived three days before. "I suppose you're here because Charles got the shit kicked out of him last night. Am I right?"

He invited them in and everyone stepped out to the backyard where the incident occurred. The police walked over to the blood stains where Charles had hit the ground and talked quietly with each other for a moment.

One of the state cops began taking statements from everyone who had been present during the fight. Every account of the incident confirmed that Charles was repeatedly warned off but assaulted the young guest anyway.

The state cop wanted to hear Connor's side of the story and was told that the four visitors had left in the dark and were headed back to Oregon.

The police had heard enough to know that Charles didn't have a case and were ready to drop the whole thing. The boyfriend ranger wasn't having anything to do with it. He became angry and began accusing everyone of lying. He approached Jonny and David and threatened to arrest them for hiding a fugitive and obstructing an official investigation.

One of the party-goers from the night before, who had no ties to the park, said, "I believe you're out of your jurisdiction here, sir. This isn't the park. The police said that they have heard enough, so please leave.

"Don't think for a moment we don't know you and Charles are lovers. You're here because he told you his version of what happened last night. But Charles is a liar and he's the only one, besides you, who thinks he's in the right."

"Well, I think, whoever this Connor guy is, he went a little overboard," the ranger retorted. "Charles is probably going to need surgery to straighten out his nose. Who's gonna pay for that, I wonder."

"You can," the young man replied. "Everyone at the party watched Charles make an ass of himself. He deserved what he got."

That finally shut the ranger up. He turned red and stared the young man down, powerless to do anything. The young man wasn't fazed, though. As a local who didn't work in the park, he knew the jerk could not wield his power over him.

David waited patiently for another moment or two, and finally said, "This is where I have to insist that you leave and allow us to enjoy the rest of our morning in peace."

All of the officials left. The ranger was reluctant to leave and had to be ushered out by the police. It was settled right then that they'd throw another party that night to celebrate Charles' broken nose and to honor the one who gave it to him.

The story spread like wildfire about how Charles got the shit beat out of him by a straight guy way smaller than he was. Over 150 people were at the party that night. So many attended they couldn't house them all, so they partied in front yard, too. At midnight, a chant rose up from the crowd, "Con-nor! Con-nor! Con-nor!"

***

Later that day, the bus headed south through Idaho along the west side of the Tetons, bound for Jackson, Wyoming. They'd all seen the iconic Grand Tetons in pictures before, but never from this side.

In the pictures, the Tetons were rugged-looking and their peaks curved slightly to the right. From the backside, though, their flanks were smooth and that defining curve went to the left. They were a geological wonder to the girls and a place to camp and to enjoy nature's beauty to the guys.

Everyone quietly enjoyed the beautiful scenery as the VW Bus made its way down the road. Becky broke the silence. "You do realize, of course, we're probably fugitives running from the law because of your new Buddhist boyfriend." She sounded pissed, but was smiling.

"Yeah, I can really pick 'em, can't I?" Carol let out a laugh.

Connor and Larry just smiled. Larry patted Connor on the back. There was nothing else to say. It was true.

They did some grocery shopping in Jackson and bought some beer and wine at a liquor store. Afterward, they headed north out of Jackson toward Grand Teton National Park.

Just outside of town, the road climbed up a ridge that Carol called a terminal moraine. It marked the southern end of a huge valley known as Jackson Hole. She went on to say that the valley was a sacred place to the American Indians, who lived there as early as twelve thousand years ago.

As they crested the ridge, the Grand Tetons suddenly came into view. It was the iconic view from the east. Their beauty and ruggedness was staggering. The mountains abruptly sprang up from the valley floor to a height of almost thirteen thousand feet, snow covering their summits and flanks. The view was so distracting they had to pull over and marvel at it.

It was some time before they had taken enough pictures and were ready to continue. They reached the Grand Teton Visitor Center a few minutes later, all the while transfixed by the stunning beauty of the peaks.

At the center, they learned about a place called Shadow Mountain on the east side of Jackson Hole. It was in the adjacent national forest where they could camp for free.

Shadow Mountain was still covered in snow, but they found a spot at the base of the mountain that looked as if it had been used as a campsite all winter. The snow was packed down and there were bare spots for their tarp and a fire pit.

The first thing that changed was the pair-ups. Carol had told everyone that she was going to share the tarp with Connor.

Larry said, "That's okay with me if Becky says it's okay with her."

"I don't bite," Becky casually replied. "As long as you stay on your side, it's cool with me."

Becky and Larry watched intently as Carol followed Connor around, listening to his ideas about a good spot for the tarp. After Connor picked one, Carol walked over to the bus and gathered Larry's half of the tarp set-up.

"Now, this ought to be real fun to watch," Larry said with amusement. To his surprise, though, the tarp went up just as fast as when he and Connor did it.

Becky laughed at the puzzled look on Larry's face and said, "We've been watching every time you guys set it up. Carol and *I* could set it up just as fast."

Soon, they had a cooking fire going. Dinner was a delicious menu of chicken fried in lard, grilled asparagus, and baked potatoes. Together with a shorty of beer and a joint, they were the proverbial happy campers.

They had finished dinner, cleaned up the camp and were settled in around the glowing embers of the campfire, ready to take in the approaching sunset. As they waited and took in the beauty of the distant mountains and the valley before them, their thoughts returned to the events of the previous night.

"I hope everything is okay for Jonny and David," said Carol.

Everyone agreed, and Connor said, "It never fails. It only takes one jackass to ruin an otherwise wonderful visit." They fell silent again and thought about Connor's words. They had no idea that back in Gardiner, a huge crowd gathered to celebrate in his honor.

As the sun perched just above the peaks, its increasing glare obscured the details of the valley. The minutes ticked by as it dropped closer to the Tetons. The moon, barely visible before, was brighter and easier to see as it followed on the heels of the sun.

Suddenly, Connor looked around at the mountain behind them. "Hey, now I understand why it's called Shadow Mountain."

The others turned and looked as the shadow of Grand Teton slowly made its way up the flank of Shadow Mountain. They looked back to the Tetons just as the sun disappeared from view.

Then, without the sun's glare, the details of valley floor popped. They could clearly see the channel of the Snake River that flowed south through the Hole as well as Jenny Lake that lay at the foot of Grand Teton. They adjourned to their separate corners and watched as the moon followed the sun's track to the horizon.

In the bus, there was silence until the moon set, and then Larry said to no one in particular, "That was one of the most beautiful things I've ever seen!"

"Yeah." Becky offered nothing else.

Under the tarp, Carol was down to her panties as she lay on Connor, kissing him and breathing heavily. Connor was in control, but just barely. He looked over at the moon as it set and whispered to Carol, "Okay, let's look at the stars for a while, then you need to get back to your end of the tarp."

They snuggled together and watched the stars slowly track cross the sky. Carol pointed to an extra bright star and told him that it was not a star, but was the planet Jupiter. Once Jupiter set, she pecked him on the lips and was gone, too.

Three hours later, she was back, teeth chattering and cold to the bone. She cuddled right in as Connor spread her bag over his and added the cotton blanket over everything. She gradually warmed and went out into a deep sleep, a slight smile on her beautiful face.

Sunday, March 28, 1976

Connor tried to get up the next morning, but Carol held on to him and wouldn't let go. So there he was, stuck with a beautiful girl he couldn't touch, who was clinging to him in the most seductive way. He lay there realizing just how uncomfortable this new sleeping arrangement was going to be. He finally got out of her grasp just as he heard Larry stirring in the VW.

Larry quietly came out through the sliding door and noticed that Connor was just getting dressed. "What? Are you sleeping in late now that you got a girl?"

"Naw, she woke up in the middle of the night, cold as hell. She crawled over to my end and shivered till I could warm her up. This morning, she wouldn't let go. I've been trying to get out of there for the last hour."

"That's funny, because they have like ten blankets in the bus."

"Well, tonight we're gonna get a couple of 'em. I don't think her sleeping bag is very thick. She was really cold and ended up sleeping next to me. Man! Is she ever hard to resist!"

"Blue balls, huh?"

"Like I've *never* had!" Connor groaned.

Soon the coffee was on, and Connor had the potatoes frying and the ham diced up, waiting to be added when the girls got up. "Nothin' like the smell of good food cooking over a fire to get people out of bed," he said. "So, how did you sleep, Carol?"

"Well, it wasn't that bad once I snuggled in next to you. You're like an electric blanket! I couldn't believe you were so warm." Carol walked up to Connor and kissed him on the lips. "I could get used to you in bed with me."

"Right back atcha," Connor said, smiling. "Tonight, let's grab some more blankets from the bus. I think you'll be more comfortable at my end of the tarp. We'll have to set it up a little different, but we'll manage."

After breakfast, they broke camp and hiked around the Jackson Hole area for the day. The Becky and Carol Geological Tour of North America continued. Their students must've asked all the right questions because they never stopped talking.

To Connor and Larry, the Teton Range was one of the more beautiful mountain ranges they'd seen. Having been to the Swiss Alps, Connor always used them for comparison. "These mountains are almost as beautiful as the Alps."

Midday found them sitting and eating lunch on the east shore of Jenny Lake. After trudging through snow for two hours, they found a clear spot that enjoyed good sunlight all day.

The mountains shot skyward from the opposite shore. They seemed close enough to reach out and touch. A chilly breeze created small ripples on the lake and blurred their reflection.

Connor broke the silence as everyone sat, absorbed in the iconic view. "So, now I know that a tectonic plate broke and the pressure pushed it up on its side. On one side of the fault, we have the Tetons, and on the other, we have the Hole.

Becky said, "That's right. You *do* listen."

"Of course I do. Now, here's a question for *you*. What was the nationality of the trappers who named the Tetons?"

"That's easy, they were French," Becky replied.

"Now here's the tough one. What does *Grand Teton* mean?" he asked with a twinkle in his eye. The girls looked at each other and shrugged their shoulders.

Larry laughed a bit and said, "Looks like you got 'em, Connor. I'll write that down. One for Connor, six hundred for the girls." Becky and Carol laughed.

"Well, yesterday at the visitor center, I read about it and found it rather humorous. You see, them there trappers had been out in the wilderness for a long, long time. They'd sit out there on the Snake River and look up at these mountains. They were reminded of what they missed most. Great big tits!"

Larry laughed uncontrollably, rolling onto his back and rocking back and forth. The girls were puzzled at first. Connor watched them both reason it out in their sharp, young minds—*Grand* meaning *big*, *Tetons* meaning *tits*—and they started laughing, too.

After lunch, they passed a joint around and sat drinking in the beauty for a while longer. A coyote scampered by, attracted by the smell of the food and interested in what they were doing. Then the ravens and jays started to gather, calling back and forth. They watched and waited for the picnickers to leave so they could hunt for scraps.

They finally summoned enough energy to retrace their steps back to the bus. They settled on some nearby logs and rested, talking about what they'd do next. Everyone grew quiet for a moment.

Larry finally said, "Hey, I got one for the girls. Do you know how much Connor and I enjoy following you two on our little walks?" Connor agreed with a nod of his head as he looked over at them with his most lecherous smile.

The girls blushed. Becky stood abruptly and walked over to Larry. He stood to protect himself. She moved too fast, though, and planted a wet kiss right on his lips. After the shock wore off, Larry returned the kiss. She pulled away and Larry said with a smile, "Guess you knew the answer to that."

Connor walked over to Carol and whispered, "You have a nice everything." He brushed her lips with his. "But I think following you on a trail is my favorite thing." Carol's smile made Connor melt, and he sat down next to her and gave her a squeeze.

They drove back into Jackson to score some fixin's for dinner and the next morning's breakfast. It was seafood linguine with three bottles of wine for dessert, accompanied by some good bluegrass on the radio.

Connor said to Larry, "I was lookin' at the park map when we were at the visitor center. Just about every slot you see going into the Teton Range has a trail. They're covered with snow now, but I bet in August all those trails will be open. You know, Larry, it might be nice to aim this way when we come back home."

Connor noticed Carol and Becky out of the corner of his eye. He nudged Larry and they looked on for a minute as the girls set up the tarp. They shared a surprised look at how quickly it was going up.

Without speaking, they went back to preparing dinner. Larry could rock a plate of linguine. Connor concentrated his energy on toasting French bread and spreading garlic butter.

They ate their fill and drank all of the wine. Larry and Connor were both a little buzzed and the girls were slurring their words.

It was time to hit the rack. Carol took a couple of blankets from the bus. Connor noticed that she had made one bed instead of two at opposite ends of the tarp. *Just like I suggested.*

Larry and Becky had been in bed for a while when the we-ain't-sleeping sounds started coming from inside the bus.

Carol said, "She told me she was horny." Connor shook his head slowly.

"What's wrong?"

"Well, I made a promise and I'm stickin' to it. Guess I'm kinda jealous."

"You know, I liked you from that first night in Death Valley. You're not my first crush, but you *are* the first guy I've wanted to have sex with. I mean, I've thought about it and you really *do* make me feel something—kind of nervous and excited. I feel out of control around you. If you had a condom, we could have sex."

"That's just not gonna happen. Your mom and dad aren't gonna hang your hymen in front of *me*. So will you do me the favor of not hanging it out there to be had? It ain't gonna happen, and I don't need the temptation. Please!"

Carol was silent for a moment. "I'm really sorry, Connor. I can be so selfish! I didn't even think of how hard this must be for *you*." She promised she'd try not to be such a tease for the rest of the trip.

They got into bed; both were fully dressed. Then Connor stripped naked. He told Carol that sleeping naked was warmer than not, so she slowly stripped, too. They slept comfortably and soundly the entire night.

Monday, March 29, 1976

It was the first time in days that Connor wasn't aching in the morning. It was late when Larry finally stirred and Connor managed to pry himself out of Carol's clutches.

They immediately built a cooking fire with aspen limbs they had gathered the night before. The fire flared up, crackling and sending sparks swirling in the air. They added a layer of small, dead branches they cut from the bottom of some nearby pine trees. This was the best wood to use because it was so dry. They worked without speaking as the fire grew into a good bed of coals.

Connor put a pan of water on the fire, looked over at Larry, and finally spoke. "You lucky motherfucker!"

"Shit just happens sometimes," Larry said unapologetically. "I mean, I was kicked into the bus. I been wantin' to thank you for that, by the way."

"Fuck you, Larry!" They both laughed.

"She's not the virgin, Carol is. I guess it's just luck, but I've never had as much lovin' as I've had on this trip," Larry exclaimed. "I guess I should thank you for that, too."

Connor just stared at the fire. He wasn't pissed, but he *was* jealous. Finally, he said quietly, "Karma."

It was quite a while before either girl got out of bed. By then, the guys had built the fire up for warmth. Becky got up and poured herself a cup of coffee. She walked over to Larry and snuggled in next to him. Everything in her movements and her facial expression said "thank you". They lightly kissed, and she sat quietly and woke up.

Larry put more water on the coal bed that was reserved for cooking. Becky was on her second cup when Carol emerged from the tarp. She poured a cup of coffee and snuggled in next to Connor.

Silence fell over the group as they took in the beauty of their surroundings. The flat expanse of the grass-covered valley lay before them. A herd of elk grazed in the distance. Behind the elk, the Teton Range bolted skyward and glistened in the morning sunlight.

They enjoyed the little warmth that the bright spring sun brought, but then a cold breeze would remind them that it was still colder than shit.

Carol whispered in Connor's ear, "I want to spend one more night here, okay?"

Connor nodded and said to Becky and Larry, "What do you guys say we spend another night here? I'd like to stay in camp so we don't have to break down the tarp again. I want a lazy day."

Larry stood up and asked Becky, "How about you and me going into Jackson to get supplies? We'll leave these two love birds here to bond."

"Okay, what's for breakfast?" Becky asked.

"Italian slumgullion," Connor answered.

Connor made the potatoes and eggs topped with diced tomatoes and jalapeño peppers, onions, and Swiss cheese as fillers. Larry busied himself with toasting bread with the green aspen branch Connor used the night before.

After breakfast, Connor and Carol watched as the bus headed down the dirt road, stirring up dust into a cyclonic whirl that nearly obliterated it from view, making it seem as if the road itself was shifting gears. Carol turned to Connor and said, "I just want to go back to bed naked with you and have you hold me."

"I have a better idea," he said. "Let's hike up this road. I bet the view up higher is incredible."

Over the course of the next hour, they walked up a very steep, dirt road and talked about their lives and their futures.

Connor also explained to Carol about the uncomfortable feelings and painful symptoms of blue balls. "Last night, just lying there and sleeping all night without getting all hot and bothered, I woke up this morning feeling great."

They spent two more days at the base of Shadow Mountain. Only after some serious prodding from Larry, did they move on. Otherwise, they might have spent the entire summer there.

Wednesday, March 31, 1976

They left Jackson Hole before dawn and drove the entire day to get to Fort Collins, Colorado. It was dark when they pulled into a motel. The girls insisted that everyone take a shower and the guys didn't argue. They had kept a back window cracked all day because everyone stank so badly.

The next day, they drove into the mountains to Estes Park, the east entrance of Rocky Mountain National Park. They paused just inside the park gate to get the epic view of the range from Longs Peak in the south, to Hallett Peak and to the Mummy Range in the north. It was too early in the year for the road over the mountains, Trail Ridge Road, to be open, so they took the road to Bear Lake.

On the way, Carol pointed out the lateral and terminal moraines left by ancient glaciers that formed the valley. She pointed out a hanging valley among the mountains, saying that it was formed by a glacier cutting across the valley at right angles and leaving it higher than the rest of the valley. Connor listened intently while Larry just admired the view.

The day spent in the park was beautiful, but cold. They decided to drive out to Fort Collins and get another motel room rather than try to camp at nine thousand feet.

The weather cooperated and the next morning was sunny and warm. They were going to the Devils Tower National Monument and had all day to make the six-hour drive. They decided to do a little laundry and clean the bus before leaving.

They found a nice campground just outside the monument that didn't charge anyone willing to camp so early in the year.

As usual, Connor had the hobo coffee ready before anyone else stirred. He was on his second cup and climbed up a rock outcrop above the camp for a moment of meditation.

While he wasn't one to worry about the future, he couldn't help thinking about what would become of his relationship with Carol. He heard the piercing half-whistle, half-scream of a Red-tailed hawk and looked up to see her glide overhead. The smaller male followed at a discreet distance, wary of any possible mood swing. It was that time of the year, and love was in the air. Connor lifted his mug in salute and said to the male, "I feel ya, bro."

"What?" asked Larry. "You feel me?" He had gotten up while Connor was lost in his thoughts and was pouring himself a cup of coffee.

"Nothin', I was talking to the hawk up there." Connor pointed upward.

"Are you okay?" asked Larry

"I guess. I don't know how much more of this I can take," said Connor. "Part of me wishes we could hurry up and get to Illinois. The other part knows it means Carol and I will have to part company.

"When did things get so damned complicated? Just a few weeks ago, I was a happy-go-lucky guy on this epic tour and now look at me. I'm done for."

"Well, I'm in the same boat."

"You mean Tanya?" asked Connor. "That's right, you never mentioned whether you were able to talk to her."

"Well, I tried many times to call, but no answer. When I called home, my mom said she had called and left her number.

"She was glad to hear from me, and a little pissed, too. But she was okay when I told her that I had written down her number wrong. I told her I must've called the wrong number a hundred times and was worried when she never answered. She asked me how the trip was going and where we were."

"Did you tell her about Becky?"

"No way!" said Larry in a hushed voice. "Tanya and I didn't promise to be exclusive. But I don't really think my heart is anywhere else. So she doesn't need to know. I'm not like you Connor, so back me up on that, okay?"

"You got it, bro." Connor turned and stared at the eastern horizon, deep in thought. "You know what we need?" Larry looked at him, waiting for the answer. "Pancakes and bacon! That's what we need!" He suddenly gathered himself and came off of the rock. He was on a mission.

Breakfast brought everyone together. They decided to have another lazy day. They spent it relaxing and wandering around the campground. They gathered a big pile of wood and were looking forward to another weenie roast that night for dinner.

In the middle of the afternoon, the temperature began to drop. It was freezing by time they started cooking the weenies. After dinner, they passed a joint and a pint of whiskey around, and then everyone hit the hay. Carol snuggled in next to Connor once again, thinking that it was strange how much she enjoyed lying on the ground next to him.

Thursday, April 8, 1976

It got to three below zero, according to the radio. Even Connor, the guy who believed his tarp could handle anything, was surprised that he was warm. He figured it was Carol's body next to his that kept him so toasty.

Everyone stayed in their cozy beds until the morning sunshine warmed the campsite up to a temperature better suited for making breakfast. Luckily, it seemed to warm up just as quickly as it had cooled the evening before.

The geology tour that day consisted of how this lava plume didn't erode away while all the soil around it did. The foursome took the time to hike the path that wound around the base of the tower. The guys were impressed with the predominantly Ponderosa pine forest with its full canopy and open, grassy floor.

Larry kept an ongoing aliens theme through the day. "I read somewhere they're gonna make an extra-terrestrial sci-fi movie here. They started shooting in Palmdale, California last December and they were supposed to start shooting again soon. How far out is that?"

"I wonder if there is a way to get to the top of this thing." Connor paused to look up and scan the side of the near vertical column. "We've been around the whole thing and I haven't seen anything that looked like a trail going up."

"I guess you could rock climb up or use a helicopter. It would be neat to see what's up there," said Larry.

Later, the guys spotted a Golden eagle chasing a Bald eagle. The birds were only about a hundred feet in the air and almost overhead. They could see that the Bald had something in its talons.

From the way the Golden was acting, it appeared the Bald had raided some food from the Golden's stash. The Golden issued a high-pitched whistle at the Bald and was almost on top of him when the Bald dropped whatever it had and flew off.

The Golden circled several times and called out in triumph. Then it turned and headed back the way it came, not even bothering to retrieve what the Bald had dropped.

"That's what I'm talkin' about!" exclaimed Larry. He spun in circles and jumped in the air. "*That's* something I can tell the grandkids!"

"You know," said Becky, "the Plains Indians consider the Bald eagle more of a carrion crow when compared to the Golden. Now I can see why. That was really cool!"

"Yeah," Connor agreed. "Balds are everywhere up in Alaska, but that's the first Golden I've ever seen. Did you see how much bigger it was than the Bald?" He smiled at the girls. "Okay, we can go back to camp now. I've seen everything I needed to see."

That drew sarcastic expressions from the girls. They wanted to hike a nearby dry creek bottom and look for fossils. They walked for two hours down the six-foot-deep wash into the grassy prairie, searching for any sign from the past.

Larry was the one who found a specimen. After the girls had given up, the four rested at the top of a short incline. Larry pulled a tuft of grass out of the sandy soil. There, below it, was a rock with a perfect impression of a prehistoric fern.

The girls went crazy, kissing and hugging Larry. In a frenzy, they dug at the rock until they got it out. It weighed almost forty pounds and a closer inspection revealed a second fern fossil.

Becky said, "This is sedimentary rock. They're the ones that'll have fossils. It's pretty cool, isn't it."

Larry and Connor took turns carrying the rock. "You found it, you should have to carry it," Connor joked.

"It's a good thing they weren't more successful!" said Larry. The travelers laughed.

They bushwhacked a straight line to a gravel road and set the rock by a fence post. A tuft of grass on top of the post marked the spot so they wouldn't miss it when they came back with the bus.

When they got back to camp with the fossil rock, Larry and Connor announced that it was breakfast for dinner and they started building a fire.

"Yesterday's pancakes were so good, we decided we needed a repeat," Connor explained. While Larry cooked the bacon and eggs, Connor peeled and mashed two bananas into the pancake batter, mixing it into a smooth consistency.

The girls pulled out their geology tools, cleaned the rock, and set it on a tree stump about ten feet from the fire. Connor walked over to the prize and, for the first time, took a close look it.

He noticed a small fissure. He pulled out his Bowie knife, stuck it in the crack and turned it. With little effort, a four-inch chunk fell to the ground, exposing more of what the girls said was the very end of a possum tail. The girls were excited at his find. Connor just shrugged. Larry was laughing.

Bacon, eggs, and pancakes done and dishes cleaned, Larry exclaimed, "Must be time for an after-dinner joint."

Connor rolled and after a short while of enjoying a Thai weed high, he announced he was putting in for the evening. He wasn't in bed long when Carol joined him, clad in nothing but panties. They lay together, exploring each other for a while, and Carol confessed, "I would really like it if we had sex before I get back home."

"That's not gonna happen," Connor declared. He paused for a moment to consider his penis, which was standing at attention, just waiting for orders.

"First impressions are the only ones that matter. I don't want your parents pissed at me for breaking a promise right off the get-go. No, you're gonna arrive back in Podunk, a virgin.

"And if you're not a virgin, then someone else is gonna get your cherry. Course, then I'd have to kill the motherfucker. I'm waiting till your mom tells me it's alright."

Carol let out a laugh. "Pigs will fly before my mom ever says it's okay."

"So when do you think we're gonna get back to your place, anyway?"

"Well, tomorrow is the Black Hills and Mount Rushmore, then the Badlands the next day. It'll take us two days to drive through South Dakota, Minnesota, and Wisconsin. Then we'll be at my place. So, four days starting tomorrow."

Carol lay there and thought about it for a moment. "I guess I can hold out till we get home, but I don't care what my mom says. Once we're there, we're having sex. I'm sick of hearing how good a time Becky's having over there in the bus!"

"Deal. On the fifth day from now, we're having sex, no matter what."

Wednesday, April 9, 1976

The day was sunny and warm, perfect for a visit to Mount Rushmore. The dead presidents' mountain was much more impressive in person than in any picture or on television. The whole tour, including the loop trail and the historical exhibits, took about three hours to complete.

After lunch, they went agate digging, which was much more fun for the girls than the guys. They sat and smiled whenever the girls brought a specimen over for them to inspect. They glanced at each other and shook their heads as the girls eagerly went back to digging.

Later, they took a hike through the forest to find a place to camp. Dinner was beef burritos. Larry had nailed the heat just right.

They were sitting around the campfire when Connor predicted that it would start raining soon. Right on cue, a slow drizzle started a few minutes later.

"How'd you know it was going to start raining?" asked Becky.

"Larry knew, too. When you grow up in rain country, you can always tell. I mostly smelled it on the wind."

Larry nodded and said, "Got here a little quicker than I expected, but it was pretty obvious."

The next morning, the precipitation had increased to a steady, sideways rain driven by a southwestern wind. It felt much colder than it really was, but that didn't stop them from going into the Badlands.

"In the rain, the Badlands really should've been called the what-the-fuck-are-we-even-*in*-this-fucking-place lands!" Connor observed.

In the afternoon, after considerable discussion and moving around, and after the rain quit, the guys finally located a spot for the tarp that wouldn't leave a mud residue on the bottom side.

The guys cooked up some soup and the girls made sandwiches. They ate in the bus and played Spades until dark, and then hit the sack. Soon, it would be time to get back to Podunk, Illinois.

Connor and Carol lay in bed for a while. Carol said, "We'll drive to a motel I've stayed at in Wisconsin. It's about an hour from my house. I want to be showered and neat for my parents. I'll pay for our room and Becky's gonna pay for her room."

"How about this, you two get our room, and Larry and I will get your room. Okay?" asked Connor. She agreed. He winked at her and she hit him in the chest.

Monday, April 12, 1976

After getting a slow start on Sunday, they traveled most of the way through South Dakota and camped at roadside park. With two more states to go through, they took turns driving.

At a pit stop, Carol called her mom to tell her they would be home around noon the next day. It was then that Carol's mom decided to finally tell her dad about the two hitchhikers.

Becky did the same, but she didn't say anything about Connor and Larry. They figured to drop the guys at Carol's, and then drop Becky at her place, a couple of blocks away.

They arrived at the motel and as they unpacked, Carol said to Connor, "I can't believe how nervous I am about you coming home with me. Other than Jonny and a few of my geology friends, I've never brought a guy home before. Certainly not someone who's gonna talk to my mom about sleeping with me."

"You make it sound like I'm really looking forward to this. I'm so fucking nervous, I doubt I'll sleep at all tonight."

"Just to let you know, this is where we're coming when you don't get my mom's approval," said Carol.

"Cool," said Connor. Then, unlike what he'd just claimed, he was asleep in no time at all.

16. The Redheads

Aviva and Ariella

They were born a day apart in October of 1949 in Shaker Heights, Ohio. Actually, it was only five hours and four minutes apart. Aviva was born at 10:17 p.m. on the evening of October 11 and Ariella at 3:21 a.m. on the morning of the twelfth.

Their parents were brothers and sisters, two Jewish brothers married to two Jewish sisters. They had a double marriage on June 12, 1944, two days before both of the grooms shipped off to war.

Jacob and Aaron fought in the South Pacific until Japan surrendered. Both had seen the worst the war could offer and walked away without being physically wounded.

They had fought in the battles of Guam, Peleliu, Iwo Jima, and Okinawa. They came away with nothing more than some scrapes and bruises. Yet, no one could witness what they had without some mental baggage.

After the war ended, they were sent to the Philippines to help rebuild the Manila Bay infrastructure. The work was exhausting, but it let them sleep without horrible visions in their dreams. They both said later that it was the best therapy they could've gotten.

The brothers returned to Shaker Heights on January 19, 1948. Couples being couples, who had been separated for three and a half years, the sisters, Sarah and Dina, announced their pregnancies on the same day. They went into labor at the same time, and both came home from the hospital with their daughters on the same day.

So were the lives of Aviva and Ariella. Both families grew to five children, but none of the cousins were as close as the two oldest, who grew up calling themselves sisters.

Most people believed that they really were sisters. They were about the same height with the most wonderful, curly red hair. They always dressed alike and a lot of people even called them twins.

The girls' mothers and fathers became doctors, and all worked at the same hospital in Cleveland. They lived in the same upscale neighborhood in Shaker Heights, a couple of blocks apart.

It was on their fifteenth birthday that the girls first became intimate with each other. It just seemed right. Because they were first cousins, they were very discreet. Later in life, they both slept with guys, and enjoyed it, but their relationship with each other was very close, and they wanted it to last forever.

They had discussed their feelings for months before sleeping together. When they finally did, it only made them feel closer. Their love was now complete. No one ever suspected them. After all, in everyone's view, they were sisters.

They both went to Kent State and studied architecture. They became active in the anti-war movement. Like so many others, they knew the evil of the war machine that was killing thousands of their generation in Vietnam. They knew the warmongers were in it for the money and didn't care how many died as long as they became more wealthy.

In their classes, when they discussed the war, no one could justify the deaths of Americans. It was a war of the have's and have-not's. The poor were drafted and the rich were ushered into colleges or the National Guard.

They had boyfriends who had been with them for almost two years. They met at an anti-war protest at Kent State. They became travelling partners to every anti-war protest in the Midwest, two in Washington, D.C., and one in New York City.

They were in Chicago with the blood on the streets at the Democratic Convention in 1968. They walked with the Weatherman Underground in Berkeley. They were card-carrying members of the Students for a Democratic Society and were an active part of the first generation of Americans that said, "Hell, no! We won't go!"

It was May 4, 1970. The girls had just graduated and earned their bachelor's degrees. It was a happy time. They were about to be taught a lesson that would stay with them for the rest of their lives.

Once again, they met with thousands of other students on the Kent State campus. They carried signs with anti-war slogans and marched to the administration building, singing "All we are saying is give peace a chance." That's when they saw the line of soldiers in front of the Dean's office.

They heard popping sounds and wondered who had the fireworks. Suddenly, two of their very best friends fell to the ground, and the girls were both covered in blood. They ran in fear for their lives as other protesters continued to fall around them. The Ohio National Guard was shooting at them for having the nerve to protest the war.

The girls fled to Shaker Heights. Their parents were very worried about them. The two oldest in the families had withdrawn into themselves. They talked very little and could be heard crying behind the closed doors of their bedrooms.

A week later, they shaved their heads and a day after that, they disappeared. Driving their VW Bug, they had just enough money to make it to Haight and Ashbury in San Francisco. They changed their names to Sunshine and Rainbow. No one would know their birth names, a common thing in San Francisco in 1970.

They both took jobs as barmaids in the same nightclub where their good looks and flirtatious ways made them a lot of tip money. One night, they brought a woman, Sandy, home with them. Later they would say she had saved their lives.

She told them of a lesbian commune in Oregon. The owner was a wealthy trust-fund baby who wanted to expand the commune and was looking for architects with a head for earth-friendly, futuristic designs. They both had graduated with honors and looked forward to the opportunity.

The next morning after a phone call, they agreed to move to Oregon. They quit their jobs the same day.

A week later, the girls arrived in southern Oregon where they finally found the seclusion they were looking for. They moved into a teepee and let everyone know they weren't sisters, but lovers. Not having to conceal their love set them free. In time, they recovered from their emotional wounds inflicted by the Ohio National Guard.

Two years later, they were married. It wasn't official, but a spiritual affair just the same. They celebrated for three days and received two tickets to Hawaii as a wedding gift. They spent a blissful week on the Big Island.

After three years, they had designed and helped build five homes and twelve community buildings. All were earth-friendly and had a low impact on the surrounding land. The owner offered them a bedroom in one of the houses, but they remained in their teepee.

They used their building designs in the commune to land internships at a big architectural firm in Portland. They left the commune and moved into an apartment where they began their reinsertion into modern city life.

The one thing that had driven them to leave the commune was their attraction to men. They certainly weren't going to find that where they'd been living.

Over the next two years, they each dated a series of men. It was never serious, just good sex. Even though some of the men wanted to get serious, their first love was for each other. After all, they were spirit wives.

They lived in Portland for two years. One night, they decided to call their parents. It was a long and joyous conversation. The phone was passed from mother to mother, from father to father and to sibling after sibling. There were tears of joy on both ends of the line.

Their internships were over and the company offered full-time jobs to both of the girls. They asked for a month to decide and explained they had some family business to attend to back home. They headed back to Shaker Heights in early June of 1975, just about five years to the day of their departure.

They arrived home to a celebration. The two families were whole again. Brothers and sisters had married. Nieces and nephews had been born. The family was growing. Unknown to the girls, they had become legends to the next generation and to the younger siblings.

They tried to explain the wounds inflicted upon them by the murders on the Kent State campus. Their fathers took them aside and, for the first time, told them of their time spent in Manila Bay and of their slow recovery.

17. The Showdown

Tuesday, April 13, 1976

Connor couldn't remember being so nervous in his entire life. They pulled up and parked in Carol's driveway. She was instantly surrounded in a group hug by her two sisters and her mom.

Carol introduced the hitchhikers and Connor got "the look" from all of them. He wasn't sure what to read into it. Larry saw it, too. It was the "what have you done to my baby" look.

Carol and her sisters got in the bus and drove Becky home. Louise, Carol's mom, led the travelers around the side of the house, down a flight of stairs, through a door and into the basement.

She pointed to a room across the large basement and said, "That's where you two are staying." As she started up the stairs, she turned and casually said, "Connor, could you come upstairs as soon as you can? We need to talk."

After she got out of earshot, Larry said, "Jesus, Connor! We may not be welcome here very long after this conversation. I ain't even gonna unpack. Matter of fact, I've got Becky's number. I think we might be more welcome there, and they don't even know we exist! I mean, I *know* you noticed the looks you got from everyone."

"Yeah, well I'll be back in no time. This don't look like a time for Type-A Connor, but Timid Connor. I really don't know what to say about the looks they gave me. I just know I brought the coveted hymen back home to Mom *intact*.

"I think the looks were because no one has seen Carol in love before. I think it's changed her aura and her mom thinks I've broken my promise. My ace in the hole is the hymen."

He headed up the stairs and found Louise in the kitchen. "What can I do for you, Louise?" Connor asked with his best smile.

"Sit down, Connor. I think you and I should talk for a while about what's been going on between you and my daughter."

She pointed to a chair at the kitchenette. Connor sat down and stared at Louise until she looked away.

"So, what is it you need to know, Louise?"

"Carol has been calling me with a surprising story of how she loves you," she said. "I never had any problems with her as long as she lived here, then she goes off to Death Valley and comes home with a boyfriend she says she loves. A hitchhiker of all things, on some tour of America, I think that's what she said. Is that true?"

"Yes, madam, that's a good description of what I'm up to."

Connor paused and stared at Louise again. As before, she looked away first. Then he started his sales pitch.

"Here's the rundown on me and my best friend, Larry. We saved for a year and a half to make this trip. We both like to hitchhike even though we own nice cars back in Oregon.

"I'm a veteran with an honorable discharge from the Army, and I work in the steel industry. Larry owns his own painting and roofing company back home. When we get back, he plans on picking up right where he left off. I'm currently on leave from the sheet metal union where I'm a third-year apprentice." While mostly accurate, Connor figured a few embellishments couldn't hurt.

Carol came walking in with her two sisters and Connor stopped his sales pitch. Carol looked at her mom and asked, "What's going on, Mom?"

Louise looked at her daughter and said, "Just talking with Connor, trying to get to know him a little.

"Your father and I have been very worried about your well-being. Connor and his friend seem to be respectable kids, though. Jonny said they were, but until you meet someone, you worry."

Connor said, "I guess there's no better time than now to tell you, Louise. I have fallen in love with your daughter. I think that's really the reason you want to talk with me.

"I know Carol has mentioned me and her feelings toward me to you on the phone. It needs to be said and I can't think of a better time than now, with her two sisters here." Carol moved up beside Connor, and he stood up and took her hand.

Louise stared at the two of them. "Did you keep your promise to me, Carol?"

Carol looked down at the floor and back at her mother. "I guess the answer is yes, and no. I wanted to have sex with Connor. But he wouldn't do it. I made him promise me back in Death Valley, before I fell in love with him. He's very stubborn about his word. So, yes, Mom, I'm still a virgin."

Carol's eyes welled up with tears, and she walked out of the room. Her sisters followed her. Connor smiled his million-dollar smile and sat back down at the table. "She tried to explain why you're so worried about her getting pregnant like her sister did. I think you just embarrassed her."

"Yes, her sister, Penny, was so bright and ready to go to college, and then she became pregnant. Now, she's married with two kids and works at the grade school as a secretary. She dreamed of being a teacher."

Connor didn't hesitate and shot back, "Is she happy?"

Louise's anger was seeping through and, for the first time, her voice raised just a fraction as she said, "I don't know if she's happy. She seems happy, but that's not the point. Her pregnancy ruined her chance for an education."

Connor got up, and as he left the room, he said, "I'll be right back." He walked down the hallway until he heard voices and knocked.

When the door opened, he said, "I'm sorry for interrupting. Penny, could you come with me? I need to ask you a question."

Puzzled, Penny looked at Carol for a second and silently followed Connor back to the kitchen. Louise looked surprised that it was Penny, and not Carol, he brought back.

"Penny, I need to know, are you happy with your place in life?" Connor asked. He could see he'd confused her, so he rephrased his question. "I guess what I'm asking is, do you regret getting pregnant and not going to college? Are you happy with two kids, a husband, and being a secretary at the school?"

"Mom never forgave me for getting pregnant and we don't talk about it. I mean, she loves her grandkids, but she's never brought the pregnancy up to me once I told her I was getting married."

Penny turned to her mom and said, "Carol was just telling me how you've held my pregnancy over her head all this time. I never told you this, Mom, but I had already decided on marriage before I got pregnant."

She turned back to Connor and continued, "Carol told us that you don't mince words when you have a point to make. So, yes, I'm happy and love my husband. I wouldn't change a thing."

Penny turned back to her mom, smiled and added "By the way, Mom. I just found out I'm pregnant with number three. We're hoping for a son this time."

Louise stood up with tears in her eyes. "Congratulations, honey. I'm so happy for you. I'm sorry I never talked with you about your decision until now."

"I love you, Mom." Penny had teared up, too. She came over and gave her mom a long hug, and then walked back to Carol's room.

Louise sat back down and stared at Connor for a moment. "You're quite a remarkable young man. You come in here and sit down in an obviously hostile situation and make me see things I've ignored for a long time."

"I hope I haven't offended you. If I did, it was the furthest thing from my mind. Carol wasn't lying when she said she gave herself to me. I guess when it comes time for sex, for a girl *or* a guy, no promise to Mom is going to stop them.

"But I made a personal promise to her, that's different. I didn't want to start a relationship with your daughter, the first girl I've ever told that I loved, by having her break a promise to you. And I want her to go to college. So does she.

"This, I think, is the point. Carol is going to become sexually active. *Someone* is going to sleep with her. I hope that someone is me, but I want your permission. Do you want her to sleep with someone on the sly, hiding her life from you? Or, do you want an open relationship of trust and well-being with your daughter?"

Louise was in shock. A look of disbelief changed to one of realization. She sat there and thought it through. Connor noticed how much Carol looked like her mom while deep in thought. After a few minutes, Louise slowly shook her head.

"I think you have made a very good point. Do you have protection?"

"Of course I do. I'm not ready to have kids yet."

"Well, I can't believe I'm saying this, but you have my blessing. I just want to point out once more that you are a remarkable young man.

"Just a word of warning, her dad's going to want to talk to you. He's working overtime at the plant or he'd be here now. He wasn't very pleased when I told him about you and your friend."

"Thanks, Louise. I guess I'll cross the 'dad' bridge when I come to it." He paused for a moment. "I've been worrying about this conversation for three weeks. I'm glad it's over. You know, I see a lot of you in Carol."

He turned and walked to Carol's room. He stood at her door, shaking for a minute before he opened it. He entered the room and stood at the foot of the bed. Looking at the three sisters, he smiled. "Ladies, I have some deflowering to do, so could you please give me and Carol some privacy?"

Carol's sisters sat in shock at first. They got up, walked over to Connor and hugged him without saying a word. As they walked through the bedroom door, he said, "This may take a few days. We both have a lot of pent-up needs."

The two sisters giggled like ten year olds, smiled back at Carol and disappeared down the hall. They both went to talk with their mom and get her side of the amazing story.

"I can't believe you did it!"

"I've been thinking for three weeks about what I was gonna say to her. Then she gave me all the ammo I needed. I'm just glad Penny was here."

He paused, while he took off his shirt. "Now, lady, it's time to get naked!"

Carol stood up and walked over to him with that million-dollar smile on her face. They embraced and kissed deeply. Carol drew back and began removing her blouse. Connor helped her.

They stood together, naked, and kissed again. Carol completely at ease as Connor guided her backward over the bed and lay down alongside her.

"You know, this will probably hurt a bit the first time, right?" he asked.

"I know, so I'm told."

"I'm sorry in advance, okay?"

Carol didn't answer him with words. She smiled and kissed him again, anxious for their long-awaited union.

The pain didn't last long. In fact, it was almost completely forgotten before they left the bed. They reappeared four hours later, half an hour before her dad was to get home. The girls, including her mom as it turned out, were there to wish her the best and, of course, to get the dirt on everything.

Poor Larry had been downstairs the whole time not knowing what was going on. Connor went downstairs and brought Larry up to date. They settled in to playing pool on the regulation table Carol had told them about.

"So you go upstairs and talk to the mom. Then she says you can go sleep with her youngest daughter. Meanwhile, you leave me down here in the dark, wondering if you're even alive." Larry smiled at Connor.

"Yep, and fuck you!"

"Connor, you friggin' amaze me! No one's gonna believe this one back home, even if I'm there to back you up!"

"Yeah, that's what I figured. I'm just glad you're here to verify the story. You know what's the best thing, though? It's my birthday today. What a present! It hadn't even dawned on me until I looked at the calendar on Carol's bedroom door."

Just then, someone they hadn't seen before came down the stairs. They figured it was Carol's dad. Connor said, extending his hand, "You must be John. I'm Connor and this is my buddy, Larry."

"Good to meet you two. I see you found the pool table. I've got winners."

A few minutes later, Jesse, the oldest daughter, came down with a shorty of beer and gave them to her dad. "This ought to tide you over till dinner."

"Thanks honey. That should do us," John replied.

Connor finished the game in a flurry and John started racking the balls. He looked at Connor and said, "What do you say we play for a buck?"

Larry answered, "You don't want to play Connor for money. He's real good."

"Well, Connor? This is my table. I play a little while most days. So, if you think you can beat me, let's make it a buck."

"One dollar, then."

Larry cackled. "Playing your girlfriend's father for a buck a game. Now I'll see if anything can get to you, Connor. Never seen anybody yet who could ruffle those feathers when he's playing pool!"

Connor broke and ran six balls off the table. John made two and Connor finished the game. "I've been playing since I was eight. Keep your money."

John threw a dollar on the table and said, "Bet's a bet. Double or nothing?"

Connor had won five straight in a similar fashion when Louise came down the stairs to announce that dinner has been served. They all went upstairs. While John and Larry sat down at the dining room table, Connor went into the kitchen and slipped the five dollars to Louise.

"John made me take it, so I figured this can be some mad money for you. I'm not gonna stay in a house and take money from my host. Don't tell him I gave it to you."

"I see why Carol likes you so much," Louise said with a twinkle in her eye.

"I don't." Connor grinned.

Carol walked into the kitchen, put her arm around Connor's waist, squeezed him and said, "We need to talk. Can you come to my room?"

Once in her room, she grabbed him, pushed him onto the bed, and kissed him. "I just wanted to say that I'm so sore down there!" She pointed to her crotch. "But it was wonderful. I feel so good! I just can't believe you did it, convinced Mom, I mean."

"Well, I just reasoned with her. But we've talked about this already."

"Yeah, but we haven't talked about my dad. I'm his little girl and he might not be as reasonable as my mom."

"I told your mom I'd cross that bridge when I came to it. I'm sure she's gonna say something to him after dinner. Besides, Larry called me your boyfriend downstairs and he never batted an eyelash." He paused. "You know, come to think of it, I've already *crossed* the bridge. Now I just have to tell your dad *why* I did it." They kissed again and went out to the dining room.

Dinner was a slow and drawn-out process of prayers, John's story about work at the auto plant, and a series of questions about the guys' Bicentennial Tour. It seemed there was a strain in the conversation.

Then John revealed his anger. "So how is it my baby daughter comes home with two vagabonds?"

"I guess *vagabonds* is as good a word as any," said Connor. "Although, I'll have to look it up in the dictionary before I can totally agree with you."

John sat and stared hard at Connor and said, "When I was your age, I was getting out of the Army, thinking about raising a family and being a respectable part of society, not some vagrant, traveling around the country like a bum!"

"So let me think here. Yes, I think you and I have a few things in common. I'm a veteran, also of the Army, who worked and saved for a year and a half to travel around the country and celebrate our nation's bicentennial birthday.

"I'm not a bum. Larry and I paid our fair share in gas, food, and motel rooms to get us here. I think the problem is that Larry told you I was your daughter's boyfriend, and you didn't know anything about it. I'm sorry about that, Larry just thought you knew."

"Well said, and you hit the nail on the head. What makes you think you're good enough for my daughter?" John scowled.

"That's easy, I don't. She does. I tried talking her out of it, but she wouldn't hear of it."

"John," said Louise, "I've talked to both of the kids and gave them my blessing. I guess you can see that Connor isn't intimidated a bit by me, or you for that matter. I think after you get to know him, everything will be fine."

Carol added in her best little-girl voice, "I love him, Daddy."

"Well, now I'm beginning to feel like a lost puppy that Carol found on the way home from school," Connor said, smiling at Carol.

John laughed at that and said to Louise, "So, you like him, huh?" He took another long look at Connor. "Okay, you two can stay, but you have to let me win a game of pool now and then."

"Maybe you can get him to lighten up," said Larry, "but if he does, it'll be the first time ever. If you want him to let you win, don't play him for money. He can't help it. He hates to lose when there's money at stake."

"He knows me well," Connor said and gave Larry a look. "Sometimes too well. But he's right. Most people learn not to play me for money. I guess it's just my competitive nature."

Connor wasn't going to tell John that he'd dropped out of high school and spent most of his days at a pool hall in downtown Portland. He had learned to play well, but there had been lessons to be learned, and it cost him. Soon, he held his own playing three-cushion billiards and straight pool with some of the best in Portland.

Even Larry didn't know about that. It had been a fun six months of his life until his parents figured out he wasn't going to school. Then he ran away to San Diego.

After dinner, Connor and John went into the TV room and talked. John gave him the third degree about his work. "What do you do for a living, Connor?"

"Well, I'm a sheet metal apprentice in the union, Local 16. I took my withdrawal when I left on the first of March. Last summer I went up north and logged on an island in southeast Alaska. In the military, I was a finance account clerk."

"What about my daughter? Are you going to move in together in Champagne while she's at college?"

Connor hadn't thought that far in the future, but answered, "If she'll have me and there's work for me, yes. Just between you, me, and the fence post, that's not up to me. I think I'll talk it over with Carol and let *her* make that decision."

The rest of the conversation was just small talk. Connor had been sized up. He didn't know if he had Daddy's approval or not, but he really wasn't worried about it.

An hour later, they walked back into the dining room and everyone fell silent. John looked a full thirty seconds at his daughter. "I've been waiting for this day to come, honey. You have my blessing." He nodded his approval and Carol smiled at him.

He turned to Larry, "What do you say we go downstairs and play pool. Maybe I can beat *you*."

"I'm not a pushover," said Larry, smiling, "if you have more beer, I might let you win a few."

Connor said, "I'm gonna walk down to the store and get some more beer and a couple of pops."

"I'm coming," Carol said, "You might get lost in this big city." Connor just laughed, and he waited for her to get ready for the walk.

It was raining, a light rain, maybe a drizzle to some. The air was damp and heavy with an odor that was foreign to Connor. When he got outside, he didn't react to it like it was a burden. He raised his face to it, breathed it in, and smiled.

Carol brought an umbrella that she opened and put over both of their heads. They walked arm in arm as she took him on the grand tour of Podunk, Illinois.

The city had preserved the Old Town section to look the way it did at the turn of the century to bring in tourists. It was a summer destination for a lot of people. The city brought in a carnival that would be set up in May and stay until September.

Carol told him that most of the town residents relied on the two auto plants in the area. One was in Illinois, where her father worked, and the other was across the border in Wisconsin.

"Dad's already talking about you getting on at the plant. He says you'll be a natural with your sheet metal training. The pay is pretty good, too."

"From what I see, that wouldn't be such a bad way to go. Except there's one thing missing."

"What's that?" Carol looked confused.

"The Pacific fucking Ocean." He laughed, and she joined him, squeezing even tighter than before.

"That's the biggest regret I have with the Death Valley trip," said Carol. "We didn't get to see the Pacific Ocean. Oh well, you'll just have to show it to me sometime."

They walked in silence for a while. Beside them, flowed a muddy river whose name was unknown to Connor. The trail they walked followed its bank as it ran almost silently past the tall trees and leaf-covered ground on its way to the Gulf of Mexico. When he strained, he could hear it slithering along, realizing that even though it was very quiet, it was still calling to him. He could feel the Om.

143

Connor had been thinking about his conversation with John. He mulled over different scenarios and was nervous about bringing up the subject to Carol. Being Connor, though, he took the plunge.

"This is the way I see it," he began. "This fall, you're gonna go to Champagne to begin your rock education. I'm sure our tour will be over by then. So, I guess I'll look for work there to be close to you.

"The thing is, though, you—we—weren't supposed to happen. So, for the rest of the trip, I'm gonna be missing you. I guess things will be moving along at a faster rate just so I can get back to you. This whole fucking trip's been turned on its ear since we fell in love.

"I guess what I'm wondering is, do you feel like cohabitating with a high school dropout from the beaver state?"

They walked a little farther. Carol waited for the rest, thinking he wasn't through. Connor breathed the dank air in deeply, wondering if it was something he could get used to.

When he didn't continue, she answered him. "I guess I wouldn't have it any other way. I love you."

"I love you, too." Connor stopped, scooped her up and spun her around. "It kinda sucks, don't it."

They laughed and walked for another hour, both deep in thought, and in love.

When they got back with the beer and pop, they went down the back steps to the basement. Larry and John were still playing pool. It turned out, John was on a hot streak and there was nothing Larry could do about it.

Carol said she needed to shower and went upstairs. Connor beat them both once and left to shower as well. Afterwards, he crawled into bed next to the most beautiful woman he'd ever dreamed he'd be with, who's pussy was so sore he couldn't touch it. It was the best night's sleep he could ever remember.

They stayed at Carol's house for a week. It was the third night before John finally beat Connor at pool. He wouldn't play for free and Louise was enjoying the cash deposits every day at the breakfast table. Connor volunteered for breakfast duty and after day two, he was left alone in the kitchen. That night, Larry helped with dinner.

On their fourth day in Illinois, Connor and Larry decided to make a few adjustments to their equipment. They wanted to leave one of their mess kits with Carol. They found that a small cutting board would come in handy and a small kitchen knife would work better than their Bowie knives. Since they would be heading south, they figured a second cotton blanket would come in handy. They found these items at a small shop in town.

When they got back, Becky and Carol and their moms were gathered at the dinner table.

"Hey, Becky," said Connor. "Good to see you again."

"Becky and her mom came over with a suggestion for you two," said Carol with a big smile.

"Really? What's up?"

"Carol and I had planned on going to Florida next month to visit my grandparents in Jacksonville. I called and asked if it was alright to come down now." Becky had a big smile on her face, too.

"They were glad to have us visit early. So, if you two want a lift to Florida, we're going your way!"

"Wow! That fits right into our agenda. What do you say, Larry?"

"I say we're two lucky people. You girls aren't sick of us yet?"

Becky laughed and said, "Like I said in Utah, I really don't like either of you, but you *are* good at camping."

"She *did* say that." Connor smiled.

"That's not all that happened that night in Utah," said Carol. "That was the night you proved to us you could cook a roast over a fire with a spit you made yourself. Remember?"

Becky said, "We told our moms about that meal, and we were wondering if we could get an encore performance."

"For a ride to Florida, we'll make you breakfast the next morning, too!" said Larry.

Sunday, April 18, 1976

The night before they left, the guys went all out to impress their hosts. It was the last chance to fulfill their promise to cook dinner over a fire. The guys got the fixings for a feast. They bought a beef loin. Larry cut slits into the roast and inserted partial pieces of garlic cloves. Connor made a spicy sauce that Larry applied to the beef regularly with a basting brush. Once the roast was on the spit, Larry never left it.

Connor pierced fifteen potatoes through about a dozen times each with a knife. Then he wrapped them in foil with a little water, butter, and garlic powder and buried them in the coals. Next, he wrapped some corn on the cob with butter and water in the foil and buried it, too. He made three foil boat-loads: one of mushrooms with a little butter, cumin, and soy sauce, one of some broccoli with butter and lemongrass, and one of the king of all veggies, asparagus, with a half cup of water and salt and pepper. They were all steamed and served al dente.

The entire meal was cooked in or over the coals. It fed Carol's whole family, including the grandkids, son-in-law, boyfriends, Becky, and her parents, too. Larry and Connor said it was the best they'd ever done. They always said that, though, it just made them want to do even better the next time.

Becky's parents weren't that concerned about Larry, but he still felt like he'd been grilled by them both. They hadn't taken the news of the hitchhikers well at first. Louise went over to explain that she had given Carol permission to give them a ride and gave the travelers a good reference.

Larry told Connor that his parent interview went well. Becky had clued him in to all her lies. The VW Bus affair apparently never happened, making it easy for him.

Becky stayed the night and went downstairs for a little of Larry's magic. Connor and Carol made a magical show of their own, not sleeping at all.

18. For Love of the Redheads

Kevin and Ryan

Kevin and Ryan were identical twins. They were born in September of 1949 in Columbus, Ohio. Kevin was nine minutes older than Ryan.

Their father was an architect. From the time they were old enough, the twins would hang out at their father's office on weekends. He would show them the tricks of the trade. By the time they graduated high school, they were accomplished draftsmen, working part-time at their father's firm.

They chose Kent State against their dad's urging to go to Ohio State University. They liked the culture of the smaller school. They met Aviva and Ariella, the redheaded beauties, in their freshman year. The girls were bashful, and it took until the next summer to form a friendship with them.

During the next two and a half years, the four transformed themselves from upper-middle-class baby boomers to anti-war-protesting hippies, and then to Yippies when Abbie Hoffman named them so. It was the time of the Youth International Party and the Street Pranksters. They reveled in their place in history.

They felt the closeness of the anti-war community. The realization that, as a generation, they were doing something that had never been done before.

They were part of a large percentage of their age group who opposed and rejected the Vietnam War. It was a war that had been started by the rich, if for no other reason than to make themselves even richer at the demise of the baby boomer generation.

It was in Chicago, at a blood-in-the-streets protest that a sexual relationship with the redheads began. After that, the four were inseparable. It was Kevin and Ryan who named Aviva, Rainbow, and Ariella, Sunshine.

At the 1968 Democratic Convention in Chicago's Grant Park, they were tear-gassed. They moved to the streets and managed to get away from the Hilton before the carnage took place.

On the way home to Ohio, Sunshine pointed out how that morning in Grant Park, everyone was singing "All we are saying is give peace a chance." Their chant evolved into "Hell no! We won't go!" and then into "Pigs are whores!" The four had seen the police turn into thugs. They were angry and vowed to protest the war every chance they could until it was over.

They went to Washington, D.C., in 1969 to march in the Vietnam Moratorium with a quarter million other protesters with black bands on their arms. It was the largest organized protest of any kind across the nation and in every major city.

Millions marched, singing "All we are saying is give peace a chance." They were honoring the fallen of the senseless war that, in the end, proved nothing except the lengths the warmongers would go to line their purses. They left Washington that week with high spirits. There had been no violence, just a general agreement that the war must end.

Everything changed for the four tight friends and lovers in May of 1970. They were walking, hand-in-hand, in protest. Suddenly, their friends were being shot down right beside them. They ran away, covered in the blood of the other protesters, their lives shattered.

The girls went home and disappeared. The guys went home, crushed and alone, longing for their first loves. They drove to Shaker Heights after two weeks. The girls, they learned, had left without a word two days before.

They drove back home, abandoned and mourning the passing of their innocence. They called Shaker Heights every week through that long, sad summer. The answer was always the same, "No word, but thanks for calling."

It was in October that their father, in a desperate need to pull his sons out of their funk, sent them to Key West for a month. They left as Earth and Sun, the names given them by Sunshine and Rainbow. When they returned, they were Kevin and Ryan once again.

They had cut their hair and were tanned and full of energy. Their father had prayed on the night of their return. He thanked his long-deceased wife for watching over their sons from heaven and bringing them back to him whole again.

Kevin and Ryan suddenly had plans for the future. They were going to form a company in the Keys and work to get contracts with the very military they'd been protesting for years.

They each met a woman and were happy, and smiling, for the first time since the shootings.

19. Parting Ways

Sunday, April 19, 1976

There was a little fanfare the next morning. Connor and Larry made flapjacks and bacon, with eggs to order. John took a sick day. Becky's parents came over for a bite and said their goodbyes and went to work.

John had Connor downstairs for one more attempt at the pool table. Connor administered yet another thorough ass-kicking, playing for five dollars a game. John came upstairs with his tail between his legs, and Connor quietly handed four five-dollar bills over to Louise and gave her a peck on the cheek.

After lots of hugs and goodbyes, everyone made their way outside to the driveway. The four loaded up the bus as Carol's parents and sisters looked on.

"Now, you be careful," Louise said. "Carol, you be sure to call us when you get to Jacksonville. Have fun!"

The four climbed in with Carol driving. She nodded in agreement to her mom's request and everyone waved good-bye.

Larry said "It's kind of like another going-away party. Last night and the long goodbyes today, just like back home."

Carol pointed the bus toward the highway as Connor and Larry sat in the back seat and talked about their terrific luck. They had managed to land a ride out of Death Valley that became a national park tour of the west with an ultimate destination of Florida!

Becky handed a map to them and asked them to pick out a spot to camp. They began pouring over the map and found a park in northern Kentucky.

It was after dark when they arrived, and the park was closed. Despite this, they decided to set up camp at the entrance and slept well. The next morning, while breaking down the tarp, they were visited by the police. Carol and Becky handled the situation with their big, beautiful smiles. The officers were very polite and didn't even ask for anyone's ID.

They spent the next night in Tennessee at a small campground. It was open, but they were the only campers.

The next day, they hiked into the magical deciduous forest of the Great Smoky Mountains National Park. Larry and Connor were surprised at the variety of colors and sounds that were so different from the evergreen forests of the west.

They left late in the afternoon, and didn't drive far before they found a nice camping spot at a reservoir in northern Georgia. The tension had been building all day. They all knew this would be their last night together.

The guys sprang for ribeye steaks with baked potatoes and corn on the cob. After dinner, they walked to the shoreline and watched the sunset.

Larry swatted a mosquito. "I've never seen a blood-sucking mosquito this early in the year back home." He was a mosquito magnet and figured he better get some repellant before the girls dropped them in Florida.

"Yeah, it's official. We're in the South," said Connor. "It's been a long time since I've seen a day this warm in April." After all of the cold weather of recent weeks, Connor looked forward to the coming warm days in Florida.

That night, no one slept. They made love and talked about what life would be like after they separated the next day.

They were up early for the sunrise and ate breakfast at a small country store. They discussed the travelers' plans at length. The day drew out and tension built as their destination grew near.

At the I-75 and I-10 interchange, Carol pulled the bus over to the side of the road. All four got out, and Connor and Larry pulled their packs out and put them on.

Becky and Larry kissed and hugged goodbye.

"I wish we were going with you," said Carol. Her voice was mixed with sadness and envy. "I almost wish we weren't expected in Jacksonville."

"Me too," said Connor. He kissed her and gave her a last hug. "I'll keep in touch."

Carol hugged Larry goodbye and said, "Now, I'm counting on you to take good care of Connor for me, okay?" Larry smiled and gave her a thumbs-up.

Connor gave Becky a hug. "Say, 'Hi,' to your grandparents for me. I hope you two enjoy your visit."

The girls climbed back in the bus. The travelers watched as they took off toward Jacksonville. They stood for several minutes as the bus grew smaller and smaller and finally disappeared over a hill.

"Well, that was the absolute best ride I've ever had! 3,000 miles and a girlfriend," said Connor. They continued to stare in the direction of the bus. Connor finally took in a deep breath and looked around.

"What do you say we set up the tarp over in those Georgia pines, Larry?" Connor pointed at a group of pines planted in one of the large loops that made up the interchange.

"Looks good to me. We need to recharge our minds and get back into hitchhiking mode. I think maybe a couple of Thai joints and twelve hours of sleep will do the trick."

Since it was so warm and the weather looked clear, they decided to lay the tarp flat on the ground rather than going to the effort of erecting it as they had been doing. The sleeping bags went down next and they slept under the cotton blankets.

Thursday, April 23, 1976

The first thing they realized when they woke up was it didn't get real cold at night and they should drop their sleeping bags at Larry's aunt and uncle's place in Golden Gate. They could pick them up when they were on their way north again.

The second thing they noticed was the condensation on everything. The cotton blankets were a bit soggy, so they strapped them to the outside of their packs. They shook the tarp as dry as they could get it, thinking they would need to dry everything out completely later in the day.

Finally, they realized they were in tick country. Larry had four ticks on him, but none had bored in yet. From that day on, they performed a tick search first thing in the morning and again before they went to bed. Now and then, Connor would find one on himself, but just as with the mosquitos, Larry drew the nasty little blood-suckers in like a magnet.

They were packed, ready to go, and standing on the southbound I-75 on-ramp. They hooked a nice ride with a couple of frat boys heading back to Gainesville. They smoked them out with three of the dwindling going-away joints, and left them with two more so they could show their frat house how good the weed was out west.

Larry thought they might make it to Golden Gate in one day. The frat boys dropped them off at the Gainesville exit and the travelers made their way to the southbound on-ramp of the freeway.

Two girls were already set up hitching a ride south, and the guys gleaned good information from them. They said the Orlando cut-off was the next good spot to hitch south. The girls also told them that, if they could avoid the Tampa Bay-St. Petersburg area, to do it. They said it was hard to get a ride out of there because the average age down there was about eighty. The guys made a mental note, and then went to get breakfast.

The girls were gone when they got back to the ramp, and a car pulled over before they could get their packs off. The driver was going to Orlando. They smiled and accepted the ride, remembering the girls' advice. Their first day in Florida was going real well.

It was just past noon when they got out at the Wildwood exit. Their ride had been air conditioned, so they had no idea of the temperature outside. It wasn't the heat so much as the humidity that smacked them in the face as they exited the car.

They walked down the off-ramp and noticed a black man selling oranges and tangerines on the side of the on-ramp heading to Tampa. They also saw the girls they'd talked to at the last exit. They were sitting in the shade of a vine-covered fence, peeling oranges and talking with the old guy running the fruit stand.

The girls spotted the travelers and one said, "Wow, you guys must've got a ride real quick! We've only been here ten minutes."

Connor noticed two guys thumbing at the end of the ramp and said, "It looks like we're third in line." He pointed at the two hitchhikers.

The second girl said, "No, you two are fourth. There's a couple ahead of us. They walked over to the truck stop to use the bathroom.

They'll be right back. She's pregnant, so they shouldn't be long once those two jerks get a ride."

"Why are they jerks?"

"They wouldn't let the pregnant couple go first. So they've been waiting down there for two hours."

Just then, the black fruit vendor came walking up with four oranges and handed them to Larry.

"I don't know if they're good or not," said Larry. "I watched him take them out of that trash dumpster over there." He pointed toward one of the two nearby dumpsters.

Speaking the same dialect as the driver of their last ride, the black guy said, "Temed joozers."

Larry, looking confused, asked, "What the heck's a *jewzer*?"

The girls started laughing and one said, "Those are oranges that are getting too ripe to sell and he puts them in that dumpster. A truck from the cannery comes every evening and takes them to make juice. So he said those are juicers. They're the perfect orange to eat. Try one, you'll see."

Larry and Connor thanked the black guy and sat in the shade by the girls. The vendor stood and watched as they peeled their oranges and took the first bite. It was their first taste of a tree-ripened orange.

Their eyes grew wide and Larry exclaimed, "This is the best orange I ever ate! I didn't know they could be so sweet."

Connor said, "The oranges in the northwest are sour most of the time. I usually pass them up when I'm buying fruit."

He stood up and walked over to the vendor, who was hooting and cat calling and dancing in circles. This wasn't the first time he'd seen that reaction from a northerner.

Connor shook his hand and said, "That's the best damned orange I've ever ate. Thank you so much."

The vendor said, "I tud yous theb be the bets joozers therd is."

Connor turned and said, "My second day in Florida and I think I understood half of what he said." He laughed and sat back down to enjoy the rest of his treat. "Another week and, hell, I'll be speaking whatever language that is." The girls laughed.

The pregnant couple came walking up. She looked like she was ready to drop. They were both bitching at each other. Connor and

Larry picked up and moved down the fence a ways so they didn't have to listen.

It was an hour before the pregnant couple got up to hitch and just like that, they were gone. Then the two girls went out and they were gone so fast, the travelers didn't notice.

They were already planning on showering in the morning, so they looked for a place along the exit to put their tarp. An opening in the fence revealed a trail that led south along the freeway. They hadn't gone far when they found a spot that looked like it was used a lot.

Connor walked over to a pizza joint and got a large, with everything, to go. Larry stayed back at the camp, swatting mosquitos and gathering firewood. They used the pizza box as kindling and had a fire going quickly. The fire kept most of the mosquitos at bay while they poured over the map, trying to figure out how far it was to Naples, a small town just west of Golden Gate.

They decided to set the tarp up lean-to fashion like they'd done all the way across America rather than sleep in the open.

20. Southern Waters

Sunday, April 25, 1976

The next morning, they realized they hadn't been harassed by the mosquitos nearly as badly and the condensation didn't soak the blankets. They were up early, did some laundry and showered before hitting the southbound on-ramp.

They turned down two rides to Tampa Bay, and then a black preacher pulled over and announced he was going to Sarasota. It was past St. Petersburg and Tampa Bay where they didn't want to get stuck. They remembered the warning from the girls the day before. The guys gladly accepted the ride.

The preacher was driving a gold Eldorado. After putting their backpacks in the trunk, they hopped in with Larry in the front seat. The car smelled brand-new. The preacher wasn't a big man—he was huge. It was difficult to tell while he was sitting, but he looked close to seven feet tall. It was just a guess, but he had to go over five hundred pounds.

After introductions, Larry thanked him for pulling over and giving them a ride. He told him about their tour and where they were headed. That was pretty much all Larry said. For the rest of the ride, the preacher was on his pulpit, extolling the gospel of the Lord Jesus Christ. Larry was once again in heaven and turned to Connor with a my-turn smirk.

Connor was glad he was in back, but still joined in when asked to bow his head in prayer. He was actually impressed. The man was well-practiced and very articulate. His pitch was smooth and polite.

"Boys," he said as they were getting close to the drop off, "I have a parish of sixteen hundred souls that come weekly to my Sunday service. Next Sunday, I'd like to make that sixteen hundred and two. It would be a blessed event if I could see your wonderful faces in our pews." He handed Larry his card.

The preacher dropped them off just south of Sarasota at the entrance to a state park and told them it was a really good place to get rides. He shook their hands, his huge hand engulfing theirs.

"Connor, that guy was incredible! I won't need another fix for a long time and when I do, I'll know right where to go."

"You're right, that guy was great. *I* might even go along. I'd like to see him up there on his pulpit, spewing that wonderful gospel of his." Connor smiled his most devilish smile and rolled his eyes.

"Fuck you, Connor!" It was Larry's only response.

The thing they were quickly finding about the weather in Florida was that, by noon, it was too hot to stand by the road and hitchhike. They decided to rent a tent site at the state park. It offered showers that were powered by quarters and security enough to leave their packs at their camp without anybody stealing their rigs.

They could smell the Gulf of Mexico, just a short walk away. They changed into their swimming trunks, grabbed some sunscreen and headed out to get their tan lines going. They both swam well, but Connor was a fish. He had spent thousands of hours on a surfboard along the Pacific Coast from San Diego to Tillamook Head in Oregon.

When Connor walked into the water of the Gulf, he was in heaven. It was warmer than any saltwater he'd ever known. The smell of brine was much more fragrant than anywhere on the Pacific coast. He walked out to his waist in the heavenly water. He began to swim, first away from shore and north for at least a mile. Then he turned south and swam back.

When he returned, Larry hadn't budged. "Holy crap! This water is so buoyant you can float with no effort at all. I read the salt content is a lot higher down here. Swimming in it is amazing. Once we get to Naples, I'm gonna go shopping for a mask and fins. This will be so cool."

"Yeah," said Larry as he continued to lie on his towel. "Maybe I'll go out with you the next time."

"Hey, Larry, your back's turning red. You should turn over or put a shirt on before you fuck up and get burned."

Connor was very aware of the potential for sunburn. His Irish skin was real sensitive for the first couple of weeks until he was a little tanned. That was all he would ever do is get a little tanned.

Larry was darker complected in March than Connor was in August. Connor knew he was going to watch Larry get darker and darker, and even when he was as tanned as he could get, he'd look pale alongside Larry.

Larry rolled over on his back as he suggested, and Connor put his shirt on and headed back to camp. Once there, Connor learned from the camp host there was a grocery store just south of the park. He showered the salt off and headed to the store.

When Larry got back to camp, he bought a bundle of wood from the camp host and gathered more wood for cooking. Then he started a fire and waited for Connor to bring the goodies.

They were becoming used to each other's moves. Larry didn't need to be told that Connor had gone to the store, and Connor knew Larry would be collecting wood and starting a cook fire when he got back.

Connor bought a small slab of pork ribs, two potatoes, a couple of ears of corn, and a small bag of tangerines. He also got a five-pound bag of charcoal and, of course, four quarts of beer and a pint of bourbon.

"The citrus may be cheap here, but those potatoes were expensive. I could've bought a ten-pound bag back home for what I paid for those two bakers. I also bought some dry rub recommended by the clerk at the store, a real nice fellow.

"It's good to see that southern hospitality really *does* exist," said Connor. "Everyone down here is so friendly. That clerk down at the store even offered us a ride when he got off of work. I know the girls were worried about the rednecks, but I don't think they pick up hitchhikers."

Their stash of aluminum foil was getting low, so Connor bought some to wrap the corn and potatoes. They unrolled the rest of it and folded it into two nice, flat pieces, and then put it away in their packs.

Larry already had a good bed of coals going and Connor helped it along with the charcoal. They poked a dozen holes in the potatoes, wrapped each tightly in foil with a little garlic and water and buried them in the coals.

They took a walk in the woods, smoked a number and were back fifteen minutes later. They wrapped the ears of corn loosely in foil, with a little salt, pepper, and water to keep them from drying out and buried them, too.

Two minutes later, they put some foil with many small holes poked in it right on top of the coals and laid the seasoned ribs on the foil. They each opened a beer and walked away for another eight minutes while they leisurely drank about half of it. They came back to turn the ribs, drank the rest of their beer and chased it with a shot of bourbon.

Dinner was served. Larry and Connor hadn't said a word about the meal during the preparation. Like a well-rehearsed play, it was as good as anything they'd ever cooked. The remaining rub went into Connor's pack for what he hoped would be many more meaty barbeques.

21. The Islanders

Rainbow and Sunshine, Kevin and Ryan

Rainbow and Sunshine stayed in Shaker Heights for two weeks. They began the search for Kevin and Ryan as soon as they returned. They had often talked about them and felt the worst thing they had done in their self-imposed banishment was to lose touch with them. They wanted to re-establish contact.

Sunshine and Rainbow were able to locate Kevin and Ryan through their father, who still lived in Columbus. They were delighted when they received a call from the girls. They had always held out hope that one day they would hear from them again and immediately invited them down to Key West.

Kevin and Ryan had successfully started the architecture and construction firm in Key West as they had planned years earlier. They were designing and building hurricane-resistant structures on the local military bases. They immediately offered jobs in their company to the redheads and the girls eagerly accepted.

This time, when the cousins left Shaker Heights, they didn't disappear. They stayed in contact with their parents and family. They also relied on their parents for financial help when they needed it. They drove a new Mercedes down to Key West, one of the perks of coming from two wealthy families.

Sunshine and Rainbow arrived in Key West and moved into a condo built by their friends, who were now their new bosses.

On their first night, Kevin and Ryan introduced them to their families. Both Kevin and Ryan had married and each had one child. The girls were glad to see that their friends had moved on and were making a wonderful life for themselves.

Sunshine and Rainbow immediately became valuable assets. The four Kent State alumni set out to establish the company as a leader in creating innovative building designs that could not only survive the most powerful storms, but also have a minimal impact on the environment.

With the addition of Rainbow and Sunshine and their creative designs they used at the commune in southern Oregon, Kevin and Ryan would quickly realize their goals.

Michael

Michael was born in June of 1950 in the Detroit suburbs. His father was a mechanic at an auto plant near their home. His mom was a grade school teacher.

For two weeks every Christmas, Michael's family came to Key West. His father had inherited a house there and rented it out during the rest of the year. During those visits, Michael spent most of his time swimming in the water and hoped to live there someday.

When it came time for college, Michael earned a scholarship at the University of Miami playing baseball. He threw a ninety-five mile per hour fast ball, had a good slider, and great change up. He was set to become the designated closer for the Hurricanes. Michael also took his studies seriously. He majored in business and maintained a 3.8 grade point average.

At the end of his sophomore year, he tore a tendon in his throwing elbow. Despite surgery, it was soon evident that he was never going to throw at the velocity needed to be a closer nor did he have the endurance to start.

About the same time, his family's vacation home in Key West caught fire and was rendered useless as a rental. Michael talked his parents into allowing him to start the rebuilding process with the insurance money.

His father did one better by signing the house over to Michael as an investment and also giving him twenty thousand dollars to do the remodel.

While much of the house was severely damaged, two of the rooms escaped with minor smoke damage. Once cleaned, he could stay in those rooms while doing the repairs.

During his junior year, he spent most of his free time in the Keys. Swimming was the best exercise for his ailing elbow and it improved greatly as he spent many hours snorkeling near Key West.

He got his business degree at the end of his junior year in June of 1971. With his diploma in hand, he moved to Key West full time. He took the twenty grand and invested it in a small, but lucrative twenty-eight unit motel that was conveniently located across the street from his house. He was able to get a really good deal because the owner wanted out from under it due to an impending divorce.

In no time at all, he was a respected businessman in the community. Using the profits from the motel, Michael made slow, but continuous progress rebuilding his home.

Jim

Jim was born in July of 1956. He lived in Key West until he was sixteen. His parents moved him north to Jacksonville after his father was transferred to the corporate office of his employer.

Jim missed Key West. He told his parents he wanted to move back after high school. His parents wanted him to go to college, but he held firm. They struck an agreement where he would go to the community college in Key West until he was ready for a four-year program.

He moved back to Key West when he was seventeen, right after his graduation, and rented a room from Michael, a childhood friend he met while spearfishing. The rent was minimal because Michael said the fish he brought home more than made up the difference.

Jim landed a maintenance job at a nearby recreational vehicle park where he worked part-time so he could pay the rent. He would get off work in the afternoon, grab his mask, fins, and spear gun and head out for hours.

He knew the area well and would let the tide take him whichever way it was going at the time. He was very successful with his spears and provided plenty of fish for himself, his roommate, and his friends.

One afternoon in September of 1974, as he was coming home from one of his fishing trips, he stopped on the west side of a key he called the Banyan Tree Island. He'd stopped on its wonderful beach many times before. The giant Banyan tree on the island was a landmark that Jim had used as a guide back home since he first started his lone excursions into the keys as a young teenager.

As Jim lay on the sand, he noticed what appeared to be the beginning of a trail leading into the underbrush at the edge of the beach. He got up to investigate and as he made his way further inland, he realized the trail zigzagged toward the interior of the island. It ended in a small clearing with the giant Banyan tree at its center. The trail was obviously man-made.

Jim was considering camping in the clearing and looked up for an anchor point for his tarp. He was surprised to see a large platform about twenty feet in the air built on the massive lower branches of the tree.

The crown of this Banyan tree was close to eighty feet high. Its main trunk was a conglomeration of the original roots and many other plants that grew together into a mass ten feet in diameter.

The seven bottom limbs of the tree really grabbed Jim's attention. They ran horizontally away from the trunk in all directions at a height of fifteen to twenty feet above the ground and were at least three feet in diameter at their base. At regular intervals, a secondary trunk extended from the branches to the ground to help support their massive weight. The branches extended into the surrounding wall of vines and seemed to go on forever.

It was this system of secondary trunks that allowed the tree to withstand the hurricane-force winds that regularly hit the Florida Keys. Jim could see more than twenty of these trunks growing straight down from the branches, some at least eighteen inches in diameter and as far away as fifty feet from the main trunk. He was sure there were many more hidden in the vines.

When Jim first spotted the platform, he also noticed that someone had used an axe to cut steps in one of the original roots that grew around the original host tree, forming a spiral staircase of sorts. With the help of a few limbs as handholds, it was a relatively easy climb up to the structure.

Jim estimated the platform was about twenty feet square with three five-foot walls and an eight-foot wall, that faced to the west. The west wall had a six-by-four-foot framed-in window that was about three feet above the floor. The opening overlooked the small clearing below. There was no glass in the frame and from the look of it, there never had been.

A roof was attached to the top of the eight-foot wall and was supported as the tree truck and limbs would allow. It was a maze of two-by-two lumber that created an irregular dome shape and covered about half of the platform.

The dome was covered with quarter-inch plywood. Galvanized corrugated steel siding sat on top of the plywood. The metal had been bent and hammered into the shape of the dome. Jim thought it looked like shit.

On the east side of the platform, remnants of canvas tarps hung, rotted in tattered strips, leaving that part exposed to the elements. Jim saw that the covered side was dry and well-preserved.

The builders had done a good job. They also left clues about when the platform had been built. Several old posters of cars built in the early fifties were still tacked to the roof and walls. A set of cast-iron pans thickly coated with rust and a box of cheap dinnerware sat on dirty, warped shelves. Two small charcoal grills that had rusted into uselessness stood in a corner.

The longer Jim was in the tree, the more apparent the enormity of the crown became to him. It was impossible to fathom its size from anywhere off of the island. It was only here, on the platform at twenty feet off of the ground in the middle of the crown, that the true size of the tree could be appreciated.

Joe

Joe was born in Raton, New Mexico, in August of 1947, the eldest of four siblings. He was born to a Mexican father who had left when he was two and an Irish mother who did a good job of raising him. She worked slinging hash at a popular roadside restaurant on an I-25 exit near the Colorado-New Mexico state line.

All three of his siblings had different fathers. His mom had gone from one man to another for ten years. The last man and the father of the youngest girl stuck around and was the only thing Joe knew as a father. He was a good influence and worked a steady job bringing stability to a once precarious life.

Joe joined the Army at seventeen and spent the better part of his first two years in Vietnam. His third tour ended suddenly on the Chinese New Year in 1968, when the North Vietnamese overran his position. He had one week until his estimated time of separation and looked forward to shipping out to Saigon the next day. During the battle, he was shot five times and left for dead. Two days later, medics discovered him during a sweep and airlifted him to Saigon.

He came away from the Army with a 100-percent disability. He would never again have full function in his right arm or leg and needed a cane to walk. He went home to New Mexico and stayed drunk and stoned for the better part of four years.

In January of 1972, a friend asked if he wanted to go to Key West for a biker rally, and he agreed. When the rally was over and his friend prepared to return to New Mexico, Joe asked him to let his mom know that he'd be back later.

In the ensuing weeks, he found some of the happiness and sanity that he had lost since his days in Vietnam. He wrote and told his mom of this. She wrote back, saying he shouldn't come home until he felt he wanted to and that she would pray for his happiness. In the months and years that followed, they exchanged letters and Christmas cards to stay in touch.

Once on his own and in a small apartment, he cut back on his drinking. Because his injuries forced him to be inactive, he put on fifty pounds. Even short walks would leave him exhausted.

Most nights, he would wake from nightmares of the war. He would dress and walk out to the beach facing the Atlantic Ocean and fall asleep, listening to the breakers. He would wake up with a start the next morning as the sun began its ascent. He always got his best sleep on that beach. He often wondered why he'd have the nightmares in his bed but could sleep peacefully beside the ocean.

Joe met Michael and Jim at a biker rally in 1974. He liked both of them very much. Their friendship made him realize just how lonely he had been. They liked Joe, as well, and readily accepted him despite all the baggage he carried from the war.

He moved in with them and, with the companionship they provided, things began to get better for him both physically and mentally. He found he could walk farther with a companion than without.

Joe asked for a bedroom facing the ocean, and he would leave his window open so the sound of the surf could put him to sleep. In no time, he began to feel at home in Michael's house. After six years of solitude, he was beginning to emerge from his shell.

The additional rent from Joe made life easier for Michael and Jim. Michael didn't charge much, and it was certainly less than Joe had paid for his apartment. In the long run, pitching in together helped everyone out.

Danny

Danny came from money. He was born in August of 1956 and was raised just outside of the Augusta National Golf Club. He grew up on a southern plantation that was over 150 years old. His grandfather was a member at the golf club, so was his dad, and so was he and all of his brothers.

He could not count the number of rounds he had played at one of the most exclusive golf clubs in the world. At twelve, he had a good game and dreamed of winning the Masters.

The youngest of five boys and eight years younger than his nearest sibling, he was spoiled from the start. All of his brothers had gone to Harvard, earned MBA's and were involved in running the vast family empire.

Smart and good-looking, his future was bright. But by his seventeenth birthday, Danny had dropped out of high school, had a bad cocaine habit and was drinking heavily. The family shipped him off to Key West to recover in an exclusive rehabilitation facility.

He stayed at the facility for six months while he recovered from his addiction. During this time, he fell in love with Key West. After his recovery, he reluctantly returned to Augusta.

At eighteen, he told his parents of his love for the Keys. He was happy there and had no urge to use cocaine. He argued that the social circles he ran with in Augusta were just going to drag him back down that same destructive road. The logical thing to do was to let him return to Key West.

His parents had already determined he wasn't a fit in the family business at the time, but they could always hold out hope. They bought the house next-door to Michael's and started a trust fund in his name to support him. They let him slip away from their lives. Danny moved in and soon began to visit with his three neighbors.

He was spoiled and had a smart mouth that would often get him into trouble. He also had an infectious energy that fueled a good sense of humor and a kindness that won most people over.

The four were soon tight friends. Danny would work for free at Michael's motel and help Jim with projects around Michael's house.

The same day that Jim found the tree house, he told his three close friends. The next day, they all went out to the Island. Joe and Danny decided to move into the structure for the summer. Using Michael's two canoes, they transported their clothes and some furniture to the Island.

They surveyed the structure and began the necessary repairs to make it livable. They built the north entry wall higher and installed a door with a small porch. Then, with a couple of gallons of paint, it began to look like a home.

Despite the improvements, Joe had troubles getting in and out of the treehouse. Jim added some additional steps and handholds, but it was still a difficult task for him.

After surviving the first tropical storm with no problems, Joe, the oldest and the alpha among them, wanted to stay year-round. It was decided in late October of 1974 that he would live on the Island full-time while Michael, Jim, and Danny would stay whenever they wanted.

Joe asked Jim if he could start snorkeling with him. Michael had told Joe about his rehab for his elbow injury and how swimming was the thing that did him the most good. It was a struggle at first; Joe was never a good swimmer.

Joe swam with Jim, and sometimes with Michael, every day for as long as his endurance would last. The results of his efforts showed almost immediately. After a month, he had more range of motion in his right leg with less pain. He dropped twenty pounds and his endurance improved greatly.

After two months, he had dropped a total of thirty-five pounds and was able to take short walks without using his cane. He was now able to get in and out of the tree house with relative ease. He also began swimming on his own early in the morning.

Joe discovered what most snorkelers and swimmers know. There's an inner peace that comes with swimming. Danny began to join Joe most mornings. They would leave at first light and swim for an hour and a half. Then they would stop somewhere to get stoned and enjoy the quiet of the early morning.

Joe's physical improvements were most apparent, but it was his mental recovery that surprised him the most. He suffered nightmares less often. Danny noticed this change and mentioned that Joe wasn't waking him up in the middle of the night with his screams nearly as often.

After six months, Joe had lost all of the extra weight. His daily workouts left him with much better muscle tone and his right arm was beginning to show more flexibility. He had an inner peace he'd not felt since before the war.

Kevin and Ryan

Jim met Kevin and Ryan while snorkeling in early November of 1974. They were all resting on the beach of a small key that was popular with snorkelers. Jim got them stoned.

Kevin and Ryan wanted to learn to spearfish and said they would barter with him using weed as their payment. Jim said he'd try to teach them, but that spearfishing was very difficult and most people weren't very good at it.

The three hit it off. Jim thought their building and designing skills would come in handy in the planned expansion of the tree house.

That evening, back at the Island, Jim brought up the two architects. He wanted to bring them into their circle of friends. Their training and skills could really benefit them and help make the Island a community. Everyone agreed.

The next evening, Jim, Kevin, and Ryan waded to the Island at low tide, when the depth of the water was just above their knees. They were treated to an exceptional dinner. They drank wine that the guests brought with them and enjoyed a couple of good doobies they brought as well.

They sat in the cooking area on second-hand lawn furniture and talked. Because of the low light and good camouflage, Kevin and Ryan didn't notice the tree house until Jim pointed it out to them. They were blown away with surprise.

Once up the tree and on the platform, they got real excited. They decided to come out on the next weekend and spend the night. They would look around for possible expansion areas so everyone could have their own bedroom. Their one requirement was that their wives could come out, too.

Sunshine and Rainbow

Four months after their arrival, in September of 1975, Kevin and Ryan offered Sunshine and Rainbow full partnerships in the company. They realized their net worth would be greater as four partners rather than only two. In addition, it would reduce the chance that the girls might leave the company.

The relationship that they'd had at Kent State was a thing of the past. Kevin's and Ryan's wives were aware of their husbands' history with Sunshine and Rainbow and welcomed them into their families.

It was settled and contracts were signed. The condo was a gift as a signing bonus. The partners celebrated with a dinner party. It was quite a lavish affair. Rainbow and Sunshine invited a few friends they'd made since arriving. They ate, drank, and smoked well.

The guests gradually trickled out and went home. It was late. The four new partners sat around the breakfast nook when Kevin and Ryan brought up the tree house. They had already talked to the guys on the Island about their friends. When they told Rainbow and Sunshine about the place, they became excited and made plans to visit the next day.

About midmorning, the four partners canoed out to the Island and met the occupants. They hit it off immediately. Not hard, considering they were four single men living on an island, and the two girls were beautiful, single redheads.

Kevin and Ryan had already been at work. They had completed four hanging walkways leading away from the main platform to four small bedrooms, each with small domed roofs.

The treehouse reminded the girls of Robinson Caruso's tree fort they'd seen on television when they were kids. They spent the night in one of the bedrooms. The girls put their bedroll on a futon already there and fell asleep to the gentle swaying of the tree branches in the breeze. The next day, they all walked the Island.

They discovered two more, smaller Banyan trees that weren't being utilized. They came back with plans of three more rooms and a walkway that would run right through the middle of the Island.

The Island was lower on the north end, and there were many spots that were swampy. The guys worried, but the girls showed them how they planned to build the walkway first. Then, they would use the walkway to transport all the materials for the rooms.

Everyone was sold on the idea when Rainbow announced that she and Sunshine would pay for the materials. So it was decided that, on January 19, 1976, the year of America's bicentennial, the girls would take up part-time residence on the Island.

They would build their own bedroom and two more for their business partners, too. Kevin and Ryan immediately agreed on the project, but they insisted on putting up the money for their own rooms.

Back at their condo, Rainbow and Sunshine lay in bed and talked about the project. "I'm almost too excited to say this, but I think this may be our coolest adventure yet," said Sunshine.

The girls kept the condo in town for the days they worked late and for when their friends and family visited. The majority of the time over the next four months was devoted to what turned out to be their biggest and most ambitious project.

As the work progressed, the girls slept with all four of the single guys. They let them know they enjoyed sex with men, but loved each other. There was no jealousy or tension, and everyone was getting laid now and then. It was a dream, come true, for the guys.

During the following months, the project hit a few snags but proceeded forward until they completed the 150-foot walkway that connected the two other Banyon trees.

After that, the construction of the three platforms and their roofs proceeded quickly. In a short time, each of the architects had their own bedroom.

When not busy building the structure, the guys' main job was to cut vines from nearby mangroves and plant them around the perimeter of the Island for additional camouflage. They even fertilized them so they would grow faster. When they finished one layer of vines, they would start another. They also camouflaged the walkway in the same way. Soon the vines covered it and rendered it almost invisible.

While the girls worked in town, Joe directed most of the labor after consulting with them. Joe, Danny, and Michael made steady headway on the project.

Jim was exempt from all duty on the structures. He was the fisherman and provided them with their most important protein source. Everyone else had tried, but couldn't get the hang of spearfishing. He was fine with that because it was what he preferred to do.

Jim had been attending the local community college for two years as part of the agreement he'd made with his parents. He was due to transfer to a four-year college in Miami in the fall. One day, in the middle of May, 1976, Jim showed up at the Island and announced to everyone that he was going to skip the fall semester.

Of the four original tenants, Jim was the only one native to the area. He loved the Keys and explained that to his parents. They figured it would save money on the gas he would spend to drive back and forth between Key West and Miami, so they agreed he could stay until Christmas. In return, though, they would need him to return home for about a month in mid-June.

One evening, soon after Jim made his announcement, all eight of the Islanders, as they liked to call themselves, sat around the fire in the small clearing under the platform. They had finished dinner and a gallon of wine, and passed a couple of joints around the circle. They enjoyed the glow of the sunset and the smell of the summer breeze. It was nirvana.

Suddenly, Joe started crying, not just sobbing, but crying hysterically without control. Everyone sat, watching their good friend and wondering what they could do. Both of the girls ran up to him and hugged him. The sobs racked his body as he held on to them.

Gradually, with an occasional sob, he began to regain his composure and started to explain. "Not since I left Vietnam, all the death and suffering, with all the pain and sorrow I've held inside, have I felt more at peace than I feel now.

"Until we moved to the Island, I'd always felt I would eventually kill myself to get rid of my demons. Right now, I'm truly happy. It's something I never thought would ever happen again. Thank you all so much!" He wiped the tears away and smiled at his friends.

Each of the girls gave him another hug and, one by one, the others walked over and hugged him, too. They lingered around the fire for a long time making small talk, and when it was time for bed, the girls took Joe to bed with them. They both wanted to add an exclamation point to his happiness.

22. Finding Family

Tuesday, April 27, 1976

After spending two days in the park, Larry and Connor were out on the coastal highway early and, in no time, hooked a ride to Naples. It turned out, the preacher who dropped them off was right. It *was* easy to get a ride from that spot.

It was about noon in Naples, and they were eating lunch outside a local hamburger joint while they waited for Larry's uncle, Don, to arrive. They noticed a cop circling the block and giving them the eye.

The third time around, he stopped and walked up to the travelers. "I'm going to need to see some ID from you two."

"Really? That's the way it is down here in Florida? Midway through lunch, you get harassed by the local law enforcement?" asked Connor. "What is it, a slow day at the office, so you thought you'd harass the new guys in town?"

"Just give me some ID."

Larry stood and pulled out his ID. "You know this isn't right. We weren't doing anything wrong."

"We're a small community, and the folks here want to know who's in our town."

"Well, officer," said Connor, "have the folks in this little hick town ever hear of the Fourth Amendment to the Constitution? You know, the one regarding privacy?"

"Listen, just show me your ID, and I'll be on my way." Connor pulled out his ID and the cop took a long look at it. "So, what are you two doing down here?"

"So you lied to us. You said you'd be on your way. Now why don't you just go?" Connor glared at the cop. "You know, we've just hitchhiked all the way from Portland, Oregon, to this place to meet up with his uncle." He pointed at Larry. "We weren't harassed *once* by the Man until we got *here*."

As Connor spoke, a Toyota pickup pulled up, and Larry's uncle got out. Connor continued, "So now that you've trampled on our Fourth Amendment rights without a care, I should tell you that you've earned the Pig-of-America Award!"

"What's going on here?" asked Don as he walked up.

"Are these two with you, Don?" asked the Pig.

"Yes they are, John. Is there a problem?"

"We had some people harassed at the beach yesterday and these two fit the description."

"Seriously, John? I monitor the police band at home. Wasn't one of those guys black, and didn't they drive off in a Chevy pickup with Michigan plates?"

"Well, I guess that'll be all." The Pig-of-America handed over the travelers' ID's and quickly returned to his car.

They watched as he drove off, and then Larry introduced Connor. The guys put their packs in the back of the truck and squeezed in the front with Don.

They drove into the country for about five minutes and pulled up to a large, two-story, cinder block home. Don said, "I heard the way you were talking back there to John. You shouldn't be too hard on him. He's just doing his job."

"I don't want to get off on the wrong foot with you, but if harassing paying customers during their lunch is doing his job, then I guess the Fourth Amendment just doesn't matter here. Especially since he lied to you about his reason for harassing us. Thanks for the rescue, by the way."

"Well, I see what Ron was talking about when he described you, Connor." Ron was Larry's dad, Don's older brother. Back in the burbs of Portland, Connor would frequently go out to the garage with Ron, and they would talk about anything that was on the news that day. They enjoyed the conversations immensely.

"Let's not tell Mary what went on just now," he continued. "She doesn't like anything to disturb her peace."

Their house sat on five acres of sand that used to be swampland. The developers dug canals that bordered two sides of their property to drain the swamps. Chickens darted through a large garden of just one crop: Cabbage.

Larry surveyed the backyard and asked, "So is cabbage the only thing that grows here?"

"No, we also grow other crops once it starts getting hot. Cabbage grows year round. Your cousin, Jeff, goes door-to-door around the neighborhood and sells it for spending money."

Don explained that his property was located inside a city called Golden Gate. The streets had already been put in and there was even a downtown area, but no buildings or anything else had been built yet. He promised them a tour during their visit.

"There's a small movement, but they have a lot of clout, to stop the state from draining swamps like this. I think Golden Gate is going to be the last area that gets drained without a huge fight."

"It seems to me the lust for money has been the reason for the rape of large sections of this country," Connor commented. "The northwest was denuded of one of the greatest forests on earth. All so the money barons of this country could get even richer.

"I honestly feel the drug of choice for the rich is money. They don't care what they destroy to get it."

"I'm looking forward to some conversations with you. Be prepared. I happen to agree with your assessment of the rich. As for the consequences of draining this swamp, I think that maybe the tree-huggers are overreacting." Don was looking at Connor with a respectful eye.

"Money is power, Don," remarked Connor. "I mean, I watched a senator from a tobacco-producing state say in a Senate hearing that cigarettes don't cause cancer.

"If you have enough money to buy a senator who will stand up and lie for you, just think who else can be bought and what rules can be bent to get things done, like draining a swamp to create a city.

"Then, when people who are armed with science come and warn what will happen to the environment if the practice is allowed, they're demonized by the people with the power to buy the press."

Don smiled and said, "I'm looking forward to your stay here. I need someone with your opinions to discuss things like world events, a young perspective."

They'd been on the back deck for two hours when Mary came out to announce that dinner was ready. She was a trained chef and had run a good steakhouse in Virginia for fifteen years before they made their move to Florida. She always looked forward to putting a meal on the table for guests.

They sat down to a feast. The chicken was prepared three different ways and it seemed there was cabbage in everything. It was a meal like nothing the two could believe.

Connor stood halfway through dinner and raised his glass. "I've never stood and toasted anything in my life," he lied. "Today, though, this excellent dinner needs to be toasted." He paused while everyone else raised their glasses. "To Mary, an artist in her own right and to the masterpiece she's created before us. This is truly the best meal I've ever eaten!" Connor sat down.

Larry and Don said in unison, "Hear, hear!"

Mary said with a big smile on her face, "Can we keep him, Don? I need to hear that more often."

"*Now* look at what you've done, Connor," Don said with a smile.

"Connor's right," said Larry. "I didn't know you were a chef, Aunt Mary. I'd like you to teach me how to cook some of what we're eating tonight, if you don't mind."

In the next two weeks, they fell into a routine. Connor and Don were up at five o'clock in the morning with coffee in hand discussing politics, sports, and weather. Then they would move on to history. They seemed to disagree about history the most. The conversations were intense at times, but never was a word spoken in anger.

Later, Larry would get up, and he and Mary would go into the kitchen for his breakfast lesson. Once the breakfast dishes were done, they'd sit down together to plan dinner.

After breakfast, Connor would go out back with Jeff, the twelve year old. He would help Jeff weed a different section of the garden every day. Next, they would feed the chickens and collect their eggs. After the chores were done, Connor would give Jeff juggling lessons.

Jeff had been a late-in-life accident. Don said he was a godsend because it made him a younger man. Connor's father had said the same thing not long before he'd left on the tour. He had been fifty-five when Connor's little sister was born and her young mind kept his from getting old. It was good to have young energy around. He said it didn't allow him to become complacent.

After lunch, the travelers would drive the pickup to the Gulf where they would spend the afternoon. Larry would lie on a towel and work on his tan while Connor swam in the ocean. Later, Connor would walk to the library and research something to back up whatever subject he and Don were currently discussing.

Thursday, May 13, 1976

Connor and Larry awoke to a commotion in Don's front yard. They poked their heads out of the front door and saw Don talking to the driver of a delivery truck. They also saw a cement mixer, some bags of cement, and a stack of lumber in the driveway.

Don told them he and Mary had wanted to put a storage shed on the back of the property for a long time. That way, they could park their cars in the garage. He figured he'd take advantage of the two young, strong bodies while he had them.

Larry and Connor were happy to help out. They all worked six hours a day on the shed. Afterward, everyone would ride to the Gulf and swim to cool off.

They had become close, like a family. It was something that was never expected when it was first agreed so long ago that the travelers would come out to visit.

It took them two weeks to finish the shed. On the day the county inspector left a signed approval form saying everything was to code, they celebrated. There was wine and beer. Larry and Mary put out a spread fit for royalty.

Don invited some of the neighbors. It was a big party that went past midnight with music playing and dancing. After all of the guests were gone, Don and Mary sat at the breakfast nook, watching Connor and Larry doing the dishes. Mary said they could wait, but Larry wouldn't hear of it, and Connor volunteered to help.

"You two are always welcome here," said Don. "Mary and I have talked about it, and we think your visit has changed us both. We were in a rut, and you have pulled us out of it. This household is happier than it's been in years. Even Jeff says your visit has been the best time of his life.

"You know, Uncle Don," said Larry, "I hardly knew you before I got here and I never met Jeff. It's been a surprise for me, too."

"I don't know," said Connor. "One of these mornings, I'm gonna push a button and you're gonna kick us both out." He smiled as he taunted Don.

The next day, after returning from their visit to the Gulf, Connor and Larry announced they were going to hitchhike to Key West. Don said he would give them a lift to Alligator Alley, a road that crossed the Everglades in a straight line from Naples to Miami. The locals called it Tami Ami, the real name being TaMiami.

Something curious happened that evening and it showed how different the northwesterners were from the Florida folk. While watching the boob tube, a special report interrupted the normal broadcast announcing that an intense weather cell was heading across Florida in a southwesterly direction. It was going to hit Golden Gate at 7:04 p.m., dropping the temperature down into the high fifties and would last thirty-one minutes with intense rain and thunder.

Immediately, Don and Mary sprang into action. Don went into the garage, brought back two electric heaters, and set them up in front of his and Mary's chairs. Mary went and got two wool blankets to cover them. When the cell arrived, they turned on the heaters and covered up with the blankets.

The two travelers, on the other hand, went out back, stripped to their skivvies, and danced in the warm rain. They hadn't seen rain in over a month, it seemed. It was paradise.

Don and Mary got up and watched them through a window for a minute. Shivering, they returned to their woollies and heaters.

Connor and Larry dried off after the cell passed by. They had been rejuvenated by the rain.

"That was the best!" said Larry as they settled back down to continue watching television.

Connor said, "I forgot how much I missed the rain. It was so warm, like taking a shower."

"You two are crazy!" said Don. "You'll probably catch a cold."

Larry said, "Not us. We grew up in the rain."

23. Alligator Alley

Thursday, May 27, 1976

*T*he next morning, after a special breakfast, Don dropped Larry and Connor off at the west end of the road called Alligator Alley, just as he said he would. He made them promise to come back and stay again before they left Florida.

Larry explained that in a couple of weeks, they were going to have money sent for their journey to Boston. He promised that when they were done with this next adventure, they'd be back. The only thing that would stop them was if they hooked a ride all the way to Boston.

With that, they said their goodbyes and got out of Don's truck. He drove off as they set up for their next ride. Their Key West sign leaned against their packs. Larry played some particularly nice blues and Connor sang his offbeat, jive-assed poetry and juggled.

Larry had to piss, so he headed off the road into the brush by a canal. As he was going, he looked down in the water. Not ten feet away, a six-foot gator lay partially submerged in the water and stared intently at him. He quickly finished and ran back to the road.

"Jesus! I see why they call it Alligator Alley! There's a gator in the water right down there where I pissed!"

Connor got his camera out and carefully went down to get a picture. "Now, when we get home, we'll have a picture to prove that story!" he said.

It wasn't long at all before a Rambler Ambassador pulled over. It was a different color, but was the same year and model as Larry's rig back home, minus the buckled front left fender.

Two very good-looking women in their early thirties got out with big smiles, and the driver opened the trunk. The travelers deposited their packs and got in the backseat. They thanked the two ladies for picking them up.

The driver said, "You two looked happy standing there. I normally don't pick up hitchhikers, but she asked me to." The driver pointed at her friend riding shotgun. "So you can thank her for the ride."

The friend said, "Hi, I'm Debbie, and she's Mags. We're bartenders in Sarasota. They make us drive to Miami every three months to take a lie detector test. I thought you two might bring a nice change to this long-assed, boring drive."

"I'm Connor, and this is Larry. We've been on the road since March third, coming up on three months now. We call it our Bicentennial Tour.

"So when you saw us out there on the side of the road, looking happy, it's what we try to sell to every car that comes along. In truth, we go under the philosophy that our ride is out there. He or she just doesn't know it yet. So, if that's the case, why not be happy?"

Larry said, "I've got a '68 Ambassador back in Oregon where we live. Push button on the dash, just like this one. Mine's tan, though."

Debbie asked, "You two are from Oregon?" She had a look of shock on her face like they'd said they were from Mars.

Getting back to her car, Mags said, "What a coincidence. I like it. It's a very reliable car. Never gives me any trouble. I get over twenty miles a gallon on the highway." She turned and smiled at Larry.

Larry was looking at the view from the backseat. The Everglades stretched out in front of them as far as he could see, to the north and south as well. Waterfowl flew in all directions. For the first time in his life, he saw an Egret, snowy white and up to his backward knees in the swamp.

"So you two have to take a lie detector test for your work?" asked Larry as he pulled his attention away from the view.

"Yes," answered Mags.

Connor said, "Jesus! Orwell's 'Big Brother is Watching You' is here, right now, as we speak!"

Debbie said, "Well, to be fair, I make more money working at this place than I've ever made before. The owners have a whole string of liquor stores with lounges attached to them. They said their profits increased by thirty-five percent when they started using the lie detector tests."

"My brother's a bartender back at a place in downtown Portland," said Connor. "I think the majority of the money he makes is from ripping off the customers, not the bar."

"The part that bothers me the most is the owners won't buy my gas to get down to Fort Lauderdale," Mags complained. "And it's almost four hundred miles round trip!"

"I tell you what," said Larry. "There's supposed to be a gas station halfway across this swamp. I'll fill your tank for the ride."

"I guess that means I'll go in half with you," Connor added.

"You two don't have to do that, but I'll take it!" Mags beamed at Debbie.

"Yeah, that's nice of you. If you get back to Sarasota, come into the bar and I'll buy you two a drink," Debbie offered.

"We've already stayed at that state park just to the south. Next time we're there, we'll look you up," said Larry. They filled up at the halfway pit stop, and then were on to Miami.

"So, on this test, do they ask if you smoke weed?" Connor asked.

"No, they don't care what we do off the job. All they want to know is if we give away free drinks or steal anything. It takes longer to hook up all the wires and stuff than the actual test itself.

"Besides, the owners smoke weed themselves. They are so cool. We get high with them every time they're in Sarasota."

"I guess that means you won't mind if I light up a joint?"

Debbie looked over at Mags and said with a smile, "I told you they looked like they were stoned."

"Well, we weren't, but we're gonna be if it's all right with Mags."

"Fire it up. I always do better on the test if I'm stoned." She paused, and then continued with a smile. "You know, you two have really changed my opinion of hitchhikers."

"I wouldn't pick up a hitchhiker if I was a girl and was alone," Connor advised. "Look them over real close. You can tell the difference between the ones who are heading somewhere and the ones who are just going."

Larry added, "Listen to him. There are really bad dirt bags out there on the road."

They got stoned and went the rest of the way making small talk and enjoying the high. The ride ended with the travelers being dropped at a city bus stop going south. Both of the girls hugged them. Debbie whispered in Larry's ear that he could stay with her if he was to stop by the bar.

They were on the bus when Larry told Connor what she'd said. "Tanya is just a figment of your imagination, isn't she?" asked Connor.

"Fuck you, Connor! What makes you think she wants to sleep with me?"

"Well, when she whispers it in *your* ear and doesn't say *shit* to me, I'm talkin' a romp in the hay! It don't matter. I'll just stay down in the park."

"You're jealous!"

"Yeah, maybe, but I think I'm just amazed at the amount of pussy that's out here on the road."

"I wonder why that is. Back home, I walk around with blue balls all the time," Larry complained.

"Well, I think it's just the mystery we represent," said Connor. "I mean, people dream of adventure, but rarely experience it. So when they see us out here doing it, it kinda turns them on. I mean, you *know* it ain't our looks!" They both laughed.

The bus driver dropped them as far south as he went. They walked until they got to a good spot for a car to pull over, took off their packs, and set up the Key West sign. Five minutes later, they were heading south once again.

"I drive to Key West twice a week. Been doing it for nine years. You're the first hitchhikers I've seen this far north. You see locals down near Key West, but most people just take the bus. It's real cheap."

"Where's the adventure in that?" asked Larry.

The driver had to make a stop on the way that would keep him several hours, so he dropped the travelers at a state park on Grassy Key, about halfway to Key West.

Since it was already late in the day, they paid for a campsite and walked to a store down the road a piece. They scored on some southern fried chicken, potato planks, and two pieces of key lime pie.

"I thought key lime pie was green, not yella," said Larry.

"Yellow or not, this is really good."

They ate at a table in back of the store, looking out at the Atlantic Ocean. Thunderheads that looked like cotton balls hung on the distant horizon. Seabirds called out as they flew by, eyeing the two for a handout.

"We both grew up eighty miles from the Pacific," said Connor, around a mouth full of pie. "You know, the Atlantic right here is like another planet. The smell, the breakers, the sounds, the colors. They're all so foreign."

"Yeah, it's like everything is a bit smaller, more civilized, I think," said Larry. "It just seems a little off. And it's *never* this warm on the Oregon coast."

"I wonder how warm the water is. If it's anything like the Gulf near your uncle's, I'm gonna be swimming a whole bunch while we're down here."

"Do me a favor and take me with you sometime. Just make me get off the beach and swim," said Larry.

They went back in the store and scored a pint of bourbon and a couple of quarts of beer. Afterwards, they walked back to camp and changed into their swimming trunks to take their virgin swim in the Atlantic Ocean.

Connor walked out through the breakers to his waist and started swimming. He went about a half mile past the breakwater and turned northeast. He turned around and swam back by Larry who hadn't even touched the water. He laughed to himself, thinking what it would take to pry him off that towel.

Connor didn't stop. He continued southwest until he came upon a mangrove. Then he dove down and looked at the schools of fish. He had been in the water for about an hour when he got back and sat down beside Larry.

"You ought to see all the fish down there around that mangrove. So many bright colors! Some of them are big enough to eat. When we get to Key West, I'm gonna find out what it'll take to get some of them. I heard people use spear guns down here."

"You can have that shit! You ever see *Jaws*?" asked Larry.

"No. I knew I was coming down here, fuck you very much! I mean, you just asked me to make you swim when we get down to Key West, then you bring up *Jaws*?"

As they walked back to their campsite, Connor started talking with everyone who seemed friendly. At the fourth camp he hooked a ride for the next morning. It was a nice Ohio couple pulling a twenty-five foot travel trailer with a suburban.

They got back to camp, twisted a doobie and walked across the highway with the bourbon and beer to cop a good buzz. Larry was saying as they were about to light the joint, "If there's one thing you do better than anyone, it's bullshitting! I can't believe you got us another ride out of a campground."

"You could do it, too. You just ask the right questions and listen to them when they answer. Before you know it, they're offering you a ride. It's easy." Connor took a long pull off of the pint and passed it to Larry.

After they finished the beer, bourbon, and weed, they walked back to camp with a glow on. The whole sky was red, orange, and yellow with silver linings. They marveled at the changing colors and intensities as the sky gradually turned to black.

"They sure do know what a sunset is around here," said Connor. "I bet Key West is crammed full of artists, just like they gravitate to the Oregon coast. You know what I mean? When you have these kinds of skies, they demand to be painted."

"There will be art galleries all over in Key West, I bet. Can't wait to see them all," Larry replied.

Before it got dark, Connor cleaned up in a quarter-powered shower and Larry followed suit. They both went to bed.

24. Back into the Fold

Lucas, Alex and JJ

Alex and Lucas sat outside a lounge close to the edge of a balcony overlooking a small pond and fragrant flower garden. They watched as JJ walked up with drink in hand and sat down. He didn't look happy.

JJ asked, "So did they give you any hint of what they want?"

"I don't know anything," Lucas answered. "They were real vague. Wouldn't answer any of my questions."

"Well, what the fuck!" JJ was really pissed now. "They ignore us since we've been down here, no matter how hard we try to contact them. And I haven't seen a *single* deposit in my account since we've been here, either. Now, out of the fucking blue, they need to see us right *now*?"

Lucas said, "Well, we can't just tell them to fuck off. But we *can* ask about the money."

"Let's do it then," Alex said. They drained their drinks and headed across the street. Looking like three ex-football linebackers, all dressed in black suits, they were very imposing.

The travel agency was a front for the Cartel. Once the receptionist got the okay, they walked into the back room and through another door that opened for them into a dimly-lit office.

The small room was crowded with no place to sit down. The three walked in and joined three other men in dark suits as they stood, facing a man behind a giant desk. He released a cloud of cigar smoke that engulfed his head, smiled and started speaking in Spanish. "You three ready to get back into the fold? Back in the good graces of our leadership in Colombia?"

Lucas answered in Spanish, "Yes, sir. We were beginning to wonder if you would need us anymore after the mix-up in Bogotá. We're more than eager to get back in the swing of things."

"Yes, Bogotá. That was a major misunderstanding on all counts. We ended up having to kill that young man's father. It isn't good business to kill someone you paid dearly to put into office, but he just wouldn't let it go."

Lucas just stood there and waited. Once he realized the man required a comment, he answered. "Like I said, it was a major fuck-up. Nothing was done maliciously. We thought we had the right guy. We all have kids of our own. Couldn't imagine how he felt."

"Well, that's behind us now." The man opened a desk drawer and pulled out three envelopes and threw them across the desk.

"Here's the money you would've received if you had stayed in Colombia. There will be five thousand more after you finish a little task. We need you three to deliver a package to a tugboat captain. It's going to take the use of two of the CIA's fancy rubber rafts. Do you guys have the clout to get them without raising any eyebrows?"

"No problem. When do you need them?" asked Lucas as he passed the envelopes to his two companions.

"You will be notified by an associate once the details come together. Call me as soon as you secure the rafts. We will need them in a week or two, maybe three. We're still waiting for the tugboat to get out of the repair yard." He pushed a card across the table with a number, but no name, on it.

"Is that everything?" Lucas asked, as he picked up the card.

"That's all."

They were at the door when the man behind the desk said, "Oh, one more thing. We want you guys to work with these three agents on this one." He pointed to the other men in the room. "They will stay with the vehicles at the boat launch to run interference with anyone who would impede the loading of the product into the trucks."

The two groups of men eyed each other suspiciously. Then the three friends left and walked back across the street before saying anything.

Lucas spoke up first. "Well, I guess we're delivery boys, which is fucking bullshit! They have their *own* people that could drop this package off."

"They took us by surprise today, but I hope they don't think we're gonna do this shit again," said Alex. "If this is what they want

186

out of us, I'll just tell them to fuck off! I didn't like the way those other agents looked as us, anyway."

"I wonder what the fucking package is," said JJ.

"They're probably Russian whores!" said Lucas. They all laughed.

The three friends headed back to the field office to see about securing use of two rubber rafts. Claiming to be working on a lead, they got permission to take the rafts in case they made an arrest. They were told that no one was expecting to use them any time soon, and they just needed to check them out.

Two weeks later, they were told to report to a different location to receive additional instructions. This angered the three agents further. This job was becoming more trouble than it was worth.

Their contact turned out to be a man they had worked with in Colombia. They immediately felt at ease when they recognized him.

The three other agents were present as well. As before, no introductions were given. They stood apart from the three friends and regarded then with contempt. The three stood their ground and chose to ignore the other agents.

They were given the logistics of the job and were told that it would be another seventy-two hours before the tugboat would be in play at the Smugglers Buoy.

"It's very important that you three deliver the package to the tugboat captain before the he drops the barge at the dock. There will be another tugboat to take the barge away in a few days. The drop-off should be done in a few minutes, so you see why you must get the package to him before he arrives. He wants to leave as soon as possible.

"You'll meet at the Smugglers Buoy. He'll slow down and you'll pull up beside the barge. His crew will drop lines with hooks and pull the package on board. Then you will head back to the boat launch, load up the rafts, and watch while the product is loaded in the trucks.

"Don't worry. It's gone off without a hitch many times. So get this done, and you're back in the good graces of everyone."

25. Far From Portland

Friday, May 28, 1976

The next morning, Larry and Connor were ready when their ride stopped to pick them up. After the proper introductions, Garrett, Sally, and the two travelers took off to Key West. The ride down was glorious. They continued west on the Overseas Highway, made mostly of bridges, that gave them wonderful panoramic views of the Atlantic Ocean and the Gulf of Mexico.

Connor said to Larry, "When I first started thinking of this trip, this was the one thing I wanted to do most of all, if we made it to Florida. I mean, think about it, this is as far as we can get away from Portland and still be in the lower forty-eight states."

Larry nodded as he looked out the window. "You know it's about as different as you can get from Portland, too."

Garrett told them they had been spending a month in Key West every summer since he retired. A friend he worked with in Toledo bought an RV park where he and Sally had stayed for the last eleven years.

Sally turned to Larry and asked, "Do you two have a place to camp once you're down in Key West?"

Larry answered, "I think we're just gonna play it by ear."

"We have a nice yard at our site. I'm sure they wouldn't mind if you set up that tarp thing there," she said.

"That's a damned good idea," said Garrett. "You'll see, once you walk around, there isn't that much land. And they don't let you set up a tent just anywhere, so you can stay with us. My buddy might even give you some work to do."

By the time they arrived at the RV park and talked to the owner, there was no saying *no*. So the travelers began to set up the tarp under the watchful eyes of about twenty locals. It seemed Garrett and Sally's arrival was a big day at the park. Their return brought out all of the neighbors, whose ages ranged from about sixty-five to eighty years.

That's the thing the travelers had noticed about Florida. Most of the people were really old. It was as if everyone on the East Coast had retired there.

After watching them set up the tarp, Garrett asked where they got the idea. They once again went on to explain that it came from a publication about World War I.

"When I was in basic training," Connor explained, "me and my bunkmate would each carry half of the pup tent. These are the type of poles we carried. I got these at an army surplus store in Portland. We used this tarp instead of canvas because it's waterproof and weighs a lot less.

"We've already weather-tested it in high wind and sideways rain, and even snow. I'll take this over any conventional tent. That is, as long as I have a partner. It's definitely a two-person adventure."

Connor and Larry left the RV park to get something for dinner. They had promised Sally that they would do the cooking. As they left, all of the old guys milled about the tarp talking about it like it was this year's model of the Mustang.

Connor said, "Christ Almighty! Who would've thought our tarp would be such a hit? It's like these guys ain't got nothin' better to do than watch our every move."

Larry said, "I think about what I'll be like when I'm that age. I think the majority of those guys fought in World War II, then spent the rest of their lives working hard. Now, they've been put out to pasture, and I think they crave anything new. I think they're bored shitless."

They walked into Key West. Connor suggested they stop in at a bar. Larry, never one to turn down a drink, quickly agreed. They walked into the first place they came to and sat at the bar. The average age of the patrons was probably sixty, and that was because Connor and Larry lowered it six or seven years when they walked in. Connor ordered two whiskeys with two beer backs.

"You know, I've read a lot," Connor started. Seeing Larry's reaction to his words, he said, "Don't sit there and shake your head like reading is perverse, you asshole!"

Connor continued on his original topic. "So, Hemingway wrote in one of his novels about the taste of bourbon. He would look forward to the cocktail hour when he could swirl it across his tongue and taste the smoky flavor of the oak barrel it was made in.

"I never could get that. I'm more of an 'across the gums, watch out stomach, here it comes, then wash it down with beer' type of guy. But I digress—Hemingway loved Key West and wrote a couple of his books down here. He also loved central Idaho. I like that area, too, and I know you do."

"Yeah, so what's your point?" asked Larry.

"He blew his fucking head off with a shotgun. Left a note saying his doctor had told him he couldn't do what he loved doing anymore. That was drinking bourbon, smoking cigars, and chasing women.

"I guess what I'm trying to say is that when I see those guys walking around a tarp, discussing the pros and cons of its use, I understand why Hemingway killed himself."

Connor sat there in silence for a moment. Then he toasted to Ernest, tapped glasses with Larry and gulped down the bourbon. He quickly flooded his mouth with beer and swallowed.

"Let's get the fuck out of here!"

"You're a weird one, dude, but I love you. You just keep on thinkin', Connor. I will always listen to your bullshit."

"Fuck you, Larry. I think Hemingway drank a better brand of bourbon." Connor was laughing with a bitter scowl on his face.

They went to a grocery store and got the fixin's for a good meal they hoped would cement their friendship with everyone back at the RV park.

As they walked back, Connor noticed some snorkeling gear in a pawn shop. Larry waited outside, and Connor went in and negotiated for a mask, fins, and a spear gun. He came out smiling and said, "I'm going fishing!"

Larry said, "How much did that set you back?"

"He wanted thirty bucks," Connor replied, "but I dickered him down to twenty-one. I'm telling you, it'll pay for itself before we leave here. Then, I'll sell it back to him." He grinned at Larry.

"Okay, but I expect fish out of you every fucking day!" said Larry. "Do you even know how to *use* a spear gun?"

"No, never used one in my life."

They walked a while in silence. Then Larry asked, "What do you think you'll do when you get old?"

"I don't know, but my Grandma still hikes in the wilderness, and she's in her seventies. She still hunts and fishes, and I think she generally enjoys herself.

"She's one strange bird, though. One day when I was fourteen, me and Gramma were up at Marion Lake in the Mount Jefferson wilderness. We were sitting, enjoying the trout and potatoes she'd just cooked when she just up and said, 'Connor, you listen close, because I believe this is gospel. All Communists and Catholics are going to hell!'

"I mean, Jesus Fucking Christ! I really didn't have anything to say to that. I'll tell you this. She was raised a Catholic and was excommunicated when she married outside the cult, and her sister was the president of the Oregon Communist Party for twenty-five years. I guess that part of the turning-the-other-cheek shit didn't take with her.

"The next day, I was hiking around a lake. We were fishing in Six Lake Basin. I came up on her real quiet like and watched her fly fish off a rock at the bottom of this huge rock slide. She landed this nice, pan-sized rainbow. She hooked the trout on her creel, and then just sat there, looking up at Three Finger Jack out there on the horizon.

"This smile came to her face, one I'd never seen on her before. It was a smile that said, 'I'm happier than fuck just sitting here.' She was a strange lady, but I loved her and will always remember her smile that day.

"So, anyway, to answer your question, I think I want to be a bad Buddhist, sitting on the side of running water, looking for the Om, and killing the food I eat. If I can, just once, achieve a smile like my Grandma's, with that look of peace, then I would have achieved something."

Larry laughed and said, "I just want to meet the right person, like Tanya, I hope, and get married and have some kids. When I'm old, I can tell my grandkids about our Bicentennial Tour. I guess it's kind of the pipe dream most people have."

Connor agreed, "Yeah, I don't know if Carol and I are going to stay an item. I think one day, though, I'll hook up with Miss Right.

"Come on. Let's impress the shit out of those old codgers at the RV park with this meal. That tent spot is the most important thing we got going."

Once back at camp, they went into action. Connor went out to find the perfect spit while Larry got the cooking fire started. He used some charcoal he got from Garrett. Next, he started to prep the roast by stuffing whole garlic cloves into slits he made with his knife and using the last of Connor's dry rub.

Larry had the roast spitted and was slowly turning it while Connor prepared the spuds, mushrooms, and asparagus all wrapped in separate aluminum foil packages. Once again, the routine of the outdoor meal was performed like a well-rehearsed ballet.

Connor would later say he felt like a stage actor in a one-act play. The audience being a group of retirees, sitting in lawn chairs ten feet away, sipping gin and tonics, and watching every move made by both of the performers. They would occasionally ask questions that the two actors answered. Through the whole process, the actors swilled a variety of alcoholic concoctions.

Two and a half hours later, they laid out their fare. Everyone sampled a small portion of each item. Larry would say later that the rub made the difference in the roast, rating it right up there with the best meat he'd ever cooked. Like always with these two, it was their latest meal that was their best.

The job was completed, and they were guaranteed a tent site for as long as they wanted to stay. Garrett and Sally's place in the social hierarchy had risen as well. The owner of the park was even asking the travelers if they might be looking for work. The things one good meal will get you.

At sunset, they crossed the highway and walked down to a tiny beach facing west over the Gulf of Mexico. Larry pulled out a pinner of the good stuff. Once again, the sky was mixing blues, yellows, and pinks with silver linings and thunderheads. It was another beautiful Florida evening.

Connor noticed a snorkeler swimming toward them and pointed him out to Larry. The snorkeler stood up, removed his mask and bent over to take his fins off. Smiling, he walked right up to them. He had a spear gun and two spears in his left hand.

Without a word, Larry offered the joint that was now attached to a roach clip to the guy as he approached. He took it and toked it. His eyes widened as the Thai weed slowly rocked his world. He offered the joint back to Larry.

"Take another hit," said Larry. The guy obliged him.

Connor took the roach from him, took the last hit and handed it back to Larry, who put the roach in his second gen container. Connor said, "So, now that you're baked—I'm Connor, he's Larry, and who are you?"

"I'm Jim. It seems I got back just in time. I've never tasted weed like that. Man! I'm really stoned off of two hits!" He looked the travelers over and asked, "Where you guys from?"

Connor gave him a short version of the Bicentennial Tour story, just saying they were from out west and had been on the road for nearly three months.

"I don't suppose you'd teach me how to use a spear gun, would you?" Connor asked. "I just bought one from a hock shop in town. I've never used one before."

Jim winced and replied, "It's harder than it looks. I've tried to teach several people, but they couldn't hit a thing." He paused and considered.

"Tell you what, since you got me stoned, I'll give you one lesson. You have to be a strong swimmer because I'm usually out for five or six hours. I'll swim fifteen miles one-way sometimes. You up for that kind of swim?"

"Connor's a friggin fish!" said Larry. "Speaking of fish, I don't see no fish with you. How often do you get any?"

"Oh, I got fish today already," Jim replied. "I just dropped them by my friends' place. I'm gonna shower and change, and I'm headed over there for dinner."

Jim took a long look at Connor as if he was trying to make up his mind about what to do.

"I'm the maintenance guy at the RV park you're staying at," he said finally. "I saw your tarp set-up at Garrett and Sally's earlier today. Kinda nice."

"Are you gonna go fishing tomorrow? I can be ready whenever you want," said Connor, anxious for his first lesson.

"I should get off at two, then leave an hour or so later. I'll stop by tomorrow and pick you up. We'll be out just a couple of hours because I got a date tomorrow night.

"I gotta warn you, though. It's not like you see on TV. The refraction of the water changes everything. Most people can't get it. They get frustrated and quit. That's why there are so many spear guns at the hock shops.

"Another thing, you always have to wash your gear in fresh water after every use. That's where I'm going now. I shower with my gear to get the salt off me and my set up."

Connor said, "Well, we'll just have to see if I'm worth a fuck tomorrow. Regardless, I'll bring a Thai joint along. You'll get good and baked."

"So that's Thai weed, huh?" asked Jim. "We don't get that stuff around here. My friends are gonna be jealous. I got a friend who was in Vietnam. He says it's the best weed he's ever smoked. Tonight, I'll be sure to tell him I agree."

"Well, if I learn anything from you tomorrow, it'll be worth the joint," said Connor.

They bullshitted a few more minutes before leaving the beach. Connor and Larry had a cocktail with Garrett and his friends back at the RV site, and then went to bed.

As they were lying down, Larry asked, "Did you see the way Jim stared at us? It kinda creeped me out. It was like he was gonna say something, but changed his mind."

"Yeah. It didn't creep me out, though. I think a lot of it was the Thai weed, man." He paused and considered his next words before speaking. "I want to say this, and I don't want to hear any of your Christian mumbo jumbo.

"I decide I'm gonna spearfish, something I've never done. I'm secretly questioning why I'm even gonna try it. Then, out of the water comes a spearfisher, who gets stoned and says he'll give me a lesson. I'll say it again, it just seems like *someone* is looking out for us."

Larry knew he'd incur Connor's wrath if he said what he believed and was quiet for a moment. "Amen to that."

"Yeah. It's getting a little freaky. I guess an *Amen* is called for, bro."

Larry said, "You know what we were talking about earlier about when we get old? I hope you're still around to verify all my Bicentennial Tour stories, because no one's gonna believe half of this shit!"

"Amen to that, too, bro. It's like I was saying. What a long, weird trip it's been."

"Yeah, that's right, and I hope it *stays* weird," said Larry as he settled in. That night, the travelers slept well.

26. Something About the Travelers

Jim, Joe, Danny, and Michael

Jim went home, showered and walked over to the Island. It was just Joe, Danny, and Michael. Sunshine and Rainbow were in town at their condo for the evening.

Michael poached the fish Jim caught that day and Danny made some curry rice. While they were eating, Jim told them of his chance meeting with the hitchhikers and the Thai weed. Joe immediately asked him if he said anything about the Island.

"I wouldn't do that without a vote. Remember, *I* was the one who discovered this tree house." He hesitated before continuing. "There's just something interesting about these two. They said they were on this Bicentennial Tour, and this is just a short stop for them. Once it gets warmer up north, they are going to Boston to visit a friend.

"I'm not certain, but I think they both have skills we might be able to use while they're here. One of them is a house painter and they both know how to roof. The one thing Sunshine and Rainbow said we really need to figure out how is to fix all the roof leaks before the rainy season. Kevin and Ryan said they weren't gonna move their stuff out here until they can fix the sieve they built for a roof."

"You know, Jim," said Joe, "the roof's one thing, but without you around, we'll have to start buying our fish."

"Yeah, I promised my parents I'd come home the week after next in exchange for letting me stay here until Christmas."

"I don't suppose either one of them knows how to spearfish," said Danny.

"Funny you should mention that. One of them wants me to teach him. That's not saying he'll be any good. None of you guys could ever hit anything." Jim pulled a cold beer from an ice chest he had floated over and popped the cap.

"Like I say, these two guys are interesting. I just got the funniest feeling when I was talking with them. It was like déjà vu, like I'd dreamed about these two or something. Kinda freaked me out."

***

Saturday, May 29, 1976

The next morning, Sally made pancakes for the travelers. After breakfast, they were talking over coffee when the park owner stopped by. He asked Larry if he wanted to paint the interior of a small storeroom for him. Larry could do it in a day, so he agreed.

Connor got his mask and fins and went to the beach. He looked around for a landmark he could use to get back to the park. Everything was so flat he finally settled on a big tree out on a nearby island. He also noticed a short-wave radio tower just south of the park.

He went out for the first time with a mask in the clear ocean waters. His fear of getting lost kept him close, but the time in the water made him happy. He saw lots of fish and was surprised at the many different kinds of birds flying overhead.

Connor got back and showered with his gear as Jim had recommended and settled in under the tarp to read a murder mystery he'd gotten from Sally. His laundry was drying and it seemed for the first time since the third of March, he was alone in camp. He fell asleep until Jim stopped by to take him spearfishing.

Connor was up and ready in a few minutes after retrieving his laundry. He had fabricated the perfect pinner under the cover of the tarp and put it in an army surplus, waterproof match container with some wooden matches. He told Garrett and Sally he was off for a spearfishing lesson with Jim so Larry wouldn't worry, and they left.

Jim had brought a weighted diver's belt with a knife on it. He told him it was easier to dive with the weight. Connor put it on and they entered the water.

Jim was a powerful swimmer and the first thing he did was set a fast pace to see if Connor could keep up. They had gone about three miles before he stopped, and then he just stood up.

"Well, you passed the endurance test."

"I *thought* that was what was going on," said Connor. "I started surfing when I was fourteen, and I love swimming in salt water. This place is a trip, though. I can't believe we swam all that way and just stood up."

Jim stopped there for a reason. He pointed out all the landmarks Connor would need to know to get back to the RV park.

He said, "Now, let's go see if you're a spearfisher."

The thing Jim didn't know was that Connor had been an expert marksman while in the Army. He led his battalion in basic training with the M-16 rifle. Over in Germany, he was a pay guard and would go out and shoot a .45 pistol at the shooting range twice a month and was rated an expert. And then, of course, there was his ability with throwing knives.

Jim took him to one of his favorite spots. It was a key that held a bounty of fish all summer long. He went over the particulars about how he shot a spear gun.

He pointed to a little cove and said, "We're gonna go in there real slow. Try not to disturb the water by splashing your fins. If you see a fish to shoot, the best thing to do is dive down till you're level with it, then shoot. Point the spear gun, don't try to aim."

Connor swam into the cove and immediately noticed a good-sized fish hanging out near the bottom. He dove down, held out the spear gun from ten feet away, and hit the fish right behind its head. He surfaced for air, took three deep breaths, dove back down, and retrieved the fish.

Jim motioned him to follow, and they swam to a nearby sandy beach. "That was amazing! You're the first person I've tried to teach that could hit anything on the first try. I mean, they're usually three or four feet away and still can't hit anything. You were at least *ten* feet away!"

Connor went back to the cove four times and brought a fish back every time. He didn't hit on every attempt, but he kept trying until he got something. The first four fish weighed about a pound or two. The last fish he brought back was a snapper that weighed over ten pounds.

Jim couldn't believe his eyes. He said, "I think that's more than enough for everyone. If you don't mind, I'll give these four to my friends. You can show off the snapper back at the RV park." Connor agreed.

The swim back was slowed because of the bounty and they were going against the tide. Jim taught Connor to avoid the deep channels when swimming into the tide because that was where the riptides were strongest.

As they neared home, they beached on a mound of sand just east of a small key and cleaned the fish. It wasn't long before gulls were diving for the guts and gills.

Connor asked "If I get you stoned, are you gonna be able to get us back to the park?"

"I'm a native. I know these waters like the back of my hand."

They smoked the Thai pinner and Jim was lost before they had gone twenty yards. After an hour of confusion, they finally rounded a key and Connor pointed out the radio tower just south of the park that he'd seen that morning. Jim was relieved.

Once they were back where they started, Connor said, "That's the thing about the Thai weed. It don't matter if you're a native or not. If you're not used to it, you're fucking *lost* for a while."

Jim sat there for a minute, realizing what had just happened and started laughing. "Some kind of native I turned out to be. Thanks for holding my hand and getting me back. I was worried it was gonna get dark and we'd have to spend the night out here."

"Hell, the first time I smoked it, I had to pull over for an hour. Didn't have the slightest idea where the fuck I was. Turns out, I was only four blocks from my apartment. Next time, we'll smoke over there." He pointed to the island with the big tree he'd seen that morning.

They returned to the RV park and showered, taking care to rinse the saltwater off of their gear. Jim gathered up all of the fish except the snapper.

He stood and said, "I'm gonna take care of these fish. I'll be back in a while."

He walked out of the park, back across the highway, and since it was high tide, waded up past his waist out to the Island.

Jim put the fish on ice, and told everyone what had just happened. The four architects were present, and they asked a lot of questions about the two hitchhikers. Jim told them that he had never seen anyone take to spearfishing like Connor had, and maybe with a little training, he would be able to fill in while he was gone.

He told them about how Larry was painting a storeroom at the RV park. He also told them that he'd talked to Larry that morning about roofing and learned he owned a roofing and painting company out west somewhere.

They decided to have a dinner at Sunshine and Rainbow's condo the following evening with all eight Islanders. Connor and Larry would be invited for everyone's evaluation.

***

Larry finished his painting project. The owner paid him and asked if he wanted any more jobs. Larry put him off on the guise that he wasn't sure how long they were going to stay. In truth, he considered himself on vacation and didn't want the work.

When Larry returned to the RV site, Connor was entertaining the neighbors while filleting the snapper. He'd borrowed a knife from Garrett, but before he could do anything, he had to sharpen it. That had drawn a series of suggestions that Connor listened to, as he went on doing what he'd always done when sharpening a blade. He used a whetstone first to bring back the edge, and then he put the steel to it to smooth out the bevel.

The snapper cut like butter. Once he had the fish filleted, he skinned it with two quick motions, leaving two thin layers of skin on the table. Connor cut the filets into steaks, wrapped them in cellophane, and put them on ice. Before the crowd left, he invited them back later for a bite of snapper. He let them know there would be enough for everyone.

The audience, realizing the show was over, moved on to the next point of interest, leaving Larry and Connor alone briefly.

"That's a real nice fish, Connor," said Larry. "So, did you get it, or did Jim?"

"I got five fish. Jim took the others to his friends. We've got to talk later. I'm gettin' some weird vibes from him."

"Really? Well, I told you how he kinda creeped me out yesterday when he was staring at us."

"Yeah, but it's probably nothing. I mean, it's not bad vibes or anything. I like the dude," said Connor. "Let's take a walk down to the store and get some fixin's for dinner. We'll talk."

After they left the park and were well away, Connor continued, "So here's what's weird. Today we were out there." He pointed out over the water to the north.

"Jim was giving me pointers on how not to get lost—this landmark, this tree, that channel. The funny thing is, I was out there this morning and the landmark I used to get back was this giant-assed tree on that island over there." He pointed at the big tree.

"I mean, that fucking tree is huge. I could see it most of the day, but to Jim, it was invisible. I didn't say anything, but it just kinda hit me as weird. I get the feeling he doesn't want me on that island."

Larry said, "Wow, man, that's fucking strange. But you won't believe what I saw just a little earlier.

"I walked across the highway and was smokin' a dube. I was way back in the puckerbrush so no one would see me. I heard someone coming and got real low. It was Jim with the fish. He walked right by me without noticing, and then he waded over to that same island with the big tree. Maybe he lives out there."

"Yeah, now it's making some sense."

"It's probably against the law to be living out there, so he keeps it a secret. I would if I was him," said Larry.

"Okay, that's probably right. I'm glad I didn't push him on it. He said he was gonna stop by later. Let's not say anything to him about it. Like I said, I do like him, and he's gonna show me some new place tomorrow that's way the fuck out in the Keys somewhere. So I don't want to piss him off.

"You know another weird fucking thing that happened today? While we were out on this little sandy mound, cleaning the fish, I swear to God I had a feeling of déjà vu like I've never had before! I mean, I knew what we were going to say before we said it. It was like I was acting in a movie I'd already seen."

"That *is* strange. I think you're getting fucking loony there, bro." Larry grinned at him.

"Fuck you, Larry. I'm not crazy, I'm just very perceptive," said Connor as he grinned back.

They reached the store and decided on red curry rice, mushrooms, and broccoli with coarsely-chopped onions. They bought the fixin's and headed back to the RV park. Connor told Larry about the fun he'd had spearfishing and how they probably won't have to buy any fish again while they were in Florida. Larry mentioned the offer that was made by the owner of the park and how he'd turned him down "on account of him being on vacation and all".

When the guys got back to the park, they started dinner. They put the snapper on the fire and everyone seemed to come out of the woodwork to observe and provide suggestions. They were *really* there for a taste.

Jim arrived just as they were serving up the meal to Garrett and Sally, who were inside their trailer enjoying the boob tube and the air conditioning. There were several other neighbors, sitting and standing around and enjoying the fare.

They served up Jim and themselves last. Jim took a bite of the snapper. It was coated with eggs and fine flour with a small amount of rosemary, cumin, cayenne pepper, and garlic powder. His eyes went wide with surprise. "I've never had snapper spiced like that. It's real good! Don't suppose I could get the recipe?"

"It's Larry's. He was the cook this evening. He's always doing things that take me by surprise."

Larry laughed. "Don't let him bullshit you. He was the one who suggested cayenne pepper. That's what made the fish. The red curry in the rice is mine. We make a good team."

"Well, I don't care who made it. This is really good."

They ate in silence until Garrett came out with three beers. "Sally says that was the best fish she's ever eaten. She says we were sure lucky meeting you two."

Larry replied, "Right back at you. We would've been SOL if you two hadn't offered us a spot to put the tarp."

Garrett smiled. "I guess we're even then."

"Just think, Garrett," said Connor. "Jim's gonna show me another spot to fish tomorrow. This could be just the beginning. Thanks for the beer and you tell Sally if things go right, we'll be cooking a lot of fish. We'll try a new recipe every night. Make her life easier, you know what I mean?"

Garrett and the neighbors quizzed Larry on the dinner, getting all the ingredients, and then they headed back to their TV sets. Once Garrett went inside, Jim and the travelers walked down by the water to get an after-dinner high going.

They smoked a Thai pinner. The sky was just beginning to give up its sunset show and was falling into a blue so dark it was arguing with black. They sat for a while and watched.

Jim said, "I told some of my friends about you guys. They're having a dinner party tomorrow night and asked me to invite you.

"They're real cool people. They live in a condo about a half mile from here. What do you say? You want to go?"

Connor looked at Larry, who shrugged, and he looked back at Jim. "Sure. Are we still on for the fishing trip tomorrow?"

"Yeah, be ready at nine in the morning. We're gonna do a long swim tomorrow. I'll show you one of my favorite spots."

"I'll be ready."

Later, after everything was cleaned and the two were getting into bed, Connor said, "What do you want to bet some of the people at tomorrow night's dinner will be from that island?"

"You sure are worried about that island. I don't give a fuck."

"I don't know what it is, but the fucking thing looks familiar to me. It's like I've dreamed about it or something. I think tomorrow we're gonna be invited out there."

"Connor, you just keep on thinkin'."

"Fuck you!"

27. Job Interview

Sunday, May 30, 1976

The next day at nine sharp, Jim arrived ready to do some serious fishing. He told Connor that this fishing hole was only available if the tide was coming in. Once they got in the channel, Connor realized why that was. The tide ripped through the keys and they just went with the flow. In a short time, they reached a wide expanse of shallow, open sea.

They stopped and rested. Jim pointed to the key that they were going to swim for. He said that once they got there, it was still five miles of swimming through the channels into the never ending maze of tiny keys north and east of Key West.

Connor found that snorkeling in the keys was fun. He was surprised the water was so shallow. He hadn't seen water over thirty feet deep the entire day, and he could stop and stand up most of the time. They saw an occasional shark or ray cruising in the channels all nonchalant, not giving the two swimmers a second glance.

Two hours later, they stood on a sandy beach. Jim pointed to the fish lying along the side of a mangrove about five feet down. He explained that, when threatened, the fish were able to swim into the roots of the mangrove and hide from predators.

They both went in the water, dove down to fish level, and fired. Jim's catch was a big tarpon, easily twenty pounds. Connor's was a small trash fish, all bone and little meat. It would be good for fish stew, though.

They made several more dives and, in twenty minutes, they had enough fish to feed the entire party that night, and then some.

The return trip was tough until they got back to the channel that had been ripping in when they left. Now, however, the tide was going out and they let it float them along until they turned southwest and made their way back in the direction of the RV park.

They cleaned the fish at the same beach as the day before. Connor pulled out a pinner, lit up, took a toke and passed it to Jim.

"Now don't worry, we won't get lost today." Connor smiled at him.

"Yeah, I've got you here to lead the way back!" They both laughed.

"So, do you go out and fish every day?"

"Nah, not when I work all day at the park. But I always have fish in the freezer," Jim replied.

"You know, you're a natural at spearfishing," he continued. "But you need to remember the spots I take you. Next week, I have to go to Jacksonville for about a month and you'll be on your own."

Connor nodded and finished the pinner. They gathered the fish and continued on to the RV park.

He immediately started filleting the catch. Larry was ready with the cellophane and packed each piece of the Mother's bounty on ice, setting enough aside for Garrett and Sally.

"By the way, Connor," said Jim. "I have a thing tomorrow, so I won't be able to go fishing." Before leaving to deliver the fish to his friends, he said, "I'll be back at seven to take you to the condo."

Larry and Connor showered and did some laundry. They wore the best of their hitchhiking gear. While waiting for Jim, they sat and talked about the party and wondered if there would be any women.

Connor said, "Mark my words. They're sizing us up tonight. I almost feel like we're going to a job interview."

"Connor, sometimes you're so full of shit. I just don't get your logic or your conclusion. I mean, what the fuck are we getting interviewed for? We ain't applying for a fucking job!" Larry was getting tired of hearing about how weird Connor felt about everything that was happening.

"I don't know," said Connor. "It's been fucking with me all day."

Jim came at seven sharp and they walked to the girls' condo. When they arrived, Jim introduced everyone. There was plenty to drink and Connor settled into a bourbon and beer back. Larry stuck with beer.

Everyone took turns asking the travelers about their hitchhiking tour and how they made a living. Larry walked out on the deck overlooking the ocean. Connor followed him and asked, "So, how many times were you asked if you were a roofer and a painter?"

"Okay, it feels like a job interview. I just don't understand what's going on."

They sat down to a wonderful meal cooked by Rainbow and Sunshine. The food was passed around and everyone ate in silence.

Rainbow spoke up first. "Jim told us about your dinner last night. He raved about the snapper you two cooked."

Larry answered, "Connor and I do a lot of campfire cooking. That was the first time in a while we've done fish. We buried a steelhead last year on the Columbia. It came out real good. Last night, that was fresh, fried fish. It's kinda hard to screw that up."

"You guys are on your Bicentennial Tour?" asked Joe. "How long do you plan on staying around these parts?"

"We'll be heading to Boston whenever my buddy says he can get some time off work. Soon, I hope, I'm getting antsy," replied Connor.

Joe said, "I know that Larry can roof and paint, what do *you* do, Connor?"

Connor looked at Joe for a long time. The room grew quiet and the Islanders began to fidget with curiosity. He stood and took a deep breath before answering.

"Well, if I may venture a guess, I could fish for you while Jim's up in Jacksonville. I guess I should let you guys know what I've figured out by watching and listening to you.

"First, the big one. You, you, you, and you"—he pointed to Joe, Jim, Michael, and Danny—"live on that island with the big tree on it real close to where I'm staying. Where the architects play into it, I don't know. But since we're here and not out on the island, I would say that all eight of you make up the sum of everyone who knows about whatever is going on out there.

"Apparently, there's some roofing and painting that needs to be done, which means there's one or more structures involved. And they're well camouflaged, because when I swam all the way around that island yesterday looking for answers, I couldn't see anything.

"So, why don't you invite us out to the paradise you keep so well hidden, and we'll tell you whether we want to work with you or not. Is that cool with you, Larry?"

Of the ten people at the table, eight sat with their mouths hanging open like they were catching flies.

"Connor told me tonight was going to feel like a job interview. I said it was bullshit until I got here, and you proved him right. He's real good at figuring things out."

Jim asked Connor, "What did I say that made you think we lived on the Island?"

"It's what you *didn't* say. That first day when we were out fishing and you were giving me all the landmarks to help me get back to the park. I had already been out that morning, and the best landmark was that big-assed tree on the island. I watched you avoid even looking at it, so I never mentioned it.

"And later, Larry watched you wade over to it with the fish I shot. I mean there's really only one conclusion. Right?"

Rainbow said to the other Islanders, "Well, if I had to vote right now, I'd vote them in. Let's drop the bullshit and let them know what we propose."

"So how did you come up with the four of us living out there?" asked Danny.

"Came to that conclusion because you three smell like a campfire. That means you haven't figured a good, freshwater containment system or a solar-and-fire water heater. I know Jim showers at the RV park and the four architects have condos. The one question I have is where are Kevin's and Ryan's wives? I mean, they've got the rings."

"Wow, you're good," said Kevin. "Our wives know about the Island and have been out there. Tonight was kind of a spur-of-the-moment thing. Couldn't get a sitter on short notice."

The next hour and a half, they sat around the table. Larry and Connor listened as the story of the Island was told from the beginning. The architects pulled out drawings showing the shapes of each roof. It was decided that the travelers would come out to the Island the following day.

"Well, that's enough business for me," said Larry. "I'm sure Jim's told you about our Thai weed. Why don't we go out on the deck and blow a couple of joints. Connor rolled two fatty's for the party. So let's smoke some dope, drink some beer, get loose, and party."

Before long, everyone was stoned. They sat around on the deck, watching the magic of the evening sky and listening to the waves lap a bluesy beat on the shore below them.

"The whole time Sunshine and I were on the West Coast, we heard about Thai weed, but never smoked any," Rainbow said. "We just thought it was an urban myth or something. Now I know why everyone raved about it."

"It's pretty hard to come by," said Larry. "There's not that much of it around. But the last couple of years with all the veterans coming home from Vietnam, it's been easier to get.

"Connor's got a nice connection, though, and we got real lucky before we left to go on our tour."

Everyone agreed it was the best weed they'd smoked. Joe said it reminded him of 'Nam.

"If you guys treat him real good, maybe he'll pull out the *real* good stuff. He's awfully protective of it, though," said Larry with a smile.

"Fuck you, Larry! Seriously, I won't do the good stuff with you until I think you can handle it. It's a hallucinogen, a mixture I made.

"The thing is, I like to be outdoors when I do my Special Smoke. So maybe next weekend, if we're still around and if you're into it, we can do it."

"You talkin' about the Yaqui Indian's 'Little smoke'?" asked Sunshine. "You know, from *The Teachings of Don Juan*?"

"Yes and no," Connor replied. "Yes, that's how the name evolved. But, no, it's my own concoction. It will help you separate your worlds, though, just like the good book says. I've had some amazing times with it.

"You're the first person in a while who's picked up on the Yaqui connection. That's kinda cool." He turned to Larry and gave him a you've-got-a-big-fucking-mouth look.

Feeling his silent wrath, Larry said, "I'm sorry, Connor. I shouldn't have said anything."

Larry continued. "If you guys get to know Connor, you'll find he's cut-and-dried about most things. I have an agreement with him that his Special Smoke is an unspoken treasure that he shares easily, but only when he's ready."

The evening moved on with more questions from everyone. The Islanders wanted to hear more about the Bicentennial Tour, and the travelers wanted to know what would be expected of them. Connor didn't want to get stuck in Key West and was worried about committing to anything that would stall the tour too long.

Connor and Larry ended up out on the deck on two chaise lounges quietly talking about what had transpired earlier at the table. The deck wrapped around three sides of the condo, and the girls were able to enjoy both sunrises and sunsets. They sat, watching giant storm clouds to the west of the Keys and hadn't noticed that all of the other guests had left.

Rainbow and Sunshine came out on the deck, pulled up a couple of deck chairs and sat down facing them.

"Everyone's gone. We would normally be out on the Island on a night like tonight because we're not working tomorrow. Instead, we'd like it if you two spent the night here with us," said Rainbow.

Connor got up and walked around behind Rainbow, kissed her on top of her beautiful, red head and began to rub her neck and shoulders. She cooed and commented on how good it felt. Then he moved to Sunshine and did the same thing. Sunshine melted into the massage.

"I'm really intrigued by your offer, but I made a promise to a girl in Illinois," said Connor. He walked over to his daypack and pulled out his little leather pouch. "Let me make you two a counter offer."

Larry said, "Your Special Smoke. Haven't seen that in a while."

Connor smiled his winning smile toward the girls, "You two want to watch the sunrise over the Atlantic with us in the morning?"

"I was *hoping* the night was gonna end with some of the little clay pipe. And girls, just so you know, *I* never made a promise to *anyone!*" said Larry. "And that's what I was talkin' about with Connor. He's cut-and-dried."

The girls were excited by the offer and followed Connor inside to the dinner table. He loaded the clay pipe and walked each of the ladies through their first encounter with his Special Smoke. Then he loaded Larry's and his.

By the time he cleaned the little clay pipe and put the Smoke away, the three others were standing at the handrail looking west at the same night sky as before, but as if for the first time. Connor moved in for a group hug.

"The energy I've felt all night from you two has been good." He squeezed even tighter. He could feel Larry tighten his grip, too.

"It's a feeling I get with the right energy. I feel a love for you both, and I hope you feel the goodness of my love."

Sunshine let out a laugh that was surprisingly low and sultry. "It's been too long since we've been out west." She gave Rainbow a kiss. "It's just a different vibe out there. We do feel your love, and we miss being around people who wear it on their sleeve like you do. You two are a welcomed gift. Thank you."

Connor pulled the pad off of a chair and walked to the east side of the deck. He threw the pad on the deck and sat down on it cross-legged. The ladies and Larry did the same thing. There they sat in silence and watched as the earth spun itself back into dawn and the sun broke over the Atlantic.

As usual, with his Special Smoke, Connor cried at the art exhibit that the Father put on for him. He looked around and was not surprised to see Sunshine and Rainbow naked and crying.

What *did* surprise him was seeing Larry tearing up, too. He figured it had to be the girls. They were beautiful. Connor took his clothes off and went back to gazing at the sky. Larry followed his lead and sat back down. Connor smiled. *Most things are better naked.*

Larry and the girls went into the bedroom. Connor had made the promise, Larry hadn't. From the sound of it, Larry was having the time of his life.

Connor found a quiet corner inside, lay his cushion on the floor, and slept for a while.

28. Tour of the Island

Monday, May 31, 1976

*L*arry and the redheads woke up about one in the afternoon. Connor was already up, and the coffee smelled good. He had started on a slumgullion omelet using some of the leftovers from the night before.

Fifteen minutes later, he served the bounty. Larry had already told the sisters about Connor's breakfasts. He had gone Mexican on them. They ate in silence, and then walked out to the deck to enjoy the dank afternoon air.

Sunshine came to Connor and put her arms around him. She closed her eyes with a smile that he'd seen many times before. The afterglow of his Special Smoke is a lot like a good night of sex, and in this case, apparently, there was the afterglow of that, too.

Rainbow came to his other side and hugged him, too. "We talked a little this morning about how much we're attracted to you. We like good sex, but usually that's it. We both feel an attraction to you that we haven't felt since college."

"Yet, I'm the one standing here this morning yearning for what I know was a very good time. But the attraction between us is something I figured out last night.

"I was born on the thirteenth of April, 1953, three and a half years before that, you two were born on the eleventh and twelfth of October. You see, we're opposites, almost exactly six months apart. Opposites attract. We're at the mercy of our own birthdates."

"Oh shit," said Larry, "there you go again with that pagan bullshit." He laughed. "Wouldn't have it any other way, bro."

He moved in to complete the circle of love. Soon, both ladies were crying and even Connor and Larry were tearing up.

Connor said, "I wonder if they're thinking we got lost out there on the Island."

Rainbow answered, "No, they're expecting us sometime this afternoon. So I guess we should take off. Thanks again for your Special Smoke. I'm still feeling it."

"No problem. But you should thank Larry. I never would've pulled it out if it wasn't for his big mouth!" They both thanked Larry for his big mouth.

Once dressed, they drove the Mercedes and parked near the path leading to the Island. Connor walked to the RV park and collected his fishing gear. He changed into his swimming trunks and headed out to his first Island adventure.

Jim stood talking with Larry on the beach where he first saw the trail to the tree house. Connor spotted them and walked over.

"So, Jim, is this the 'thing' you had today?"

"Yup." Jim smiled at him.

The smell of food hung thickly in the air as he led the travelers to the small clearing where they cooked. Larry looked up and spotted the platform in the Banyan tree. He pointed it out to Connor who finally understood why he couldn't see it when he swam around the Island. It was completely covered in vines.

"Wow! Did you guys build that?" asked Connor.

"Not the central platform," Jim answered. "We *did* make some improvements and put up the other structures." He pointed out toward the curtains of vines. "You'll see them once you're up there. We also brought over all this furniture down here."

"That's a nice cookstove you got there. Looks like it was built in the thirty's. How the hell did you get it out here?" asked Connor.

Joe told the story of the cookstove and how hard it had been to get the heavy hunk of steel out to the Island. All four of the original Islanders had pinched a finger or had smashed a toe by the time they got it into place.

They had done it at night and just getting it across the highway and down the trail to the water had been tough. They floated it over on a platform lashed between the canoes. Everyone had been happy to get it for free, but felt they'd paid plenty by the time it was in place.

They sat down to a good meal of poached fish and rice. Larry immediately realized he needed to bring some spices out to the Island. These folks needed to wake up their taste buds!

While they were eating, Connor said to Larry, "Do you remember the first night I brought up the tour to you? We were at Bob's cabin, and you had trouble finding it because he had camouflaged the trail so well. You noticed the three switchbacks and all of the vines that work like curtains?"

After the meal, Connor walked back to the beach. He stood by himself at the water's edge for a while and opened his senses to this little paradise. After putting on his mask and fins, he walked out to his waist in the warm water. He leisurely rolled onto his back and floated away from the Island until he felt the tide gently grab him.

Once out a ways, he swam over to a neighboring, C-shaped key with a lagoon. He swam into the lagoon and dove along the roots of the mangrove to survey for fish. With the lingering glow of his Special Smoke filling him, the water felt like warm oil. He seemed to slide through it with no resistance at all. The feeling was like nothing he'd ever experienced.

He dove, surfaced and spun in circles enjoying the feeling. Then he dove and swam across the bottom for as long as his lungs would allow. He burst out of the water at full speed and lay on his back laughing in his bliss. He floated on the surface staring up at the sky and imagined himself a seal, like he'd seen on television.

Suddenly, the sound of nearby splashing tore him out of his revelry. It was Jim, Joe, and the ladies.

Jim said, "You look like you're having too much fun out here."

Connor replied, "It's my Special Smoke. The water feels so warm and the smell of the brine is electric to me. I've always loved the water, but never the way I do right now."

They joined him and swam around the little lagoon. Connor thought this would always be a place in his mind where all things were good. At everyone's urging, he swam back to the Island for his first tour of nirvana.

The main tree house led to a little city in the branches. The scope took him by surprise. All of it was perfectly camouflaged.

He saw the influence of the architects on the Island. The style of construction had changed as soon as the ladies were included. Their designs were an adaption of the roof joist connections they first used in Oregon, interlocking and secured with two stainless bolts that enabled them to create low and sweet curves in the roofs over their bedrooms.

Connor counted six small structures other than the original platform. They all conformed to the tree and were connected by elevated walkways. Each roof was unique, presenting a complicated set of problems for Larry to figure out.

The redheads built their platform under a perfect slightly sloping dome. They briefly explained about the energy of the shape. Ryan and Kevin's platform had two rooms and was the biggest building in the trees. It was covered by a geodesic dome. Next door, a seventh platform, still in its infancy, was intended for their kids once they were old enough to be trusted with the secret of the paradise.

After the tour, Rainbow and Sunshine explained that they had six pallets of cedar shakes leftover from a previous project. Now, they wanted to put them on the roofs of all the buildings to eliminate their biggest headache, the leaks. They described the summer monsoons that were about a month away.

Larry asked about felt paper, tar, flashing, and other materials that would be needed to do the job right. They said all the materials were in a storage shed. They were leftovers from other projects they'd finished over the past year.

So they decided that Larry would supervise the roofing and Connor would take over the spearfishing while Jim was up in Jacksonville.

Larry told them they could get done before the monsoons, but they had to start soon. He figured it would take them about two or three weeks to complete the project.

The next evening, the Islanders, that now included the travelers, ferried over all of the supplies they would need. It took many trips with the canoes.

Larry was curious and asked "What did you use cedar for down here?"

"The government was going to test them on several buildings for durability." Ryan answered "We did just one small out building, and then they cancelled the project. We were stuck with all these shingles. They were stuck with the bill." He had a devilish smile.

"I guess it all worked out in the end, right?" Larry laughed.

They had all of the materials stacked on the ground below the main platform. There were over a hundred bundles of cedar shakes, twelve bundles of ridge wood, twenty gallons of tar, and twenty-five rolls of felt. Using some rope, they pulled the materials up and distributed them throughout the complex.

Over the next week, Connor and Jim went out to fish. Every day they went to a different place, and then every evening, they studied marine navigation maps to help Connor with his headings.

One day, Jim took Connor fifteen miles through the Keys to a buoy in the open water west of the Island. It was the beginning of a shipping lane into the north side of the keys, left over from the days of the fish canneries.

One cannery in particular had long since been torn down, but the dock was still there. The road to the dock was still in good shape as were the boat ramps and parking lot. It was a popular place for the locals to launch their boats and park their trailers.

Jim and Connor sat on the buoy as it gently rocked back and forth. It rose fifteen feet out the water with a bright red flashing light at the top and had a twenty-foot platform surrounding it.

Jim said, "This is what the locals call the Smugglers Buoy. Florida has more coastline than any other state in the lower forty-eight. The cops can't watch it all, so it's a good place for drug smugglers to run their weed.

This is where they turn northeast and head into the Keys. They push small barges up to a whole bunch of landings and unload tons of weed. They put it into trucks and ship it all over the states."

Jim pointed south and continued, "Cuba's only ninety miles south of here. Before Castro took over, there used to be quite a big charter business ferrying people to and from Havana. That's all gone now. They say the Cartel flies its weed to Jamaica and ships it up here."

He pointed to the northeast at another flashing light. "That's the next buoy following the north edge of the Keys.

"One night, I lay here waiting for the tide to turn and a barge full of bales came within twenty feet of me. It scared me shitless! I didn't want them to see me, so I hid over the side. Luckily, everyone on board was busy looking for that strobe light on the next buoy.

"A couple of days later, I canoed up that way looking for their landing. Sure enough, not two miles past that buoy, they had unloaded their booty. The barge was still there. I got a couple of ounces off the deck. Kept me stoned for a while."

Connor pointed out a dark blue line in the water several miles to the south that ran to the east as far as he could see. "What's that dark blue water?" he asked.

"That's the beginning of the Florida Current," said Jim. "It goes around the south tip of the Keys, then turns to the north and into the Gulf Stream. It runs all the way to Norway. It's deep and swift.

"I swam down to it once. I don't recommend it. It swept me five miles east before I could get out of its current. It took me a while to find my way back home, too. Hell, I didn't get back until after dark.

"It wasn't a total loss, though. I discovered a couple of good fishing spots on the way." Jim grinned at Connor.

They began the swim back when the tide turned. Before getting back, Connor shot a big grouper he'd spotted on the way out. He swam down about twenty-five feet and shot the fish in the head while it was still another ten feet below him. The fish swam for ten more feet when Connor grabbed the spear and pulled it up to the surface.

Connor smiled at Jim and said, "There's no way I could've done that a week ago."

Jim said, "I don't think I could do it *now*! That was amazing! It looks like I'm leaving my friends in good hands."

They tethered the fish through its gill and Connor pulled it all the way back to the sand mound and cleaned it.

When they got back, Jim told the Islanders that they had swum close to thirty-five miles, and he thought Connor could do it again tomorrow with no problem.

Larry and Connor got busy cooking dinner. They liked to grill the fish with the skin on. The fish absorbed the smoke of the cook fire, adding a flavor that no store-bought spice could deliver.

"That's really good, how did you do that?" asked Danny.

"Well, Connor and I just play it by ear. There really isn't a recipe as such. We just use our imagination and experience. We *have* done a lot of campfire cooking. You should just watch what we do, and you'll get the idea."

"Yeah," said Connor. "It's really not that hard."

After dinner, Jim said, "I don't think you guys are gonna miss a meal when I'm gone. Connor will be showing *me* a few tricks when I get back."

"I don't know about that. You got way more years of fishing these parts than me. I can't wait till you get back. We'll have a good swim, once I'm in shape."

Everyone wondered what Connor, in shape, would be. He already seemed to be in better shape than any one there.

29. Nearing Completion

Wednesday, June 9, 1976

Jim left early in the morning and Connor went on his first solo fishing trip. He got back at midday with two fish, and then went to town for supplies. Joe tagged along. With his bad limbs, roofing wasn't something he could do. He became the designated gofer.

They walked and after a bit of probing, Joe told Connor a brief version of his war experience and about how he ended up on the Island.

Connor told him of his idea of capturing rain off of all the roofs to use as drinking water and setting up a shower reservoir that could be heated by using the cook stove.

"Why waste all that energy on just cooking. You guys will be surprised how fast a little copper tubing coiled in the cookstove will heat water. That way, I won't have to put up with your smelly asses all the time." They both laughed.

They bought supplies and were back on the shore ready to wade over to the Island when Joe asked, "Do you mind if I ask you a personal question?"

Connor answered, a little surprised. "I guess that depends on the question. Shoot."

"Are you gay?"

Connor laughed hard for a moment, and then said, "The girls must've told you that I turned them down. That's because I promised a girl I would be faithful. Don't get me wrong, I really wanted to sleep with both of them, but I'm taken.

"You don't have to worry. I'm not admiring your ass as you walk away." They both laughed again.

He went on to tell Joe about his run-in with Charles back in Gardiner, Montana. Connor also told him that both he and Larry had gay brothers.

"I will say this," said Connor. "I *do* carry around a certain resentment for the gay population. In the sixties, I was proud to be gay. I tried to stay gay all the time. Then, when I got back from the Army, I was forced to be happy. If I said I was gay, men would start hitting on me. You know how easy it is to rhyme the word gay? It's really the poet inside me that carries the resentment the most."

"Larry's gonna get a kick out of this," he said as they arrived on the Island.

For the first time, Connor noticed that the wade to the Island was very secluded. The only way to be seen crossing was from the trees where Larry had been when he saw Jim cross or to be in a boat. There weren't any boats in this area because of the shallow water, so they could cross without being seen by outsiders.

Like everything Larry did, he excelled at it. The roofing was coming along faster than anyone expected. He couldn't stand around, pointing a finger and supervising. He was a hands-on guy and only knew one speed. That meant the roofing was going to go fast.

The architects had been coming out every evening to see how the work was progressing. Sometimes the girls stayed the night, usually with someone different. They did like to spread their sexual needs around.

After dinner one night, when all of the Islanders were present, Larry brought up the painting job. He wouldn't commit to that part of the project.

"I have to get back to my uncle's place to get some mail. After that, I might be willing to teach someone how to paint."

Then he said to Connor, "You must be enjoying yourself, swimming all day while we work our asses off around here." He was smiling, but his voice held a trace of envy.

"I get to swim and you get the redheads, right? No more complaining. I don't want to hear about it," Connor shot back at him with a smile. There was envy in his voice, as well.

"I tell you what, Larry. When you finish the roofs and before we leave for your aunt and uncle's, what do you say you and me go out for a day. Jim left his gear here.

"Why don't we take a little swim right now? No spear guns. Then you can tell me if you want to spend a whole day doing it."

"You got a deal, as long as we have an after-dinner joint first."

"Well, of course, you couldn't get me out there straight."

After the joint, Connor took Larry on a three-mile swim. He did just like Jim had done on Connor's first lesson. He threw on the afterburners, and Larry kept up just fine. Connor came to a stop and stood up in the same spot Jim had. Afterward, they swam the three miles back, nice and easy, because they were fighting the tide.

Standing on the beach back on the Island, Larry said, "That was more fun than I thought it would be. You know, I should be done with the roofing on Friday morning, maybe even Thursday evening. Why don't we go out on Saturday?"

"Cool," said Connor. "It sure took a long time to finally get you in the water!"

"Well, I haven't forgotten what happens in *Jaws*!" said Larry.

"And I'm *still* glad I never saw it!" They both laughed.

When they got back to the cooking circle, Larry told everyone that he would be tagging along with Connor that Saturday for the whole day. He didn't want to shoot anything, so he would just swim along and enjoy a day of Key West snorkeling.

Then Connor dropped the bombshell. "On Friday, after dinner, what do you guys say we try my Special Smoke adventure? I feel the closeness here, and on Friday, I hope you'll feel that closeness in a way you can't imagine."

He turned and walked away, back toward the water. When he got to the narrow beach he started running and dove in. It was a nice, shallow dive, and he skimmed right over the sandy bottom. He gave his best Olympic swimmer imitation and sped off to his favorite lagoon. He was starting to get muscles he didn't know he had.

Larry sat there with a sheepish look on his face as the Islanders silently stared at him, waiting for an explanation.

"Honestly, he doesn't confide in me when it comes to his Special Smoke. Ever since I opened my big mouth at the condo, he's been real quiet about it. He told me not to do it again.

"Back home he'd walk into a party, and I never knew if he'd pull it out. He told me he had to feel the vibes of the group before he'd let anyone smoke it. He wanted to have a good time, not babysit a bunch of crybabies."

Everyone walked to the water and swam out to Connor's little lagoon and joined him. Whenever Connor was in the water, he always regressed to his childhood. It was all fun and games in the lagoon.

Friday, June 11, 1976

On Friday, after dinner, Connor said, "Let's go up to the tree house to do this. You'll all end up in your rooms contemplating life anyway, so we may as well start this trip up there."

Everyone sat in a close circle. Connor stood in the middle and administered the Smoke to one person at a time, and then he sat and took two hits for himself.

"All this does is magnify what you already know and who you really are. I hope you all enjoy it as much as I do. If you're game, let's watch the sunrise before we go to bed."

Everyone laughed as the effect of Connor's Special Smoke overtook them. Connor stood up and climbed down to the ground and went to swim for a while. He could hear everyone talking and laughing as the sounds rolled out across the water, making him chuckle to himself. His Special Smoke was doing its job of bringing everyone together on a plane that they wouldn't be able to explain in the morning.

He lost track of time, and thought he must've fallen asleep while floating. He stripped naked and went to snuggle with the ladies. Larry was already there, so he found an unoccupied corner and snuggled with Rainbow, while she snuggled with Sunshine, who had Larry wrapped like a cocoon.

Saturday, June 12, 1976

He woke hours after sunrise. He smiled and felt well-rested and hoped someone had enjoyed the sunrise. It turned out that everyone had enjoyed it, except him. He was the only one who could sleep well and long on his Smoke. Larry had explained that he'd seen it before and advised them not to wake him.

The sunrise had been magical, and they cried at the beauty of it. Connor's Special Smoke could take a normal sunrise and turn it into a life experience, one not soon forgotten.

Everyone had returned to bed before Connor woke and slept into the afternoon. Connor, not wanting to wake Larry, went out and shot dinner. The fish fillets were on ice and he was swimming around in his little lagoon when he heard Larry calling his name.

Connor swam over to the beach and said, "Hey, Larry. Sorry I went out without you. It was getting late and you were still in bed."

"No problem, I needed the sleep. Maybe I can go out with you tomorrow."

"Sure thing."

Everyone was up and went around hugging each other as the last feelings of Connor's Special Smoke flickered away. It left them filled with the joy that Connor could feel everyday while living with the Islanders.

30. Making the Transaction

Alex, Lucas, and JJ

As the Islanders ate dinner that Saturday evening, Alex, Lucas, and JJ were getting into one of the two rubber rafts the CIA had provided them. They had four black, waterproof, and virtually unsinkable duffel bags stuffed with 7.2 million dollars loaded in the second raft.

The wind was coming out of the southwest at a constant twelve miles per hour, creating a two-foot, choppy surf that would make running into it an unpleasant adventure. They disembarked from a dock at the end of a long, gated road.

The dock had been bought by the Colombians through an American subsidiary. They would park long-haul truck trailers there, and when a shipment came in, they would bring semi-trucks in and load the trailers under the cover of night. Then they would send the trucks out to unload at many drop sites across the east coast.

The three other agents left at the dock were not happy. They had been saddled with agents they didn't know or trust. They had been in Miami longer than the three in the raft and were pissed that the new guys were given the job of delivering the money. They had no idea how important and influential their coworkers were to the Cartel.

All six agents were dressed in camo fatigues. The three friends felt out of place not being in their usual black suits, but the fatigues were cooler. They all wore baseball caps saying "DEA".

They had gone over the instructions at least five times before they left the Cartel's office. If for any reason they felt threatened, they were to throw the money overboard. The duffel bags would float. The bags also had a homing beacon that would automatically start transmitting if it contacted the water.

They were to attach the four duffel bags together before they threw them overboard. The ropes they needed were laid out lengthwise on the bottom of the raft bow to stern: one port, one center line, one starboard. They had laid the duffel bags on the ropes, wrapped them and tied off the ropes. They ran a fourth rope through the handles of each duffel bag and tied it off, too. If they needed to jettison the payload, they were ready.

The three friends left an hour before dark, pulling the raft that carried the money. Alex steered while Lucas navigated, using a marine map of the area. JJ was on the bow in the never-ending spray looking for debris.

It was slow going until they hit open water and could see the beacon of the Smugglers Buoy. Alex increased the throttle, and they weathered the rough seas until they got to the buoy.

Once there, they moored to the northeast corner and managed to get on the platform. Despite the slack tide, the buoy was not much better than the lurching raft. The sky was a light pink, and they silently watched the show as they waited for the tugboat pushing a small barge loaded with bales of good, Colombian Gold weed.

Lucas had been quiet most of the day. They were made to go over their instructions until they could recite them word for word. When they were finished with their handler, they went to lunch. JJ and Alex had asked him if anything was wrong, but they got no answer.

Now, with both rafts moored to the buoy and in the deepening twilight, he finally broke his silence.

"You know, I've been thinking about getting out. You know what I mean? Take a step back and disappear for a while. I don't know about you two, but I've got just over three million and some change. I haven't said anything, but I bought a little place about twenty miles out of Berne, Switzerland. I could retire and live very nicely off the interest."

"Hell yes!" said JJ. "If this whole drop tonight goes according to plan, we're gonna be more important and more trusted, and the money should come pouring in. I've been thinking the same thing for quite a while. Only, I want five million and I'm getting close. I have just over four right now."

Alex said, "I guess great minds think alike. I think it's hilarious that we make a pact not to talk finances, and yet we're all thinking along the same lines. I bought a small house a few miles northeast of Milan. I planned on inviting you guys over this summer so we could discuss our retirement.

"I just don't like living with the knowledge that, if we get busted, we're not gonna see that Swiss money for a lot of years, if ever, because we're gonna be in Leavenworth! I think I'd rather have my kids thinking I suffered from burnout and moved away. It's a double-edged sword here. We fuck up one way, we're in jail. We fuck up the other way, we're fucking fish food.

"And like today, dealing with that arrogant Colombian son of a bitch, making us recite the directions over and over. I felt like taking my gun out and drilling the motherfucker!

"And by the way, I have five and a half million. I made a couple of very profitable investments."

"Yeah, cocaine does turn a good profit," said JJ. "We ought to make one more, big score before we call it quits. I'll go in on it with you. What do you say, Lucas? You want to pad that retirement fund a little bit?"

"Okay, we're all in this together," said Lucas. "One more, big coke deal. We'll use my connection in New York. Bring the coke in from Colombia to Miami in an embassy package. Then I'll take it to New York and in forty-eight hours, we turn our three hundred thousand into four million.

"I'm gonna resign from the DEA citing that I just don't believe I'm doing any good and walk out of there and disappear. I'll hang a private detective shingle outside on the front porch in Switzerland in case I get bored."

The slack tide slowly reversed and was now flowing into the Keys. They heard the low drone of a diesel motor for thirty minutes before they first spotted the tugboat pushing the barge. It was coming north, around the west end of the Florida Current.

The tugboat was a converted minesweeper from World War II. Its teakwood hull and shallow draft made it perfect for getting into the shallow bays of the South Pacific islands that the Japanese had left mined when they retreated. This one had been refitted with push skaggs on the front that were designed to mate with a shallow-draft barge. It was the perfect tandem to get into the Keys.

They watched as the tugboat turned and slowly came at them. It was almost on them before they saw the crew tossing the bales of weed overboard. Suddenly, the bright searchlight of a Coast Guard cutter came on, trained on the barge. The crew of the barge continued to throw the bales overboard until they all floated in the water.

Alex and JJ jumped into the raft with the duffel bags, slid the money into the water and watched as it drifted off with the bales of marijuana on the tide. Then they went to intercept the cutter.

After showing their DEA badges and explaining they were acting on a tip, they helped the Coast Guard arrest the crew. The captain of the cutter wasn't pleased that the DEA had shown up to take some of the glory from him. When Lucas tried to press him on his plans, the captain told him his immediate plan was to put the three DEA agents back in their rafts.

The crew of the cutter took control of the tugboat. They planned to take the barge and the tugboat to Miami. Before the three agents disembarked from the barge, they overheard the captain say that they would return in the morning to retrieve the bales of marijuana.

They got back into the rubber raft and began searching for the duffel bags, keeping an eye out for the blinking red light on the transmitter's battery pack. They searched for three hours on the dark, choppy sea, weaving in and out of the bales of weed, circling many of the tiny keys, and searching the roots of the mangroves. Their portable spotlights were very powerful, and they assumed that the bags would be easy to spot. They were wrong.

"Where the fuck are those duffel bags?" JJ yelled. "I mean, this receiver isn't receiving any signal! I wonder if those 'unsinkable' bags sank. It would be just our luck."

They finally gave up the search. With concern on their faces, they headed back to the landing. They talked about how fucked they were if the Coast Guard found the money the next day, or even worse, if they couldn't find it at all.

JJ drove the raft at the stern with Alex and Lucas mid-raft, port and starboard. They pulled the other raft, now empty. All three stared straight ahead, slacked-jawed with similar visions of the reaction their handler would have when he heard their story.

They got back to the landing and explained what had happened to the other agents. The biggest of the three stood up, walked over, and began yelling at the three friends.

"I been working southern Florida without a problem since the beginning! Now they hitch me to you hot shots and everything's gone to hell! What the fuck are we gonna do now?" He turned to the other two agents and spoke to them in Spanish.

JJ and Lucas turned and started talking in English. Alex looked as though he was part of the conversation, but was listening to the big guy telling the other agents that they ought to kill the new guys and take their chances with the handler themselves.

The two other guys said that they should let the handler deal with them. They looked at Alex, who had drawn his .45 automatic. Lucas and JJ saw this and drew theirs, too.

Alex pointed his weapon at the big guy who wanted to kill them and said, "Let me tell you, big mouth! You shut the fuck up, or I'll strip you naked and fuck you right up the ass! You got me, you stupid, fucking asshole?"

Lucas pointed his gun and said, "What do you guys say we all calm down and get these two rafts loaded, and then find out what the fuck we're gonna do back in Miami."

Alex watched with his .45 drawn as the five other agents got the rafts loaded. They drove back to Miami in separate rigs and trailers. Once the three friends were alone, Alex said, "I thought we were gonna shoot it out for a minute."

JJ was pissed, "I'll tell you, if that big fucker runs his mouth again, I'll triple-tap him and leave him floating somewhere."

"That's a little project we'll get done before we retire. Fucking guy's a douche bag," said Lucas.

31. Colombian Gold

Sunday, June 13, 1976

*E*arly the next morning, Connor and Larry took off swimming to the north. The wind had died down from yesterday and it was mostly clear. The sky was thick with gulls, more than at any time since they'd been in Florida.

"So, here's the deal," said Connor. "We're gonna swim and let the tide carry us about two miles northeast. There's a nice beach there, and we'll rest for a while. I'll swim a short distance away and fish. Once I've shot our dinner, we'll get stoned and wait for the tide to turn. We'll let it give us a ride back to the Island.

"Lead on, great white fisherman," Larry said. He was nervous, but was doing a good job of covering it up.

"Be cool, little brown turd."

About an hour later, the two were sitting on a small, secluded beach lighting the perfect pinner that Connor had twisted before they left. They passed it back and forth without saying a word. Larry stowed the roach and they sat back as the high enveloped them.

Larry said, "I can't believe how quick we got here. It was kinda like swimming hard down a river. We were flying there for a while."

"Yeah, Jim taught me pretty good. Knowing the tide times is the secret."

They sat on the sand, glowing in the peace of the high for about twenty minutes when Connor said, "I could get used to this, I think. If Carol and I don't work out, I could really enjoy myself down here. If they let me live on the Island, and I could get a job. Man! That would be paradise."

"I don't know, bro. It would be hard to leave the northwest for a long time. Before you knew it, you'd be missing walking outside and seeing a snow-capped mountain. And fishing with a pole rather than a spear. I know I'd miss it."

"Yeah. Fuck, I hate being homesick. I guess it would happen. It always has, no matter where I'm at. I always end up wanting to be back home in Oregon, eventually."

They sat quietly perusing their own little worlds when Connor got up with his spear gun, mask, and fins in hand. "I'll be back in a bit. We should get out of here as soon as the tide turns."

***

Half an hour after Connor and Larry left to go fishing that morning, the first of the Colombian bales reached the Island coming from the southwest. Joe was on the beach and noticed a bale that had already landed and the long line of bales following it.

He called out, and soon, Michael and Danny joined him. They rushed to collect the bales into nice neat stacks. It was a hard job requiring a person on each end of the bale. Michael just kept pushing them to the beach while Joe and Danny stacked them. The stack grew to about five feet high, eight feet wide and about forty feet long. It was slowly filling up the beach.

A little over an hour later, they stood and stared at their retirement fund and wondered how they were going to sell it all. They heard a motor and turned to see a shallow-draft Coast Guard boat coming right at them.

"Well, I hope they don't think this shit is ours," said Joe.

The guy operating the boat did a nifty sideways landing and the man in charge stepped out like a young version of MacArthur landing at Manila. "How are you guys doing today? I see you've been very busy."

Just then, three landing crafts came into view. They were holdovers from World War II. It looked like a scene from *Sands of Iwo Jima*. They came right to the water's edge and dropped their front gates, revealing five or six Coast Guard grunts in each craft who poured out and stood at attention. One of the launches already had about fifteen bales inside.

"It looks like they've been here awhile," said Joe. "I wonder if they watched us stack this shit."

The guy doing his best MacArthur impersonation smiled at the three and asked, "You guys feel like helping us load?"

229

Danny answered, "Not really. I think stacking it here was enough for one day."

"Let me rephrase," he said, still smiling. "If you guys help us load the marijuana bales, I won't see any reason to call the local sheriff and have you arrested."

They helped, but had lost their enthusiasm. The Coast Guard grunts loaded most of it. The young MacArthur didn't even ask them for their ID's. The Islanders told them they had been canoeing and spotted the bales.

The Coast Guard was happy they recovered it before it sank. It would be good public relations for them when the story broke. Of course, the DEA wouldn't be mentioned at all.

Before getting back into his boat, the young MacArthur said, "You saved us a lot of time. You have a good day."

The launches raised their gates, backed down the beach, turned and left. The Islanders stood and watched their dreams of millions sail off toward the horizon.

"Well," said Joe, "I guess we'll have to keep buying weed. But on the bright side, we just had twenty-five Coast Guard walking all over this beach for two hours, and not one of them noticed the trail or any of the structures. The camouflage really does work, huh."

"Yes, it does," said Danny, "but I'd rather have the weed."

Suddenly, Michael spotted a bale that had sunk in about fifteen feet of water about seventy feet away from the beach. They got some rope and two buoys from camp.

With Michael diving down several times, he got the rope around the bale. He ran it through the eyes of the buoys and back to shore. With Joe and Danny pulling on the rope and Michael keeping the buoys above the bale, they managed to get it floating. Then they dragged it onto the beach.

They hauled it back to the cook stove in the clearing and tore it apart, separating the water-logged outside layer from the dry center. They burned all of the wet stuff in the cook stove. The exploding seeds sounded like miniature popcorn and smelled like heaven.

Danny quickly set to work on a joint. He sifted seeds and rolled a four-paper spliff out of the dry weed. He held it out for the others to see and quickly lit it. He took a hit and passed it around.

"Well, we aren't millionaires anymore," said Joe. "But we can sell most of this and buy the parts we need for a water reservoir like Connor's been talking about."

"That sounds like a good idea," said Danny. "We should get a couple thousand out of this, easy. Let's celebrate! We really should have a barbecue. Jim keeps saying that those two hitchhikers can do it up right. Let's get the fixin's. They'll be happy to cook."

"That sounds good," said Michael. "I've been craving a good steak dinner for a while."

Connor and Larry got back from their swim with five small fish. As they approached the beach, they saw the many footprints and impressions left by the gates of the three landing craft.

They walked back to the clearing to Joe, Danny, and Michael, who were more red-eyed than the guys just getting out of the ocean. They looked at Connor and Larry through tiny slits for eyes and with big, shit-eating grins. In front of them sat about ten or twelve pounds of great-looking, Colombian Gold bud on a tarp.

Connor and Larry stopped short in shock, their eyes bugged out and mouths gaped open. Larry recovered first and asked, "Anything strange happen while we were gone?"

Joe, Danny, and Michael started at the same time. They were so stoned that getting a complete sentence out of any of them was like proving there really was a Sasquatch: Impossible. After a lot of repeating, the entire story finally unfolded.

"Where were the architects while all of this went on?" asked Connor.

"That's what I was doing out on the beach. I walked out there to say goodbye to them," answered Joe. "I mean, they no more than got out of sight when I turned and spotted that first bale as it hit the beach. After that it was just a blur. Like I said, before we knew it, the Coast Guard was on the beach, all looking around. Not one even had a clue there was a trail leading back here." He smiled proudly.

Danny said, "We're going to town to buy some steak. We'll buy if you guys cook. We need to celebrate. You guys have been a godsend. Now you're our good luck charms, too."

Larry said, "What do you say, Connor? You want to go get the fixin's so we can't blame these guys if we fuck it up?"

Michael, Joe, and Danny grabbed the two travelers and started to dance them around in a circle, jumping up and down and laughing at the top of their lungs.

Connor and Larry broke free, and Connor said, "You guys should find a bale of weed every day!"

The travelers quickly changed, and they left for town. They stopped by to invite the architects to dinner, but everyone had family stuff going on later or was in a business meeting and couldn't talk. No one mentioned what went on after they had left the Island that morning.

"Their loss. We'll tell them tomorrow," said Joe.

Danny bought the meat that Larry picked out. Joe shadowed the travelers and paid for the side dishes. Connor bought a quart of medium-priced bourbon he'd never seen before, thinking he might be able to get "the Hemingway effect" with a better grade of bourbon. Everyone bought beer and ice. They'd thought ahead and had a canoe stashed alongside the highway to float everything back to the Island.

In no time, the travelers cooked and served the five-course meal. They fielded questions from the three Islanders the whole time they were cooking.

Connor said to Larry, "You know, I been thinking about a TV show where you and I travel around and teach people the art of outdoor cooking. I mean, we've been cooking in front of people asking questions this whole trip. You know, it could be a fifteen-minute spot on some fishing show on Saturday at five in the afternoon." Connor smiled.

"I love you, Connor. You just keep on thinkin', buddy!"

"Fuck you, Larry." They laughed.

Everyone sat in a circle around the big, wooden spool that Jim found when he first moved out to the Island. It had been stuck in a mangrove and he floated it back to the beach. Then, with everyone's help, they rolled it into the small clearing.

It had been the centerpiece of the clearing for almost two years, and this was the best meal ever to be laid out on it. It was covered with bread, asparagus, Brussel sprouts, corn, and mashed potatoes. In the center was a pile of spicy, rare beef. Connor had even made a boatload of gravy for the spuds.

For the next hour, it sounded like feeding time on a hog farm with a continuous variety of audible grunts and burps. One by one, they got up from the table and moved their chairs to form a circle under the platform.

Connor cracked the bourbon, took a pull and passed it to the right followed by a spliff. He winced yet again and decided that Hemingway must not have had taste buds. When the bottle and spliff came back around, he took another toke, chased it with the bourbon, and washed it all down with some ice-cold beer. The bourbon was gone first, followed by the spliff. Everyone was pretty much toasted by the time the beer was gone and the sun was down.

Connor said to Larry, "What do you say, bro? One last swim in the morning, then we'll split back north Tuesday or Wednesday?"

Larry answered with a slur, "Tell you what. I'll go, but we gotta get out of here early. The architects are gonna be here around noon with a couple pieces of flashing for the girls' roof. I'm gonna give the tenants a walk-through for their final approval.

"I say we leave Thursday. You've been swimming, and I've been roofing. I'd like to go downtown and bar hop for a night."

Connor stood and was up the tree in a flash. He poked his head out of the window and said, "I got the girls' bed, you got Jim's bed, bro." He was gone.

Larry stuck around long enough to help Joe up the tree and everyone else, too. He was the last one up and only fell twice before he made it onto the platform.

32. Consequences

Alex, Lucas, and JJ

When the Coast Guard arrived in Key West to pick up the jettisoned weed, the agents were back in the same room where they'd first received their instructions. They had been searched and disarmed. Four Colombians in fatigues stood behind them with assault rifles pointed at their backs. A fifth, with a silenced .45 automatic, stood to their side. He was obviously their commander.

Their handler, the same one they'd talked to on the previous morning, who had repeatedly made them recite their directions back to him before they left with the cash, was seated on a couch. A coffee table stood between him and the six agents.

The big-mouthed agent, who had stayed at the landing and wanted to shoot the three friends, started talking to the handler in English.

"We stayed on shore like you told us. Then they came back six hours later saying they lost the money. They told us they had to throw it in the water to avoid the Coast Guard getting it. Then they couldn't find it again.

"I don't believe them. I think they know where the money is, and they're using the Coast Guard to hide the fact that they stole it!"

The handler stood slowly. He looked up at the big agent who was throwing the three friends under the bus until he finally finished babbling.

"You should shut your mouth!" He pointed at the agent.

He turned to Lucas and asked, "What happened?"

Lucas told him the facts, exactly as they happened. They put the money in the water and watched the flashing light as it floated off with the bales of weed. The receiver had picked up the signal right before they boarded the barge.

They were on the barge for about an hour before the Coast Guard captain told them to leave. When they got back to the raft, the receiver was no longer picking up the signal.

He explained that it was dark, and they drove through all of the floating bales of product, searching with their spot lights. Then, they returned to the buoy and circled every island they had passed, but were unable to find the duffel bags.

"We'll go back out there before first light with both boats, and we'll find it," declared Lucas.

The handler confirmed the Coast Guard bust. He also confirmed that no cash or weed had been recovered yet. The captain and crew of the tug and barge were to be released to the Colombian embassy and the vessels impounded.

Alex realized the Cartel had a Coast Guard member on their payroll. *Why the fuck not?*

Suddenly, a commotion came from the next room. The handler went quiet and grew ashen. He turned and moved away from the door which suddenly burst open.

A man, who couldn't have been more than five foot two, walked in with a cleaver in his hand. He was the same man the three friends had first met with three weeks before.

He spoke in Spanish to the Colombians in the room. "Do you think these gringos stole the money?"

With no hesitation, the handler answered, "Well, I've known these three"—he pointed at the three friends—"since they were in Colombia, that's been three years now. They've always done what was asked of them with no problems. They've handled much more cash than this on numerous occasions and never let us down."

He pointed to the other three agents. "These other three are yours. I don't know them at all."

The little guy with the cleaver pointed at the big agent. He signaled to one of the guards. Without warning, the guard hit the agent with the big mouth in the head from behind with the butt of his rifle. Stunned, the agent went down, crashing into the coffee table and rolling onto the floor. Everyone watched as he slowly came to. When he tried to get up, two of the guards held him down as they forced his hand onto the coffee table.

The man swung the cleaver and, with a smooth stroke, cut the agent's little finger off at the base, nicking his ring finger in the process. The two guards quickly hauled the screaming agent out of the room. His severed finger remained on the table in a small pool of blood.

The man swung the cleaver back and forth in a threatening manner. He spoke in Spanish, "My name is Sebastian. The Coast Guard will be picking up all of the marijuana bales they can find today, all day. You are to stay away until tomorrow morning. Then, you will go back into the area and search for the money.

"Since your receiver quit working, you'll be given two more. If the Coast Guard finds the money, we will get it back after a sizable finder's fee. But they don't *know* about the money, so they won't be looking for it. Chances are, *you'll* find it." The five remaining agents quickly nodded their heads.

He continued, "I will have men waiting for you at the landing tomorrow. If you don't have the money when you return, you will be brought back here, and I will cut your balls off and feed them to you!"

The man buried the cleaver in the table right next to the little finger and left the room. As the door shut behind him, the agents started talking all at once.

"Shut the fuck up!" the commander shouted. "Sebastian is in Miami because of your fuck-up in Colombia." He pointed to the three friends. "It will be a while before he can return. He doesn't like being so close to you agents. You stay here until I get back. Then you will go out at first light tomorrow and do as you were told." He left the room in disgust.

The five agents stood silently, looking at each other nervously. After a very long half hour, their .45 automatics were returned, each one with a brand new silencer. They admired their new toys and relaxed, knowing they were again able to defend themselves.

The door opened and the agent with the missing finger walked through, cradling his hand that was now bandaged. His eyes looked dulled by pain killers.

Sebastian walked back into the room followed by the commander who had five manila envelopes in his hand. The agent with the bandage started speaking rapidly in Spanish. Sebastian

236

pulled a silenced twenty-two from his coat pocket, turned to the agent and put a bullet into his forehead. The agent collapsed in a heap to the floor. The gun hardly made a sound. Sebastian looked at it and smiled.

The commander said, "There's five thousand dollars in each envelope. When you bring the money back, each of you will get fifty thousand more. Sebastian says you did the right thing by putting the cash adrift. Our man on the Coast Guard cutter confirmed that you convinced the ship captain you were there on a tip and that there was no money in your raft."

Without a word, the agents took the envelopes and put them in their breast pockets. They quickly left the room and got into the elevator. Now the three friends were in complete control. They turned on the two other agents.

Alex moved to within inches of one and said, "We're in this together, bitch! Either of you try to snitch like your buddy did back there, it won't be the Cartel that kills you. Do you understand? That stupid fucking idiot actually thought we would rip off the people who pay us so well. Lot of good it did him!

"That guy with the cleaver is crazy. When he was in the next room, he was talking with the bosses in Bogotá. I think he wanted all of us dead. So you two just stay with us. Tomorrow an hour before daybreak, we'll be at that boat launch. Bring your sea legs. It could be a long day."

The guy smiled back at Alex and said, "We'll stay with you and we'll pull our asses out of the fire you three put us in. If we don't find the money, we'd better dig a big fucking hole and cover ourselves because this could turn south real quick.

"So, I guess we'll be hangin' together until tomorrow. Are you guys hungry? I haven't eaten since yesterday."

"Hell, yeah! Lead on."

Once they got into their separate vehicles, JJ said, "If we don't find that money, I'm not going back just to fucking die."

"Yeah, we're fucked, and we need to form an escape plan," Lucas agreed.

33. Justice is Served

Monday, June 14, 1976

The next morning, an hour before dawn, the five DEA agents launched the two rafts and moored them at the dock. They stood, waiting and keeping their distance from one another. They heard the rigs long before they arrived.

JJ said, "Well, *they* aren't gonna sneak up on anyone."

Just then, four Suburbans, riding a cloud of dust, pulled into the parking lot and circled around. An American got out and walked up to Lucas. "What's going on, Lucas?"

It took a second before Lucas recognized his first handler from New York. He smiled and said, "What's goin' on, Dom? Been a while. Wish it was better circumstances."

"Me, too. You're in a world of shit if you don't come back with the money. Shit, man! Where did the duffel bags go?"

"We didn't lose them on purpose. They have to be out there somewhere, but they must be hid real good if the Coast Guard didn't find them.

"Don't worry, we'll be back soon. I mean, it was fucking dark when we lost them. You know all three of us have always been straight with you guys, and none of us are gonna rip off the hand that feeds us!"

As it began to get light, the five agents were already on their way to the Smugglers Buoy. Once there, they talked about what happened on the night they lost the money. They agreed to begin the search by following the white foam of the tide line, just as the bales had that night.

After three hours with no results, the tension mounted. The three friends pulled their raft alongside the second raft to discuss the search strategy. As the agents argued, a movement on the beach of a distant island caught JJ's eye. He watched as the four architects walked across the beach and disappeared into what looked like a wall of jungle.

He pointed at the beach and said, "What the fuck do we got going on there?"

Alex said, "I bet you that's the beach where the bales landed. Think about it. If all the bales floated to that beach, why wouldn't the money?"

One of the two agents in the other raft said, "That makes good sense. Let's go shake them down."

"If we go there," said Lucas, "we're letting the public in on the missing money, and tomorrow there's going to be a thousand boats out here searching for it. I think it might be a little early to let anyone else in on this."

"We don't have to let them know about the money," said JJ. "Maybe we should just go see what they have to say. We *do* have a reputation for getting the answers we need." JJ's smile let the other two friends know that his sadistic juices were beginning to ooze, and they liked it.

That was the way it usually happened with the three. JJ would always want to get violent, and the other two would gradually get pulled in. It was never pretty and almost always ended up with someone dead.

A few seconds later, they watched as Danny and Michael came out of the jungle, grabbed a canoe that magically appeared from its hiding place and headed off east. In a couple of minutes, they were back with several parcels that they deposited on the beach, and then they put the canoe back. The two picked up a couple of the packages and vanished the way they had come. A moment later, the architects and Danny were back, picked up the rest of the packages and disappeared once more.

"I count six," said one of the other agents. "I wonder what the fuck we got going here. They could be dividing up the loot as we sit! We have to look into this."

JJ looked at his friends, his smile becoming even more fiendish. "I think he makes a good point."

"I say we look for a while longer," said Lucas. "I don't want to go in there unless we're sure that the duffel bags aren't stuck in one of these keys. Let's keep an eye on that beach and continue the search in that direction. Okay?"

Reluctantly, the others agreed with nods, and they continued the needle-in-a-haystack search.

***

At first light, Connor and Larry floated on the tide heading northeast. Their destination was a key Jim had showed Connor on one of their outings. He said that he always saw plenty of fish there early in the morning, and Connor wanted to see if that was true. After the tide turned, it would be easy to get back in time for Larry to get the Islanders' final approval on his job.

Before leaving, they had stood on the beach and Connor went over the itinerary. Larry was inquisitive and had grilled Connor about the tides and the time schedule.

It wasn't until Connor guaranteed him that he'd be back in time to sell his job to the architects that Larry eased up and agreed to go that far from the Island.

As they took off, Connor quipped, "You ain't even getting paid for the job. That red-headed luxury tax you're charging must be really good!" He dove in and started swimming when he saw Larry moving fast to hit him.

After a hundred yards he stopped to put his mask on. Connor spotted the two rafts circling a small key a couple of miles to the west. He didn't think anything of it, just some fellow snorkelers.

A line of thunderheads on the eastern horizon stretched north as far as the eye could see. He said, "I don't like the look of those clouds. They look like what-the-fuck-are-we-doing-out-here kind of clouds."

"What the fuck, Connor? They're over there, we're over here. We will be back on the Island getting stoned and drinking beer before they get here. Besides, if it rains good and hard, it'll be a good test of my roofing job."

"Just like the businessman you are. You just keep on fucking thinkin', Larry!"

"You know, I would've made a pretty penny had I bid the fucking job. The ladies got me thinking with the wrong brain. I guess I'll never fuckin' learn. Right, Connor?"

"I really don't ever want to stop thinking with my small, little dick brain. That'd mean no women. You know what I mean?"

Connor smirked and pointed at the two rafts that had just come into view once again. "I wonder what the fuck those guys are doing over there."

"Probably having a good time not having to swim to where they're fishing," said Larry.

"I'd rather be swimming. I bet you both of those guys get hung up on a sandbar today. They don't look like they're fishing, but they're so far off I can't really tell. They're probably out having a good time. Fuck it, let's get going." Connor set a nice, fast pace and never slowed for more than an hour.

***

The agents continued to search and slowly made their way closer to the Banyan tree island. The rafts were almost silent when they were running slow. The CIA had the diesel outboards designed for clandestine landings with saddle tanks large enough to give them a three-hundred-mile range.

Alex looked at the two agents in the other raft, "You two know if we go in there, bad things are gonna happen. I don't know what you've done for the Colombians or for whoever else, but this works well for us. We know how to get information from people.

"It's not what we were taught at Quantico. So I don't want either of you whining about how we do things. You just keep your mouths shut and your eyes open!"

He paused as the other agents nodded in agreement and added, "Whatever you do, don't mention the DEA or who we are. Let *them* worry about that. Ignorance will bring us the answers we want quicker, and maybe we can leave them alive." They stowed their DEA hats out of sight in the rafts.

They beached and stood next to the rafts, looking at the row of thunderheads as they moved closer. After a short search they found the path. They admired the camouflage as they quietly walked into the middle of an excited conversation about the weed that was left behind. Everything came to a halt as JJ put a finger up to his lips and quieted the group with a *shush*.

The Islanders were in shock as five brutish-looking men in camo fatigues stood before them. With mirrored sunglasses and grim faces, each man pointed a pistol with a silencer at them. It was impossible to tell exactly who they were. They wore no rank or insignias.

"Go ahead and take it," said Joe. "The Coast Guard left it here yesterday." He pointed at the weed that was now in a cardboard box covered with a small tarp.

Alex moved his gun a little to the left and fired. The gun barely made a sound and the bullet struck a tree with a thud near Joe's head. Joe instinctively ducked and shrank back.

"We don't give a fuck about the weed, dumb shit! We want the money," he said.

Joe asked, "What money? We didn't find any money."

"There were four black duffel bags full of money floating with that weed. Now, where did you hide it?" Alex demanded.

Danny made the mistake of looking up. JJ followed his eyes and spotted the tree house. He walked toward Danny.

"Well, what do we have here? I bet the fucking Coast Guard didn't even notice that!" He pointed up with his pistol so the others saw the platform and continued, "Now, what do you say we head on up there?" He pointed his gun at Danny's head. "Get going! You're gonna be Alex's little bitch if you don't tell us where the money is!"

Danny said, "Man, we don't know anything about any money. Maybe the Coast Guard found it."

He was answered with a slap to the back of his head and a kick to his ass. Danny almost went down, his hands stopping him from going all the way to the sand.

"Just get your ass up the fucking tree!" JJ ordered him with a motion of his gun.

JJ followed Danny up the tree trunk and once on the platform, he started searching for the money. Not finding it, he yelled down, "Send them all up here and you two follow them. You aren't gonna believe it. I think these guys *live* up here. There are walkways leading all over the fucking place!"

Lucas herded the other Islanders up the tree trunk. Alex told the other two agents to keep an eye out for anyone else. He followed Lucas up the tree, onto the front porch, through the door and onto the platform. They walked to the outlying rooms and searched. Nothing was found.

When they returned empty-handed, they were angry with lust in their eyes. Having mentioned the money, they knew they couldn't leave anyone alive. The idea of torturing and killing the seven civilians was all the three friends could think of. They would have to silence the two other agents as well. Their sadistic juices were flowing, and they were going to have some well-deserved fun for a while. As always, JJ took the lead.

He walked over to a hibachi they used in the tree house and poured some charcoal in it. Then he squirted some starter fluid on the charcoal and lit it. He took two kitchen knives from the counter and shoved the blades into the coals. It would be a while before they would heat up.

Alex knew he had plenty of time for the interrogation. With growing excitement, he walked over to Danny and said, "You're kind of cute, aren't you. Tell you what, why don't you strip. NOW!"

"I'm not taking my clothes off! Who in the fuck *are* you people?"

The move was fast and fluid. The shot from Alex's revolver hit exactly where he intended, taking off the top of Danny's right ear. Danny covered his ear with his hand and screamed in pain. The other Islanders gasped in surprise and shock.

"Okay! Alright! Don't shoot again!" Danny pulled his hand away from his ear and looked at the blood.

Joe rushed at Alex. "Hey, man! We don't have your fucking—"

That's all he got out when JJ hit him in the head with the butt of his pistol. He went down seeing flashes and hearing bells. Blood flowed down his forehead.

Sunshine and Rainbow pulled him back to where the rest of the Islanders huddled in fear. Lucas followed and delivered a boot to Joe's groin. He screamed and grabbed his groin, staring at the agent with rage.

"You people are in for some fun here! We want the money. We think you have it. The Coast Guard didn't find it or they'd be announcing it all over the news! The money was last seen floating toward *this* island with a bunch of bales of weed," said JJ, smiling and breathing hard.

JJ's anticipation mounted. Alex and Lucas had seen it numerous times. It was part of the reason they were in their situation. JJ had flipped out on that kid in Colombia and killed him. But now, they weren't concerned. They knew what was to come. While they weren't as pumped as JJ, they were excited, too.

"Now strip!" demanded Alex.

Danny reluctantly took off his T-shirt and dropped his swimming trunks. Blood ran down his neck and back. Once undressed, he stood back, holding his mutilated ear with one hand and covering his dick with the other.

Alex turned him and shoved him toward a chair, and then bent him over it and threatened to rape him. It had been too long since he'd felt this thrill. As he held him over the chair, JJ tied Danny's hands to the handrail of the platform and his feet to the legs of the chair. Danny couldn't go anywhere.

The three agents huddled in a corner whispering in Spanish. They discussed what they were going to do with the bodies when they were done. They figured they'd just leave them in a pile right on the island. Who knew how long it would be before anyone came looking.

At this point, returning to the landing without the money was not an option. They decided instead to go to Key West, rent a car, and go to Miami International. They could use their diplomatic passports to escape to Europe without arousing suspicion.

Alex grabbed a magazine from a shelf and fanned the coals in the hibachi. They quickly began to glow red. He took one of the knives out of the coals. It was slightly red, too, and he was breathing hard as he pressed it against Danny's back.

Danny lurched and screamed in pain. It was a loud and mournful scream, with death all over it. Alex held him in place, pressing himself against Danny's ass and becoming sexually excited.

He turned to the other Islanders who stared in disbelief, powerless to help Danny.

"I *know* you know where those duffel bags are. They were floating with the weed and all the weed ended up here. So this could all end well for you if you just tell us where the fucking money is!"

All of the Islanders talked at once, denying any knowledge of the money and pleading with the agents to stop torturing Danny. They promised not to tell anyone about them. Lucas fired his gun above their heads, silencing them. The Islanders huddled together against the wall. Kevin and Ryan tried their best to shield Sunshine and Rainbow.

JJ grabbed a washrag and pressed the other knife to Danny's ass. As he screamed again, JJ stuffed the rag into his mouth so far it muffled his scream.

Alex walked back to the coals and put the first knife back in until it was red-hot once more. He returned to Danny and laid it on his back again. The smoke curled up off of his skin and the stench filled the air. Danny let out a muffled scream and passed out.

To revive him, Alex doused Danny with water from a nearby bucket and returned to the hibachi to reheat the knife. He returned to Danny and opened his pants. As he laid the knife on Danny once again, he slowly worked his penis inside him. Danny lurched, fighting desperately to get away, his howl of pain stifled by the rag in his mouth. Alex rode him like he was a bucking bronc, an evil smile of pure pleasure on his face.

JJ walked up to Sunshine and shoved Kevin aside. With a quick move, he grabbed the front of her blouse and ripped it open, exposing her breasts. Rainbow growled and lunged at the agent, scratching his face.

"You bitch!" He stepped back and slapped her across the cheek. She fell backward against the wall, stunned by the blow. He tore the front of her blouse open as she slid downward, and then he pulled what remained of Sunshine's blouse off.

"I can't wait till you're strapped to the chair!" he said while rubbing his face and looking at the blood on his hand.

Sunshine went to care for her love. Rainbow had not lost consciousness, but she was numb. They huddled on the floor and embraced each other, fearful of what would happen next. This was far worse than any of their most paranoid thoughts.

Suddenly, JJ grabbed Sunshine by the hair and pulled her up to her feet. She cried out and instinctively reached up with both hands and held on to his fist. Her toes barely touched the floor as he groped her breasts. She fought as he tried to shove his hand down the front of her pants. She twisted away from his reach and Kevin moved

245

toward them. Lucas stepped forward and hit him with a backhand, sending him down.

JJ laughed and threw Sunshine back at Rainbow, who quickly gathered her in. "You two are gonna be fun!" Then he kicked Kevin in the ribs, "And you need to watch yourself or you'll be next. Or better yet, I'll make you watch your twin first."

***

The air was heavy in the heat of the day. The long line of thunderheads had turned into a long line of tropical rain showers. Large raindrops began to fall as Connor and Larry neared the Island.

Connor said, "I ain't liking this shit! We're the tallest thing out here. Let's get the fuck back to the Island before it starts raining lightning bolts!"

They were still a little over a mile away from the beach, but with the help of the tide and the adrenalin rush, they were flying along. As they drew closer to the Island, Connor pulled up and pointed at the two rubber rafts on the beach.

He looked at Larry and said, "That can't be good. Those are the two rafts we saw this morning when we left."

Larry asked, "Who do you think they are?"

"Looks like the military. God! I'm glad our packs are back at the RV park! Did you bring anything that could get us busted, bro?"

"There's nothing but rolling papers in my daypack. But I got tobacco with it. What about you?"

"I brought my throwing knives, like always, but I hid them out at the beach close to the trail. Didn't want anyone to see them and start asking questions."

"So what do you want to do?" asked Larry.

"I'll bet this is about the weed those guys found. Come on," Connor said, "We better go face the music. They might need us to corroborate their story."

Larry nodded in agreement and they swam toward the beach.

***

Danny lay over the chair convulsing in pain as Alex continued to rape him. He had stopped his attack several times only to reheat the knife and yet again press it against Danny's back. Each time, Danny lurched to escape the hot knife and Alex violently thrust himself inside, a look of ecstasy on his face.

Rainbow puked in a trash can while Sunshine, naked from the waist up, stood with the others, staring helplessly at the rape. They were in shock, horrified at the inevitable conclusion that they were all going to be tortured.

After Alex was done, he turned to the Islanders and pulled his pants up. He smiled at them and said, "We're gonna be here all day until you tell us where you put the money. I'm looking forward to fucking you all!"

"Let's save the redheads for last," said Lucas. "We'll *all* have a good time with them!" He laughed as he saw the fear in the girls' eyes.

Contemplating a way out, Ryan composed himself and said, "If it's money you guys want, we can come up with a pretty nice sum. Please! Just stop what you're doing and let us go. We won't say a word about what's happened here."

Lucas, eager to share in the fun, ignored Ryan's plea and took a hot knife and laid it across Danny's ass. Danny had spit out the washrag and screamed louder than at any other time, and he passed out again.

JJ didn't hesitate. He pointed his revolver and fired, hitting Danny in the back of the head. Blood sprayed all over the curtains and walls.

The Islanders shrank back and screamed in unison. They quickly fell silent again when the agents trained their guns on them, threatening to shoot.

Lucas and Alex cut Danny loose and threw his body out of the window. He fell, lifeless, to the ground.

"*Now* do you see there's nothing you can do to stop this from happening?" yelled JJ. "Except produce the four black duffel bags full of money." He moved quickly, hitting Ryan with the butt of his revolver. Blood sprayed against the wall from the three-inch gash in his scalp.

Ryan grabbed his head and would've fallen if his brother hadn't caught him. Kevin pulled him as far away as possible against the wall, and they stood there in shock. The hopelessness of the situation was becoming clear to them all.

***

Just as Connor and Larry neared the beach, Danny let out what was to be his last blood-curdling scream. It was followed almost immediately by the horrified screams of the Islanders as they watched the murder of their friend.

Larry and Connor looked at each other, eyes wide with surprise.

"What the fuck?" exclaimed Connor in a hushed voice. "Quick! We need to get in there and see what the fuck is going on!"

They crept onto the beach, past the two rubber rafts. Connor quickly moved to the hidden throwing knives and harness. He put the harness on with a smooth motion that came with hundreds of hours of practice. Larry moved up to his side.

Connor whispered in his ear, "I think the screams came from the platform. Let's go in quietly. If everyone is up there, we might be able to get the jump on them."

They hadn't gone far when they spotted the two agents standing under the platform and talking to each other. Suddenly, Danny's body fell out of the Banyan tree and bounced when it hit the ground, narrowly missing one of the agents.

Both Connor and Larry started in surprise. Their movement would have given them away, but the two agents' attention was diverted to Danny's body.

"What the fuck are you doing up there, man?" One of the agents yelled up to Lucas.

Lucas yelled back, "We're going to get an answer out of these motherfuckers in a short time, or there's going to be a *pile* of dead bodies down there. Don't worry. We'll give you guys a turn with the redheads."

The two agents on the ground smiled at each other, and turned away from Connor and Larry. The travelers were shocked at the sight of Danny's dead body. Anger filled Connor at the mention of Sunshine and Rainbow.

JJ grabbed Joe and pulled him toward the chair. Joe resisted, and he hit him again with the butt of his gun. Stunned, Joe ceased his resistance as more blood began to stain the front of his shirt. Sunshine and Rainbow screamed at the thought of what would come next. Lucas rushed them, and they quickly stopped.

Hearing the girls' screams, Connor froze and his hands began to shake. He pulled Larry close and said "I can't let this go on. Stay here and go for the police if they shoot me."

Larry whispered back, "I'm not going anywhere, because you're not gonna get shot!"

They heard Joe's protests as JJ and Alex bent him over the chair and tied him off. Alex pulled his shorts down and readied himself for another rape. Lucas returned to the window and stared out into the jungle. He thought he'd seen a movement. He watched for a moment for any sign of trouble. Seeing nothing, he turned from the window and directed his attention to the captives.

Connor sprang into action. He ran toward the two agents on the ground. They turned toward him and reached for their revolvers, but neither was fast enough. Connor threw the first knife overhand, and then dove to the side like he'd practiced so many times before and threw the second, side arm. Both agents fell to the ground, each with a knife lodged in his throat. Not a sound came from either except for the slight thumps of their bodies hitting the ground.

To Connor, everything moved in slow motion. The fear had him shaking and the adrenalin had him moving faster than he ever remembered. Larry came running up and helped him pull the two bodies out of sight.

They heard Joe scream and yell, "You fucking perverts! Don't you understand we don't know where your fucking money is?"

They heard an agent reply, "That may be, but that's not gonna stop me from fuckin' you up the ass, you motherfucker!"

Then they heard Joe let out another scream.

Connor pulled both knives from the bodies, surprised at how difficult it was. He wiped them on one of the dead agent's fatigues and sheathed them.

He took a pistol from one of the agents and Larry grabbed the other one. Connor pulled Larry close and whispered, "You stay down here and keep an eye out for any new arrivals. You ever shoot a forty-five?" Larry shook his head.

Connor held his .45 up with two hands. "Point and gently pull the trigger. You may not hit 'em, but you'll scare the shit out of 'em."

Larry nodded and whispered back, "I don't want to watch you die, so don't even give them a chance!"

"They'll get the same chance these two got. They killed Danny, them motherfuckers! I wonder how many are up there."

Up above, Michael whispered to Rainbow, "If you two can slide out of here and get back to your room while these guys aren't looking, go down the fire escape rope and get help for the rest of us. These guys don't know you can make it out of here from your room, so they aren't paying close attention."

Lucas came up beside Ryan and kneed him in the stomach, sending him to the floor. "You're next, big mouth!"

Rainbow whispered back to Michael, "I don't think anything is going to work. We can't make it!"

Without hesitation, Connor climbed the tree as quickly and quietly as possible. He stood outside the door looking through a crack until it was the right time to introduce himself. He quietly opened the door. What followed happened so fast that no one but Connor could say exactly, and even he wasn't really sure.

Alex had his back turned as he raped Joe. Lucas and JJ were looking on with smiles on their faces. Lucas saw Connor first and raised his weapon. Connor, holding the .45 two-handed just like he was taught, fired at him. Lucas fired back at the same time, the bullet hitting the floor in front of Connor's toes. Connor's bullet hit Lucas in the heart. The impact propelled him backward and out through the window.

For an instant, everyone on the platform froze. They watched in surprise as Lucas' body flew out of the window and hit the ground with a thud.

The bullet Lucas fired went through the floor of the platform and missed Larry by just a few feet. He turned at the sound of the bullet hitting the ground and jumped as Lucas' body landed in the sand next to Danny's body.

JJ turned and fired at Connor just as Connor fired back. His bullet whistled past Connor's ear. Connor's bullet took JJ in the eye and left a three-inch hole in the back of his head. Blood and brains sprayed all over the wall right before he slammed into it and slid to the floor.

Alex made a move toward his weapon. It was just out of his reach as Connor put his pistol to Alex's ear and pulled the trigger. Blood covered Joe's back as the bullet went through Alex's head and lodged in the wall.

Connor kicked their weapons away from them and turned to the Islanders. He calmly asked, "Are there any more of these assholes?"

Realizing they were all in shock, he suddenly raised his voice and asked again, "Are there *any more* of these assholes?" Michael slowly shook his head.

Everything stopped for a moment as they took in the ghastly scene. Connor stood in the middle of the room, the pistol still in his hand. The Islanders continued to huddle against the wall, the girls instinctively covering their breasts. Joe remained strapped to the chair.

Joe struggled to free himself. Michael cut him loose from his bindings and helped him stand up. Rainbow and Sunshine hugged each other and cried. Kevin helped Ryan sit and examined his head.

Connor walked over to the ladies and scooped them up in a big hug. He kissed each on the top of the head. Although he began to shake and felt weak as the adrenaline wore off, his mind was still in overdrive.

"You two should go back and find some other clothes. Be quick about it." He raised his voice just enough to let them know they should start moving. "Hurry now, we've got a lot to do."

He walked over to the two agents still on the platform. "We need to get these bodies out of here. Michael, you and Kevin help me throw them to the ground, okay?"

He called down to Larry, "Look out below, Larry."

"You okay, Connor?" Larry called back. "Is everyone okay?"

"Yeah, we're okay. Stay clear of the window."

The bodies were heavy, and they struggled to get the two agents through the window. The ladies returned just as they managed to push the second agent over the ledge.

Everyone climbed down to the ground. They gathered around Danny's body and began to cry for their friend.

A lightning bolt struck nearby. The ensuing thunder was immediate and deafening. Then the rain, which had been sporadic, big drops, turned into a deluge.

Rainbow came over to Connor crying as she wrapped herself around him and said, "Connor, you saved us! You're my hero, you're my hero!" She began sobbing and was joined by Sunshine and the rest of the Islanders. They surrounded him saying that the men were going to kill them all.

It was always the case in Connor's life. As everyone around him panicked and seized up with fear, he remained calm and fluid in his thoughts. This, however, was so over the top that he started shaking again. He held everyone close and slowly collected himself.

Larry had been listening to everything. Finally, he asked, "What the fuck was going on here? Who were those guys, and what did they want? And why on earth would they want to kill Danny?" He stood next to Connor and the story unfolded before them.

Connor took a deep breath. His mind still racing, he took charge of the situation. "We need to wash off all of this blood. Let's all go to the beach and clean up."

Everyone did as he asked. Afterward, Connor told Michael and Kevin to get the first aid kit and patch up Ryan and Joe.

He was worried that others would see the rafts and come looking for the dead agents. "They might have friends. Let's get their rafts over to the lagoon and ditch them out of sight under the mangrove branches."

Larry and the girls helped Connor move the rafts into the lagoon, and then swam back to the beach. Everyone stood in a group, still in shock, and waited for Connor's next order.

"We need to clean this mess up. Larry, you take the ladies home and go to the store. We need large garbage bags and all the bleach you can carry. Take Kevin with you." The girls hugged and kissed Connor a last time and left with Larry and Kevin without saying another word.

Back in the clearing, Connor continued issuing orders as he regained his composure. "Ryan and Joe should go to the hospital and get stitched up. Give them some bullshit story, I don't care. But don't mention anything about what really happened out here. We need time to collect our thoughts and get some answers, like who the fuck *were* these assholes?"

Connor walked over to one of the agents and pulled his wallet out of his pants pocket. Inside, he found an ID. He looked up at Ryan, Joe, and Michael.

"I just murdered five DEA agents." Connor shook his head in disbelief.

"They were enjoying what they were doing," said Ryan. "They deserved what they got. You didn't *murder* anyone, that's for sure. What Rainbow said about you being a hero is the truth. You and Larry saved our lives."

"It was a good kill, man," said Joe, reverting back to his Vietnam days. He was visibly shaken by his torture. "I was next. If you hadn't showed up when you did, I'd be dead right now."

Joe put a hand on Connor's shoulder. "Connor, you need to leave here. We'll take care of the bodies."

"I don't think so. I slept in this bed, now I'm gonna make it, real neat."

Connor continued to search the dead agent and found the manila envelope in his shirt pocket. He opened it and quickly counted five thousand dollars. He went to the other agents, throwing everything from their pockets into a pile. He found five identical envelopes.

Connor picked up one of the envelopes and handed it to Joe. "Take this with you to pay the hospital bill."

He paced back and forth, running different scenarios through his head. "Here's the deal. I'm the killer here. I'll clean up this mess. I want you guys to stay away for at least a week."

"Connor," said Michael, "I just want you to know those guys were evil. They killed Danny. They tortured him and raped him. That guy there shot him in the back of the head. Then they raped and tortured Joe. They told us Ryan was next."

"Michael is right," Ryan agreed. "We didn't do anything to deserve what we were going to get. It's like the girls said, you're a hero, Connor."

"I'm a hero, they're fucking evil, I understand. But when Larry and Kevin get back, you all need to get the fuck out of here!"

253

Michael asked, "I know how you killed those three, but how did you kill these two?" He pointed at the two agents that had remained below. "We didn't hear anything going on down here."

Connor pulled one of his knives out of the harness still strapped on his back. He turned and threw it at a young Banyan trunk just two inches in diameter, burying it in the tiny trunk from fifteen feet away. Then, in a flash, he buried the second blade a half an inch away from the first. "That's how I took these two out. Never thought I'd use them to kill, but I guess it's all I ever practiced for."

A short while later, Larry and Kevin returned with five boxes of the large, heavy-duty garbage bags Connor asked for and a quart of bourbon.

When he heard what Connor wanted, Larry said, "Not me, bro. Them, I can understand, but I started this trip with you. Now, fuck you, if I'm gonna leave you here on your own."

He deposited the garbage bags by the bodies and handed the bourbon to Connor. "Here, this should help calm you down. I bought all the bleach I could find. It's back on the shore."

Connor knew Larry when he dug his heels in. There was no budging him. He turned to the Islanders and handed them three of the envelopes.

"Take this. We'll meet you guys at the ladies' condo after we're done here. Michael, make sure Joe doesn't get all macho and get him stitched up along with Ryan."

Connor hugged the four Islanders and said, "Now, you guys get the fuck out of here. Make up a good story, okay?" He chuckled and said, "Tell them some kung fu dude numb-chucked you. Anything but the truth, you hear? Then Larry and I will meet you all in a week or so."

The storm was petering out and the sun broke from behind a cloud. They were too numb to argue and slowly nodded and left the clearing.

34. Loose Ends

Connor turned and walked over to Larry. He handed Larry the fifth envelope.

"Here's the deal. I'm gonna cut these guys up and dump them into those rubber rafts out there. You don't need to be here for that.

"I want you to go to Miami on the morning bus and use this money to get us a good car. One that won't get us pulled over. Make sure it's in good shape, has good tags, and runs good. And don't go to a car dealer. Look for one in the paper."

Larry stood and stared at Connor for a moment. "I keep thinking of that day in the rock pit when you showed me and the girls your knife throwing. It made me feel safe. It really did. But I never thought I'd watch you kill two guys like that. Jesus, Connor! Do you think we'll go to jail over this?"

"I might, but you won't." Connor stared out over the water. "If you can get out of here and get us a good ride, we should be alright. By the time you get back, I'll have this mess all wrapped up."

Connor was silent again as he pondered the task ahead of him. "Let's go grab the bleach and get the tree house cleaned up, and then you go to the condo. Leave out in the morning from there. I'll take care of this. I have a plan. I think it'll be alright."

They went up to the platform and washed the blood off of the ceiling, walls, and floor. They pulled the curtains down and threw them to the ground. Afterward, Larry went down and began ferrying five-gallon buckets of saltwater that Connor pulled up and used to rinse the platform. Two hours later, it was clean and the blood stains were gone. The air was thick with the smell of bleach.

Connor came down from the platform. "Okay, now get the fuck out of here and leave the rest to me."

He collected the bloody curtains and rags that they had thrown down and piled them beside the firepit.

They walked to the beach and saw the bow of a small Coast Guard cutter just as it emerged from behind the trees. They quickly ducked back into the jungle before the bridge came into view. The cutter slowly made its way along the shoreline and disappeared.

Larry stayed out of sight and watched in case the cutter returned while Connor returned to the clearing and stripped all of the bodies. He was surprised at how difficult it was to get their clothing off. He finally just cut them off with his throwing knife and added them to the pile next to the firepit along with the agents' wallets.

Larry walked into the clearing and said, "They turned around and split. I haven't seen them in forty-five minutes."

As it turned out, the Coast Guard couldn't get a crane barge for forty-eight hours, so they sent the small cutter to see if anyone was trying to recover any of the bales that had sunk. When they didn't find anyone, they returned to Miami.

"Good, now you go. I got this. I'll see you when you get back." Larry walked over to Connor and gave him a hug and a stern look. He left without saying another word.

After he was gone, Connor went to the Banyan tree and picked up a machete. He returned to the bodies and with five powerful strokes, took each of their heads off. He put one head in a bag, added some sand and tied the bag off, and then doubled it. He went to the beach and threw the bag down on the sand. He repeated the process four times.

He did the same thing with their hands, slicing each off with a stroke of the machete and bagging them. Connor put all of the agents' jewelry, watches, and contents from their pockets in the last bag.

He went back to the lagoon and retrieved the two rubber rafts. He tied them together, bow to stern, and struggled to put the headless bodies into the second raft. As he loaded the garbage bags in the first raft, he discovered the DEA baseball caps. He collected all five and searched the rafts for any other items left by the agents. Finding nothing else, he returned to the clearing and added the DEA caps to the pile of clothing beside the firepit.

He siphoned enough fuel from the second raft to fill the tanks of the first. Wading into the water, he took the bowline of the lead raft and slowly pulled them back to the lagoon. He pushed them under the mangroves once again, tied them off to a limb, and swam back to the Island.

Just as he got back to the beach another downpour hit along with more lightning and thunder. Connor got the five-gallon buckets and made several trips with seawater to pour over the ground, washing away any blood that remained.

Finally, he went up to Danny's room and picked out some clothes. He washed Danny and dressed him in the clean clothes, wrapped him in a tarp and hid him in one of the canoes.

It was done. He was exhausted. He grabbed the bourbon and two cold beers and slowly walked to the beach. The same beach where Jim had first discovered the camouflaged trail that led to what, a short while ago, Connor thought was paradise. He sat and tried to think of anything he might have forgotten. He opened the bottle and took a long pull and downed one of the beers.

He slowed his breathing and relaxed. The tears began to flow. Slowly at first, and then harder and harder they came, until he was racked with the grief of what he'd done. He lay on the beach in the fetal position, crying for the dead.

Connor was asleep when Larry showed up. He shook him awake and handed him a note he'd brought from the condo. It was from the girls and said they were going to Ohio, that they would be back in two weeks, and asked them to stay around until they got back. Then they called them their heroes again.

"That hero shit is getting old. I only did what needed to be done, you know?" Connor paused, thinking about what else he needed to do. "I guess when you leave tomorrow, I'll ditch the bodies. I don't know what we're gonna do with Danny. He needs to be found somehow. I guess I'll figure that out when you get back."

Connor was hyper once again. His mind jumped from one thing to another. "Fuck it. Listen, Larry. There's a bus leaving for Miami in a couple of hours. Take that money and leave now.

"I'm not gonna make it back to the RV park tonight, so tell Garrett and Sally we needed to go to Miami to pick up some money that our mothers sent us. They'll understand."

"You sure you got this, bro? I really feel like shit leaving you here by yourself."

"You just buy a car and get back here. That's as important as anything I'm doing here."

Larry walked into the clearing under the platform. All evidence of the horrific scene, apart from the materials left by the firepit, was gone. He walked back to the beach.

"Where's Danny?"

"I dressed him and wrapped him in a tarp. He's in one of the canoes. We'll move him when you get back."

Larry had turned to wade back to the highway when Connor said, "One more thing, after you get back with the car, park it down at the ladies' condo. Don't let anyone at the RV park know about it, okay?"

Hours later, after the sun went down, Connor swam out to the rafts. He untied the bowline and got into the first raft over the bow. Surprised at how much rainwater they contained, he bailed out both rafts. Then, just in case his plan fell through, he put on a pair of gloves from the first aid kit and wiped down both rafts with a rag to remove any fingerprints.

He slowly drove the rafts to the Smugglers Buoy. Separating them, he tied the one holding the bodies to the buoy on the protected northeast side.

With the other raft, he went south to the deep water. Suddenly, he felt the Florida Current begin to carry him to the east, just as Jim had described. He quickly dropped the weighted bags with the heads, hands, jewelry, and watches into the water.

He turned and sped northward to escape the current and made his way back to the buoy. At first, he was worried about finding it again and was relieved when he saw the flashing beacon.

Once back, he tied the rafts together again, headed due north for a half mile and turned south again. He secured the steering wheel of the lead raft with some rope and made sure it wouldn't veer off course. He set the throttle so it would power the two rafts slowly at about five miles per hour.

He put on his fins and mask, and slipped over the side as the rafts passed the buoy. He was numb with exhaustion as he swam back and crawled up onto the platform. Once there, he waited for the tide to change.

He fell into a fitful sleep and awoke screaming several times. He kept seeing the agents falling off the platform with the holes he'd put in them.

Tuesday, June 15, 1976

The tide had reversed and the eastern sky began to turn pink as he dropped into the water. He hadn't eaten dinner the day before and his hunger pangs were getting bad, but he wasn't in a hurry. He was going to swim the fifteen miles back at a leisurely pace letting the tide do most of the work.

He was about two miles from the buoy and was coming around the end of a mangrove when he noticed the duffel bags. At first, he thought they were logs. He swam over to them thinking they might be a life raft. It wasn't until he got right up to them that he realized what they were.

They had lodged in such a way that they were invisible to anyone but a swimmer. It was pure luck that he saw them at all. Had he been any higher than six inches above the water, the duffel bags would have disappeared into the mangrove. He wondered how close the agents had gotten to them in their search that morning.

He fought for a while to free them from the branches. Using them as a raft, he climbed on top and let the tide steer him right to the Island. *Just like the weed.* He noticed they were equipped with a homing transmitter, but it had been crushed by the mangrove as the bags were forced under the limbs.

Connor steered his impromptu raft into the lagoon of the C-shaped key and tied it off. Then he swam to a good spot to watch the Island for a while. Before he had left, he wiped the beach clean of footprints and the high-tide line could easily be seen from his vantage point. No one had been to the Island by way of the beach.

When he felt it was safe, he swam over and quietly pulled one of his knives from its sheath. Then he got one of the agent's guns he'd stashed by the trail and searched the Island for intruders.

He also looked for any sign left behind that would betray that six people had died there. The smell of blood came from the sand where he'd cut the agents into pieces. He filled the five-gallon buckets with seawater and dumped it all over the area. He repeated this until the stench was gone. Finally, he mixed bleach in the water and spread it over the same area to insure the smell wouldn't return.

Only then did he swim back to the lagoon and retrieve the duffel bags. He floated them over to the Island. Once he beached the bags, he pulled them apart and dragged them one at a time into the cooking area.

With some difficulty, he opened the first bag. It had a triple fold over two zippers. In it, he found bundles of one-hundred-dollar bills wrapped in cellophane and labeled "$100,000". Counting eighteen separate bundles, it didn't take long to figure out that added up to 7.2 million dollars.

Now he knew why the Cartel had sent the goons. He realized that if he didn't move fast, he was going to be shooting whoever they sent next. He resealed the bag and dragged all four back to the beach. He pulled the empty canoe from its hiding place and loaded the duffel bags in. He floated the canoe out to the lagoon, shoved it as far as he could under the mangrove and tied it off.

He was famished and returned to the Island to make himself some breakfast. He started a cooking fire in the firepit and prepared a simple breakfast of fish and eggs. While eating, he burned the pile of bloody rags, curtains, wallets, and clothing left from before using kerosene as an accelerant.

A disturbing thought came to him. He was sober and had not been stoned for the first time in a long time. His stash was back at the RV park with his pack, and he'd hidden the remainder of the Colombian weed on the roof of the platform with some difficulty.

He remembered the bottle of bourbon that Larry had bought. *God damn, Larry, how'd you know?* He poured three fingers in a glass and gulped it down. He grimaced. *How could Hemingway love this stuff?* He laughed softly as the alcohol began to take hold.

He felt exhaustion overtake him and decided to try to get some sleep in Rainbow and Sunshine's room. It was farthest away from the beach. Anyone coming would be felt a long way off by the sway of the walkway under their weight.

As an added safety measure, he stashed the last remaining items he'd kept of the DEA agents—their guns, ammo, and badges—in the bedroom with him.

Even with the bourbon, he didn't think he would be able to sleep. After lying down, he realized he'd swum close to thirty-five miles in the last two days. The events of the last twenty-four hours kept going through his mind. He wondered if he'd forgotten anything. He was exhausted and his body ached with fatigue. Finally, after a lot of tossing and turning, sleep took him.

35. Karma

Ninety Miles to the South

As Connor slept, two of the finest rubber rafts made beached themselves on a strip of sand near a remote fishing village just under ninety miles to the south. A young man walked the beach at low tide, looking for anything the ocean might have deposited on the shore.

He saw the rafts before he heard them. The CIA had designed them for stealth with muffled diesel outboard motors. The young man watched as the rafts quietly slid onto the beach. He ran and turned off the one motor that was running. He smelled the headless bodies before he saw them. He stepped back in shock and ran for his father.

After hearing the young man's story, his father went to the barn and got his ancient tractor with its front bucket loader. He found his other son and together, the three went to inspect the boats.

After a long discussion, they decided to bury the corpses. They dug a shallow grave well above the high-tide line. Then they put the headless, handless, naked bodies in and covered them up. They pulled the rafts one at a time back to the barn on an ancient flatbed trailer.

Over the next two weeks, the young men cleaned every inch of the rafts removing all evidence of the bodies. They were shiny new when they put them back on the beach and brought their neighbors out to see what had just washed up.

The young man, who everyone knew was an avid beachcomber, was lauded for his find. His father took one of the boats and his sons kept the other.

The sons used the raft to fish every chance they could. It was a boon for the whole village as the catch was shared in a communal way, like everything else.

It was only natural that they buried the bodies and kept the rafts. This was Castro's Cuba, stuck in the early sixties and even earlier with most things mechanical. What they had found would make them good money as fishing boats.

Their village was poor and very remote with less than a hundred, closely-knit people and no official law enforcement. It was the kind of village that people moved to after the revolution if they'd been loyal to the previous regime.

Every family was excited about the good fortune and would work together to keep the secret. They shared a unanimous opinion that was rarely voiced aloud: "Fuck Castro!" Most of these families had been well-established and wealthy before he came to power. Now, they were forced to make a subsistent living off the land. The rafts were just a little payback, karma.

***

Wednesday, June 16, 1976

It was early the next morning when Connor felt the footsteps coming toward him. He eased up from the bed, carefully picked up one of the pistols and hid behind the door. Larry called out and Connor relaxed.

He opened the door and said, "You scared the shit out of me!"

"What the fuck you doing all the way back here?"

"I figured it would be hard to sneak up on me," Connor answered. "It worked, too. If you hadn't called out, I might've shot you!"

He stuffed the pistols, ammo, and badges in a couple of canvas bags he found in the room and headed out.

"I picked up a '68 Ranchero for two thousand dollars. It has a topper on back and looks real sharp. It's got a straight six in it with four on the floor, it sounds real nice and quiet. I don't think we'll be noticed by anyone."

"Sounds perfect. Let's pack up this afternoon. Make up a story about getting a ride all the way back to Naples," said Connor.

"After dark let's get Danny in the back of the rig. We'll drop him on the side of the road south of Miami. Then we'll head on out."

He suddenly remembered another detail. "Oh yeah, I almost forgot. I got four duffel bags full of money I found yesterday."

"You got what?" asked Larry in disbelief.

"You remember what they said about those agents looking for money? Well, yesterday when I was swimming back from getting rid of the bodies, I spotted four duffel bags. There looks to be over seven million dollars in them."

"You're fucking kidding me!"

"I've been thinking on it since I found it. We're taking the money," Connor declared. "I mean, think about it. No one knows who we are. The Coast Guard didn't even ask the Islanders for their ID's. We weren't even there. The Islanders don't know I found the money. And I guarantee the government didn't know where their agents were while they were torturing and killing Danny."

Connor saw the look of reservation on Larry's face. "If you want, we can come back down here in a while. We can get with the Islanders and talk to them about it. I'll be all for it. But you think it through. We might be the only ones who can get away free. This is drug money headed to the Cartel in Colombia."

"It's your call," said Larry. "You killed five people who were looking for drug money. You found the money. You make the call, but I don't think I want any of it."

Connor laughed, "Who says I was gonna *give* you any?"

That evening after dark, they loaded up Danny's body, the four duffel bags, and their packs without a hitch. Twenty miles south of Miami, they dropped Danny into the bushes alongside an isolated pullout on the road. His wallet was in his pants for easy identification.

They drove to Naples, paid cash for a motel room, and despite being completely exhausted, neither slept much.

36. Finding the Om

Thursday, June 17, 1976

*T*he next morning, they ate a big breakfast in the motel restaurant and paid for four more nights. They put a Do Not Disturb sign on the door and left.

Once at the same hamburger joint where they had been when they first arrived, they gave Don a call. He showed up a half hour later. It was just like the first day, minus the pig.

"We can't stay long," Larry lied. "We met some people from Naples and they're gonna give us a ride all the way to Boston."

They picked up their mail and everything else they'd left with Don. After many hugs and invitations, he gave them a ride back into town. After he split, they returned to the motel.

They watched the news in their motel room every night for three more nights looking for any mention of the agents. Nothing was reported.

Each night, the travelers struggled to get much needed rest, but neither slept much. Visions of the dead agents and nightmares plagued them whenever they closed their eyes.

The police found Danny's body two days later and started an investigation. Danny's family lawyers were there to insure his murder wasn't swept under the rug. The police hit a dead-end at every turn.

Monday, June 21, 1976

After four days, they drove to Sarasota and rented another motel room. That night, they called a cab and told the driver they were looking for a bar and liquor store combo. There were several places that fit that description, and he said he needed more information. They told him it was a big chain and the employees had to take a lie-detector test to work there. The driver took them right to the place. It was only a half mile away. They tipped the driver big hoping he would come and give them a lift home in case they got drunk.

They walked in and sat at the biggest bar they'd ever seen. Eight bartenders worked different sections of the bar. They spotted Debbie and walked over and sat down. She greeted them and asked what they would like. She paused and looked again saying, "I know you two, don't I?"

Larry answered, "I don't think you *know* us, but you asked us to stop in and you'd buy us a drink."

Once she heard his voice, she said, "Damn! You guys clean up real nice. Let's see now, you're Larry and you're Connor, right?"

Connor nodded and said, "I'll take a double shot of bourbon and a beer back."

"Make that two, and you don't have to buy," said Larry.

They had six shots and three beers in no time at all. Larry and Debbie talked, and Connor just sat there for a while, saying nothing.

He told Larry he was going back to the room. He stopped by the liquor store next door for a pint of bourbon and a quart of beer and slowly walked back to the motel room.

He never felt so helpless in his entire life. He lay down and started to cry again. Angrily, he took a long pull off of the bottle. It calmed him. He took another long pull and the bottle was empty. He tossed it on the floor. He chugged the quart of beer in three long draws and lay back as the alcohol put him to sleep.

Larry dragged himself in after closing time. He lay in his bed and listened to Connor cry for a while. He shed a few tears of his own, and then finally drifted off.

Tuesday, June 22, 1976

Connor woke up with God's own hangover. He said to Larry softly, "I'm not handling this very well. I can't stop crying. When I closed my eyes last night, I saw those two with the knives sticking out of their throats."

Larry replied, "Me, too. I don't think I could've slept without the alcohol." He paused and thought for a moment.

"I tell you what. Let's stop at the first rest stop north and roll a fatty. Maybe it'll help us."

"You just keep on thinkin', Larry. That's what you're good at." They both chuckled, checked out of the motel and left.

After they stopped and smoked the fatty, they took off north to the first fruit stand they spotted. They bought a bag of assorted citrus fruit and some boiled peanuts.

Connor drove and Larry peeled the tangerines and oranges. The radio played some classic rock-and-roll from the fifties and sixties. Connor wasn't sure whether it was the music, the weed, the peanuts, or the fruit, but he was feeling better.

"I was thinking last night while you were at the bar. When I was in the service, I spent a three-day weekend in West Berlin. Friday and Saturday, then back out Sunday. There was about thirty of us and we had to stay in our Class A uniforms and sleep in the barracks, so the night life was limited. Although, I heard a couple of guys got lucky even in their uniforms." Connor paused for several minutes thinking back on that weekend.

"And so, what about that weekend?" asked Larry after Connor went silent.

"Anyway," Connor continued, "on Saturday, we had the option of seeing the Berlin Symphonic Orchestra, or we could do a tour of the local museums. Two of the guys and I picked the symphony. They were playing Beethoven's *Ninth Symphony*"—Connor hummed a few bars of the theme—"I know you're gonna think I'm weird because I know this shit, but the fourth movement is called the 'Ode to Joy' and it deals with this poem written in the 1600s by a guy named Fredrick Schiller.

"I've always loved that poem. It's about the warriors, heroes, and gods of war, and how they go to this plane of heaven called Elysium when they die. There are large fields of grain and lots of wine, and they all sit around and talk about their feats of glory while they were alive."

Larry asked, "Where the fuck you going with this Connor?"

"Well, I've always thought about the 'Ode to Joy' and all those warriors drinking and talking about their conquests. Those guys down in Key West are all calling me a hero, and all I want to do is cry.

"Then I started thinking about everyone I know who was in Vietnam, Korea, and World War II. Well, not a single fucking one of

267

them talks about it. I guess, once you've walked a mile in a warrior's shoes, the 'Ode to Joy' is a bunch of fucking bullshit! There's no *joy* about it."

"I see what you mean bro, but you did what you had to for everyone's. We just need to take a deep breath and figure out what we're gonna do now."

They drove in silence for a long time when Larry asked, "You know, I been wondering, just where the fuck are we going?"

"I was just thinking about that. Maybe we ought to just continue the tour like we planned. First, we got to figure a place to put this money.

"What do you say we head to Champagne and rent a storage locker? I think that's where I'm gonna end up anyway. Then we'll go up to Podunk and see Carol and Becky again. Maybe you can get laid, too. I just need a little love."

Larry asked, "Are you gonna tell Carol about what went on down there?"

"Do you remember what I said when you asked me if I would grow a crop with you?"

"Sometimes I wish the fuck I never *asked* to grow a crop with you!" Larry scowled at him.

Connor continued, ignoring him, "You tell just one person and the whole world will know. I mean, we're not talking about a patch of weed here! We're talking about five killings that would be considered murders if the government got wind of it. Let alone the Colombian Cartel. Jesus! We just can't take that chance! I'm not saying a word to anyone."

Larry's next question was the hard one. "What do you plan on telling Rainbow and Sunshine and the rest of the Islanders?"

"I've thought about it," said Connor. "When they get back to Key West, we definitely need to sit down and talk with them."

"Okay," said Larry, "the next question is, how are we going to register this rig?"

"I think I'll get my Illinois driver's license. I'll just use Carol's address and register it in Illinois. How's that sound?"

"Well, it's *my* rig, I bought it," said Larry.

"Okay, here's the deal. *You* get an Illinois driver's license then."

"Okay, I see your point."

They drove in silence most of the way to Tennessee and spent the night in another motel.

Wednesday, June 23, 1976

The next day, they made it to Champagne. Connor found a storage locker and paid six months in advance. He took out a couple of grand apiece for the road. Larry accepted the money, but only after Connor talked him into it.

While eating dinner, Larry came up with the idea of apartment shopping. Connor could rent an apartment, get a driver's license and register the rig.

That evening, from a motel on the outskirts of Champagne, Connor called Carol with his plans. He asked her if she wanted to do some apartment hunting with him. She was excited and talked with her mom and dad about it. She called back to say that she and Becky would be there.

Thursday, June 24, 1976

By the time the girls got to the motel the next day, Connor had a list of rentals near the college.

Carol ran into Connor's arms, and they hugged and kissed and hugged again. Connor held on tightly and realized how much he'd missed her. His pain eased as he held her, and he didn't want to let her go.

After a moment, Carol pulled away and kissed him again, and then looked in his eyes. He was different somehow. She saw a darkness in his expression despite the smile on his face.

"Is everything okay?" she asked him.

Connor didn't have any words for a moment. "I'm just really happy to see you. I've been missing you more than I thought." He hugged her once more. Meanwhile, Larry and Becky were hugging, kissing, and laughing together.

After a brief visit, Carol and Connor went to look at the apartment rentals. Thinking nothing of it, Connor got into the Ranchero and Carol stood back and asked, "When did you get a car? I thought you guys were all about hitchhiking?"

While Connor valued the truth more than most, he also knew this truth could not be told. It pained him to have to lie to her. "We got it as payment for some work we did in Florida. Do you like it?"

"Yeah, it's real nice," she said as she got in.

Larry and Becky decided to stay at the motel room and talked about the first thing that popped up.

They rented the third place they looked at, a very small one-bedroom apartment that was just four blocks from the campus. It was semi-furnished with a couch, a bed, and a table with four chairs in the kitchen.

They paid the landlord and got the keys. Then they went into the apartment, stripped naked, and had sex on every piece of furniture in the place. When Connor took out a condom, Carol stopped him and said, "You don't need that. I started using the pill after I got back from Florida." Connor smiled at her.

They went back to the motel room and picked up Larry and Becky and showed them the apartment. They went out and bought TV dinners and plastic cutlery for their first meal in the place.

Becky had driven the VW bus to the apartment, so she and Larry took off back to the motel, leaving Connor with Carol. They snuggled under sleeping bags through the night. Connor felt the pain inside him gradually dissipate.

He told her that he and Larry planned to leave the next day, and he would use the apartment as a base. He explained that he still planned on seeing a few friends. He mentioned Boston, Kentucky, and Louisiana. Carol asked if she could come to Baton Rouge with him, and he said he'd talk with Larry about it.

Friday, June 25, 1976

The next day, Connor became an Illinois resident, getting a driver's license and registering the Ranchero. The girls headed back to Podunk and the travelers got back on the road.

"So, I was thinking," said Connor. "We got another few days until everyone is gonna be back in Key West, and I don't feel like being around any of my Army friends with all this shit weighing on my mind. What do you say we head into the Smoky Mountains again and do some good old car camping?"

Larry let out a laugh that showed his relief. "I was gonna say that I really wasn't up to meeting a bunch of strangers. We need time to think about what we plan to do down south. I think camping is a great idea."

They drove south and then east until the Smokies came into view. They rented a campsite and had the tarp up in no time. After scoring two bundles of firewood from the camp host, they burned some hamburgers for dinner.

Larry chased his last bite with some cold beer. "We should do burgers more often. They're easy as fuck to cook and fast. Not to mention, they're tasty as fuck, too."

"Yeah, you're right." Connor was just finishing up a perfect pinner for an after-dinner treat. "What do you say we grab a couple of beers and get lost for a while?"

They walked up a trail that circled up onto the bluff overlooking the campground and stopped to smoke the pinner. Afterwards, they lit a couple of cigarettes and fell into silence.

As they sat quietly, Larry sensed the tension growing in Connor. He waited patiently. He knew that when he was ready, Connor would come up with a solution to fix the situation in Key West.

Connor suddenly said, "I think on it, and it's just real hard to get past the fact that I killed five guys. And to top it all, they're fucking government agents! This is so fucked up!"

"Why don't you tell me what you did with them? When I got back to the Island, I couldn't tell anything had gone on there, other than that real strong bleach smell."

Connor told him about the details of the disposal and how he'd found the money on the way back.

"Jesus, Connor! You sure those rafts will make it to Cuba?"

"No, I ain't sure of anything. I just remember all those Cuban refugees making it to Florida in a lot worse boats than those two rubber rafts. I don't see why it wouldn't work in reverse.

"I topped off the diesel tank of the lead raft. It didn't take shit to fill it. The agents were out there running around all morning and weren't even a gallon down. Shit, they both had two ten-gallon tanks, at least. I think those rafts could've made *Brazil* if Cuba wasn't in the fuckin' way.

"Those garbage bags are in a current that heads to Norway. I don't know if they'll make it there, but Jim says scuba divers stay away from it because it's so dangerous to swim in.

"I don't even know that, if they find the rafts, they'll announce it on the news. But if they *do* find them, it ain't gonna take long to figure out that there are five DEA agents missing and that those agents were last seen in Key West a couple of days before they went missing.

"I know there's a lot that can go wrong. If the rafts make Cuba, and I think they will, I don't see the Cuban government calling the White House and asking them if they're missing a couple of boats."

Connor rambled on as he paced back and forth in front of Larry, kicking the dirt and cursing his fucking luck.

"Connor, you need to calm down, and let's talk this through. What's done is done. Now we just have to stay calm and wait."

"Yeah, I know. This is what's got me worried. Ryan comes home with a four-inch gash in his scalp, freshly stitched. His wife freaks out and asks what happened.

"Now, Ryan isn't wired to lie to his wife. Christ! He told her about Rainbow and Sunshine! What do you think he's gonna say? He's gonna tell her the fucking truth. So is fuckin' Kevin. *I* would in their shoes.

"So we've got Rainbow, Sunshine, Ryan, and Kevin, and their wives and kids, all heading to Ohio to their folks' place. Now what do you think are the odds that they spill the beans?"

"But I don't think anyone's going to the police. It's their own kids who could go to jail." Larry tried to ease the stress level. "I guess it's not going the way we imagined, bro."

"The way we *fucking imagined*?" asked Connor in disbelief. "The way I imagined it was us hitching to Boston to see my friend, Scott. Not having to look over my shoulder for the rest of my life wondering if some FBI agent's gonna arrest me. Or worse, having a cartel thug coming to ask about the seven-fucking-million dollars I just happen to have!

"Look, I think we should head down to the Island in a few days. Everybody should be back by then. If anything was gonna go down, they would know it."

"We should try to give Michael a call at his motel," Larry suggested. "I wonder if anyone's even been back out to the Island since we left. *I* wouldn't feel very comfortable out there."

Connor sat, his mind spinning with the different scenarios. Larry waited for a reply. He watched as his friend quietly went over everything in his mind.

"Shit! I've had the answer to my problem all along." Connor said suddenly with a smile.

He returned to camp followed by a curious Larry. Connor walked to the rig and rifled through his pack. When he turned around, he was swinging the leather pouch containing his Special Smoke in one hand and the little clay pipe in the other. He walked back to the fire and sat down.

"I guarantee we'll feel better in the morning."

"Let's do it." Larry sat close and waited patiently as Connor readied the pipe. "Well, I guess this will prove your whole LSD Theory of Compatibility. I should write that down." He laughed nervously.

Connor loaded the bowl over full. Larry took three big hits. He got up and walked away before Connor could load the pipe again. Connor took his three hits.

He put the pipe away and went to put it back in his pack. When he turned, he faced Larry with a big smile. Larry was smiling back.

They sat around the fire and laughed at the strangeness of their situation. With the influence of the Smoke, they both seemed to suddenly except their circumstance.

Soon, Larry went and lay on his sleeping bag, covered up with a cotton blanket, and swatted at the occasional mosquito. Connor walked to a nearby tree and climbed as high up as the branches would allow. He found a comfortable perch, sat and watched the night sky revolve over him.

37. Closure

Saturday, June 26, 1976

*I*t didn't seem long at all before the light of dawn came to the eastern sky and the Father's Morning Greatest Hits show began. Once he was satisfied with the sunrise, Connor climbed down the tree and crawled into bed opposite of Larry.

He slept soundly until Larry nudged him with a cup of morning joe in his hand.

"Not very often I'm handing *you* the coffee." He turned and sat by the fire.

Connor walked over and joined him. They sat in silence, enjoying the benefits of the Smoke.

"Thanks for the smoke, bro," said Larry. "I wouldn't of believed my peaceful feeling if I wasn't experiencing it."

Connor pointed to the tree he climbed and said, "I spent the whole night up there and a lot crossed my mind. This morning I teared up for the sunrise. I realized that the Smoke had done its job.

"You snored most of the night down here. I probably was, too, once I hit the hay. But I do feel like a huge fucking weight has been removed from my psyche. I guess it's time to head south, bro."

"Yeah, I think so, too."

They didn't eat, but packed up and started south. They stayed on secondary roads, using a road map they scored at the Kentucky border. In four hours, they were through Tennessee and in Georgia, sitting at the counter of a small café, drinking average coffee and eating really good ham and eggs.

"They dry-smoke their ham back here. Can you tell the difference? This shit really rocks. Too bad we had to get grits with it. But if I swirl my over-easy eggs into it, it ain't bad. I saw a trucker doing it down in Florida and thought I'd try it. So, two eggs and ham and grits ain't that bad, bro. Remember that."

After eating, Connor came back inside from the outdoor phone booth. He was smiling.

"Michael says that the Miami police talked to him about Danny. He told them Danny had said he was going to Miami for a couple of days, but he didn't know why. Danny's parents and brothers all came down, packed his shit and left. And there's a For Sale sign in front of Danny's house.

"Kevin and Ryan are back, and Sunshine and Rainbow are due back tomorrow. So, what do you say we find the Interstate and fly south into Florida? We can spend the night in a motel room and shower. Tomorrow morning, after breakfast, we can bust ass for Key West."

"So, we just play it by ear once we get there, right?" asked Larry.

"Yeah, by the fucking ear. I just hope we don't have to babysit these guys.

"Remember this, they know we're from out west, but they don't know for sure *where*. And, they don't know either of our last names. I think we ought to keep it that way.

"The less they know, the less they can tell. I mean, shit, in two years, I'll be the Masked Avenger, and you'll be my sidekick, Little Brown Turd."

"Very funny, asshole! I'm just glad you're getting your sense of humor back."

"The Special Smoke is working its magic, bro."

Sunday, June 27, 1976

The next evening, the guys pulled up and parked the Ranchero at the RV park. They gave everyone a line about waiting at Larry's uncle's place until their cash arrived and said the car was borrowed from Larry's cousin. As an extra precaution, Connor made sure the rig was parked out of sight of the highway.

They walked over to Michael's place and knocked on the door. He answered, and it took him a minute to recognize the two. They had come wearing their bandanas and backpacks.

"Well, come on in." He stepped aside. They passed him and walked into the main room. "We should go right out to the Island. Let me get ready. It'll be just a minute."

They walked to the beach. Holding their packs over their heads, they forded the crossing like they'd done so many times before. They walked into the clearing and found Jim and Joe there.

Jim had returned soon after he heard about Danny. He had heard only bits of the story, but Joe had lived it. He ran to Connor and threw his arms around him. Connor hugged him back. Soon, he was sobbing with convulsions and heaves. Jim stood back in awe. He'd never realized the grief Joe had bottled up inside.

Connor slowly pried himself away from Joe as he softly whispered calming words into his ear. Joe finally released him and stood there looking at his feet.

Larry patted Joe on the back and said, "Good to see someone out here. We weren't sure we'd find anyone."

"We've been out here during the day," said Joe, "but no one has stayed here overnight until Jim got back a few days ago. Michael and I still haven't stayed over. Jim's the only one. I decided not to let what happened chase me out of here. I *do* own a gun now, though."

Jim finally crossed the clearing and gave both of the travelers a hug. "It seems I missed out on all the excitement. I heard about you and your knives."

He walked over to the Banyan trunk and rubbed the knife wounds that Connor's knifes had left. "I don't mean to bother you, but I'm having trouble with what they told me."

Just then, a knife lodged with a thud in the trunk about an inch above the first two wounds. It startled Jim, causing him to jump.

Connor said, as he walked over to the trunk, "They weren't lying. It's not something I let on to people. You guys are the first outside of a small group of friends back home to learn that I'm really good with throwing—"

Jim's anger began to show as he interrupted Connor. "Wait a minute. What *really* went on here? I've been getting bits and pieces, but no one has told me *shit!*"

Connor stared for a moment at Jim. "You'll know the whole story tomorrow. I'm sorry if you feel left out, that's not anyone's intention. It's my fault. I guess I was the one who swore them to secrecy." He turned to Joe and Michael. "So, how was Ohio?"

"The architects went to Ohio, we didn't," Joe answered.

"Joe and I went to Miami," said Michael. "We holed up in a motel for two days until we saw the police report about Danny's body being found. Then we figured we should be down here at my house when the police came. They got here a couple of hours after we did.

"Like I told you on the phone, Danny's parents and brothers were all here. We told them he had said he was going to Miami for a couple of days.

"They seemed satisfied with that. They were over at Danny's all day. There was a theory that it was a coke deal gone bad. They said the blood test results would take a couple of weeks.

"The next day, a moving truck showed up. The family loaded up everything in the house that wasn't tied down and left. Two days after that, there was a For Sale sign in front of the place."

"The day we got back from Miami," said Joe, "the Coast Guard showed up with a barge and crane. Everyone in town knew what was going on by then. There were some crowds in the evening watching the whole thing go down.

"They had scuba divers looking for sunken bales. When they found one, they used the crane to lift it out of the water and onto the deck of the barge. It took three days.

"Michael and I watched, but they never got closer than a couple hundred yards from the Island. When they left, it looked like they had another hundred and fifty bales, or so. There was no sign of anyone setting foot on the Island.

"The day after the Coast Guard left, there were a bunch boats out there looking for anything they'd missed. But no one found anything, though."

Michael added, "There was also a group of Colombians out there for a week looking every day. I watched them real close. They didn't find anything, either.

"It was kind of strange knowing they weren't looking for weed. I could tell they were looking for something stuck under the mangroves. They finally gave up and left. That was just a few days ago. We haven't seen anybody since."

Connor said, "In that case, I guess we'll sleep out here tonight. Is that okay with you, Larry?"

"Sure, I guess I don't have a problem with it."

"We all need to meet somewhere safe from anyone overhearing," said Connor. "I really think everyone should come out here. But, if anyone's uncomfortable with that, then at the ladies' condo.

"When we get everyone together, I'll tell you all at once what happened after you left that day. So tomorrow, let the architects know I'd like to say goodbye at their convenience, whenever they feel comfortable.

"Now, we've been driving all fucking day and need some sleep. I'll be back in the ladies' hut."

He flew up the tree and was on his way to the north end of the Island before anyone could say a thing.

"Don't mind him," Larry said. "He's been a little on-edge the last couple of weeks. I'll take Ryan and Kevin's pad. You guys want to smoke some weed before I go to bed?"

They walked to the beach and smoked a joint of the good stuff. They stood around for a while making small talk, and then they all headed for their beds.

Monday, June 28, 1976

The next morning, Connor had already walked to the store for breakfast fixin's and was cooking sausage and drinking coffee as the sleepyheads came down out of the trees.

Larry said, "I was noticing that Kevin and Ryan's pad still needs a little work yet. So, I'm gonna finish hanging their shelves. Then I can say I kept my end of the bargain."

"I think I'm gonna take my spear gun and kill something with it," said Connor. "I'd like some fresh fish for dinner. It's funny, but the thing you guys taught me most was how much I love fish."

Jim asked, "Do you mind if I tag along?"

"Not at all."

They finished breakfast and went their separate ways. Connor didn't say it, but the other thing he had learned about himself was just how much he loved swimming in the Keys.

He took off that morning, and for the first time, Jim was following *him*. There was no hurry. He planned on being out most of the day, so he lay on his back and floated along, letting the tide take him down the path of least resistance.

They ended up at the beach where they'd smoked that first Thai pinner and were laughing about how lost Jim had gotten. They both had two nice fish, and Connor lit a pinner. He was describing the fish bisque he was planning on cooking that evening.

It had been nagging Jim all day, so he finally asked Connor. "Something really bad happened while I was gone, didn't it?"

Connor looked at him without saying a word. Jim continued, "No one is the same. It seems like everyone is suddenly afraid of the Island. And what the hell was Danny doing buying drugs in Miami? I can't believe he's dead." Jim paused and thought about his friend.

"It seems like everyone keeps looking around for something, but can't find it. I mean, Joe has walked every square inch of the Island, searching. He just shakes his head and keeps looking."

Connor thought about it and laughed a bit. "I forgot about the bale of weed that they found. Shit, I guess I'm a better camouflage artist than I thought. I hid their weed before I left and forgot to tell anyone where."

Jim sighed. "Yeah, they told me about the bale that sunk. I wondered what happened to it. I figured that's where Joe's been coming up with all that cash he's been spending. He paid for steak dinners two nights in a row."

Connor, wanting to change the subject before Jim could ask any more questions, said, "I came out here to swim. Let's get back to the Island. Larry might need our help.

"Don't worry, Jim. You'll get your answers soon. But you've got to know, you're the *lucky* one here."

When they got back to the Island, everyone was gathered on the beach. When Joe stopped by with Connor's message, everything had stopped. Everyone came out to wait for him. They had helped Larry fix a small leak in the ladies' roof and hang the shelves in Kevin and Ryan's room. Now, they were just waiting.

Connor came out of the water to tears from all of the architects. He was crying, too. Seeing Ryan's and Kevin's wives, he said, "Wow! You people really *do* want answers. Looks like you told your wives. I guess I would've, too."

Connor hugged Kevin's wife, Sarah, first, and then he hugged Ryan's wife, Melanie. They were both sobbing.

They walked to the clearing. Everyone found a place to sit while Connor pulled a package from his pack and raced up the tree. A few seconds later, he appeared at the window where they had thrown the bodies off of the platform.

He threw the string of prayer flags he had bought so long ago out of the window and tied one end to the window's edge. He swung his legs over, jumped the twenty feet to the ground, rolled and came to his feet. He tied the other end of the flags to a piece of wood and buried it where Danny had landed. "That's for Danny, may his spirit flow with those in the flags, forever."

He stood in the center of the group for a moment, trying to decide where to begin. Finally he said, "First things first." He looked at Joe. "I hear you've been looking all over the Island for something. The best camouflage is usually right under your nose."

He walked over to a rope that was tied off to a tree branch. It was used to pull supplies up to the platform. Connor untied it and gave it a tug. Two large garbage bags full of weed came sliding off of the platform roof. "I thought I'd never get them to stay up there, but there you go."

"I wasn't looking for the weed," said Joe.

"Yeah, that's what I figured. I just didn't want to tell Jim that you were looking for graves."

Jim shot a look of shock at Connor. "Graves?"

For the next hour, the story slowly came out. First, Kevin described their encounter with the agents, and Sunshine gave Jim the story of how Danny had really died. Then Joe told of his rape and showed Jim his wounds from the knife burns that he had suffered before Connor got there. Finally, Connor and Larry told the story from their side.

Joe asked Connor, "What did you do with the bodies?"

"Well, I can tell you what I *didn't* do with them," Connor explained. "I didn't bury them anywhere you'll find them. That's a guarantee. But this is where it gets a little sticky, so I'll just say this. Larry, remember when you asked me to grow that ten-plant crop with you?" Larry nodded and rolled his eyes.

"Well, I'll tell you the same thing I told Larry. You tell one person and it's no longer a secret. I haven't even told Larry," he lied.

"It ain't gonna do you any good to know what I did with the bodies. On the other hand, I can see lots of shit going wrong in the future, and I pray it never comes to this.

"Let's say one of you is being questioned about the disappearance of five federal agents. Right now, you could give them the truth. All the truth you know will point them to a hitchhiker from out west somewhere. You guys don't even know my last name. I'm keeping it that way.

"I love you all and plan on keeping in touch. But there will be no letters or phone calls. I'll just show up and catch up on what's been happening, then leave."

Connor was suddenly silent as he stared at the ground. Several moments went by as everyone waited for him to continue.

Finally, he said, "Never in my wildest imagination would I have ever believed what went on here. You know, I *dreamed* about this Island before I ever got here. But it wasn't the nightmare that went on here. My dreams were all happy ones. I told Larry about how Jim had been so familiar and why I loved Rainbow and Sunshine, who are more like family than anyone I've ever met."

The redheads exchanged a glance and looked back at Connor, smiling. Rainbow said, "We feel the same way about you."

Connor returned their smiles and continued, "It just seems to me that this whole thing has been a set-up. Destiny.

"When I saw Danny fall to the ground, I just reacted. I mean, Jesus fucking Christ! When I look back on it, it's like it wasn't real. It's like I'm watching a movie, standing on the outside looking in."

Connor went silent again for a moment. "I just hope I don't spend the rest of my life in jail for killing five corrupt government agents who would've killed me given the same chance."

Sunshine stood and walked over to Connor and said, "You are a hero, so is Larry. I *still* can't believe what I saw you do! I know you cringe when I say that, but we would all be dead if it wasn't for you and Larry."

"I didn't really do much but move the bodies after they were already dead," said Larry.

"That's not true," Connor said, looking at Larry. "You had my back. Without you there, I wouldn't have been able to do what I did."

Connor looked back at Sunshine. "When I lie down at night, I run the events through my head. I figure my whole life has been a preparation for that day. But that doesn't make it any easier to live with. Most nights, I cry myself to sleep.

"I know we all have the same dark cloud of Danny and those agents hanging over our heads. I know what I did was necessary. But there's no statute of limitations. No matter what the story is, when it comes to the government, we all would be left swinging in the wind. The only way we can all be safe is to keep this secret between us. So, please honor me and Larry by doing that.

"You know, I love you all like family. So, let's have a good meal, and then Larry and I are gonna go west, back the way we came."

All of the Islanders sat in silence considering Connor's words. From the beginning, they knew the travelers would leave at some point, but never under these circumstances. The days ahead would be very hard without them around, without Danny.

Connor walked over to Larry and whispered, "I think that's all I have to say. Let's say we're going to the store and just split."

Connor walked over to a note pad, wrote down his bisque recipe and said, "You guys get this started. We'll be right back from the store with the rest of the ingredients."

They grabbed their packs and left. Once on the highway and walking to the rig, Larry said, "You know, it's getting late, Connor. I think we ought to rock their world with our seafood bisque and give them a Special Smoke closure to this thing. I mean, you were right about the Smoke. I do feel better the last couple of days."

Connor walked in silence for a minute. "Okay, let's put our packs in the rig. Then we'll go back and teach them—what did you call it?—the LSD Theory of Compatibility. Yeah, that's the fucking ticket."

They got back to the Island and water was simmering with chunks of fresh fish, onions, and garlic. The aroma was intoxicating. Connor opened two cans of minced clams, one can of a seafood mix he'd never seen out west, and a can of crab chunks. Larry made a nice rue for a thickening agent. They added a little table cream and some half-and-half, and let it simmer until all the ingredients married. It was bisque.

They sat around the clearing under the treehouse eating the bisque. Everyone loved it.

Connor said with a smile, "It must be the Atlantic air or maybe it's the quality of the eastern cream. This is the best bisque I've ever been a party to."

Larry agreed saying, "I think it's all the hot air and bullshit!" Everyone laughed.

Dinner was over and joints had been smoked when Connor pulled out his Special Smoke and the little clay pipe. The Islanders grew quiet.

Connor said, "I know I gave you the spiel about the healing properties of my Special Smoke. Larry and I were all fucked up when we left here. I mean, you just don't experience that kind of trauma without some kind of aftereffect. So, let's do this, and you guys can tell me how you feel in the morning."

Larry just smiled and nodded.

Everyone climbed the tree and sat in a circle as Connor loaded the pipe for each of the Islanders. Twenty minutes later, each had adjourned to their bedroom.

Connor and Larry quietly climbed down the giant tree for the last time and waded to the highway. They walked to the Ranchero and were gone.

The story continues in:

Better Left Unsaid Than Dead
The Chronicles of Connor, Book 2
(coming in early 2018)

Better Left Unsaid Than Dead
The Chronicles of Connor, Book Two
(coming in early 2018)

It's five years after the killings in Key West and the gruesome images still wake Connor from his sleep. Now, on the eve of telling Carol his terrible secret and introducing her to the Islanders, he gets the call he'd always dreaded. The FBI has been asking questions about the missing DEA agents. How could that be? Someone talked, but who?

Five years had changed Connor. The killings had done something he never expected. It had hardened him into a man who knew he would kill to protect himself and those he loved. A business owner and upstanding member of the community, Connor wasn't going to allow those he'd saved from torture and death get him convicted of his actions on that terrible day. The beast he'd hidden deep inside was going to take on the very people he had protected.

ABOUT THE AUTHOR

R.G. Shannon was born in the northwest hills of Portland, Oregon, the youngest of four rough and rowdy boys. He spent his youth camping and fishing in the wilds of Oregon and Washington. As an adolescent, he was active in the anti-war community and participated in protests from 1968 to 1971.

He volunteered for the draft at eighteen and earned an honorable discharge after two years of service. He spent two summers logging in Alaska and joined the Boilermakers Union, where he worked as a welder in Oregon, Washington, and Alaska. After leaving the Union, he worked in several national parks as a maintenance man.

His short story, "The Artifact Conspiracy", was published in *Artifact*, the 2016 Anthology of the Northwestern Independent Writers Association. He now lives in the outskirts of Portland with his wife of ten years.